MEN WITHOUT MERCY!

As a curl of smoke rose from a sod house on the horizon, the leader of the nightriders turned to the confederate on his left. "How long have those sodbusters been there? I thought I had them all pinpointed."

The rider shrugged. "It's a big country, Cap. Homesteaders are coming in like locusts and it's getting hard to keep track."

The dozen-odd horsemen didn't slow as they rode in, and the farmer gasped as they came his way, trampling his young wheat under hoof. The girl—for she was little more than that—ran to the edge of the wheat before she stopped, hoe upraised, suddenly aware of the intent that was written on their faces in evil, leering grins.

The nightriders spread out like a pack of hungry wolves, and the farmer realized that his only gun was in the distant hut.

As the men converged on him, he screamed to his young wife. "Martha, run for the house!" She ran desperately, but a rider cut her off, and, as she fell to the ground before him, he smiled obscenely down at her. With a gleam in his hardened eyes he unfastened his belt, and Martha sobbed uncontrollably. "Oh God *no! Please help me!*"

But there was no salvation forthcoming.

THE HOME-STEADERS

Lee Davis Willoughby

A DELL/BRYANS BOOK

Published by
Dell Publishing Co., Inc.
I Dag Hammarskjold Plaza
New York, New York 10017

Dell ® TM 681510, Dell Publishing Co., Inc.

ISBN: 0-440-03628-3

Printed in the United States of America

First printing—April 1981

THE
HOMESTEADERS

THE NIGHTRIDERS SLOWED their mounts to a walk as they moved in on the lonely dot of lamplight from downwind and by the dark of the moon. They knew their victims had a brace of redbone hounds and while an early bay of warning wouldn't be much help to one man against a dozen, the durned old sodbuster had a Henry Repeater and some said he'd fought at Cold Harbor. The nightriders didn't consider what they were up to a cowardly act. They figured they were acting with admirable gumption, considering. But they hadn't come all this way to get shot. They'd come to do some shooting.

The feedsacks they wore over their heads to conceal their features would have made it hard to see in better light. Under the star-spangled vault of a clear Nebraska sky it was a bitch to make out up and down from sideways. Save for the little

7

yellow square of light from the window ahead, they seemed to be riding waist-deep in coal-black nothingness. The dead, flat horizon all around was visible simply as a hazy line where the stars and slanted arch of the Milky Way ended and a man who studied overmuch while riding the prairie at night could be seized with sudden vertigo. For, as the sky appeared a vault above, the logic of the human eye could form the blackness under it into another deep bowl curving the same way down and down to God knows where!

But the masked nightriders had followed the owlhoot trail before so they took comfort in the soft hiss of horseshoes through the invisible dry grass just beneath them. They knew a pony saw better in the dark than most folks, too. So they didn't fret themselves about the prairie dog holes and such a body could ride into in these parts at night.

One of the masked men had gotten ahead of his companions and as his pony suddenly stopped without warning he grunted in surprise as his weight threw him forward and the saddle horn caught him in the gut. He swore and spurred his mount as he straightened up. But the pony still balked. The leader of the expedition moved up alongside and called out softly, "Hold on, you poor ignorant greenhorn. That old hoss has more sense than its rider."

As the leader started to dismount, the confused rider growled, "Greenhorn my ass! I guess I et some trail dust in my time, pardner. I rode north with Captain Goodnight and ten thousand Texas cows when all they growed in these parts was buffalo and Sioux, God damn your eyes!"

The leader said soothingly, "Sure you did, old son," as he groped ahead of himself in the darkness. Then he felt the cold steel strands, invisible in the darkness, and his voice dripped venom as he muttered, "I thought so. It's the sod buster's fucking *fence!*"

The others had of course reined in to sit their mounts in a ragged line. The first rider who'd stopped stared hard ahead of his pony and muttered, "I don't see no fence. I don't see *nothing!*"

The leader moved to take a pair of wirecutters from his saddlebag as he replied grimly, "Of course you can't see bobwire at night, old son. You can hardly see the infernal stuff in broad daylight. The sons of bitches invented the stuff just to gut a cow or tear some poor rider's leg off at the knee. Fill your fists, gents. This wire sort of twangs when you cut it and we ain't all that far from the soddy, yonder."

There was a crackle of saddle leather as the men shifted their weights to draw their weapons. Most of the dozen favored sawed-off shotguns for this sort of social call. A couple drew Winchesters. One kid who'd sort of tagged along drew a .44 S&W. Kids were like that, but nobody commented. It was hard to find enough riders with hair on their chests, these days. For all their brag and war talk, most cow folks still drew the line at the out-and-out extermination of the vermin infesting the range of late.

The leader's wirecutters made short work of the three strands of barbed wire. And though he'd warned them of possible noise, in truth there wasn't much. The one old sod buster, working alone, hadn't been able to string his wire as tight as it was supposed to go. The leader, afoot, could just make out the sheen of starlight on the dry grass stems. So as his followers waited, he hauled the severed wires well clear before moving back to his mount. He started to remount. Then his eyes narrowed thoughtfully under the feedsack mask as he gauged the distance to the soft lamplight that betrayed the isolated sod house's position. He said, "We'd best leave the ponies here with the kid. We'll move in the rest of the way on foot."

There was a murmur of undecided semi-protest. The boy who'd only brought a pistol said, "Now hold on, damn it. I never rode this fur to hold anybody's infernal hosses! I come along to see the elephant and have me some fun."

The first rider who'd stopped said, "I'm a top hand. I never walk where I can ride. That infernal house is a good quarter-mile away!"

The leader slapped the wirecutters against his leather chaps for silence as he snapped, "Shut up, all of you. You boys elected me to lead you 'cause you know I rode with Mosby's Guerrilla in the war. In the first damn place that soddy ain't no quarter-mile off. The whole blamed homestead ain't but a quarter-mile across. In the second place, we're going in on foot because that son of a bitch has two hounds and a Henry and a man can't shoot for shit aboard a spooked pony."

As he met sullen silence if not complete agreement he added in a mollified tone, "We never rode all this way to whoop and holler and torch a chicken coop, boys. I told you when we started out that I aimed to do things *right* this time. You don't get rid of nesters by shooting out their windows and tipping over their shithouse like a passel of kids playing it's Halloween. If any of you boys is having second thoughts, now that we're here, you can just turn around and git and we'll say no more about it. The rest of you dismount and follow me. I've talked about it all I aim to."

There was another low and more ominous murmuring as the nightriders got down from their saddles and started handing their reins to the protesting kid assigned the task. When he said something about wanting to get at least one crack at the infernal nesters, durn it, an older hand growled, "Just hesh and do as you're told. Your chore's important enough, considering you don't shave regular. They'll hang you alongside the rest of us if ever you brag too much about this night, kid!"

The leader waited until he saw his men were ready. Then he put the wirecutters away and drew his own sawed-off scatter gun from its saddle boot and said, "Form line of skirmish on my left and keep it down to a roar. Nobody fires 'til they hear from me or Old Rufus, here."

The eleven masked men walked abreast through the brittle stubble toward the sod house. One man was wearing Texas spurs that jingled for God's sake, but it was a mite late to worry about that. As they got close enough to see the checks in the curtain hanging in front of the coal oil lamp inside the soddy a hound began to bark. The leader hissed, "Steady as she goes. It's inside the house. The more fools they."

A second hound took up the challenge as the skirmish line parted to pass the outhouse on either side. The light from the window cast a faint glow on the packed bare earth of the barnyard, and as the hounds inside began to bay a plowhorse nick-

ered from the nearby corral and the chickens in the
lean-to against the south wall of the soddy awoke
to add their foolish cackles to the sudden uproar.
The leader strode toward the doorway, shotgun
braced against his hip with its ten gauge twin
muzzles leading the way. The door flew open, out-
lining a tall thin man in bib overalls against the
lamplight behind him. He held his Henry rifle
foolishly at port, arms across his chest, as he called
out, "Who's there? What's going on out here?"

The leader of the nightriders didn't answer with
human words. He replied to the sod buster's worried call by squeezing both triggers. The heavy
gauge weapon in his hands filled the night with
roaring flame as both charges of number nine buck
slammed into the nester in the doorway, folded
him like a jack-knife, and blasted him backwards
into his one-room soddy!

As the homesteader lay spread-eagled on the
floor with his unfired weapon across his twitching
shins the leader of the nightriders shifted the shotgun to his left hand and drew his Walker .45
without breaking stride. A pale woman in a thin
cotton shift came into his line of vision, now, as
she knelt, screaming, by the body in the doorway.
One of her knees was in the spreading pool of
blood around her man as she tried to raise his head
and shoulders, shouting mindlessly down at his
slack-jawed face in the yellow lamplight. The leader stepped to the threshold, revolver cocked and
aimed. As she heard the scrape of his boot she
glanced up, eyes like saucers. He said, "Evening,
ma'am," and fired, the shot catching her through
the chest and flattening her across her husband's
corpse.

As his followers crowded around he smiled under his rough mask and said, "Don't that look nice? A loving couple, all cozied up together friendly as anything."

He holstered his pistol and said, "All right, boys, the fun part's over. Now we have some chores to do. I want this fucking soddy burned out total. We'll kill or run off all the stock and fill the well in afore we leave, too. Let's get cracking. We've only a few more hours to turn this infernal place back into open range."

His companion shrugged and picked up a tin of coal oil from another corner as he said, "We knowed there was a family here. We got our own families to think about. If this game's too rich for your blood, stay home with the womenfolk next time. Stay home and just wait 'til these infernal sod busters fence you in and starve you out!"

The man who'd spoken opened the tin and proceeded to splash coal oil over the sod walls and furnishings. One man who'd betrayed a certain softness moved over by the stove and rummaged around until he found a gallon jar of turpentine. He uncorked it and began to pour it over the bedding and mattress. "Once the flames eat into the roof beams up there the whole kit and kaboodle ought to come down. There won't be all that much left of these folks. You reckon the Sheriff will think they was just sort of burned up accidental-like?"

The man splashing coal oil said, "They ain't supposed to think it's no accident. We'll leave plenty of sign aside from the cut fences and run off stock. There's no sense burning sod busters out unless you make sure the others get the message."

Joseph Barrow stared up at the pearling dawn sky from his sleeping bag, wondering why he still felt so tired. He'd turned in the night before as soon as it had gotten too dark to work and he'd slept like a log, too bone-weary to dream, on the tolerable mattress of the thick prairie sod.

Thinking about sod had him fully awake with a groan. There was no sense laying slug-a-bed with the sun ball about to pop over the horizon at him any infernal minute. He threw the blankets off and sat up, shivering in the dawn chill as he hauled his boots on, then stood up to strap his gunbelt in place around his lean hips. He knew a man looked sort of funny wearing a buscadero gunrig over bib overalls and a red flannel union suit, but he was alone out here and they'd told him in town about some odd goings on, considering the Sioux were said to be peaceable this year.

His back felt stiff. He braced his hands against his floating ribs and stretched with a grimace as he had himself a look-around. As always, out here, there wasn't a hell of a lot to see.

The land was flat. A tawny hide stretched like a drum-skin on the steel rim of the horizon all around. He'd never been able to see that far back in Penn State. No matter which way a body looked there seemed to be a hill, a tree, a house, or *some* damned thing. Out here the sky and earth just met razor-sharp, maybe three or four miles away. He'd spied some cows at sundown far to the west, with the damned sun shining between their legs as they grazed at least two or more miles away.

When he peered to the south he could see the black dots of the railroad town of Pittsburgh Landing. Just the roof tops, he judged, since the town he'd left his women folk in whilst he proved their claim was a good two or three hours' ride.

Pittsburgh Landing was a funny name for a prairie town. He'd heard other Penn Staters were out here, but there sure wasn't any lake or river to go with that "Landing" part. It was just a cluster of frame buildings around the siding and loading pens of the U.P. Railroad they'd freighted themselves west aboard. Ma said the rooms they'd hired in town were outrageous, considering the bugs and threadbare furnishings, but Ma was too old to rough it on the open prairie until he got the house up. Ma was over forty and the spunk had sort of faded from her eyes since Pa died just as they'd sold the old played out farm to head west.

Jessie was younger than he and a willing worker, too. He sure missed her joshing as she helped him chore. But his half-sister was needed in town to look after Ma.

Leaving the bedroll spread on the grass to sundry, young Barrow moved over to his dead fire on the cleared earth of what he meant for a barnyard, Lord willing and his back didn't give out first. He hunkered down to pile cow chips on a couple of clumps of cheat-grass tinder. He struck a sulfur match and lit the otherwise useless grass stems. Critters refused cheat-grass and it could fuel a nasty prairie fire, but it had its uses. Pa had raised him to understand that everything the Lord had put here had some use or other. A weed was just an herb no man had found a use for, yet. But there sure was a lot of cheat, growing on this quarter section they'd claimed. That likely accounted for the handy cow chips, too. The land was overgrazed. The price of beef was up, back east. The stock men who'd been grazing free in these parts until recent had abused the range a mite. Some folks were like that, with land they didn't really own.

He knew it would take a spell for the cow chip fire to coal enough for his morning Arbuckle. So, as the morning sun rose shy in the east he got up, went to the long-handled spade he'd left standing with its blade in the earth, and decided he may as well cut some more sod whilst he waited.

The beginnings of the house that was to be now rose as high as his knees in a fifteen by thirty foot rectangle. Cutting the first sods had cleared the floor space inside and the beginnings of the surrounding yards. Joe stepped to the cleancut edge where sod as far as one could see dropped

down a good six inches to the bare, cleared top-
soil. He carefully placed the sharp edge of the
square-tipped spade in place. Then he put his
heel next to the shaft and drove down, letting his
weight do most of the work. He only had to cut
two sides before he could lever back on the long
handle and move the square of sod the few protesting inches it took to sever it from the soil. He
grimaced and muttered, "I know you were aiming
to stay put, grass. But this is as rough on me as
it is on you."

As he worked, cutting sod after sod in a string-
straight line, he saw the rising sun was lighting up
a distant smoke plume, far to the west. He went on
working, but frowned thoughtfully as he gauged
the wind. It didn't seem likely the grass fire, if
that was what it was, could be headed his way.
It was south of the U.P. tracks and ought to sweep
well south of town, if it burned that far east on
the prevailing wind. He stopped a moment, wet
his finger, and held it up to double check. There
wasn't much wind at all this morning. He'd keep
an eye on that smoke, but it wasn't really a
danger. Some fool had likely lit a campfire on the
grass without clearing it down to soil. Lots of fools
had come out here to get in on the Homestead Act,
now that Uncle Sam had opened up the Nebraska
prairie. He'd met some on the emigrant train as
didn't speak English, for God's sake. A quarter
section of free land sounded good, 'til a man had to
prove it. Many a man who'd never held the
handles of a plow before seemed to think a quarter
section was 160 acres of gold dust, and that all
you had to do was file on it and sit back, rich.

Joe Barrow knew better. He'd grown up on a

hard scrapple farm, and digging that well, over yonder, had taught him a mite about Nebraska soil. It was fair soil. Hell, it was good soil, given care and water. But he'd dug straight down, a good fifteen feet, before he'd come to the water table, and this was early summer. The land figured to dry some between now and the fall rains. Folks in town had said the last few years had been drier than usual and last winter's snow hadn't been all that much. It was no wonder the cheat-grass had invaded the overgrazed, impoverished range. He'd likely have to dig the well deeper by August, but that could wait. He had other things to do.

He straightened with a groan and stared around, fighting the hopelessness that crowded in on him when stiff muscles refused to limber up on a man. There was so *much* to do. The well and even the infernal house would only be the first drops in the bucket. He glanced at the coils of Glidden wire leaning up against the lumber pile between the wagon trace and his camp. He still needed to find some infernal poles. They told him in town they were fresh out of fence posts. There sure weren't any poles a man could *cut* out here in the middle of nowheres. If and when he found his damned poles, each and every one would have to be set a good three feet in the ground, below the God-awful frost line out here. His quarter section was one mile around. The poles had to be set no further than ten feet apart if they meant to hold up a fence that would stop anything important. It made his back ache just to think about it.

He cut another square of sod and then he stood the spade in place and limped back to the fire. The first cow chips were glowing nicely and the punky

scent of burning cow shit wasn't all that unpleasant, despite the way Ma had bitched when he
explained the fuel situation out here. He put a
couple of extra cow chips on. Then he settled the
battered coffee pot on the coals. He knew he'd
feel wider awake once he downed a couple of
mugs of Arbuckle. But meanwhile, the sun was
still rising and the water would take a spell to
boil. So he got up again to chore a mite whilst he
waited.

He picked up one of the sods he'd cut and carried it toward the low walls he was building. A
sassy horned lark was pecking at the roots of the
overturned sods atop the wall. It eyed him suspiciously and chirped sort of ornery. Joe said, "Oh,
shut up," and the bird flew away.

He placed the sod on the wall, upside down, of
course, so the grass would die and dry. Little sow
bugs and an earthworm wriggled in complaint as
he wedged the inverted sod firmly in place. He
said, "Sorry, this is our house, now. But you boys
can just dig down and mosey off somewheres else.
It ain't like this is all the prairie there is, you know."

As he turned away, he spotted a distant rider
coming from the north. He walked back to his fire
and hunkered down to see how his water was
doing. It wasn't doing anything. The rider wasn't
likely up to anything he had to worry about, either. The string-straight wagon trace, out front,
was a county road. It led to Pittsburgh Landing,
over the horizon to the south. The rider was likely
headed there. If he figured it was any of Joe's business he'd say so as he passed. If he didn't, he
wouldn't. If he stopped to jaw neighborly, Joe
would offer him some coffee. If he stopped to pick

a fight, he'd fight him. Joseph Barrow was on the comfortable side of six feet tall and he hadn't lost a fight since he'd started shaving regular. He hadn't, in truth, *had* that many fights, but he hadn't backed out of one in living memory.

As the stranger approached, jingling in the clear morning air, Barrow saw by his duds that he was a cowboy. That meant a serious fight, if a fight was what he had in mind. Cowboys were a funny breed. Proud as sin, but too lazy to walk a hundred yards or fight a man with their fists. The one headed his way wore a cross draw rig and had a Winchester hanging next to his coiled throw-rope. So Joe stood up. He knew a man can't draw sudden when he's hunkered down. But since the cowboy's free hand rode polite on the far side of his holstered six gun, Joe kept his own hands polite, too.

The stranger cut in at an angle as he left the wagon trace. He reined in on the far side of the fire and said, "Morning. My handle is Mackail. Pete Mackail, but you can call me Brazos. I am looking for some strays as wears the Double M brand. Our spread lies just over the sky line to the northwest."

The young homesteader nodded politely and said, "I'm Joe Barrow and this aims to be the Barrow Place, one of these damned days. I spied some cattle last night about sundown. They was too far off for me to see brand one."

Mackail shifted his weight in the saddle as he stared morosely off at the empty horizon Joe had pointed his chin at. He sighed and said, "Hell, if that was them, they either turned back at the U.P. tracks or they never. Looks like a grass fire to the south. They wouldn't be headed *that* way."

Joe asked, "How did they get loose? Hole in your fence?"

Mackail stiffened and turned to stare thoughtfully down at Joe, who met his gaze unwinkingly with a sincerely puzzled smile.

Mackail smiled back and said, "I see you called 'em cattle instead of cows, too. So you likely meant that friendly."

"I did. I was about to have me some Arbuckle and you're welcome to join me, uh, Brazos."

Mackail studied on that before he nodded and said, "I'll just take you up on that, Pilgrim. For I can see you're a neighborly cuss, considering, and them fool cows is either headed back to water or they're long gone."

As he dismounted he added, "It was a queer as led 'em off. I told old Trinity we ought to shoot that queer, but he's a stubborn cuss. You wait 'til Trinity gets back from wherever the hell he rode off to and we'll see who was right or wrong about queers."

Joe noticed the cowboy's mount was trained to stand quietly with its reins on the grass. As Mackail joined him at the fire, Joe knelt again to open the tin of Arbuckle and pour some grounds in the pot. Mackail frowned and said, "You sure make fancy coffee, considering your other habits. You make it fresh ever' morning, Joe?"

"Tastes better that way. What's this queer whatever you keep talking about, Brazos?"

The cowboy shot him a curious look, saw he wasn't funning, and said, "Hell, I know you call cows cattle, but ever'body knows what a queer steer is! Ain't you ever even cut a milk cow he-critter, farmer boy?"

"I've castrated veal. My name is Joe to my friends. Folks who don't aim to be my friends had best call me Mister Barrow unless they're a hell of a lot bigger and meaner than anybody I see, hereabouts."

"Hey, don't get your bowels in an uproar, uh, Joe. I was only funning, and that Arbuckle do smell good. Getting back to what I was saying about them queers; if you've cut critters, you know you have to get all of both balls or it don't count. You leave even a speck of he-stuff in a steer and it gets all mixed up about its station in life. It don't know if it's a he or a she and the other critters get confused a mite, too. Some queer steers act she-male and get all worn and torn from the others trying to mount them. Others suspicion they're bull brutes, only they don't have the wherewithal to treat a she-critter right. It do vex a cow in heat to be mounted over and over by a sissy who can't get it up."

Joe chuckled at the grotesque pictures the visitor was painting and said, with a nod, "I can see how a messed-up neither-nore could get your herd to milling about and fussing some. You figure this queer steer of yours caused a stampede and they busted through your fence and—"

"Hold on one cotton picking minute!" Brazos cut in, adding, "Fair is fair, God damn it! If I don't hoorah you about *your* ways, you got no call to hoorah me, and that's the *second* time you've accused me of stringing God damned triple-titted Glidden wire!"

"I don't understand. Didn't you say you have a homestead claim nearby?"

"Well, shit yes we got us a homestead claim.

Two of 'em, in fact. One in my brother's name and one in mine, right across the way from one another. That's the only way we could *get* us a home spread in these infernal parts, now that President Arthur has opened up this stretch of Nebraska to settlers. Our combined holdings is the headquarters of the Double M. 'Course, we share the water from the single sunflower windmill. The main house and bunk shacks is on my claim. The tanks, corrals, and stables is on my brother's. You likely already know that the fool government requires you to build 'provements on the land you've filed on. So we sort of shared it out. But what's this bullshit about *fences*?"

"Don't you have a boundry line? Your combined holdings would make up a half section and—"

"Boundry lines? Hell, ever'body in these parts *knows* when they're on Mackail land. If you can see our windmill, you're on our land, God damn it."

Joe shot a thoughtful look at the far horizon and muttered, "Seems to me you could see a windmill quite a ways off, Brazos. You did say you only filed on half a square mile, right?"

"Yep. That's all the fool law allows. But you see, Old Son, this has always been sort of open country, until recent. Us old boys who got here *first* sort of picked out home spreads, here and there, and let our cows sort of graze wherever they had a mind to. Anybody can see it takes at least five or six acres of this prairie to keep one cow alive. How big a herd could anybody keep on a little over three hundred acres? That's all there is to a half section, you know."

Joe divided in his head and said, "Yeah, sixty

odd cows wouldn't make much of a herd, as beef,
would it?"

"Hell, old son, sixty head wouldn't be a big
dairy herd, and none of us know how to milk anyways. So what we've been doing, up to now, is
holding a few acres on paper and grazing the open
range all about. There's never been no need for
fencing. The cows all drift back to water, sooner
or later, and those as stray to another spread get
returned at roundup time. That's why we brand
'em in the first durned place."

Joe heard the pot starting to perk. He said, "Arbuckle's almost ready. I'm starting to see why we
got some ugly looks when we came out here. Tried
to strike up a conversation in town with a gent
dressed much like you, the other night. He looked
right through me and walked away, sort of muttering."

Brazos Mackail shrugged and said, "Well, I can't
say I welcome sod busters with open arms. But I
was raised polite and, what the hell, none of you
will *be* here long enough to really vex us."

"Is that a warning or a threat, Mackail?"

"Shoot, it's just common sense, like I keep telling old Trinity. There's no sense getting surly just
'cause Washington slickered you poor sod busters
into coming out here to pay taxes as you starve to
death. This bitty quarter section, here, is just a
pimple on the prairie's ass. You and yours will be
long gone and your fence will rust away in no time
at all."

Joe tested the pot again and said, "We came to
stay, Brazos."

The cowboy nodded and said, "Sure you did.
Nobody ever came all the way out here to be

busted and dusted out. But you ain't the first gent I've had this conversation with." He pointed at the horizon to the east and added, "There was a family from West-by-God Virginia just over the sky line, yonder, until last year or so. I disremember their name, but they was nice folks. Some of the boys talked foolish about nesters that close to our spread, but I told Trinity and the others to leave 'em alone and they'd larn, and that's what happened."

"What happened to them? Were they attacked by Indians or something?"

Brazos laughed and said, "Shoot, we ain't seen Sioux since '76 or so in these parts, and *they* was afraid of *us*, then! What attacked them folks was grasshoppers. They hit us at the Double M, too, only we didn't have no standing crops worth mention and the prairie heals itself sudden after the hordes has passed. We had to lay out some hay bales 'til the grass greened up again, but, you see, we *knowed* grasshoppers come through every few years, so we keep extra fodder on hand. Those poor sod busters only had lots of empty acres to show for all that hard work and, I dunno, I reckon they just quit whilst they could still make it back east with the few cents they had left. I rode over to see if there was anything I could do to help, but they was gone when I got there. Sort of spooky and sad to see a house just setting owl-eyed and empty in the middle of nowheres. They left the stove and some furnishings, by the way. Once you're set up, here, you might want to wander over and see if there's anything you need. I doubt they'll ever be back to argue the matter with any of us."

Joe decided he had Brazos pegged now. The Texan was a live-and-let-live type who, like himself, saw no reason to pick a fight he didn't have to. He poured two mugs of coffee as he said, "Well, I reckon it's only fair to warn you that I've an ace in the hole. I mean to plant a barley crop once I have the house up."

"Hell, Joe, I ain't a farmer and I can tell you there's a fifty-fifty chance your crop'll get frosted off afore it's high enough to matter."

"I know. I ain't finished. I'm more than a farmer. Back home I worked a spell as a blacksmith. If push comes to shove, I can always get work in town to tide us over."

Brazos started to say something, changed his mind, and took a sip of his coffee before he asked, "*Us*, Joe? I don't aim to pry, but I see you, and I see them rolls of Glidden wire, yonder. But I don't see nobody else."

Joe nodded and said, "I know. I left my Ma and kid sister in Pittsburgh Landing while I made things fitting, here."

"You got two female mouths to feed, with no male kin, Joe? The folks I just told you of had two husky boys to help, and they still got et out."

"I follow your drift. But, like I said, I have a trade. Our original plan was for me to homestead this claim with my Pa, but he took the ague and died on us. We'd already sold everything off, so what the hell and here I am. My Ma's wore out and not fit for much these days. But Jessie's a good worker. We'll make out."

"Jessie is this kid sister of your'n, right?"

"Yeah. She's really only my half sister. Our Ma

was married twice and the Pa I keep mentioning was really my step-father but . . . Thunderation, I don't know why I'm telling you all this, Brazos."

"I'm a good listener and you've been working out here all alone for a spell. It's sort of interesting, but you don't have to tell me about your folks if you don't want to."

Joe chuckled and said, "You're right, I've been talking to birds and such, too. There's no deep dark secrets in our family, Brazos. My real dad marched off to the war and got himself kilt at Shiloh. Ma married up with Jessie's pa when I was a baby and he treated us both right. I always thought of him as my Pa and I miss him, albeit not as much as Ma, I fear. That's all there is to our story. I reckon things like that happened a lot during the war.

Brazos nodded, soberly, and said, "I had an uncle killed in the same battle, Joe, only, we called it Pittsburgh Landing, on the other side."

Joe blinked in surprise and half turned his head to stare south at the distant roof tops as he marveled, "Pittsburgh Landing was what the *Rebs* called the Battle of Shiloh? That explains a lot. How many of you Southerons *are* there in these parts?"

"Enough to name the town, Joe. You see, when they cleaned out the Sioux, and Texas cows come north, they was drove by Texas riders. Until a few short years ago, there weren't enough Yankees in these parts to shake a stick at."

"Then most of you stock men are Southerons?"

"Not most, Joe. *All*. Mebbe that's why some of the old boys have acted sort of mule-headed about you new homesteaders. But don't let it fret you. We ain't all like that. Hell, me and Trinity were too young to ride on either side in the war. I figure it's sort of dumb to held a grudge until it's old enough to vote, and that's how long ago it was since your kin and mine were swapping shots at Shiloh, Pittsburgh Landing, or wherever."

Joe Barrow sipped his own coffee, wondering why it tasted so bitter despite being a mite weak. Had it really been twenty-two years since his real father, the father he'd never known, had died at rebel hands on a soft spring day, far from home?

This Texan's kin had been there. For all Joe knew, a Mackail trigger finger had orphaned him to be raised by another man. A man he'd liked well enough, but had never really respected. Pa had meant well. He'd tried. But they'd been poor, dirt poor, all their lives. It was a thought he'd often blocked out, but it rose like bile in his throat as he tried to swallow this bitter brew. His real father had been an officer, from a prosperous family up the valley. Ma had been too proud to approach them on his behalf the time he'd wanted to go to college. He understood why. But he couldn't help wondering, sometimes, what his life would have been, if some dirty rebel bastard hadn't killed his real father and . . . "You're right, Brazos," he said with a weary smile, "It was long ago and far away and there's no sense crying over spilt milk. I'll try to remember that cattle are cows and I won't ask anyone in town how it got its name, thanks to you."

Brazos shrugged and said, "Don't matter to me one way or the other, Joe. Neighborly is as neighborly does. You leave me alone and I'll leave you alone. But don't string that infernal wire too close to the road, hear?"

By LATE AFTERNOON the mysterious smoke on the horizon had faded away, it was seven times hotter than it had any right to be, and despite being totally worn out Joe Barrow couldn't see that he'd accomplished enough to matter.

The walls of the soddy to be now rose as high as his chest. He knew he had to allow for sinkage and that the roof, when he got to it, had to stand at least nine feet the first winter if he wasn't to bump his head on the beams by spring. The sod squares got dustier but no lighter in his weary hands as the day wore on. Big green flies pestered him as he worked, sucking the sweat from his exposed flesh and sometimes stinging. Big grasshoppers, the exact tawny gray of the prairie, buzzed up like rattlesnakes in a startling display of butterfly wings as he disturbed them with his spade. Overhead, two carrion crows circled, as if they were trying to tell him something about fools who worked like that under the merciless Nebraska sun. As the sun began to sink in the west Joe went to the well to fetch a pail of water for his supper. The well was dry. He stared down at the muddy bottom, far below, and cursed mindlessly for a time. Then he sighed, got the spade, and lowered himself forty feet on the rope ladder to dig it deeper.

At least it was cool down there. The vertical walls of soft loam were sobering to think about as he started digging. For if they caved in with him down here, that would be it. But they needed water, damn it, so he didn't think about it.

Joe was a good shovel hand, thanks to Pa. It was funny how Pa had never managed to amount to anything, back home. For though the old man had failed at every scheme he'd followed through the years, he'd been a good farmer and a good teacher. As Joe dug it seemed he could hear Pa saying, "That's it, Joseph. Let the tool do the work for you. Don't fight the spade with your arms. It'll whip you sure. Don't drive the blade with your hands. Put your foot on the step and lean easy. Give the earth time to make way for your weight. Now, don't pick up that dirt with your skinny *arms*, boy! Brace your down arm against your knee and *lever* it up, easy. That's right. Use the long handle to push down and the dirt just rides up, see? Now, you have the blade full. Don't you go *lifting*, hear? Swing it on the pivot your forearm makes agin' your thigh. Now, just twist your hands and *roll* the spoil off into the bucket. You're doing fine, boy. A man can dig all day, if he does it right. It's easy if you know how."

But it wasn't easy, damn it. It was back-breaking labor, even though he was strong and had the knack to keep going long after many a stronger man might have quit. Joe had to climb all the way to the top, haul the bucket up, dump it, and then climb back down to start all over again. He did this seven times before the earth he was digging in began to turn to liquid mud around his boots. He scooped the heavier muck until the water stood like brown soup around his ankles. Then he said, "That'll larn you to sink on me, old well. You'd best settle some before we use you for Arbuckle, though."

He climbed back up, hauled the bucket after himself, and emptied the slop on the ground. He saw a buckboard coming north along the wagon trace. The sunlight flashing on red hair told him at a distance who the girl driving the rig was. It was his buckboard, too. Like most of the gear they'd brought from Penn State, it had been left in town until things out here on the homestead were in order. Where Jessie had gotten the painted pony she was driving was a total mystery. He noticed the wagon bed was loaded with a mess of some-things under a tarp.

As Jessie swung off the wagon trace Joe went to meet her. The painted pony had a wall-eyed look and spooked as he caught its bridle. As Jessie got down he saw she was wearing the same green poplin skirt, but she had on a new and frilly blouse. He wondered where she'd spent their meager savings on such a foolish notion, but he didn't say so. Old Jessie was starting to blossom a mite as her teen-age baby fat gave way to the high cheek bones and feline grace of her Scotch-Irish ancestry. She was getting to be a real looker and it fretted a gal to dress poor, even if she was.

Jessie came over to give Joe a peck on the cheek, and she only had to rise a mite on her toes to do it, for Jessie was tall for a gal. She said, "I fetched some furnishings out for the house, Joe. How's it coming?"

He shot a disgusted glance at the sod walls and said, "See for your ownself, durn it. Where'd you get this critter? He looks spooky as hell."

Jessie laughed and said, "I hired him at the livery, of course. I got him cheap. The colored boy there said he was mean."

"I'd say he was telling you true, girl. Pa always said never to buy a horse who showed you the whites of his eyes. And look at them three white stockings! Don't you know that a pony should have all four hooves white or none at all?"

"Pooh, I didn't *buy* him, Joe, I only hired him to drive out and back. Why don't you ride back with me after we unload? Ma's worried about you. She says she just knows you're out here living on nothing but coffee."

He unhitched the painted pony and left the buckboard standing as he led it to the lumber pile to tether it, with Jessie tagging along. The pony shook its muzzle and tried to bite his hand. He slapped it across the face with the hat in his free hand and they started to get along better after that. He tied the reins to some bound two-by-fours. Then he turned to his half-sister and said, "You'll ride back alone, after we sup and jaw some. What do you mean about furnishings? I won't have any roof up for at least a couple more days. That's why I left everything in town with you and Ma, Jessie."

Jessie said, "Ma says some of our things will be safer out here with you. She hasn't been getting on with that landlady at the boarding house. She found out her kin rode for the South during the war and she fears they'll steal us blind."

Joe rolled his eyes heavenward and put his hat back on as he said, "I asked folks in town about that widow woman as lets rooms, Jessie. They told me she was a decent old gal."

"You don't have to convince *me*, Joe. I haven't had words with the poor old critter. But you know how Ma is about old rebs. They killed a couple of her cousins aside from . . . you know."

Joe knew. He and Jessie hadn't talked much about having different fathers, growing up. Pa had treated them both like his own and it hadn't seemed important, when they were kids.

Lately, since Pa had died and Ma had taken to brooding about the past so much, it had sort of changed. He wondered, sometimes, if Jessie felt as odd about him as he did her. He wondered what there was to feel odd about.

Lots of kids had had different fathers or mothers. Since they had the same Ma, they were kin, half-ways at least. But it sure was funny how, well, *different* they'd turned out. Neither one of them seemed to take after Ma. How could anybody look like a negatively pretty, washed-out-looking old gal? Joe had never even seen a tintype of his real father, but he must have favored him. When he looked in the mirror he saw a firm-jawed face that didn't look at all like Ma or Jessie. He had heavy brows and curly light brown hair. His eyes were wide-set and gunmetal gray. He knew eyes like that must have glazed in death long ago under the blossoming fruit trees in the lovely hell of Shiloh. Nobody else he'd ever known had eyes like his.

Jessie favored Pa's Scotch-Irish kin. Her feline green eyes gazed at him friendly enough. Sometimes, when they got to jawing, he could see her dead father's pleasant ghost in their depths. Yeah, he could see she was Pa's daughter, right enough. But Pa hadn't been his father, and there was nothing of his mother in her smiling face. He wondered why, lately, that had started to spook him.

He said, "Well, it'll likely rain and ruin everything, but if Ma's still fighting the war I'd best unload the stuff and put it inside the walls. I reckon it'll be safe enough, under the tarp. Why don't you fix us some grub whilst I unload?"

Jessie said, "Pooh, it's early and you look like you've been drug through the keyhole backwards. I'd best give you a hand. Has it been hard out here, Joe?"

He rolled the tarp away and stared soberly at the pathetic treasures Ma and Pa had accumulated from a lifetime of unremitting toil. He said, "We never expected a farmstead to just grow all by itself out here, girl. The sods are hard to cut, but at least they're free. Ever' other damned thing out here except the cow turds costs the earth."

Jessie laughed as he looked away, aware he'd cussed in front of a gal. He picked up a silver chest and toted it away. It was heavy enough to be filled with a real silver service, but of course it was only tin and pot metal, with any artificial surface it may have once had long since polished away by Ma's nervous fussy hands. Jessie picked up a bird cage that hadn't held a bird in living memory in one hand, then gathered some quilts in the other to follow him. He led her through the gap left for a doorway in the walls. He put the chest down in a corner. Jessie placed the other shoddy treasures atop it and said, "My, these walls look sort of *shaggy,* Joe."

He said, "I know, When I get around to it, I mean to plaster the insides with mud and maybe whitewash 'em. I've heard some soddys even have wall paper. But they say you have to let 'em settle a year or so first."

"Ma's likely to have a fit about this dirt floor, too."

"She's been having lots of them things, lately. I studied on laying some planks, Jessie. We can't afford it. The lumber for the roof alone costs enough, out here, to build a whole frame house back east. I wanted to lay tarpaper over the roof planks afore I layed the sods of the roof, but it costs too much. They tell me the roofs stop leaking, once the grass up there comes back to life and roots together solid."

"Good Lord, a lawn for a roof? How will we ever mow it, honey?"

"Don't see as we have to. This buffalo grass don't grow all that high."

He sure wished he could get her to stop calling him Honey. But he didn't see how he could say so without hurting her feelings. Ma had always called both of them Honey and he knew it seemed only natural to old Jessie. There wasn't anything wrong with a sister calling her brother "Honey", when you studied on it. Maybe it was just that they didn't *look* like brother and sister. He remembered how that old gent on the train had referred to Jessie as his wife, and how funny it had made him feel. He'd have felt even funnier setting the old gent straight, so he hadn't, and that had made him feel sort of, well, sneaky. Like he and old Jessie shared some guilty secret.

There was more junk on the buckboard than he'd remembered and after they had made a few more trips it was coming back to him how hard he'd been working all day. Jessie was sort of sweating, too, by the time she'd staggered from the buckboard with her last load.

The sun was lower, now, and the western sky was blushing red and painting the prairie a soft orange with purple shadows. But it was still hot. Joe knew it would stay hot until well after the stars came out. He went to the fire, hunkered down, and poked the embers alive before tossing on more cow chips. Jessie went to the buckboard, took off her blouse, and hung it over the wagon tongue. She was wearing a thin cotton shift under it, of course, but as she began to remove her green skirt, Joe gaped at her and asked, "What in thunder are you *doing*, girl?"

Jessie said, "I don't want to sweat-stain my duds, honey. What's the matter with you? You've seen me in my shift before, Lord knows. We used to take baths together, naked as jaybirds, remember?"

"God damn it that was a long time ago in the first place and we are right next to a public highway in the second!"

"Pooh, it'll be dark in a few minutes. Nobody's coming. I'm wearing my shift, anyway."

She draped the skirt over the wagon tongue and came to join him at the fire, saying, "Oh, that feels ever so much better. I should have taken off those duds before I got all sweated up."

As she sat in the grass across from him, Jessie raised her bare knees and hugged them. He looked quickly down at the fire. The fool girl had no stockings on above her high button boots. He couldn't tell if she had drawers on or not from where he hunkered. Her legs were in the way. But if she *didn't* have drawers on, and if she moved her shins apart a mite . . .

Joe glanced around. There was nobody in sight as far as the eye could see and it was getting darker. He knew that if he insisted on her covering herself proper she'd just pester him to tell her why. How the hell did a man tell his own sister that it made a man remember why boys and girls were built different when she traipsed about him half-naked?

She'd think he was dirty-minded. But, damn it, Jessie was old enough to know better. He remembered, back home when she'd been about eleven or twelve and he'd surprised her primping stark naked in front of the pier glass in Ma's room. She'd just laughed and said Hi and he'd crawfished out sudden, but not before he'd seen the budding little breasts and the shadow of soft red down between her long kid legs. They'd never talked about it, after, but they were both a lot older, now. He could see the nipples of her fully matured breasts in the flickering firelight, for the cotton shift was a mite outgrown as well as thin. He knew her groin would be fully thatched with flaming red hair, now, and that he'd likely see it any infernal minute if he wasn't careful.

Damn it, Ma must have told her *something*, by

now, about the birds and bees. He knew *he* wasn't about to. She'd likely just laugh and say it didn't count with close kin. She was right, too. It was downright unseemly for a brother to even be thinking about his own sister's pubic hair, red or otherwise. Maybe Ma was right and he should be thinking about marrying up with some gal, like she said. He'd sparked a few gals in his time. Even had a few who hadn't been no better than they should have been. That was likely what was making him so dirty, lately.

It was easy enough for a virgin boy to keep his thoughts pure when he had too much to do to worry about courting some sassy gal down the valley. But once a man had lost his cherry and found out why peckers got hard all by themselves, there was just no controlling the thoughts that sprang out at him, unbidden.

Jessie said, "I'd best see about supper. I brought some pots out. You fetch the water and I'll rustle the grub."

Then she started to rise, opening her upraised shins to brace herself as she leaned forward. The firelight flashed for a split second between her thighs and though her groin was exposed, it was covered by a V of startling white cotton. Joe wondered, as he turned away, why the momentary glimpse of innocent undergarment seemed more exciting than anything he could have imagined. He rose, himself, and went to the well to draw a bucket of water. It smelled muddy, but when he brought it to the fire it was clear enough to use. As she filled the pots and put them on the fire to simmer he told her about the water table. It seemed awfully important, right now, to keep talking about things like that.

There were two sides to the coin of Jessie's disturbing unconcern about her feminine identity. You could talk to Jessie man to man.

As much a farmer as many a man he'd met, Jessie was genuinely interested in details that even Ma and other housewives didn't see fit to worry their heads about. Ma always said it was a woman's task to cook and sew and it was up to her menfolks to supply the food on the table and the notions from the store.

Jessie found the deep water table interesting as hell and had some right sensible suggestions about the layout of the homestead, for a gal.

As she put turnips and spuds in the pot and began to slice the side of bacon she'd brought from town Jessie said, "I see you figured smart about the doorway facing south, Joe. I ain't sure you ought to have windows in the north and west walls, though. The east window's all right. It'll catch the morning light, winter and summer. The south windows on either side of the door will give us plenty of light, too. But I mind you'd best block up those other gaps you've started. The afternoon sun is cruel out here. The north wind in the winter is said to be a pure bitch. I'd leave those two walls blank."

"You would, huh? When did you start cussing, girl?"

"Cussing, honey? Bitch ain't a cuss word. It's a she-hound."

"Well, you hadn't ought to call anything else a bitch, then. As to the windows, I don't feel all that comforted by a blank wall facing north. North is where the Sioux and other spiteful folks would ride from. The Nebraska Sand Hill country is up thataways, a few days's ride."

"Shoot, I hear tell the Sioux were cleared from the Sand Hill Country long ago, honey."

"I heard that, too. It's cattle country, now. Feller in town was telling me it was more peaceable out here when they only had the *Sioux* to worry about!"

"Heavens, you're not afraid of cowboys, are you? I met some in town just today and they seemed friendly enough, to me."

"That figures. Mebbe I'll just leave a couple of small windows facing north. Big enough to shove a rifle barrel out. Too small for a blizzard to blow through."

Jessie shrugged as she dropped a couple of slices of bacon in with the turnips and spuds to boil. She said, "At least leave the west wall blank, then. It's still hot as blazes with the sun ball down. The afternoon sunbeams frying on the floor inside would make our new house an oven."

Joe frowned and said, "Hell, there has to be some light inside."

"Well sure there has to be, honey. But how many windows do you think we need in a one room house?"

Joe said, quietly, "I mean to divide it up a mite, once there's time. I figure the bedrooms ought to be set aside from the main."

Jessie looked at him innocently across the fire and Joe wondered why he felt like he'd said something dirty. Jessie shrugged again and he wished she had her bare shoulders covered. There was nothing wrong, really wrong, with a female's shoulders, for God's sake. Gals had shoulders just like everybody else, except maybe punier and, well, sort of oddly flirty-looking.

She said, "Well I sure would like to have my own room. But we've got so much work to do, Honey. I don't mind sharing one room with you and Ma for now. It ain't like the three of us are strangers, you know."

Joe didn't answer as he stared down at the coals. As a Victorian, Joe of course had no true grasp of the mind-bending contradictions of the moral code he'd been brought up under. The puritan morality and sniggering preoccupation with impossible modesty that "decent" folk had drummed into them from birth made for very confused mental gymnastics that only the smug and stupid could feel comfortable with.

In an era when almost everyone was involved with agriculture and even city folk kept livestock in the backyard, a proper Victorian maiden was supposed to blush, or hopefully faint, if anyone was crude enough to say "cock" instead of "rooster" or "bull" instead of "he-brute."

Women were not supposed to have legs. "Leg" was a word avoided by the primmer, even when referring to the legs of a table. The human body was a shameful object and in theory not even the lowest prostitute would expose her naked body fully, while a proper Christian wife, of course, went to bed clad head to toe in a flannel gown. Nobody, ever, admitted any carnal knowledge of another living soul.

But in practice, it simply wouldn't work. Only the more prosperous could afford separate rooms for every member of a family. Few of the really rich had indoor plumbing. So the thunder mug under the bed or the outhouse used by one and all just had to be ignored. People who *noticed* one another heeding the call to nature simply were not genteel.

It was impossible to do housework or farm chores with every inch of skin covered as the code demanded. Women mopped bare-footed with their skirts hiked up, but since women didn't have ankles, nobody was supposed to notice. Men working stripped to the waist in the privacy of their own residence were somehow invisible to the female members of their household. In the heat of summer in a stuffy Victorian house, both sexes moved in a state of deshabille they concealed behind lace curtains to the outside world. Like the double standard that allowed boys to be boys on the shady side of town, Victorians assured themselves that "relations don't count" when the cramped conditions of a crowded household forced them to drop the awesome standards of modesty they were expected to uphold in public.

But Joe Barrow had a logical mind. It refused to "see" that a glimpse of stocking on the street was shocking and that his Ma squatting on a piss pot or his kid sister taking a bath by the kitchen stove were things a man just didn't notice. He knew Jessie would think he was some sort of maniac if he allowed it didn't seem right for a man to share one room with two women. He felt mighty ashamed of his secret. It wouldn't have been any comfort to him had he known about the rampant incest the forced intimacy in other households of the hypocritical era often led to. Like any other proper Victorian, he'd have been shocked. The thought of actually doing anything to Jessie, or, God forbid, his Ma, had never crossed Joe's conscious mind. Any decent gal he wasn't married to would be safe in bed with Joe, stark naked, and the Good Book said you couldn't marry up with your kin. He just knew he'd feel more comforted if the two of 'em slept somewhere else, and for God's sake kept their duds on when he was about.

He and Jessie talked some more about the future farm over supper. Then she put on her proper duds while he hitched the pony to the buckboard for her. She kissed him again before he could get her to drive back to town. It was pure dark now, but town wasn't far and she'd be all right if that fool pony didn't bolt. He meant to have a talk with the livery the next time he was in town. Jessie was strong, for a gal, and knew how to handle horseflesh better than some men. But she was still his kid sister, dammit, and they had no call hiring her a mean-eyed pony.

He let the fire die as he laid another row of sods by starlight. He kept at it until he ran out of cut sods. It was too dark to cut more. They had to be the same size and squared true. So he stopped. He had to stop, but, Jesus, there was so much to do out here and so little time betwixt sunrise and sunset. It was late in the season for planting and he couldn't even begin to plow until he strung the fence. He knew what free ranging cattle would do to sprouting barley spears. Barley was a piss poor crop, next to the more profitable wheat. It grew faster and could take some frost. That was why you couldn't get a good price for it. Any durned fool could grow barley. But at least it was a crop. It'd be a crying shame to let a hundred and sixty acres lie fallow until next spring, just because they'd been late getting out here and he couldn't seem to work no faster.

Joe sank down on the open bedroll and hauled off his boots. He undid his gunbelt and placed it on his hat nearby to keep it from the dew on the grass, come morning. He sprawled luxuriously and sighed, "Oh, Lord, I've needed this for quite a spell, now."

It was still a mite warm. But he pulled the blankets over himself anyway. He knew that if he fell asleep exposed to the night air, even fully clothed, he'd wake up with cramps from head to toe. He'd worked his fool head off all day and a man had to keep his back muscles warm if he aimed to use them the next day.

His body was exhausted, but sleep refused to fill his active mind. He had so many plans and so little time. He knew he needed all the sleep he could get. So he told himself to forget the chores and think about something else. The only thoughts he seemed to have that didn't concern the work at hand all seemed to be dirty.

"I need a woman." he decided, trying to ignore the unbidden erection he suddenly noticed. It had been a long time since he'd had that Crawford gal in the hayloft, back home in Penn State. Good Lord, it had been just afore Pa died. He'd been too busy since then to trifle with gals.

Ginger Crawford had been sort of trashy, like all her kin, but, Jesus, he sure could have used her tonight. He wondered who Ginger was fooling with right now. He knew she hadn't gone without it all this time. For a seventeen year old, she'd sure screwed like she'd been at it some time. He wondered who'd broken old Ginger in. Mike Harris, the old boy who'd fixed him up with Ginger, had said all the trashy Crawford women screwed like mink. He'd sure been right about Ginger. He'd allowed the whole durn family rutted like pigs in their one-room shanty down by the river. Joe had no notion how Mike had learned this, but he said they did it. Mother, father, brothers and sisters, just going at it hot and heavy every time they felt like it. It sounded mighty wild, even though Ginger hadn't hesitated much as soon as they were alone in that hayloft, and hadn't worn a stitch under her threadbare dress, neither.

He knew the Crawford brothers weren't much. He'd had to whip Seth Crawford's ass for stealing his pencil in school that time. So mayhaps Mike was right about the Crawford gals and their brothers, but, Jesus, that part about them taking turns with their own Ma just wasn't possible. Nobody could do a thing like that to their own Ma, even if a shiftless Pa would stand for it!

Old Mike had sniggered when he said that Pa Crawford didn't mind, since he enjoyed his daughters so much. But Joe had said it was crazy as well as disgusting. Good God, Ma Crawford was old and fat and ugly. Who in thunder would want to bed the old bawd even if they weren't related to her?

Of course, if folks were really dirty as hell and had a nice looking Ma, it was barely possible a total randy asshole might go crazy some night and forget hisself. But even if his Ma was young and sort of pretty, like his own Ma, he'd have to be drunk or something, even if he caught her naked and alone and . . . "Jesus!" Joe groaned aloud as, unbidden, the picture of that time he'd walked in on his mother bathing in the kitchen filled his mind with forbidden pictures.

"If you have to think about naked women," he told himself, "Think about some other naked women, you damned fool!"

But that wasn't as easy as it sounded. For in truth, the few women he'd had in his time had all been partly dressed. He'd never really seen any naked women in his whole life, save for his half-sister and his still reasonably good-looking mother.

Hence, even as he tried to fantasize about other women, and Joe was a healthy young man who hadn't had sex for far too long, he was ill equipped to do so. Almost every woman he'd ever had or wanted had been almost fully clad. So no matter what sort of face he put on an imaginary sex partner, when he got them undressed they were either tall willowy teen agers with red pubic aprons, or a smaller more voluptuous and mature woman with a white rounded belly and a wet mop of dishwater blonde between suddenly shyly crossed creamy thighs.

"I've got to get me a fancy gal," Joe decided. "As soon as I get the roof up, and afore I move Ma and Jessie out here, I'll just stride into a parlour house bold as brass and lay my money down. It don't matter if we can afford it or not. I've got to see me at least one saucy brunette gal, stripped naked as a jay bird. Might even get me a Mex or Breed gal, too. I got to set my mind straight afore I daydreams any more naked ladies. A man who jerks off with his own kin in mind would likely eat shit, too!"

As JOE LAY torturing himself alone on the prairie, the nightriders were moving just over the horizon. As they passed a soddy, the masked leader laughed and said, "There's one we don't have to worry about, boys. Grasshoppers run that bunch out for us."

The rider at his side said, "Let's torch it anyways. Some other infernal nesters are likely to take up the abandoned claim and there's no sense leaving a house standing for the bastards."

But the leader said, "No. The fence is gone. Scavengers from town took the posts and wire. That's all that really matters. Yonder soddy will melt back into the range afore anybody can sort out the papers filed on this old spread. Besides, they'd see the flames from town and I don't like ducking the Sheriff's posses unless I've done something important. You boys have to pay attention to business. I told you where we're headed this night. Them folks who filed on the water hole the Bar Seven's always used was told in town they was committing suicide. I aims to prove to them that the warning was serious."

"That old waterhole's a smart ride from here, pard. What about them new folks, just to the west on the wagon trace? I hear there's only one kid over there, still building his infernal soddy. Do we ride over that way, we'd likely catch him alone. He ain't even got a watch dog."

The leader snorted in annoyance under the feed sack over his head. He said, "God damn it, old son, if I've told you boys once I've told you a hundred times. This ain't a Halloween party! We don't ride ever' which way whoopin' and shootin' like trail drivers coming into Dodge. We picks our targets with care, and once we picks one, we sticks to it. We can't wipe out every damned one of these sod busters. We has to pick off good examples. Tonight we're going to larn those sons of bitches not to file on water rights other folks saw first."

"Well, hell, can't we hit that sassy Barrow kid on the way back? He's a pure sitting duck, and we don't even have to work at cleaning up after him. His fence ain't strung and his soddy ain't finished. We could just stuff him and his supplies down his well afore we caved it in. They wouldn't see *that* from town would they?"

The leader reconsidered as he rode on. They'd said in town the son of a bitch was another Yankee from Penn State. So it was sort of tempting. But then he shook his head and said, "Not yet. Not until we have to. It's too close to the Double M spread. Goddam Sheriff would be out there asking questions in no time at all."

"Shoot, old Trinity Mackail lies good. Old Sheriff wouldn't get much out of Trinity."

"Mebbe. I reckon we'll just leave the Double M out of the Sheriff's calculations, for now. That fool Barrow's dirt poor and figures to go busted anyway."

"Yeah? What if he makes it? They say he's a working son of a bitch and he has a trade to tide him over 'til he gets a crop, too."

"We'll worry about that when the time comes. Nobody in town's about to hire the son of a bitch. If he pulls a rabbit out of his hat, we'll just drop by some night and shoot the critter."

A rider on the leader's other flank growled, "Might have to pay us a call on the Double M, too. For a cow man, old Brazos Mackail is too friendly with farm folk for my tastes. His brother's all right, but—"

And then the rider was out of his saddle with a gasp of surprised pain as the leader reined in, whirled his mount, and snapped, "Don't *do* it, damn it! He didn't *know!*"

The rider who'd ridden up to pistol whip the man who'd threatened the Double M from his saddle sat his own mount quietly, holding the gun in his hand thoughtfully as the man he'd dismounted rose to his feet, holding a hand in wonder to the blood welling from under his feed sack mask. He shook his head groggily and gasped, "For God's sake, why'd you have to go and do a fool thing like that? Who the hell *are* you?"

The leader snapped, "Shut up, both of you. You

boys know you ain't to question each other's true names or outfits. Nobody but me needs to know who each and ever' one of you might be. That way, if one of us gets caught . . . But never mind. Get back on your pony, old son, and we'll say no more about it."

The fallen nightrider hauled himself back aboard his bronc, still dazed and too dumb to drop it. He muttered, "You busted me right after I said something about the Double M, you skunk. I'll bet you must be—" and then, as the silent masked rider who'd dismounted him leveled the pistol in his hand he quickly added, "Right. We'll just forget the whole deal. I stand corrected that we have no friends riding for the Double M."

The leader nodded and clucked his own mount into motion, leading off, as he reconsidered his options. Behind him, the man only he and a few others knew as Windy Travis had recovered from his pistol whipping and was still jawing, albeit innocently.

But Windy wasn't stupid, despite his big mouth. He had to know now why he'd been attacked by the other masked rider the moment he threatened the Mackail brothers. The man riding for the Double M knew too, and he'd just proven he had an unpredictable temper.

There was a chance the whole thing would blow over, but the wily ex-guerrilla in command didn't believe in leaving things to chance. Windy had been humiliated. Despite the care they'd taken in keeping most of their true identities a secret from one another in the lower ranks, Windy now held a dangerous set of guesses to go with his often careless talk. The other rider, knowing this, would probably go for Windy, later, on his own. For, despite the mask, anybody who'd ever heard Windy sound off would know who he was.

The poor bastard was still talking back there, for God's sake. The leader paid the words no mind, for the brags of a dead man didn't matter and Windy was dead, although he hadn't figured that out yet.

The leader decided he'd do it after they burned out the sod busters by the Bar Seven water rights. When the gang broke up, he'd offer to ride part way with Windy and as soon as they were alone, Old Rufus would do the rest. It was too bad. Windy had been a good old boy. But, like he kept telling them, this was serious business they were on, and what the hell, if he worked it right, they might blame it on the sod busters.

The sun ball read almost high noon and Joe Barrow had the sod walls above the level of his head when the buckboard stopped out front. Joe stopped what he was doing, wiped the sweat from his brow and mosied over to greet the tall stern figure holding the reins of a bay horse between the shafts. The stranger had a Winchester across his knees, pointed sort of casually in Joe's direction. A nickel-plated star was pinned to the lapel of his dark frock coat. So Joe kept his own hands well clear of the pistol on his hip as he nodded at the man and saia, "Howdy."

The stranger said, "I'm Deputy Brody. If you're Joe Barrow, climb aboard. Sheriff MacLeod wants to have a word with you in town. If you're aiming to say you're somebody else, don't. You fit the description they gave me to a tee."

Joe frowned and said, "I'm Joe Barrow and I'll be proud to ride in with you, if it's important. My Ma and kid sister ain't in trouble, are they?"

Brody said, "Not hardly. You may be. Sheriff will decide that after he sizes you up. Get aboard, boy. I ain't got all day."

Wordlessly, Joe climbed up on the spring seat beside the deputy. Brody waited until he was settled before he added, "You'd do well to unbuckle that gun rig. Just keep your hands polite and where I can see 'em. I'll put your gun in the back, for now."

Joe did as he was told. As the deputy pulled the rig away with his own free hand and dropped it behind them in the empty wagon bed, Joe asked, "Am I under arrest? What's the charge?"

Brody clucked the bay forward and swung them around before he replied, "Sheriff didn't say. My orders was to bring you in. I have had some past misunderstandings with gents who argued a moot point whilst wearing a gun, so, all in all, we'll both ride in more relaxed with me holding all the hardwear."

As the bay broke into a trot, Joe shrugged and said, "I was raised never to argue with the law unless I'd done something, which I ain't. If I allow you're the boss, would you be neighborly enough to tell me what this is all about?"

Brody said, "I ain't one for talking. Sheriff MacLeod's right good at it, though. So suppose we let him explain, eh?"

Joe nodded and kept silent, his mind in a whirl. The obedience of his suspect seemed to mollify the older man. After they'd ridden a time in silence he said grudgingly, "I can see you was raised

polite, boy. It do be tedious dragging folks in
kicking and screaming. They told me you was a
Yankee, too. I guess that only goes to show. There's
good and bad most ever'where."

"I take it you're from Texas, too, Mister Brody?"

"Nope. Old Virginia. Rode with the South in
my day. Likely afore you was birthed."

Joe didn't answer, aware he could be in trouble
no matter what he said to this infernal old Reb.
Deputy Brody nodded as if to himself and said,
"Understand your Daddy rode for the Union Cavalry, as an officer."

Joe sighed, knowing Ma had been at it again in
town. He nodded and said, "He did. He was killed
at Shiloh. I seckon you'd rather hear me say it as
Pittsburgh Landing, huh?"

Brody's voice was sober as he said, "You just call
it what you feel like calling it, son. By any name,
it was one hell of a fight, with lots of good men
killed on both sides. I wasn't trying to hoorah you
about your Daddy, Joe Barrow. I was *in* the war.
I don't have to prove what an unreconstructed
rebel I am by mean-mouthing folks who wasn't
there. I fit for the side I felt I ought to. Your daddy
did the same for his own. You have no call to feel
ashamed of a man who died for his cause, whatever it might have been."

Joe nodded and said, "Thank you. I'm not
ashamed of my father. I never knew him, but if
you must know, I'm sort of proud of him."

"There you go. I said you acted like a boy raised
decent. Now that we've got that straight, I'd best
tell you something about Sheriff MacLeod. He *is*
a Texican. Rode for the South as a full colonel. He
was wounded some and decorated all to hell. The

Federal Government refused him a U.S. Marshal's badge, but they can't keep an old Southeron from getting hisself elected fair and square, can they?"

"I reckon not, when the county is filled to the brim with Texas cowboys."

Brody drove silently for a time before he sighed and said, "Now, talk like that is what I was aiming to warn you agin', boy. As I was about to say afore you smart-mouthed, Sheriff MacLeod don't have to prove he's a Hero of the Lost Cause by picking on bitty Yankees. He's got a whole drawer-full of medals and citations to prove it. So listen sharp. You'll find the sheriff firm but fair. He'd hang Robert E. Lee in the flesh if he caught him doing something as called for a hanging. On the other hand, he'd let Beast Butler and U.S. Grant ride off together if they had proper papers on the horses they was riding. Do you follow my drift?"

"Sure. Like you said, there's good and bad no matter where you look."

Brody laughed and said, "There you go. When we get into town, I want you to look Sheriff MacLeod in the eye and tell him true. Don't try to bend things even a little bit. Old Mac is sort of gentle-spoke, considering, but he's hell on fibbers and I've never seen one fool him yet."

"I've got nothing to hide. But I thank you for the advice."

He waited a while before he added, "I guess I'll just have to wait until we get there before I hear the charges, huh?"

Brody thought and then he said, "Well, hell, it says in the constitution that a man has a right to know. So what the hell: If you did it you already know. If you didn't it don't matter. The crime you're suspected of is murder. Murder in the First Degree."

Sheriff Ewen Angus MacLeod, Colonel, C.S.A., Retired, was a balding courtly man on the comfortable side of sixty. He sat behind his desk with his fingers steepled thoughtfully and, save for the deep tan and old saber scar, his face resembled that of a friendly family doctor more than it seemed a feared and respected lawman ought to look like. On the paneled wall behind him MacLeod displayed a tattered, bullet-riddled Confederate flag. On a staff-stand nearby hung the Stars and Stripes of the Union. Sheriff MacLeod saw no contradiction in this. For he'd followed the Stars and Bars in victory and defeat, and today he was an officer of a different kind who'd sworn to uphold the laws and stand by the constitution of These United States.

As the deputy ushered Joe in the sheriff rose and stepped around the desk to extend his hand. Joe shook with him, noting the gentle steel in the tough older man's grip and responding with just enough pressure to let the sheriff know he was sort of strong his ownself. Sheriff MacLeod said, "It was good of you to come, Mister Barrow." Then he noted the gunbelt hanging over his deputy's elbow and raised an eyebrow to say, "I don't feel that was called for, Deputy Brody. Surely Mister Barrow, here, offered to come forward as a willing witness?"

Brody said, "The boy didn't offer me no resistance, Sheriff. We just figured he'd be more comforted without all that hardware around his hips as we rode the bouncy old buckboard."

"Well, none of us are riding a buckboard, now. Give the man his property, Deputy."

Brody handed Joe his gunbelt, sans comment. Joe strapped it on and as he buckled up he noticed Brody had casually unbuttoned his frock coat to let it fall away from his own holstered hogleg. The Sheriff wore a serious-looking Patterson Conversion in a waxed cutaway crossdraw rig. He obviously didn't worry much about other folks having guns on, and of course Brody was backing his play, whatever in thunder it might be.

MacLeod waited politely until Joe stood more manly before he nodded and said, "Please follow me, Mister Barrow. Got something I want to talk to you about."

Joe followed the older man out with the deputy bringing up the rear. They moved back through the county building along a narrow corridor. The Sheriff opened a door and led them into a little room. A body lay under a sheet on a trestle table. The Sheriff pulled the sheet down. Joe saw the body of a stocky stranger, dressed cowboy. The pale face stared at the ceiling with a look of numb surprise. The checked shirt was blown away at the side near the dead man's waist line. The exposed flesh under the tattered edges of the shirt looked like ground meat. Sheriff MacLeod strode around to the far side, facing Joe, before he smiled and said, "Well?"

Joe frowned down at the body and said, "I can see this gent is dead. If you want an educated guess, I'd say he was took from behind with a shot gun. You didn't need me to tell you that, though."

"That's true, Mister Barrow. We thought you might know him."

Joe shook his head and said, "Never seen him before, alive or dead. I'm sorry, but if you brung me in to help you identify him, I can't help you."

The Sheriff said, "Oh, we know who he is, Mister Barrow. His name was William Travis. They called him Windy. He was a rider for the Circle Six. We haven't notified his kith and kin yet. People do act silly when a man's been bushwacked and the law has nobody in the lockup to answer for it."

Joe shrugged and said, "Well, I see you've decided to hang this on me, but I didn't do it and you can just believe me or go to hell."

"Watch your mouth, boy!" snapped Deputy Brody, adding, "You are talking to the law!"

But the Sheriff just smiled and said, "That's all right. I can see Mister Barrow doesn't understand the situation." Then he swung his glance on Joe and said, "We don't work like that in this country, son. I don't accuse anybody of anything until I know he did it."

"Then what am I doing here? I never saw this dead man afore. I was nowheres near him when he got shot."

"That's not exactly true, Mister Barrow. The body was found near your claim. Windy's mount came home without him at sunrise. Lucky for you, his sidekicks notified us he was missing as they started searching. Some of my men checked the old abandoned claim near your place. He was just inside the doorway with his toes in the grass outside. We figured he had to be under some kind of cover, since you can see carrion crows a long ways on the prairie and they'd have been circling anybody down in the open."

Joe nodded with a slight shudder and said, "I knowed about the old claim just over the sky line from our'n. I can't see why you say it was lucky for me they found him next door."

"You can't? Funny, you looks like a bright lad. I said it was lucky for you he was found by *us* and not a posse of pissed-off cow hands. What do you reckon they'd have done to the first sod buster they could find, Mister Barrow?"

Joe blinked in sudden understanding and muttered, "Jesus."

"That's the way I see it, too. What was Mister Barrow doing when you came upon him, Deputy Brody?"

Brody said, "Nothing important, Sheriff. He was working on his sod house, now that I study on it."

"I see. Well, you can see the problem we have here, Mister Barrow. You're the only man I can come up with who was anywhere near the scene when Windy was shot. Are you sure you didn't hear anything last night? Coroner says he was hit with two charges from a ten gauge and sound carries far on the still night air."

Joe thought before he shook his head and replied, "Nossir. I slept through it if it was anywheres near enough to matter. How far off is that old claim?"

"Don't you know? I thought you just said you'd been there."

"Well I ain't. I heard *tell* the place was near our'n. I've been too busy to go exploring."

"I see. Who told you the place was there, Mister Barrow?"

Joe started to answer. Then he thought better of it and replied, "A cow hand told me. He stopped for Arbuckle a few days back. Disremember his name, if he offered it."

"What did this mysterious cow hand look like, Mister Barrow?"

"Like a cowboy, of course. Had on a big hat and them leather chaps they all wear. I remember wondering why they all wear them chaps, out here on open prairie."

The Sheriff sighed and said, "Nobody did, until a year or so ago. They say it do smart to ride into a bobwire fence unexpected at sundown. But let's get back to this gent on the table. Do you own a shotgun, Mister Barrow?"

Joe said, "Yes. Only it's at the boarding house with Ma and kid sister. I reckon that makes them suspects too, huh?"

MacLeod smiled thinly and said, "Not hardly. I know about the ladies. Know where they were last night, too. In a small town, things like that are easy to check on with a few questions. I'll take your word the family scatter gun was safely stored away. But we did find some new shells. They tell me at the general store that they don't stock that brand of ammo. So the killer must have brought them from somewhere else, like maybe from back east. We found one under the old stove and another under that bin in the corner. I reckon that in the dark the killer didn't notice he was leaving evidence, eh?"

Joe shrugged and said, " 'Peers to me he didn't give a damn. You don't drop shells from a double barrel scatter gun by accident. He must have broke it in the soddy to reload if you found his spent brass."

The sheriff nodded and said, "You can go now, Mister Barrow. I thank you for your co-operation."

Joe looked surprised and asked, "You believe me?"

MacLeod didn't nod, but said, "I believe you either didn't do it or you're a liar worthy of my total admiration. You see, I asked you some trick questions. If you were anywhere near the scene, you shouldn't be trying to homestead. You belong on the stage, making a fortune as one hell of an actor."

Joe looked blankly at him. The Sheriff smiled and said, "The body wasn't in the doorway. It was inside, on its back. You never blinked an eye when I said we'd found him face down in the doorway. You didn't take the hook when I mentioned a stove and bin that folks salvaged long ago, either. But what I really liked was that remark about brass shells. We never found two rounds inside the soddy, Mister Barrow. There was only one. My deputies found it in the grass outside. It was an unusual cartridge, like I said, only it was red paper with a metal base. Ten Gauge DuVal."

"DuVal? Never heard of that make."

"I know. It's a small company down Texas way. I was wondering how a Penn State newcomer could have come by shotgun shells made in Austin, but you have to understand I have a job to do. I hope you'll forgive me for joshing you with a few foolish questions, son."

The Sheriff led the way back to his office as Brody, behind Joe asked, "How come you left your guns with your womenfolks, boy? Seems to me you'd need 'em out on your claim."

Joe patted the gun on his hip and said, "I got me a sidearm. Too busy out there right now to go hunting and my sister Jessie could need a gun, too."

"You never knows when anybody might need a gun. Your sister sounds like a tough little lady."

"She's all right. Ma is sort of spooked out here and keeps thinking folks is out to rob her. Jessie has the shotgun under the bed as a sort of comfort, if you want to see it."

Ahead of him, MacLeod said, "I told you we were dropping it for now, Mister Barrow." Then, back once more in the office, he turned to add, "I'd best fill you in on a few things before you leave us though. Meaning no disrespect, you carry a tolerable chip on your shoulder, for a sod buster."

"Mebbe that's 'cause cowboys keep hoorawing me."

"That's to be expected, son. I disremember anybody in these parts asking you homesteaders to come out here in the first place."

"I guess we got a right to file on government land they've opened to settling, Sheriff."

"Well, sure you have. And I mean to back the law no matter how foolish it gets. But my job would sure be a lot easier if both sides had better *manners* in these parts."

"We never come out here looking for trouble, Sheriff."

MacLeod smiled crookedly and his voice was sympathetic as he said, "Sure you did, son. You just didn't know it."

Before Joe could protest, he quickly added, "I know what they told you back east. They told you the Golden West was a land of milk and honey where you just had to plant a seed and jump back before a corn stalk grew up your pants leg and hoisted you into the sky. The railroads want folks out here. Washington wants folks out here. Hell, the *folks* want folks out here. It's a big, raw lonesome land and it wouldn't look so tedious if there was a rose-covered cottage every mile or so. But roses don't grow out here, son. The only thing this prairie grows is grass and livestock. The folks who got here first figured that out a long time ago. That don't give them any right to pester you homesteaders. It says in the constitution that any man has a right to pursue his happiness as foolishly as he's up to, within the law. But try to understand the feelings of your stock-raising neighbors."

Joe said, "They told me at the land office that this flat prairie land had been opened to farming and that the cattle men had lots of open range set aside for all time in the sand hills to the north."

MacLeod sighed and said, "Sure they did. They probably told you about the Tooth Fairy, too. It's true there's cows grazing in the sand hills. You'll see how many this fall, when they drive the herds to the railroad to ship east. Those slickers in Washington aim to collect grazing fees or land tax on every square inch out here. The stock men in *these* parts can't move to the sand hills, even if the law said one man had to move just because another man wanted to move in on him. The sand hill outfits have already claimed all the water rights and likely headquarters spreads up north. Stock raisers who beat you out here have all their money and dreams tied up to the claims they hold right now. And this land won't take crowding, son!"

"So I've been told, Sheriff. But how much crowding is our bitty quarter section, when you get right down to it?"

MacLeod shook his head and said, "How much does one grasshopper eat? Since 1880 over eleven thousand new homestead claims have been filed in Nebraska alone. Some of you have already been dusted out, after ruining the range and gutting a mess of cows on that infernal wire. Nobody figures any *one* of you will put him out of the cattle industry. Nobody figures any of you will last long enough to prove your claim. But meanwhile you do make folks nervous. So try to act polite and speak softly to your elders while you conduct your experiment and we'll say no more about it."

Joe saw he was free to go. But he couldn't resist saying, soberly, "I'm here for the foreseeable future, Sheriff."

MacLeod opened the door for Joe as he smiled and said, "It's a free country, as long as you pay your taxes. You foresee all the future you like, son. You're one whiz of a prophet if you're able to predict dry farming in a land of little rain. You'll get less than twenty inches in a wet year out here, mostly in the winter when you can't use it. The growing season's too short for any crop but grass even when there's enough rain. Last year we had less than ten inches. So just you run along and try to stay out of other trouble until you're ready to go back east where you belong, hear?"

JOE HADN'T PLANNED this trip into town and he didn't admire the idea of walking all the way back to the claim. He'd been too proud to beg for a ride home from the Sheriff. For all his courtly rebel ways, the old bastard hadn't offered, either. Joe wasn't sure whether they'd thought he packed a pony in his hip pocket or if they enjoyed hazing greenhorns a mite themselves. He decided as long as he was here he'd see how Ma and Jessie were before he started legging it. The law's ridiculous notion had already cost him the best part of the day, so what the hell.

The dusty streets of Pittsburgh Landing were hot as the hinges of hell under the afternoon sun and as it was a weekday he saw few others as he headed for the boarding house. It was just as well. Joe grimaced at his own reflection in a glass store front as he peered. He hadn't put on a proper shirt

over his red union suit and bib. He needed a bath
as well as a shave. But how in thunder was a man
supposed to know he'd be frog-marched into town
at gunpoint when he rolled out of his sleeping
roll? Water was scarce as hen's teeth out here and
you needed some advance notice if folks expected
you to come in looking civilized.

A couple of cowboys rode past, whooping and
lashing their mounts at a full lope down the street
toward the depot. Joe wondered why they did
that.

He came to the mustard-colored frame house of
the Widow Palmer. He mounted the steps and
twisted the brass handle of the door bell. The
Widow Palmer came to the door. She was as old
as Ma but sort of pretty in a pressed-flower way.
There was a frosting of gray in her parted black
hair but you could see she'd been a looker before
Time's cruel shark had robbed her of her husband
and the stars in her eyes. He said, "Forgive my
appearance, ma'am. I wasn't expecting to come
calling."

The Widow Parker dimpled prettily, considering, and said, "Come in, Mister Barrow. Thank
heavens you've come. I fear your poor mother is
feeling poorly."

As he followed her inside he asked what was
wrong with Ma. Over her shoulder she replied she
wasn't sure, but it was likely homesickness. Joe
followed her up the stairs and it was funny how
young she looked from behind. She wore her
skirts in a saucy Dolly Varden flounce and though
she was a widow, her dress was cornflower blue
instead of black. He admired the way it fit her
narrow waist. She'd likely never had many kids

and sure kept herself trim for such an old lady.

Joe suddenly flushed, grateful for the gloom in the stairwell as he realized he was thinking dirty again. What in the pure hell was wrong with him? The poor old gal was at least forty if she was a day!

They got to the top of the landing and she turned to say, softly, "You know the way, Mister Barrow. Forgive me if I don't conduct you proper, but for some reason your mother seems vexed with me."

He nodded understandingly and soothed, "She's never gotten over Pa. I'll just show myself in, ma'am."

She dimpled again and left him to his own devices. As she went back down he wondered why Ma couldn't see she was a nice old lady. Sure, she had a soft southeron drawl, but hell, she didn't look like she'd led many charges dressed in butternut gray. He was glad he didn't remember the war. Life was complicated enough without old grudges to nurse like a viper to one's bosom.

He knocked on the third door, expecting Jessie to open it. But Ma herself opened it a worried crack to call out, "Who's there? What do you want?"

Then she saw it was Joe and let him in, sobbing, "Oh, thank the Lord you came today, Joseph. I want to go home!"

He stepped inside, saying, "It'll be a few more days, Ma. I hope to have the roof up come Saturday. Where's Jessie?"

"Out galavanting about, of course. You'd think she'd be willing to sit with a woman who's feeling poorly, but she says she feels cooped up in here. Never mind your sister, son. You don't understand,

I don't want to go home to some infernal sod hut. I want to go *home* home! I hate it out here! You have to take us back to Penn State right away!"

Joe looked down at her soberly, searching for the right words. The room he'd hired for them was clean and cheerful, despite her odd notions about the Widow Palmer. It was costing them more than they could afford, too. If she found it dirty and buggy here, he knew all too well what she'd think of a dirt floor and walls of shaggy sod that smelled like an open grave. Gently, he said, "Ma, we don't own the old place no more."

"Then we'll just have to buy another, back where I can see trees and flowers all about."

"We'll have us trees and flowers someday, Ma. They say cottonwoods grow well out here, if you get them started with extra water the first few summers. I've got some land by the house already cleared and I'll scatter some sunflower seeds for you as soon as I have the time. We can't go back to Penn State, Ma. There's nothing back there for us as we can afford. We staked our future on this claim out here. It's all we have."

Ma started to say something. Then her eyes filled up with tears and she suddenly grabbed at Joe and threw herself against him, to bury her head against his chest and bawl like a little girl.

He held her gently, feeling awkward. He could see the two of them in the mirror across the room near the foot of the big brass bedstead and it was funny, but a stranger peering in on them would have been surprised to know it was a grown man comforting his old ma. Women didn't show their years much from behind and with her agin him like that it looked like he was holding a young gal in his arms. Ma felt sort of like a regular gal in his arms, too. She was built a lot like that sassy Crawford gal back home and her breasts were firm against his own chest and the part of her ash blonde hair smelled like that other gal's had in the hayloft and . . .

Joe moved his mother firmly away from him and said, stiffly, "Get a hold on yourself, Ma. What in thunder has come over you? You never acted like this when we was planning to come out here. It wasn't me or Jessie's notion to sell the old place and try for a new start out here. It was you your ownself who said we ought to carry out Pa's plans, remember?"

She shuddered and moved over to the bed to sit down and bury her face in her hands. She sobbed, "I know I'm being foolish, Joseph. I know I'm all mixed up inside my head since your Pa left us. It seemed like a good notion, back then. I just wanted to get away from Penn State and its hurtful memories and I wasn't thinking about what it might be like out here until I saw them awful empty plainlands from the train. I need things, well, sort of wrapped around me, like. Back home I never noticed it. Back home there was always a tree or a bush or something near enough to matter. It ain't natural out here, Joseph! You can feel the earth spinning under you and you want something to hold on to!"

He couldn't ask any woman the obvious questions her wild talk brought to mind. He wasn't sure he understood that "Change of Life" business in any case. But Ma sure was getting crazy. Stiffly, he said, "I got me some errands to tend, as long as I'm here, Ma. I'll see if I can find Jessie and I'll tell her to get back here and mind you better, hear?"

"Don't go, Joseph. You just got here and I've missed you so."

"Well, sure you have. That's why I've got to get a roof over our heads so we can all be together again, Ma. Just sit tight, I'll have Jessie back here directly."

He let himself out as she went on blubbering. He met the Widow Palmer in the hall downstairs. She asked, "Is there anything I can do to help, Mister Barrow? I'm afraid some of this may be my fault."

"Your fault, ma'am? My sister Jessie says you've treated them both decent and I thank you."

She sighed and said, "I'm afraid I made a foolish mistake soon after they moved in. You see, I'd forgotten folks from the Ohio Valley all talked the same and, well, I'm afraid I assumed when she told me her first husband had died in the war that he'd ridden for the South."

Joe nodded understandingly and said, "Some of our kin migrated north from Kentucky a spell back. Pennsylvania Dutchmen twit us about our southern way of speaking, too, but I fear we're Yankee to the core. No offense."

She dimpled and said, "None taken, sir. It was a long time ago, even for those of us who remember it." Then she added, "At least, it was for me. I feel I'm a westerner, now. I fear your mother's still dwelling in the past."

"Yes, ma'am. I reckon she was happier there. There's nothing any of us can do, ma'am. But I purely thank you for your kind thoughts."

The pretty widow lowered her eyes and mur-

mured, "Uh, the price I quoted you on the room, I
mean, if there's a problem with that . . ."

"We're paid up 'til Monday, ain't we, ma'am?"

"Of course. Please don't think I mean to pry, but
I do have ears and eyes. If you folks are having
trouble about money, well, my late husband left
me reasonably comfortable and maybe we could
work out a more reasonable rate."

Joe frowned and said, "I can see you're a Christian woman, ma'am, and I admire your delicate
way of putting things but we ain't broke yet. I got
some credit and a few dollars left in the bank down
the street. They told us afore we come to you that
you hired rooms reasonable and we have no com-
plaints with you if you have none with us."

"I never meant to insult you, I assure you, sir!"

"Ma'am, you didn't insult me. You made a kind
gesture in a land where such things are hard to
come by. I follow your drift and I said I admired
you for it. I'd take you up on it, too, but before
Ma went crazy she raised me honest. It wouldn't
be fair to take advantage of a widow woman. So I
don't aim to do it. But I thank you just the same."

The Widow Palmer smiled a Mona Lisa smile as
she murmured, "Sometimes a widow woman
doesn't mind being taken advantage of, but we'll
say no more about it, for now, then. You just call
on me if there's anything else I can do for you,
hear?"

Joe nodded and let her show him out. He smiled
crookedly as he walked away. He knew the widow
woman would faint dead away if he ever told her
the advantage he sure would like to take of her.
He of course had no idea she'd meant it exactly as

his frustrated mind had twisted her seemingly innocent words. For Joe was not alone in being trapped by the prim code of the times and he had no idea how attractive he was to a healthy woman who remembered things she wasn't supposed to think about.

Upstairs, his mother watched from behind the lace curtains as he strode away, strong and tall as the youth who'd left her to march away to war. The Mary Ann he'd left behind had never been held in those strong arms again and it had never been the same with her second husband. Unconsciously, the woman ran her hand down to relieve the tingle between her trembling thighs. Then, as she cupped her mons through the folds of her skirting, she suddenly gasped in awareness at what she was doing and snatched it away from her own forbidden flesh.

"Crazy, I'm going crazy!" she moaned, moving over to the bed and throwing herself face down across it. That was the second time this week she'd caught herself starting to play with herself. What on earth was happening to her? It was bad enough she'd started talking to herself of late! Everybody knew folks went crazy fooling with their own privates, for land's sakes!

Down on the street, Joe watched for Jessie as he strode toward the bank. He didn't see her. If she was in some shop spending more on frills and play pretties he'd skin her good. But how in thunder could a grown man stick his head in a milliner's or notion shop and ask if they'd seen his fool kid sis?

He went to the bank and drew ten dollars. He couldn't pack home much by shank's mare, but while he was thinking on it he'd pick up some flower seed as well as more coffee and tobacco at the general store. There was a chance Jessie was in there, spending like a drunken sailor, anyways.

Jessie wasn't in the general store. The only other customer was a funny-looking little rascal wearing steel rimmed specs and a high-necked blouse that hung outside his pants like a skirt. He had on a funny little cap with a visor, like a sea captain's. Joe was too polite to ask him where the ocean was. He looked like a furriner anyways.

The stranger had finished buying his sack of chicken feed and Joe moved out of his way as he headed out with it, sort of staggered by its weight. Joe figured the wagon out front must be his. It had looked sort of furrin, too, now that he studied on it.

As he bellied up to the counter the storekeeper gazed after the man leaving and said, "Rooshin. Ain't that a bitch? Him and his woman don't talk enough American to matter."

Joe shrugged and said, "It takes all kinds, I reckon. I'll have me some Arbuckle and a sack of Bull. You don't carry flower seeds, do you?"

"Flower seeds? Not in living memory, friend. Never had a call for flower seeds before. What sort of flowers are we talking about?"

"Don't matter, if you don't stock 'em. Sounds sort of foolish to me, too."

Then both of them turned as they heard a rebel yell out front and the storekeeper sighed and said, "Oh, hell, they're at it again. But at least the Rooshin paid, poor little bastard."

Joe peered out the dusty window to see two cowhands had the little four-eyed man cut off from his wagon out front. As one of them jeered at him the other had slipped up behind to slash his sack of chickenfeed with a barlow knife, and feed was cascading in a golden stream as the greenhorn protested weakly.

The storekeeper yelled, "Hey, what about your supplies?" but Joe was headed out the door. He stepped closer to the little man they were hazing and nodded at the familiar face of the one cowboy blocking the immigrant's escape. He said, "Afternoon, Mackail. Ain't two on one a mite unfair?"

Mackail looked him over with undisguised loathing and said, "Well, well, we got us two fucking farm boys to play with now, Spike."

Spike must have been the name of the one with the knife, for he grinned and said, "The more the merrier. You take the big one and I'll handle this bitty Rooshin, pard."

But despite the brag, nobody moved right away, for Joe was big and Joe was packing a gun on his hip. Mackail was armed, too, as Joe had noticed on a friendlier occasion. Spike had a nickel-plated Harrington Richardson tucked in his belt. Mackail looked thoughtfully at Joe's holstered weapon and said, "We're a mite close to the courthouse for gunplay, pilgrim. But seeing as you're feeling so brave, why don't we just all drop our hardware and take us a little trip to Fist City?"

"Joe said, "I'm willing, but you sure are a moody gent, Mackail. I reckon you need someone to back your play afore you show your true colors, huh?"

"What are you jawing about, sod buster? Drop that gun rig and let's fight quiet, or slap leather and we'll fight noisy. It makes no never mind to me, as long as we have it out, you hog-slopping chickenshit bastard!"

Joe said "Well, as long as you put it that way . . ." and reached for his belt buckle as he told their earlier victim, "You just put what's left of that feed aboard and drive off, little feller. Me and these cow fucks can likely manage without you."

The smaller man dropped the sack on the boardwalk and said, in a thick accent, "*Nyet*, I, Yasha, stand by you, Big Tovarich!"

Joe nodded and said, "I'm waiting to see you drop your own guns, Mackail."

Mackail said, "Spike, lay your pistol over on yonder barrel and whup the little one's ass. Before I tear your face off, stranger, what's your name, in case your kin should ask?"

"My name? Hell, I told you my name when we met the other day. But since I can see you have a mighty spooky memory, it's Joe Barrow, the same as always."

Mackail unbuckled his own rig and hung it over the hitching rail the Russian's team was tethered to as he said, in a surprisingly pleasant tone, "Well, I'm pleased to meet you, Joe Barrow, and now I aim to kick the shit out of you."

He sounded like he meant it. But before it could go any farther Deputy Brody came around the corner, stopped, and just stood there, looking at all four of them with one eyebrow raised.

Brody waited a spell. Then he said, "Sheriff sent me looking for you, Barrow. Said you might need a ride back to your place. Is anything going on here that I should know about?"

Joe looked at the others. Then he shrugged and

said, "I've got nothing *I* mean to report to the Law. These other gents can speak for themselves."

Brody stared down at the spilled chickenfeed and the sack at Yasha's feet. He asked, "Accident?" and Mackail laughed and said, "Yeah, Brody. This little feller's sack ripped open and we was fixing to help him clean up this awful mess."

"I see. That's why you all took your guns off, eh? What have you got to say about this, Mister Ivanov?"

Yasha Ivanov licked his lips and said, "*Pravda,* is true like cowboys say. Feed sack is ripping on nail in door."

"Well, you just load your wagon and head on home then, Mister Ivanov. I can see the Lord helps those as helps themselves, and if a man don't feel he needs the Law he's on his own."

Then Brody smiled at the two cowboys to add, "You boys said something about being ready to leave, didn't you?"

Mackail shrugged, got his gunbelt from the rail and as he hitched it back on he smiled at Joe and said, "Another time, pilgrim."

Joe said, "You know where I live, Texas."

Spike picked up his own gun and tucked it away as they walked off, sort of growling. Brody told Joe, "Don't ever do that again. You ain't paid by the county to keep those assholes from bullying folks. You just made an enemy you didn't need. Mackail's not just ornery. He's a mite loco in the head."

Joe said "I noticed. He sure had me fooled, though. I thought he was a sensible gent, 'til just now."

"Yeah, he's treacherous as they come. His

brother's okay, but watch your step with *that* side
of the family. You still want that ride? My buckboard's back by the office."

The smaller homesteader, Yasha, had put the
ruptured feed sack on his wagon bed and rejoined
them to slap Joe's back jovially and say, "Wait, Big
Tovarich. Before you go anywhere, Yasha buys you
drink, *da*?"

Brody said, "You can do better than that, Mister
Ivanov. I just remembered you two boys don't
live all that fur apart. Barrow, here, lives a few
miles north of you and your sister on the same
wagon trace. We passed your spread on the way
in, now that I study on it. It's pure ned keeping
all you new folks straight in my head. But if you'll
ride Barrow home for me, I'll buy you both a
drink."

So the three of them went across to the saloon
and each bought a round of beer in turn. It was a
hot day.

Three beers hardly cooled a man off enough to
matter, but they were busy men, so that had to be
it for now. Brody headed back to his appointed
rounds and Joe went back to the wagon with
Yasha. Yasha had apparently been telling them
the story of his life, but his English was so funny
Joe hadn't got much of it sorted out in his head and
what he understood didn't seem all that interesting. Some gents called Cossacks had been pes-
tering Yasha to join some army he didn't want to,
so he'd come over here with his own kid sister to
grow wheat, which Brody had allowed wasn't
possible. The chicken feed was for Yasha's sister,
he vowed. Joe figured he must mean the sister
kept hens. He didn't know what Rooshin gals et,

but chickenfeed seemed sort of odd, even for a furriner.

As they were getting ready to light out, Joe heard the pound of running hooves and turned just in time to see his own buckboard, with Jessie at the reins, tear by lickety split in a cloud of dust! That infernal painted pony with the three white socks had the bit in his teeth and was headed anywhere else, sudden, no matter where Jessie had a mind to go!

Joe cursed and automatically started running after the buckboard. Not because he had a hope in hell of catching up with a running pony but because a man couldn't just stand there and watch a kinswoman smash up. As he saw how futile his efforts were, another man way down the street sprang into action and darted out to grab the runaway's bridle in one hand and lash it across the eyes with the cowboy hat in his other hand. The pony fought like hell, but between Jessie standing up and sawing away as she leaned against the reins and the cowboy skating aways on his high boot heels, they had the brute halted and just cussing by the time Joe caught up with them.

He shot a grateful look at the man who'd saved Jessie and said, "I owe you, friend. You just saved my fool sister's neck!"

Then he saw it was Mackail.

Mackail said, "Howdy, Joe. Are you all right up there, Little Missy?"

Jessie sank back down on the spring seat with a relieved look and said, "Thanks to you and the Good Lord, sir! For heaven's sake, Joe, aren't you going to introduce me to this gallant gentleman?"

Joe frowned and said, "Uh, this here's Mister Mackail, Jessie. Brazos Mackail."

Brazos bowed his head to Jesse and said, "Pleased to meet you, ma'am. Your brother and me met the other day, out to your place."

He glanced at Joe as if for confirmation and Joe said, "Yeah, we been meeting a lot lately. I see you're in a good mood again, Mackail. Does Spike put powders in your drinks or something?"

Mackail looked puzzled and replied, "Spike? Spike Long? I didn't know you knowed him, Joe."

"You didn't, huh? I get it, new manners for new occasions. I think she's pretty, too, and I meant what I said about owing you for saving my kid sis just now. But I don't have your convenient memory, so if you'll just take your hands off that bridle I'll see she gets back to the livery in one piece."

Mackail let go as if the straps he was holding had gotten hot and his smile faded to a hurt look as he said, "Suit yourself. I meant no harm to you and your'n, Joe Barrow. But if that's the way you wants it, I can take a hint."

He bowed again to Jessie and turned on his heel to stride off stiffly.

Joe said, "I'd best lead this brute on foot" and Jessie called down, "What on earth's gotten it into you, Joe? That cowboy acted neighborly as anything. You had no call to insult him like that."

Aware others were listening as the commotion began to attract a modest crowd, Joe said, "Just be still and I'll expand on it later."

He led her up the street past Yasha, who called out that he'd wait. When he got her to the livery he led the pony through the gate and told the colored stable hand, "If you ever hire this pony to my sister again you can give your soul to Jesus, for your ass will belong to me!"

"The lady said she liked old Calico, cap'n."

"Yeah, well, she's a poor judge of man flesh, too. You just remember what I said. I'll tell her what sort of horse to drive and what sort of cowboy she's allowed to talk to. Some women don't have a lick of sense."

THE IVANOV HOMESTEAD lay between Joe's and town as Brody had said. Joe hadn't paid it much mind on the way in, having more important matters on his mind at the time. Yasha insisted Joe stop and sup with them before he drove him the rest of the way and what the hell, the day was shot in any case.

The first thing Joe noticed was the greenery around the dooryard of the otherwise nondescript little spread. They had the house, a barn, and a hen run-up. As they reined in before the soddy a blonde girl dressed as funny as Yasha came out to greet them and the Russian said her name was Nadja. She was taller than her older brother, which wasn't all that hard when you studied the little draft-evader. Joe figured she and Jessie were both about five-seven or so. They were about the same age, too, but that's where they parted company.

Nadja's eyes were as blue as Dutch tiles and her face was heart-shaped between the two long golden braids on either side. Yasha spouted at her in their own lingo and as she stared at Joe in dawning understanding, she suddenly lit up the world with a radiant smile that made his legs go all mushy as she said, in better English, "You are brave good man, Friend Josef!"

He said, "Just a neighbor, ma'am. Are those sunflowers you've planted all around?"

"*Da*, I mean yes. Russian sunflowers. You will see, when they are taller. Brought seeds from old country. Do you want sunflower seeds? Ask anything of us and is yours. But come inside. First we eat and then we talk about rewards for hero."

Joe snorted in embarrassment and offered to help put the team away. But Yasha insisted he go inside and wait in comfort. As Joe followed the blonde inside he saw they'd fixed the place up nice, considering what they had to work with. The earth floor was swept clean and a big tile stove occupied one corner. Nadja said they'd had it packed in a little box and put it together over here, when he commented on it. It hardly seemed possible.

She ushered him to a seat at the plank table and glanced out through the braided twine curtains before she put a glass of tea from their big brass whatever in front of him and said, softly, "You were kind to poor little Yasha. Many laugh at him. Is true he is a coward, but he is still my brother and I love him."

Joe wondered how you drank hot tea from a durned old glass, so he let it set to cool some as he said, "Your brother's all right, Miss Nadja. He could have crawfished out, but he never. He ain't all that big, but a man has no say about that. He stood tall enough beside me when push come to shove."

"Is true? Yasha said the two of you faced down those bullies, but you know Yasha."

"Mebbe I know him better than you do, Miss Nadja. He was scared all right. I was scared too, and I was more lucky with the way I growed. That ain't being a coward. You're only a coward when you back out of a fight."

"I know. In old country, when we were children . . . but maybe you are right. Maybe new country makes men different, I hope."

"He told me over beers about not wanting to serve in some army. Is that what you're holding agin him, Miss Nadja?"

She shrugged as she poured her own glass of tea from the samovar and said, "Partly so. Our father was soldier. Two older brothers soldiers, too. They died fighting Turk. When Yasha's turn came up . . . He told you."

"Yeah. My father died in a war one time. I ain't sure I'd like to die in another. Mebbe he figured a father and two brothers was all your family owed your king."

Nadja said, "*Pravda*, the Tsar has plenty peasants bigger than little brother Yasha. Was not just running away from conscription gangs I worry about. But I bore you with long sad story and now Yasha comes and we can eat."

So they ate and Joe had no idea what it was, but it sure smelled good and tasted better. The little soddy was filled with the warmth of hearty peasant cooking and the lavender or something you could notice coming from Nadja's low bodice when she got near you, serving. Joe figured it was alright to dress like that indoors, but Rooshin gals shure wore their duds cut low. She had a little gold cross on a chain and that likely meant they were Christian folks, despite their funny ways, but it was hard to keep one's mind on Christian teachings when a pretty gal bent near you and the bitty cross sort of hinted at further delights down the valley it nestled in.

She seemed as bad as Jessie about letting folks see her hide and he wondered what the world was coming to, the way the younger gals was starting to act these days. But at least she wasn't improper as a sister to think dirty about. Joe let himself go a mite in imagining what lay under that brocaded outfit as he watched her from the corners of his eyes. It gave him a hell of a hard-on and he told himself to stop. He'd heard gals could tell when a man was lusting after them and it wasn't decent to lust after a proper gal, even a furriner. He knew that if he didn't get into town one of these nights and rut like a hog with one of them shady gals a man was supposed to think dirty about, he'd wind up sick in the head. Men who didn't do things right wound up playing with themselves in lunatic asylums.

By the time they'd et and smoked a spell it was sundown. So Yasha said he'd run him on home.

Joe had forgotten how God-awful bleak his own unfinished place looked 'til he faced it alone in the sunset. He'd almost forgot what it was to have a proper home, let alone a woman once in a while. He stared wistfully after the homeward-bound neighbor as Yasha and his rig became a dot on the horizon. Then Joe shrugged and picked up his spade. There was a little light left and he wasn't going to get his own place fixed up so nice if he just stood around like a big-ass bird with a hard-on.

IT WASN'T EASY, but Joe had the soddy roofed by Monday and his mother, sister, and the rest of their belongings moved out to the homestead by the latter part of the week. Young Yasha helped by freighting for them and Nadja came over with a big bucket of beet soup that even tasted good cold. She threw in a couple of her fresh killed and plucked chickens for luck, and even Ma seemed interested in that red paprika stuff old Nadja showed them. It was nice to see the gals all got along. The Ivanovs were over the horizon line and nobody had the time for much gadding back and forth, but it seemed to comfort Ma to know she had a neighbor gal, even if you couldn't see her yard from your own. Jessie asked about the neighbors to the north and Joe said to forget about them. He'd told her Brazos Mackail was crazy, and though she allowed it seemed impossible that such

89

a "Nice Boy" would pick on little immigrants, she knew Joe never lied.

It was after he had his little family settled in that Joe found out what real work was like. Building the infernal place had been bad enough. Keeping it going was harder.

Jessie worked like a beaver, mostly about the house. Joe knew that without her choring some he'd have just had to pack it in, for Ma just sat. She sat in the dooryard, staring at the distant dots of roof tops of town like she purely loved it, now that she couldn't sit in the Widow Palmer's hating it. At night she sat in the dark by the stove, just staring in the dark. It made Joe feel spooky, but he was too tired to study on it. It seemed he'd just get to sleep when it was time to rise and shine again. One morning as they ate his Ma said something about how much she hated it out here and before he thought Joe snapped, "You don't hate it half as much as you would if you had to *work* the God-damned place, you crazy old woman!"

So of course Ma started to bawl and when he tried to say he was sorry she picked up the sugar bowl and threw it at him, so Joe went outside, red-faced and wanting to hit something.

But there wasn't anything to hit. You could empty your gun at the far horizon and see the dust puffs long before they reached the sky line. Joe picked up the spade and went to the well. But the damned well had water in it. He shrugged and walked over by the road to start another post hole. He knew he ought to have a post hole digger to do it right, but he knew how much they had left in the bank, too. He cursed and started. They still had no fence posts, but if he ever figured out where the hell he could get them he meant to be ready.

Jessie came from the house, her own eyes red-rimmed. She stopped nearby and just stood watching. Joe growled "I said I was sorry, damn it."

Jessie said, "I know, Joe. Ma's sorry, too, but she can't help herself. I think she has a worried mind."

He snorted and said, "You figured that out all by yourself, huh? The woman's been telling us she's touched since before we *got* here, girl!"

"I know, honey. I know you already have enough on your plate, but we've got to study on Ma. I think she's going crazy. I mean, *really* crazy."

Joe stopped digging and leaned on the handle, staring off across the prairie as Jessie insisted, "Joe, she's been talking wild as anything."

"I know. I got ears."

"I'm not talking about her complaining about this place, honey. You've only heard her polite crazy talk. She's been telling me all sorts of things from back when she was young, like us."

"What sort of things?"

"Nothing I could repeat in front of any man, even you. You know women tell each other things they'd never tell a husband. I don't know how much of it's real and how much is the might-have-beens she never got around to. Some of it's ugly and some just makes no sense at all. Joe, I think we might have to put Ma away. They got a hospital for folks like her in Lincoln. She needs help, honey."

"Hell, we all need help. You're the one who's talking crazy, girl! Old Ma's going through that, uh, thing old gals go through. I know it's harder on you, being more cooped up with her and all, but she'll get over her hysterics after we get this place looking decent. The Ivanovs are coming over later to sup with us some more. Ma likes old Nadja and she may stay over tonight. I got to get into town and Yasha's driving me. Be a good change for you gals to have a hen party, all to yourselves."

Jessie repressed a shudder as she said, "If Ma don't start talking crazy to that Russian gal, you mean. I can keep family secrets as well as the next person, but you don't know the half of what Ma says when no men are about!"

Joe knew he wasn't going to get the details out of Jessie, so he just shrugged and said, "Well, Nadja don't understand half what we say, anyway. She's a smart gal. She'll understand about female troubles."

Jessie half turned away. Then she asked, "Are you paying court to Nadja, honey?"

Joe laughed and said, "Hell, I can't even study on such fool notions until we get us a fence up and a crop in the ground."

"She's pretty and strong-looking. Ma said she was sure you and her had already . . . never mind."

Joe frowned down at her and demanded, "Don't you drop it *there*, little sis! If Ma's saying things like that I have me a right to know. Nadja Ivanov has a *brother* watching out for her and talk like that can get a man bushwacked!"

"Oh, pooh, Yasha likes you."

"Jessie, no man likes another that much! Just how serious did Ma accuse me and Nadja? I'll tell you here and now I've never trifled with her."

Jessie looked down at the grass at her bare feet and said, softly, "It's no never mind to me if you have, but I'll take your word for it. Ma said she could tell when a gal had been . . . you know. She said if it wasn't Yasha she'd been, uh, getting it regular from, it had to be . . . you."

"Oh for God's sake, Jessie, Yasha is Nadja's own brother."

"I know. Ma said, back home, she'd known of such things happening. She asked me . . ." and then Jessie turned and ran away as Joe watched, bemused.

Jesus, Ma was really crazy if she'd accused him and Jessie! He turned to drive the spade viciously into the sod as he growled, "Crazy old bawd. If you're so infernal sure you can tell when a gal's been screwed, how come you had to ask Jessie a question like that, huh?"

He rolled a spadeful of spoil aside, feeling better, as he nodded in reply to his own question and said, "You can't tell no such thing. I don't know about Nadja, cause I ain't been there all her life. But I knows for a fact that Jessie is pure. So there goes your whole dirty notion and, hell, I'll bet Nadja's pure, too!"

He wondered where in the hell Ma had gotten all these ideas about incest all of a sudden. It was only natural to feel a mite shy about kin of the wrong sex, after you were growed enough to know about such things. But it took a horny dirty mind indeed to come right out and *say* a gal was being wicked with her own brother. Two gals, now that you mulled it over. It was lucky for the Widow Palmer she didn't have a brother or even a . . .

"Stop thinking crazy and study on this fence line, damn it," he warned himself. But that only made it worse. He knew that if the poor Widow Palmer had had a grown son living in her boarding house that Ma would have likely said something sick about that, too. What in God's name was wrong with Ma? He knew he never had many dirty thoughts unless he was hankering for a gal. But women weren't supposed to hanker like that, damn it! Women who lusted after sex were wild and wicked, even if they were young ones. An old forty-year-old gal dwelling on it was just disgusting. Maybe Ma should talk to a doctor about her head. Maybe there was something they could do to help her.

He grimaced as he remembered, without wanting to, the time he'd been at the vet's with Pa, back home. There'd been this crazy-acting old mare in the stall and one of the stable hands had been shoving a greased pick handle in and out of her whilst she shuddered and whinnied fit to bust. He'd been as curious as any other kid, so he'd asked what they was doing and the vet's helper had said the mare was in heat but too old to breed, so he was helping her out. He'd said the old mare just needed a good screwing to set her head right again. The other men all around had laughed sort of dirty and one had said a lot of crazy old gals he was too polite to name could have used the same treatment.

He'd never thought about it again until just now. Jesus, they wouldn't do *that* to Ma at the lunatic asylum, would they? It didn't seem lawful to help a human female out that way, no matter how bad she might need it. Hell, he'd rather see Ma, well, improper with some nice old gent. He knew a lot of that went on. He'd been hearing gossip about old maids all his life. So some of it was likely true.

"I'd kill the son of a bitch!" he decided, getting

back to work. He felt sorry for Ma and he could see how some discreet sinning could help her out. But he knew he couldn't stand for it. A man who'd let another trifle with his Ma was no better than an animal. It'd be as bad doing it to her himself, for God's sake and that was too crazy to even think about. So he told himself to stop thinking about it.

It wasn't easy.

NADJA HAD SAID they were bringing over some vittles but Jessie had a pot of stew going anyway. For, in truth the young Russian nesters weren't living all that high on the hog despite their head start. Joe had noticed that while Yasha had his quarter section fenced and Nadja had their soddy downright civilized, they hadn't plowed yet. The one time he'd commented on it, Yasha had laughed and said it was way too early.

It was funny, the little jasper didn't look lazy and he had two horses, but it was high summer and he hadn't made a move to plant a crop. Joe hadn't pressed him. Telling a fool how to manage his own business was a waste of time as well as impolite, and fair was fair. The Ivanovs had a going spread and the Barrows were having trouble keeping the water bucket filled. The durned well was dangerously deep for him to go down in, now, and still the infernal water table kept dropping. He still hadn't found anybody who'd sell him one damned fence post and it was getting late for even a catch crop of barley. It was starting to look like they could forget farming this summer and somehow survive eighteen months or more on the savings in the bank. Every time Joe tried to figure out how with a pencil and paper, his answers came out all wrong. Simple arithmetic allowed they had enough to make her to spring. But that couldn't be right. Anyone could see they had to eat until the fall harvest could be sold.

Yasha was tardy getting there this evening, too. Ma was muttering to herself inside and even Jessie was starting to talk mean about starting without them. But Joe said he wasn't of a mind to say Grace twice and to get away from their bitching he went outside to study on the well as he drew some more water.

The sky was turning red and the little star of well water down there at the bottom of the shaft winked up at him from the darkness like the planet Mars on a clear night. He lowered the bucket on the windlass he'd erected over the frame well-head and he could tell by the sound it made down there that the bucket had bottomed in the mud and had to turn on its side to half fill. He swore and cranked it up. As he'd expected, it was only a quarter filled and such water as he'd fetched was a quarter mud, with a couple of drowned grasshoppers and a still swimming cricket to season the unwholesome-smelling mixture. He'd hauled the rope ladder out a day or so back. Jessie had told him it was pure suicide to dig any deeper without timber shoring,

and right was right. He knew he had to find some
timber at a price he could afford, and soon. He
was willing and able to dig as deep as the water
table had a mind to go, but he knew the prairie
had stood aside polite about as long as it could.

He toted the bucket back to the doorway and
set it down without going inside. He walked
around to stare down the wagon trace toward town
and the infernal furriner's homestead. The western
sunset looked redder and spookier than usual this
night. Seemed a mite early, too. He could still see
the sun ball through those billowing orange and
purple clouds over on the sky line. It looked like
rain. A real gully-washer at that. So the local
weather prophets weren't all that smart after all.
They kept saying not to figure on real rain afore
October or November and there the rain was,
towering to the zenith in an old-fashioned anvil
head like they had when it thundered back home
in Penn State. He wondered if the roof would leak
bad and if the one lightning rod he'd installed on
the north-west corner of the flat sod roof would be
enough.

Joe swung his eyes south along the sky line and
there, way down the wagon trace, came a wagon
drawed by two pokey old plow brutes. They were
little more than a growing dot, but he knew it was
Yasha and Nadja and it was about time. He knew
he was between them and the soddy behind him,
so they couldn't see him on the north horizon. He
knew it looked impolite to stand anxious by the
roadway when guests arrived a mite late, so he
started to go back inside. But as he turned he spied
a ragged line of horsemen to the west. They'd

come over the horizon with the blood-red sunset behind them and they seemed to be headed his way, sudden.

He judged the distance and the pace they were setting. He nodded and walked over to the house. He opened the door and called in, "Jessie, fetch me my shotgun. But stay inside with Ma."

"What's going on out there, hon?"

"Don't know yet. Do as I say, sis."

Jessie got the old twelve-gauge double-barreled duck gun and had it in one hand as she stepped out the door with the Winchester in her other. Joe nodded and said, "Good thinking. Repeater hasn't the stopping power, but it fires further and keeps firing." He took the rifle and added, "I thank you, and now get back inside and bar the door."

Jessie started to ask him what on earth was going on. Then her own keen eyes took in the immigrants coming one way and the mysterious riders coming another. She hefted the shotgun and said, "I'd best stand by you, honey. I know I'm a gal, but I've hit me some ducks with this old scatter gun in my time."

Joe said, "This ain't your time. Do as you're told and stay indoors and out of sight with Ma."

"Joe, I want to help."

"That's what I just asked you to do, damn it. Those riders look like cowboys on their way to town likely looking for, uh, excitement. I'm hoping they won't find one old boy in bib overalls all that exciting. But you know how boys show off in front of a gal, and we ain't got a picket fence for them to walk."

Jessie's eyes widened in sudden understanding.

She nodded, but asked, "What about Nadja? She's a gal, and prettier than me, too."

Joe shrugged and said, "I'm hoping they'll just make it here ahead of them others. If they don't, it can't be helped. I'll do what I can. One gal is less tempting than two, in any case, so get inside like I said and make sure Ma keeps quiet."

Without looking to see if his command was obeyed, Joe moved casually to the wagon trace and the edge of what was his by rights of the Homestead Act and a lot of hard work. Yasha had a lead on the others over to the west. But it was a near thing, in the end. As Yasha drove close enough to hail him, Joe pointed at the riders coming in out of the sunset and called back, "Swing around to the back of the house and get your sister under cover."

"What is wrong, Tovarich Joe? Who are they? What do they want?"

"I don't know, God damn it! Doesn't anybody hereabouts ever do what they're told without debating every point with me?"

Nadja said something to her brother in Russian and it must have made sense to him, for Yasha whipped his team into a trot and cut off the wagon trace toward the soddy.

Joe didn't watch them. He had his eyes on the riders coming in from the west. There were at least two dozen of them and he didn't have that many rounds in his Winchester. So Joe's mouth felt a mite dry as he waited, quietly, for them to swing south toward town like he hoped they would, or keep coming and do whatever.

They didn't swing south. They rode up to the

wagon trace and reined in just across from Joe.
They were black as pitch against the ruby sky that
outlined them. One held his hand up and said, "I
know you told me to stay clear of your and your'n,
Joe Barrow, but we're in this together and I'm
asking for a truce until it's over."

"Is that you, Brazos Mackail? What are you
talking about? What are we in together?"

Brazos swept his arm back toward the billowing clouds to the west and replied "Hell, can't you
see it coming? It's no wonder you act so spooky.
You must be blind as a bat or else you're just plain
dumb."

Joe shrugged and said, "I see a thunder storm
headed this way, but . . ." and then he saw the
bright red pencil line of flame on the dark horizon
and gasped, "Kee-rist! You're right, I was dumb!"

Brazos said, "Wind's from the northwest, so the
burn is headed here, there and ever'where. We've
got it backfired away from our headquarters spread
but there are some Double M cows out here, and
the fire could swing toward town if the wind
shifts a mite. I figured this wagon trace would be
the best place to make our stand, if that's all right
with you."

Joe nodded and said, "Hell yes it's all right with
me. I've got a well dug and we can form a bucket
brigade."

There was a ragged outburst of laughter from
the line of riders. Brazos laughed too, but not as
nasty, before he said, "You can wet down your
soddy and such, if you fear falling sparks. Me and
the boys has fit prairie burns afore. We don't need
your help. I just thought I'd best fill you in on
what we was doing before we started. Had a

greenhorn fire a shot at me one time when he mistook my intentions during another fire."

Brazos swung himself out of the saddle and Joe saw he'd drawn a short-handled spade from among the gear hanging from his work saddle. As he came closer, Joe saw he was wearing bib overalls himself, so Joe knew the cowboy meant to do some serious work. Brazos called out, "All right, Concho, you take your boys north a ways and wait my signal afore we back the burn. Trinity, would you like to take the south flank?"

A surly figure still sitting his mount under a big Texas hat spat and said, "I'll do her, but you know damned well I won't *like* to! I don't see why we have to pull this sod buster's chestnuts or anything else out of any fire."

"Damn it, Trinity, we ain't here to make friends. We're here 'cause this bare dirt wagon trace is the best place to stop the burn. You just ride on home and sulk, if you've a mind to."

The Mackail called Trinity swung his mount around sullenly and growled, "Come on, Spike. You and Shorty help me set up down there. May as well get her over with."

The commotion and conversation had attracted the attention of those in the soddy and despite Joe's orders, Jessie came out to see what was going on. Brazos Mackail took his hat off to her. But before he could start up with her Joe said, "Prairie fire. These men are fixing to stop it here. I'm fixing to help. Tell Yasha to get out here with a shovel. Tell Ma to brew a mess of Arbuckle. You and Nadja get all the water you can on the sod roof. Be faster if one of you was to stay up there and wet things down as the other handed buckets up."

Jessie nodded and ran back for the house. Brazos said, "Nice little gal. I can see why you're worried about her, Barrow, but you got me all wrong if that was what made you so surly the other day in town."

"We'll talk about it another time, Brazos. Right now I aim to back your play. So I'd best get me a spade and you just tell me and the Rooshin what you want us to do."

Joe trotted off before Brazos could answer. He kept his gun belt on but leaned the Winchester against the wall of the soddy as he picked up one of the spades there. Yasha came out and Joe handed him another as he snapped, "Let's go."

He ran back to the wagon trace where Brazos and the others were already at work. He saw they were using spades and hoes to hack away all the weeds and cheat that grew between the ruts where the wheels had scalped the sod away. That part made sense. What they were doing with the dry tinder they were clearing didn't. Brazos had moved up the line somewhere.

Joe fell in beside a burly cowboy and started scraping with his own spade as he asked, "Shouldn't we be piling the stuff to the east, *away* from the fire front?"

The cowboy snorted in disgust, tossed a mixture of weeds and dust across the trace toward the fire and growled, "Go teach your granny to suck aigs, tenderfoot."

Joe moved off a mite and started doing it his way. He looked around for Yasha, but the Russian was nowhere in sight. It was getting hard to see as the rising smoke blocked out the setting sun's rays and the ruddy glow on the horizon reflected shifting red and black illumination from the smoke.

Some of it was overhead, now, as the prevailing winds drove it ahead of the flames. Joe could smell the pungent ropey smell of burning grass, now. It gagged a man worse than wood smoke. He rolled a spadeful of spoil toward the house and saw Jessie up on the roof with her skirts kilted almost to her bare knees as she sloshed water over the sods. The gals were doing a good job and if any of these cowboys commented on her ankles he'd just do what a man had to do about a thing like that. He rolled another spadeful of spoil off the road and another cowboy tapped him on the shoulder to say, in a more reasonable tone, "Wrong way, pilgrim. Toss as much shit as you can towards them flames. We ain't got much time. They're coming sudden."

Joe started to ask why but the man had moved on. He looked around for Brazos. He didn't want to look dumb, but he didn't want to act dumb, either. He wanted somebody to tell him what the hell they thought they were doing.

He moved down the line and asked another man, "Where's your boss?" The hand pointed his hoe at a familiar figure three men down. Joe moved closer and when he saw Mackail he said, "I'm mixed up, I reckon. How come we're feeding them oncoming flames instead of getting ever-thing as'll burn out of it's path, Mackail?"

The cowboy straightened, frowned at him in the red glare, and growled, "If you don't know how to fight a prairie fire, stay the hell off the prairie, Sod Buster!"

Joe snarled back, "Oh, we're playing that way again are we?"

Mackail spat and started to turn away. Then he

spotted Jessie on the roof over Joe's shoulder and his face became less sullen, but not much prettier as he said, "Well, well, what have we here? Who's the nice little piece of ass up yonder, Farmer Boy?"

Joe hit him. For a man with such a big mouth he hadn't been braced for it worth a damn and the hat flew straight up in the air as Joe's big fist slammed into his sneering face. The blow put Mackail on the ground and as a couple of men grabbed Joe from either side the man he'd flattened sat up and said, "Let him go, boys. This is personal."

Mackail rolled a leg under his center of gravity and rose with the feline grace of a man who'd been thrown from his first pony before he was old enough to walk. The Double M riders who'd tried to break it up stepped well clear of Joe as one of them sighed, "Oh, shit, I don't want to see this."

Joe said, "You spoke out of line about my kid sister, Mackail. I'm ready to call us even if you are."

The cowboy put his left hand to his mouth, stared bemused at his bloody fingertips, and said, "We ain't even by half, Sod Buster. I can see you're armed and that makes two of us. Fill your fist, you son of a bitch!"

Joe stood his ground, but waited. He knew the man who slapped leather first was in the wrong in the eyes of the law. He doubted he'd get a witness from among this crowd, but he knew they'd hang him sure if he drew first and won.

Mackail must have been thinking the same way. He sneered, "What's the matter, skeered? All right. Spike, you count to three for us, hear?"

Spike Long said, "Not hardly. I'll back any sidekick in innocent fun but Sheriff MacLeod has warned us personal, and we're close as hell to the county courthouse, Boss."

Mackail said, "You just ride in and have a drink then, for you're fired. I'll tell you waddies and this infernal farmer what I aim to do, then. I aim to count three and then I aim to slap leather. Anybody else around here can just do whatever they've a mind to."

Joe took a deep breath and braced himself. Bu* before anything else took place a man in bib overalls stepped between them and shouted, "Have you both come unglued in the head? We come to fight a fire, not each other!"

For a moment Joe Barrow thought he was seeing double. Then, for the first time, he realized the man he'd been brawling with was wearing trail duds and not the overalls he'd first seen. Joe laughed incredulously and gasped, "For God's sake, you Mackail boys are twins! Identical twins!"

The one who'd jnst challenged him to a shoot out frowned and said, "Hell, ever'body in the country knows that. That don't give no farmer the right to bust my head open!"

Joe turned to the more reasonable one and said, "I've been a fool and some of this here is my fault. You must be Brazos and this here is your brother Trinity, right?"

The Mackail twins nodded, albeit with totally different expressions. Brazos asked, "What are you two fussing about? Can't you see we don't have time for kid stuff?"

Joe said, "Trinity and me had words in town the other day. When you stopped my sister's runaway pony I thought you was him and I'm pure sorry for the way I spoke to you. I'll say I'm sorry to Trinity, here, too. Fair is fair and I busted him for what might not have called for a busting if I'd known you boys were two brothers instead of one maniac!"

Trinity spat and said, "It's a mite late to say you're sorry, Sod Buster."

But Brazos said, "No it ain't. The man apologized handsome for an honest mistake. I want you to shake and start over with a fresh deck."

Trinity hesitated and Brazos said, quietly, "I mean it, Trinity."

Trinity Mackail shrugged and said, "I'll drop the fight, for now. I'll be damned if I'll shake."

Brazos asked, "Is that jake with you, Barrow?" Joe nodded and said, "War's over, as far as I'm concerned. I ain't one for formalities."

Brazos laughed and said, "There you go, Trinity. Let's light the back burn."

He took out a match box and as Joe watched, confused, Brazos bent to pick up a clump of cheat, twist it into a torch, and light it. Up and down the long line, other dusty men were doing the same. A couple were moving ponies to the east side of the road and as Brazos knelt to light the windrow of weeds and grass they'd cleared from the wagon trace, Joe gasped, "Have you gone crazy? We ain't a hundred yards from my house!"

Then he saw the fire was acting crazy, too. The clouds were moving east overhead and the ominously approaching prairie fire was following the same winds towards them. But, as the dry grass closer to hand began to burn brightly, he saw the flames were leaning west, toward the larger burn!

He wet a finger and held it up. The damned

wind was from the west, at least, at shoulder level. He hunkered down and tried again, holding the wet finger toward the ground. He frowned, puzzled. There was a strong draft just below knee level. Going the wrong way. Brazos came over to join him after tossing his burned out torch on the grass west of the wagon trace. He said, "That's right. That praire fire is sucking air from all directions."

Joe said, "I get it. The bare roadway keeps your back burn from moving east and the rising heat of the bigger fire moves it west. When the two fronts meet out there a mile or so, There'll be nothing left to burn and it'll have to die out."

Brazos nodded and said, "That's why we call it a back burn. I'm sorry about my brother acting so surly. I told you he didn't cotton to new neighbors."

"I noticed. They told me in town that one of you boys was neighborly and the other one wasn't. Might have saved me a lot of confusion if they'd told me you were identical twins. Don't it mix you up sometimes?"

Brazos shrugged and said, "Used to get me in a few fights as a kid. Old Trinity has a certain knack for making enemies. But he's starting to settle down. You see, our Ma died when we was little and when our Pa died a year or so back we had a little trouble sorting out who was supposed to ramrod the outfit."

"I take it you wound up the boss?"

"Sort of. I've always been able to whip old Trinity in a fist fight and he's not mean enough to shoot me."

"Well, I'm glad he listened to you about shooting me! I told my women folk to brew some coffee and now that we seem to have this burn under control—"

"I'd admire having some more of your Arbuckle," Brazos cut in, "but we only have it under control here and now. Me and the boys has to ride south and make sure it don't shift towards town."

"I'd ride with you if I had a horse. But won't the townees see the smoke and make their own back burn?"

"Sure they will. But they'll expect us to help."

"I had no idea folks were so neighborly out here."

"Yeah, I heard nobody will sell you fence posts in town. I'll tell you true, Joe. We don't want you to make it. We'll do whatever we can to help you fail, within the law. But the law says it's every man's duty to fight fire, flood, Injuns and outlaws."

"That's comforting to hear. They told me in town that another homestead was burned out the other day. I figure that was the smoke we was watching together the first day we met. Remember?"

"Yeah, I heard tell about it in more detail, for I rode with the Sheriff's posse later that night. We never cut the trail of the nightriders as done the deed. It was an ugly deed, too."

"I heard about the nightriders, too. Are you telling me you cowboys don't approve?"

Brazos looked surprised and replied, "Approve? Hell, Joe, they *killed* that nester family over yonder!"

"So what? I thought the idea was to run us all off your range, Brazos."

"Well, sure we want you off our range, God damn it. Everybody out here with a lick of sense wants this prairie left the way God made her. But that don't make us ogres who'd stand by and see women and childer killed! Those folks they burned out had a little baby daughter. The men in our posse rode on sort of hard-eyed after we found what was left of her in the ashes. Most of 'em was cow men, too."

Joe nodded and said, "I suspicion I have a lot to learn about you Texas men. Now, if I could just get you to study *my* ways some . . ."

Brazos laughed boyishly and clapped him on the shoulder as he said, "Hell, you can't teach a cowboy farming, Old Son. Most of us come out west as farmers. Texicans larnt a long ways back that you can't raise nothing but cows west of the twenty inch line. Get over your notion that this is some sort of infernal contest, Old Son. It's like I keep telling the other cow folks. There's no need for nobody to get all surly. A man learns to work with nature out here, or nature runs him under."

Joe stared morosely west at the burning prairie. The back burn was half way to the main burn, now, and he had to admit that had been a trick he'd never seen before. He said, "Maybe I'll figure out how to grow me a crop. Where will that leave us, Brazos?"

Brazos shrugged and said, "I'll be eating crow if you do it. But you won't. You sod busters just can't understand that we're out here raising crops, too. Cows just happen to be the crop this country's good for."

Joe started to protest and Brazos added, "Hold on. Before you say something foolish about our primitive methods I'd like to mind you that wheat is a *grass*. So's oats and barley, and even corn's a

big old kind of thirsty grass when you study on
it. Do you deny that, Joe?"

"Of course not. Ever'body knows most grain
crops are domesticated types of grass."

"There you go, and the one thing any cowboy
has to know, aside from cows, is grass! I don't
have a kid wrangling for me who couldn't name
you ever' breed of grass and forb they have out
here on this prairie. We know where to bed a
calving cow on big blue stem in some well-watered
draw. We know where they can make it through
the summer brown on gramma and buffalo. We
know when the cheat gets thick that it's time to
move 'em to better grazing. We know some forbs
will poison a critter and we know others that act
as a tonic. You show the average stock-raiser a
clump of sod you found ten miles from a place
he's never rode and he'll tell you what kind of
soil it was growing in and how many inches of
rain fell that year."

Brazos stared eastward across the quarter section the Barrows had filed on and his voice was
gentle as he added, "You show me a bushel of
wheat you say you growed on this land, Joe, and
I'll have to call you a liar, nice a gent as I think
you are."

Then he turned away and called out, "All right,
boys, saddle up and let's see if we can keep her
from drifting south."

Joe dragged his spade blade in the grass as he
headed in the opposite direction. Jessie had of
course climbed down off the roof as she saw the
danger moving west. He nodded at her and said,
"You and Nadja did a good job, sis. Where is she,

by the way? I lost track of that fool brother of hers on the fire line, too."

Jessie said, "They both lit out to the east. I can't tell you why."

Joe frowned. The Ivanov's wagon and team were still in the yard behind the soddy. Ma was standing in the doorway, wiping her hands on her apron. She called out, "Where on earth is everybody? I thought we were fixing to sup."

Joe peered at the eastern skyline. The sky was dark over that way and the first stars were out, but the slanting rays of the sunset and dying fire made a pink dot on the horizon of Nadja's white blouse.

Joe moved to the neighbor's wagon and untethered the team. He told Jessie, "Stay here with Ma. I'll drive after them and find out what in thunder is going on."

He clucked the two old plow horses into motion and a cluck in English must have sounded like Russian, for they headed east after Nadja without any argument. He figured the team had to be American horseflesh, anyway. Yasha had told him they'd brought a mess of furniture and this wagon from the old country, but two old plugs in steerage sounded silly.

The Russian girl had a good start, but there was no way to lose sight of her and as he began to gain she heard him and stopped. He drove up to where she stood, rosey on one side and lavender on the other in the funny light, and as he reined in he saw tears running down her cheeks.

He said, "Evening. Do you have some particular reason for running a couple of miles toward nowheres, Miss Nadja?"

She came over to him and as he helped her aboard she sobbed, "Yasha has done it again. You can see he was too frightened to think."

"Yeah, a thinking man with a wagon and team would hardly run hull down over the horizon, even if he had some place to go. I reckon you want to catch up with him, huh?"

She nodded, choking back a sob, and Joe clucked them forward. He said, "I've been meaning to visit an abandoned homestead they say lies over yonder. He might head there. But I reckon you'd be the best judge of that, Miss Nadja. I don't mean to pry, but you seem to know which way he's headed."

"Poor he. He will just run until he can't keep running. Try not to hate him, Friend Josef. Is sickness Yasha isn't helping. I am telling you this before, *nyet*?"

"You said he was a coward and I told you that you had your brother wrong, Miss Nadja. He stood with me in an edgey situation, the other day in town."

"You make kind joke. What do you call this thing tonight? I was in doorway. I heard you tell Yasha to help you and other men fighting fire. I saw Yasha's face. Was like other time he ran away."

"He just lit out, huh? What other time are we jawing about, Miss Nadja?"

The Russian girl stared down at her hands in her lap as Joe drove, searching the dark horizon ahead of some sign of her panic stricken brother. Nadja licked her lips and said, "We came with, how you say, party of other young men who are not wanting to be soldiers for Little Father? Was two, no, three years ago we came to place called Dakota."

"That's the territory just north of Nebraska, right? We was thinking about Dakota Territory. Easier to get here on the U.P. You folks had another claim up there?"

"*Da*, was how you are saying, commune? All Russians, like us. Was trouble. *Nyet* big trouble. Army troopers telling us was only band of what they are calling Reservation Jumpings."

"Indians? I do remember reading in the papers about some sassy Sioux raising a little ned up that way, now that I study on it. Don't remember them hurting anybody important. Burned out a few spreads and tried to wreck a train afore the army rounded 'em up. What happened? Did you Rooshins get hit by Sioux?"

Nadja sobbed, "Don't know what happened! Yasha ran away! Our leader, Boris, is handing out guns. Is saying we must be brave and not let Indians see we are afraid. Indians come, making much noise, shooting flaming arrows and making little children cry. I, Nadja, am afraid, but not screaming like silly woman. I am looking for brother, Yasha, to loading his rifle for him. That time, he take wagon. This wagon. Was not his wagon, but when I saw he was driving away I ran after and jumped on back. I am saying, Yasha, are you crazy, and he is just driving over prairie like mad man. Later, is saying he did it to save me. But I know this is lie. If I had not caught up he would have left me with others. I am so ashamed."

Joe whistled softly and said, "I can see why you moved a ways south. Be sort of rough to explain to your Rooshin friends if you'd gone back after the Indian raid, wouldn't it?"

Nadja looked away and said, "Not possible, either. This was not our wagon. Things in it were not ours. All our friends from old country think Yasha and I are worse than cowards. We are thieves."

"Oh, hold on a spell, Miss Nadja. You ain't no thief. You just went along with your brother. I ain't sure Yasha's a thief, neither. Let's just call him nervous for now. You left your old gear as a fair exchange, didn't you?"

"*Pravda*, and I had pretty dress in hope chest I was saving for wedding some day. Is not point. Yasha and I ran away. Even little children stayed that night to yell back at Indians. Yasha was big coward, like I said."

They drove on a time in silence as Joe mulled her odd tale over. He spied the dark mass of another sod house and swung the team toward it. He said, "Yonder's the house I was telling you about, Miss Nadja. They was right about it looking spooky." He didn't think he ought to tell her about the dead man they'd found in the deserted soddy, right now. She likely had enough on her plate without ghost stories in the gloaming.

It took a spell to get to anything worth notice on the dead flat prairie. As they headed for the dark, deserted claim he said, "I'm no educated expert on spooky behavings, Miss Nadja, but I've studied your tale and I've been going over what happened in town the other day. Your brother ain't all that scared of folks. The two rascals we tangled with was both armed and a lot bigger than Yasha. He backed my play like a man, and that's the truth. I ain't making it up to comfort you."

"Maybe, Friend Josef. But he is running from recruiters of Tsar and he is running from Indians and—"

"Now just back up and let's study on that, Miss Nadja. Not wanting to fight a Turk for no sensible reason could be considered sort of unpatriotic, but it don't sound like blind panic if he took time to pack and buy you both a steamboat passage. He ran off wild-eyed from that Indian raid. Tonight he ran off just as crazy from another fire. There wasn't no Sioux whooping and hollering at us back there, Miss Nadja. Just the fire. Both times he ran when he saw flames. Do you follow my drift?"

Nadja swung around to stare at him, her eyes glowing in the slanting light from the west as she gasped, "You are saying Yasha is afraid of fire?" She shook her head and added, "Is possible, but that is crazy, too."

Joe said, "Well, they do say Napoleon was scared of cats. Crazy scared, I mean. Couldn't abide a cat anywhere's near him. He was willing to let folks shoot cannon and such at him, but whenever he seed a cat he'd get all ashen-faced and rubbery-laiged. I'll allow it made old Napoleon sort of odd, but I disremember anyone ever accusing him of being afraid of a fight."

Nadja nodded and said, "*Pravda*, I have heard of such things. Some people afraid of high places. Brave men fainting at sight of blood."

"There you go. I don't know what they call it, but that's likely what old Yasha has. My Ma's sort of spooked about the open space out here, I suspicion, for she's sure acted odd since we come west. I ain't saying your brother's right to get so excited by the sight of flames, but it might help if you understood it wasn't exactly his fault. Think on it as some sort of condition, like hay fever."

Nadja smiled radiantly and threw her arms around him to plant a moist kiss on his cheek. He grinned sheepishly and said, "Aw, mush. You had no call to do that, girl."

But it had surely felt good and he might have gotten in more trouble had not he thought to rein in first to call out, "Hey, Yasha? You in there, old son?"

The silly little son of a bitch was, just as he'd started to really enjoy looking for him, too. Yasha appeared in the doorway, pale-faced and covered with vomit down the front of his peasant blouse. Joe said, "We come to fetch you back to the house, Yasha. Supper's waiting and that fire's out, now."

Yasha licked his lips and avoided Joe's eyes as he said something to his sister in Russian. Nadja answered him in kind and it would have been more interesting to Joe if he'd understood word one.

While she was trying to coax him over to the wagon, Joe got down for a look-see around the played out homestead. They'd been right about the fence having been carted off, damn it. The door and window sashes were missing, too. But there had to be a tolerable mess of planking under the roof sods. Be a chore to scalp the soddy and haul the lumber home, but he had a buckboard and they'd been figuring on buying a mule, as soon as he had time to plow. Getting the mule early would cut into their savings some, but this lumber would pay for it and he'd have something to ride to town aboard. There wasn't a woman around here he could trifle with and the smells and sounds of the infernal critters was getting him too flustered to sleep right. Yasha wasn't the only gent out here with a troubled mind. If he ever told another living soul about that disgusting dream he'd had the other night they'd call the law and have him locked up as a dangerous lunatic.

He wanted to see inside. So he moved over by Yasha in the doorway and asked, quietly, "See anything worth salvaging in there?"

He stepped inside the gaping doorway and struck a match as Yasha started to blubber at him. He said, "Yeah, why don't you get in the wagon? I see they got all the furniture and the stove. There's a flower pot over there Ma might like."

"Tovarich Joe, I don't know what to say."

"Don't say it, then. I'll just fetch that pot and we'll drive back and have supper. You'll be able to wash up by the well, outside."

"What am I to say to your mother and sister? How can I facing them?"

"You don't have to say anything, save that you're ready to sup. Facing 'em won't hurt you. They're both tolerable-looking gals. You want to drive back or shall I?"

Yasha swallowed and said, "You, Joe. I am too crazy to drive. My sister will be afraid if I drive."

Joe looked up at Nadja and raised an eyebrow. The Russian girl nodded and said, "You must drive, brother. Is your team. Josef had trouble getting them to follow you."

So Yasha climbed up in the driver's seat as

Nadja handed him the reins. Joe got on the other side of her. It was a snug fit. Her soft, strong thigh felt nice against his denim-clad leg. He wondered what it would feel like with big legs like that around his waist and that made him wonder if it was true the Mex gal by the depot did it three ways for three dollars. He couldn't afford no three dollars, but he didn't need it three ways. One old-fashioned screw would likely kill him, and be sort of rough on the Mex gal by the time he got himself calmed down a mite.

He knew it was too late to study on going into town with Yasha, like they had planned. His Rooshin friend was starting to talk sensible again and even told a joke as they drove back in the gathering darkness. Yasha was likely going to be all right, but, Jesus, if them nightriders ever found out how scared he was of fire . . .

"LOLITA" THE NOTORIOUS "Mex Gal" of Pittsburgh Landing was sitting in the doorway on the shady side of her crib near the railroad depot. The shade didn't help much. She was still sort of ugly. Joe had no way of knowing her name wasn't Lolita or that she was really a Red River Breed. Nobody would ever tell him the other whores in town had decided one "Indian Mary" seemed enough and that there'd been an opening for a "Mex Gal" as well as the still vacant slots for a "French Gal" and a "Pretty Quadroon" when "Lolita" had come down from Deadwood after a financial dispute had led to some cutting the Law up there was still interested in.

Joe circled the block, pretending he didn't notice Lolita as he passed her in the doorway. She pretended she didn't notice him, either. Business was slow in the middle of the week and at least he looked clean. Those bib overalls would come off quicker than chaps and jeans, but the young fool was sober. Lolita prefered her customers drunk. It was easier on both of them. More profitable, too. The big farmer looked like all he wanted was a simple screw and it was hardly worth getting undressed for one lousy dollar.

Joe turned the corner and told himself he'd best tend to first things first. He'd have been mortified at the suggestion he was too shy to approach a whore in broad daylight. He just had to use common sense. A man had no call throwing away money on luxuries before he had a clearer idea on just how much he had to spend.

They'd told him at the livery they had no mules for sale or hire. They wanted a ridiculous twenty dollars for that spooked paint pony few people ever hired. Joe might have taken him as a gift. Any horse was better than none. But he was blamed if he'd pay for the privilege of teaching that critter how to turn a straight furrow hitched to a John Deere.

As he headed back up Main Street, he saw Trinity Mackail and Spike Long coming his way on the shady side. He hadn't thought Trinity meant it when he'd said old Spike was fired. He could tell the twin cowboys apart now. Brazos wore sensible cattle working duds or even overalls whilst choring. Trinity always looked like he was dressed for the cover of Buntline's Wild West Magazine in his ten gallon hat and bat-wing chaps.

Joe cut across the sunlit dusty street for the overhang across the way. As he clomped up the board steps in front of the hardware store he met

Deputy Brody standing there. Brody nodded and said, "Smart move. I heard you've tangled again with Trinity Mackail, son."

Joe frowned and said, "I was coming over here anyways. Folks sure do jaw a lot in these parts."

"I'm paid to listen, son. Paid to study on how serious the gossip is, too. It's my understanding that this time killing words was spoke. Do you want to put a peace bond on that ornery cuss? If he started up with you again after we had a talk with the Justice of the Peace I could do something serious about his manners."

Joe shook his head and said, "I don't reckon I need to act so sissy. He brags a good fight, but, so far, he's never really gone for me."

"*So far* can wind up a mite late, if you're face down when I come across you, boy. I know his brother, Brazos, stopped that other fight. You can't count on me or Brazos always being there. I know you feel you can handle him. Mebbe you could, alone. But he generally has Spike or one of his other hands backing him."

Joe nodded, but said, "Spike ain't as crazy as he acts. He'd back his boss in a trip to Fist City, but he's just funning with that nickel-plated whore pistol. Didn't your informers tell you Spike refused to go along with gunplay the other night?"

Brody looked surprised and said, "No, they never. But that's good to hear from the horse's mouth. It's good to know I misjudged young Spike, but I do wish folks would be more consistent, hereabouts. My job is tough enough. The Sheriff gets sore if I bend a pistol barrel over someone who was only funning. My wife'll mourn some if I take a round some night from a gent I had in my book as harmless. You, ah, headed home after you finish here at the hardware?"

"Not hardly. Got to find me a work horse. Aim to ride it home. I hitched a ride with some new folks, but they said they'll be staying in town tonight."

Brody nodded and said, "I met 'em. Swede family named Olsen, right? I directed them to the Widow Palmer's, but they hired rooms at the Drover's Rest. Told 'em not to file on that waterhole up near the county line, too. But they don't seem of a mind to take advice on anything. Where's that fool Swede now, over to the Land Office?"

"Can't say. Gus Olsen said he meant to leave his wife and kids bedded down afore he went to file his claim. Ain't seen any of 'em since they dropped me off. They're all right. Old Gus is sort of set in his ways, like most furriners, but he was neighborly when he spied me trudging down the wagon trace to town."

Brody shrugged and said, "Well, I don't have to worry about 'em today. Be a week or more afore the fool Swede starts putting his bench marks around that waterhole near the wagon trace to the north. Sure wish the judge'd give us a peace bond on him. But the law's foolish that way. You can get a peace bond on a man making threats on another's life. You can't get one preventing suicide."

"You think there'll be trouble when he files his claim, Deputy?"

Brody spat and said, "Think, hell, I know there'll be trouble. The herds coming down outten the sand hills ever' fall roundup have been using that waterhole for years. It's the only open water betwixt the rails, here, and a day's drive north of the county line."

"Hmm, I follow your drift. Can't they water at the Double M? Brazos Mackail's a friendly cuss and he told me they have a windmill and water tanks."

Brody said, "Sure they can. If they don't mind driving thirsty cows miles out of their way, which ain't as easy as it sounds. The Double M ain't on the trace. It's a couple of miles off to the west. Seven or eight miles north-north-west from your place. Those trail herders are going to be expecting to water where they always has. Going to take some talking to get them to drive a thousand head or more around and almost another day to water."

Joe frowned, consulting the mental map of the county in his head. It was a simple enough map. The county was just a square rug cut out of dead flat prairie with the railroad bisecting it from east to west and this town in the center. He said, "County line's not that far, Deputy. I doubt it's twenty miles and Olsen's claim is well this side of her."

Brody looked disgusted and said, "I can see you've drove few herds to market, boy. You don't run cows. Not if you aim to deliver 'em full weight at the loading scales. You walks cows on the trail, and unless you walks 'em slow they'll still sweat off a mess of weight on you. Cows is sold here by the pound. Figure out what it can cost if ever' cow in a herd of a thousand just sweats off a pound or so, and you'll see why nobody hurries 'em all that much. Ten, fifteen miles is a long day's drive to a trail herd. Them Swedes are nigh a day's drive out. The sand hill drovers will be counting on watering overnight there and drifting them in the rest of the way slow to sell as much water and cow shit as they can to the buyers down to the loading pens. How do you figure you'd feel if that fool Swede was costing you a couple of hundred dollars ever' time you drove past free water you'd been counting on?"

Joe whistled softly under his breath and said, "I'll have a talk with Olsen. He might listen to another farmer. What if he was to leave the water hole unfenced beside the trace? He could still use the water and the herds could graze across the way, right?"

Brody nodded and said, "That'd help, if he'd go along with your neighborly notion. I was right about you having sense as well as manners. Some pure somebody had better talk some sense into that Swede and he's already told me he don't need any advice from me. I reckon he don't like my Old Virginia ways. Might listen to a Yankee. No offense."

Joe shook with the deputy and went inside the hardware store. He asked the storekeeper if they'd gotten in the fence posts he'd ordered. The older man behind the counter shook his head and said, "I fear not, Mister Barrow. I ordered them like I said I would. Ever'body seems to want fence posts these days. Just talked to a furriner who said he needed some, too. I got wire and staples. Not pole one to string 'em on. He acted sort of unfriendly about it. Like it was my fault the train only stops here once in a coon's age."

Joe nodded and asked, "Big blonde gent named Olsen? I was looking for him."

The storekeeper nodded back and said, "That was his name, sure as hell. Looked like a Swede or German or something. He as much as accused me of refusing to sell him supplies."

The thought had crossed Joe's mind, but he said, "Well, it's hard getting started out here even when you can get supplies. How soon do you reckon you'll get some poles in?"

"Can't say. You know any sort of lumber is rare as hell in these parts. But what the hell, it's too late in the season for planting in any case. I told that Swede he'd be lucky to have his soddy built afore the nights started frosting the grass. But he just stomped out, cussing."

Joe nodded and moved toward the door, saying he'd try again next week. An open crate on the floor caught his eye. He stopped and stared down at the dismantled sheet metal blades in the crate and asked, "Ain't this a windmill kit?"

The storekeeper nodded brightly and said, "It is, and I can let you have her cheap. Ordered it for a customer who never come to claim it. Understand they went busted and left. Seeing you bought all that wire off me, I'll sell you the fixings of that mill for a flat hundred dollars."

Joe grimaced and said, "I'd have to study some on that."

The storekeeper came around from behind the counter and handed him a little booklet, saying, "Here, take along this catalogue to help you. It tells how easy a Sunflower is to set up and how much water it can pump and all. I know it sounds a mite steep, but I ain't trying to cheat you on my just mark-up. Give yourself a dollar a day for the time you waste drawing water by hand and you'll see how soon these critters pay for themselves."

Joe thanked him, folded the booklet, and put it in his pocket before he walked back outside. He didn't have any hundred dollars to spare. He couldn't afford that whore down by the depot and he needed that badly, too. Maybe worse than he needed a windmill. A man could always draw another bucket of water. But he needed help with a chronic hunger and the dreams he'd been having of late were driving him crazy.

He started toward the depot. But as he passed the cribs the Mex gal wasn't there. He knew he'd look dumb as hell knocking on her door. She was likely entertaining another customer. Joe's nose wrinkled as he pictured that. The whole business was plumb disgusting, when you studied on it. He sure wished there was a nicer way to relieve the pressure. But the few ways he'd heard about that didn't involve a woman were even more disgusting.

He circled back and homed in on the sound of metal on metal coming from the smithy near the livery. He walked over under the overhang of the wide entrance and stood polite until the smith at the anvil noticed him. The smith hit the shoe he was working on a few more licks and put it in the forge to heat up again. He nodded at Joe and Joe said, "I used to work at that, back home."

"Do tell?"

"Yeah, I was sort of wondering if you could use some part time help. I was planning on a catch

crop of barley to tide us over, but with one thing
and the other I can't seem to get started. I'm a fair
hand at shoeing. I know which end of the hammer
you hang on to, too. Made me a tolerable wrought
iron gate one time. Sold it for sixty dollars."

The smith looked him over some more and said,
"Not much call for gates in these parts. Folks don't
cotton much to fences."

"So they keep saying. How about my helping
you shoe?"

The smith took the reheated horseshoe from the
forge with his tongs, placed it on the anvil, and
gave it a harder lick with his hammer as he
growled, "Don't need any help. Couldn't afford
to hire you if I did."

"That forge'd run hotter if you had somebody
cranking her for you whilst you worked."

"That hard coal burns hot enough between the
times I crank some air my ownself. I got me a kid
who comes in after school to clean up a mite.
There ain't enough work here for two men, and,
like I said, I couldn't afford to hire you if there
was."

"You didn't ask me how much I wanted, friend."

"Don't have to ask. I ain't your friend and you
ain't mine. Most of my customers are stock-raisers."

"I see. That's why you can't afford to hire me,
huh?"

"Now you're starting to get the picture, Nester.
It's nothing personal, you understand. But I have
enough on my plate without taking sides."

"Seems to me you've already taken sides, ain't
you?"

"Have it your own way. Just go pester someone else for a job."

"You reckon anyone else in town would give me a part time job?"

"Doubt it. But it's a free country. So you're welcome to try."

Joe took a deep breath to hide the fire and salt in his voice as he said, softly, "I'll pass on how free it might be, for now. I don't reckon you'd want to say if somebody's sort of passed the word about you townees being smart to sort of freeze us out, huh?"

The smith looked down at the shoe he was working on and replied, "You are right. I wouldn't want to say."

So Joe thanked him for his time and walked away, a cold hard knot of helpless anger in his gut.

He told himself not to go off half-cocked. The livery might have really not had a mule they could sell him. The hardware man had acted friendly enough and it stood to reason fence posts were hard to come by, these days, with all the new homesteads springing up all around. He passed two women in sun bonnets and stepped aside, polite, to let them pass. He knew he had no call to hold mean thoughts against everybody hereabouts. Some were for him and some were agin' him and most likely didn't give a hoot one way or the other. The hell of it was that a man had no way of knowing. Save for Trinity Mackail, who was sort of a fool, nobody but that smith had come right out and said they was agin' him. The smith was more a scared man than an enemy, he knew. But if they'd scared the smith into surly

manners they'd likely scared others. He knew it
was a waste of time looking for part time work in
town, even if he'd had another trade save smithing.

As he passed the Widow Palmer's, she was
sweeping her front steps. She waved him over to
ask how his Ma and Jessie were. He told her they
were tolerable and she invited him inside for a
cup of coffee. So he went. It felt good to get out
of the hot sun and the widow woman had lied.
For she put some cake in front of him with the
coffee on the rosewood table in her front parlor.

She sat beside him on the settee, not crowding
him, but closer than he'd expected. As she reached
across him to serve them both he noticed she
smelled good. She had on fancy perfume and her
gray-streaked hair had been washed recent, he
could tell. She seemed a mite flushed from housework on a hot day, but all he could smell, aside
from soap and perfume, was a whiff of honest
sweat on clean cotton. He wondered why it
speeded up his breathing so. He was likely bushed
from traipsing about in the sun.

As they made small talk about the way things
had been going since his women folk had boarded
with her, the widow nodded sort of sad and said
it was a shame it took so long to get set up. After
he'd called her Ma'am a dozen times or so, she
said to call her Gloria.

He said, "I'm willing. But are you sure you
won't get in trouble with your neighbors, ma'am?"

"Gloria," she insisted, adding, "I doubt the
nightriders will bother *me* for acting like a Christian, Joe. I own as many cows as many a man in
this county."

"Do tell? I thought this was a boarding house. Where in thunder do you have all these cattle hid, Gloria?"

She laughed, sort of girlishly, considering, and said, "Out on the range, of course. I own the Circle Six, over to the west of town. I prefer to live in town, of course. I leave the herding and such to the boys I have working for me."

Joe frowned and said, "I didn't know. That Windy Whomsoever they found near my place must have been one of your hands then, huh?"

She grimaced and said, "Yes. I've no idea what on earth he was doing so far from my spread. He hadn't worked for me long. I hired him last year when he drifted north after some trouble in Dodge. He talked an awful lot for a top hand, but he never did explain that too clearly. I told the sheriff it's my notion he was gunned by someone who must have had a score to settle with him. I can't think of a single enemy he had here in this part of the country. Poor Windy was a good hand and sort of puppy dog friendly. But he did ride a long ways for a job, so—"

"Is that why you asked me in here, Gloria? To talk about that dead cow hand of your'n?"

She shook her head and said, "No. I have some things to show you, after you coffee and cake some."

He put down his cup with an inquisitive frown. She said, "Oh, all right" and rose to her feet, adding, "Back this way. I'm afraid I like to gossip. That's one reason I let rooms. It's sort of lonely living all by myself in this big house. I heard you were having a hard time, Joe. Your poor sick mother is enough of a burden for one young man, in my opinion."

He followed her, confused, as she led him down a hallway toward the rear of the house. She opened a door to a small musty room and said, "I keep this as a store and tack room. Forgive the smell. I've been meaning to air it, but it's sort of depressing."

Joe saw a dusty army saddle on a sawhorse in one corner. A bridle and a pair of horse collars hung from nails on the plank wall, along with a man's battered hat and an old cavalry saber. The rest of the stuff was just furniture, covered with dust cloths.

Gloria Palmer said, "My late husband owned the saddle. I found those work collars in the attic when I bought the place. No cowboy has any use for a saddle he can't rope with, but you're welcome to all this gear if you can use it, Joe."

He swallowed and said, "I can use it, but how much do you figure it's worth, Miss Gloria?"

She started to say something, saw the firm look in his eye, and answered, "I'll let you have it all for one dollar. Does that sound fair?"

"No, Miss Gloria, it sounds right generous and I oughtta be horsewhipped for taking advantage of a widow woman, but if you don't want the stuff I sure do."

"It's settled, then. The next time you're in town with your buckboard you can just pick them up."

They started back to the front parlor. He said, "I'll pay you now and you can hold them, then. I don't know just when I'll be able to take them home. I've been trying to get us a mule, but right now it's starting to look like I'll be walking home again tonight."

Gloria waited until they were seated again before she asked, "Could you settle for a team of Morgans? I don't have any mules."

Joe blinked and said, "Miss Gloria, a team of Morgans would have mules and almost ever'thing else beat by miles! Are you saying you have a team for sale?"

"Over at the livery, getting fat. I only use them once in a while to drive out to my cow holdings. I've been meaning to sell them off and get a saddle horse. A woman has to watch her figure and a ride once or twice a week is little enough exercise, don't you think?"

He started to say her figure was all right, but he didn't think that would sound polite, so he said, "I'll take your team sight unseen, but how much money are we talking about, Miss Gloria?"

"Oh, I don't know. Would ten dollars be a fair price, Joe?"

"Ten dollars apiece for Morgans?"

"Silly, I meant ten dollars for the team. I told you they were fat and lazy."

He shook his head in wonder and said, "Miss Gloria, you can't buy no sway-backed scrub for no ten dollars. Unbroke cow ponies cost more'n that, and if your Morgans are a trained team, why, they'd be worth Lord-Only-Knows to anybody with some money to spend."

She smiled, sort of motherly, and said, "You don't have that much to spend, Joe. You forget your mother and sister lived with me a spell. The team is yours for ten dollars and I'll just throw in the saddle and other gear for good measure, hear?"

He wanted to take her up on it, but he knew it wasn't right to take advantage of a crazy woman. She must be getting like Ma, he thought. Old women all went crazy living alone, it seemed. He said, "We got to work this out fair, Miss Gloria. That team's worth fifty or sixty dollars and the saddle alone's worth twenty if it's got a busted tree. I'll just go over to the bank and—"

"Wait," she cut in, "I've some say about my own property, Joe. If you won't be sensible, I'll tell you what we're going to do. I'm going to sell you the horses and gear on credit, hear? You just give me a one-dollar deposit and we'll say no more about it until you have your first crop sold. That sounds fair, doesn't it?"

Joe hesitated. Fair was fair, but a man didn't get far being foolish, either. He said, "You got yourself a deal, Miss Gloria, and I'll shake on it."

She laughed as she took his work-hardened hand in hers and then as they locked eyes, she sort of stopped breathing. His own heart was racing like a trip hammer, too, and he wondered what in thunder was going on inside his chest. They both rose, as if in agreement he was finished and it was time for him to leave. But she didn't move to show him out. She just stood there, holding his hand, for a long, quiet but excited time. He licked his lips and said, "Well," and she sort of swayed in toward him, closing her eyes. He started to step backward but the fool settee was in the way and he couldn't. Her face was turned up to his and though he knew she'd likely call the whole deal off if she didn't just faint dead away, it seemed only natural to haul her in and kiss her good.

She kissed back, sobbing, as she wrapped herself around him. Joe was suddenly aware her body was against his, and moving sort of longingly against him. He tried to sit them both down again, but she murmured against his lips, "No, let's go to my room, Joe."

So they did. Her shuttered room was downstairs just off the hall and the big feather bed had any hayloft beat by a country mile as he lay her across it and started to feel under her dress, still kissing her. He'd kept the Crawford gal too busy to say no, either. She hissed against his lips as he slid a rough palm up the smooth inside of her thigh and when he got it to her groin she wasn't wearing a thing under her Dolly Varden. He tongued her and slid a finger into the moist desire he felt in other quarters. That felt just like a young gal's, too. He didn't know what he was supposed to say to a woman old enough to be his Ma, but he sure knew what he wanted to do! How in the hell was he to get his fool bib overalls off without giving her time to cool off? He couldn't even drop his gunbelt without taking his hand away and . . .

"Joe, stop and let me get undressed," she murmured with her lips still pressed against his. She kissed a lot better than old Ginger or any other gal he'd ever fooled with, and she sounded like she meant it. But he'd been told that if you let go of a gal's privates before you'd gotten 'em good and hot they'd turn all prim and proper again and, Jesus, if there was one thing on this earth he didn't want, it was for her to change her mind on him right now!

She spoke more firmly but her eyes were laughing as she insisted, "Stop it, you sweet fool. Let's not waste it by starting with our clothes on."

He raised his head a mite and stared down at her smiling face. She was sure smiling bawdy for such a nice old lady. There wasn't a trace of shy second thought in her knowing eyes as she said, "You just turn your back as you undress yourself. It'll only take me a second."

So he kissed her again and rolled away to start shucking his boots as he perched on the edge of the bed. The boots and gunbelt were no fuss, but he had to rise to shuck the overalls and the union suit he wore under it. He sat back down as she said, behind him, "Oh, God, you do have a lovely body. Turn around and let me see!"

Red-faced, Joe turned his head to look back over his shoulder. He gasped in surprise as he saw she'd stripped herself to the buff and was lying there with her dark hair unbound on the pillow and her thighs open in welcome. He couldn't think of a thing to say. So he rolled over and got on top of her. He'd never known a naked woman could look that good in broad daylight! Her face was somehow younger, with the hair hallowing it all soft and her eyes glowing up at him like a fawn's, but she was still too old to be doing anything this bawdy in broad daylight and he knew she thought he was bawdy, too, but it didn't matter. He lowered himself into her and as she arched her spine to accept him with a moan of pleasure the tight wet pulsations of her frustrated flesh made him cry out, "Kee-rist!" as he ejaculated on the first good stroke.

She felt it running out of her and down between her buttocks and sighed, "Oh, no! You can't be through already!"

He growled, "Not by half, for I've been saving

up for this a spell!" and as he began to pound her, sobbing with relief, she wrapped her ankles around his waist to croon, "Oh, my, I can see you have. There certainly is a lot of you, isn't there?"

Aware of his own strength he asked if he was hurting her and Gloria said, "Yes, and I love every bit of it. Don't hold back, darling. I want it all. I want you to lose yourself inside me, completely."

So he did. And it would have been hard to say who was getting the most out of it. Old Gloria was obviously starved for the services of a strong lusty man while Joe realized the sniggering barnyard affairs he'd had up to now didn't hold a candle to the real thing. For this, he knew, was the grown-up way that married folks and such made love, and while it was a mite shocking it sure did pleasure a man.

It pleasured old Gloria, too, and after they'd shared a couple of long moaning climaxes the old-fashioned way she made him roll over so she could get on top. Joe was really shocked as she took command up there. For the bawdy widow woman was the third woman in his life he'd ever seen completely naked and the first he'd seen in such a saucy position. He started to laugh as he watched her dark nipples bounce in time to her pelvic thrusts. She had her heels on the mattress with her knees spread astoundingly and when he glanced down between them he could see her pubic hair was grayer than her head, considering how young the rest of her was acting and feeling. She frowned slightly as she stopped moving and asked, "What's so funny?"

He answered her by thrusting up into her as he soothed, "You ain't funny. I am. I've never done this afore with a lady stripped total and it's sort of wild, at least, to me."

She grinned roguishly and rolled off him to move to the nearby dresser as he watched, bemused, enjoying the rear view, too. Gloria adjusted the mirror over the dresser drawers so that they could see themselves in it from the bed. Joe flushed to see how silly he looked laying spread-eagled with an erection across the clean but rumpled sheets. Gloria came back to remount him, saying, "There, don't they look like they're having fun? What say we join them?"

And so, in the next few hours, Joe Barrow learned about sex from a mistress of the art who had few if any inhibitions. He was glad he hadn't been able to get up the nerve to visit the Mex Gal, now. Not even the widow woman could know the service she was performing in allowing Joe to grow familiar with naked female flesh he was allowed to touch. When she later proposed a temporary truce and went to get them some more coffee and cake he was able to lie semi-sated and watch her comings and goings in the nude without feeling at all embarrassed. It was odd, but as she sat on the edge of the bed, pouring and serving with the tray between them on the sheets, it seemed perfectly natural and sort of casual, despite her not having a stitch on. He no longer worried about her seeing him that way, either. He still found her desirable, for in truth Gloria Palmer had a lovely body and he knew a little snow on the roof hadn't put out the fire in her furnace. Now that he'd grown used to the idea, it did seem sort of odd that folks thought clothes were so important. Joe chewed and swallowed some cake before he commented on his discovery. Gloria smiled and said, "I've often wished people didn't have to wear so much, at least, on a hot day. They say the Sandwich Islanders get by with nothing but grass skirts and it doesn't seem to cause rioting in the streets."

"Well, they're heathen furriners, so they likely know no better. I ain't talking about ever'body traipsing about naked, Gloria. Folks'd never get their chores done. What I meant was enough to preserve modesty, without having to pack so much nobody really needs. When you get right down to bed rock, nobody could see the parts as counted if men just wore pants and a gal could go out on a hot day with just her breasts and privates covered."

"Oh, surely she'd have to cover her limbs, wouldn't she?"

"I've been studying on that, just now. I like your limbs just fine and I can see they're smaller and softer-looking than my own. But, hell, arms and legs ain't all that different. Despite all the screaming, I don't see how looking at a gal's ankle is much worse than looking at a skinny boy's, when both has socks on, anyways. All you gals hike your skirts up to do housework when nobody's looking. What harm would it really be if you went to Church with your ankles showing?"

Gloria laughed and said, "My, you are getting depraved, after your first shyness."

He grinned sheepishly and said, "Yeah, I reckon I did act sort of schoolboyish, at first. This open way of loving takes some getting used to. You likely suspicioned I've not had many women in my time."

The experienced older woman replied with a fond smile as she lifted her cup to her lips. She knew what he meant, but it didn't jibe with her previous conceptions of the sweet strong farmboy she'd rather brazenly seduced. She said, "I hope I haven't robbed you of your virginity, dear. Robbing the cradle was bad enough."

"Now don't go mean-mouthing a man who tried sincere, Gloria! I reckon I've had me more'n one gal, even if it was with most of our duds on. Back home in Penn State I was considered sort of wild."

"I can believe that. But you haven't been that long without sex, have you?"

He nodded and said, "Yeah, but it wasn't shyness so much as lack of opportunity. You know I've been too busy to look at a gal, until recent."

"Really? From the way your mother and half-sister were going at one another one day I thought . . . Never mind."

Joe frowned and said, "Don't go saying never mind, now, Gloria. You was about to tell me something when you dropped your lashes like that, weren't you?"

She said, "It's not important, Joe. Your mother seems to be going through the change of life and it's made her, well, a mite odd."

"I already knew that. What were she and Jessie fussing about?"

"Oh, just gal-fuss, cooped up as they were together. I tried to be more friendly but your mother seems convinced I'm a Confederate spy. Jessie is a sweet girl and she never started any of the spats."

"Old Jessie's all right. What were they spatting about? Come on, Gloria, I can tell when folks are keeping their thoughts close to the vest."

The widow woman laughed as she glanced

down at her bare breasts to say, "I seem to have mislaid my vest. Your mother was just being cruel, Joe. I can see Jessie's protests were truthful and it's small wonder she got a mite hysterical."

"But you wasn't sure, until today, huh? Are you saying Ma accused me and Jessie of, well, this?"

"I'm afraid so, dear. I wouldn't let it upset me, since it's not true."

"Good God on the Mountain! Ma must be crazy as a bed bug! What makes old ladies talk and act so dirty?"

Gloria Palmer grimaced and looked away as she murmured, "Those who talk and those who act aren't the same kind of lunatic, dear. Your mother can't be much older than me, and I know all too well how lonely a healthy woman feels in bed. Before she got mad at me she mentioned that you favored your long-lost father to a tee. I never bore a son to my late husband, let alone one who was his spitting image. But I can feel how it could mix a lonely woman up. I wanted you so bad I could taste it the first time I clapped eyes on you. If you'd reminded me of someone I used to sleep with a lot I don't reckon I'd have taken this long to have my wicked way with you."

Joe knew better than to ask her if other men in the county had been sharing her favors recently. It was obvious as hell old Gloria had her own notions of what could go on behind closed doors. He wondered why it bothered him. He'd been willing to do this very thing with that slut down by the depot, once he got up the nerve to ask. No matter how many lovers the widow woman had, she couldn't be as dirty as that Mex gal. She was a lot better looking, too.

Later, they lounged side by side on the bed and shared a most unladylike smoke as well as what he realized was a sort of afterdinner conversation. He was afraid the offer of the horses and gear had been meant just to entice him into being wicked, but old Gloria sais she was no Injun giver and that she'd meant what she said about the Morgans and his paying up after he got paid for a catch crop. He took a drag of smoke, handed her the cheroot, and said, "God damn, I *like* you, Gloria Palmer!"

She smiled, sort of maternally, considering, and said, "I like you, too, Joe."

He said, "I don't mean I like you 'cause you've, uh, acted so friendly. You mustn't take this as an insult, but I've been studying on how I feel with you, uh, betwixt times. This may sound dumb, but I reckon I like being with you even when we ain't . . . you know."

She let smoke curl out her nostrils as she lowered her lashes and said, "I like it like this, too, dear. You see, I like men. I mean, I like them as more than something to take pleasure with. The love-making is just the icing on the cake. The things I miss most about being married are the, well, moments like this. Don't it feel like we're all alone, snug and cheerful, with the rest of the world off somewheres else?"

"Yeah, that's the way I was too dumb to put it. Out in the real world folks got all sorts of chores and worries, for it's broad daylight and I ought to be ashamed for wasting a whole afternoon like this. But I sure feel, uh, comforted. I got ever'-thing that really matters here and now for this stolen time. It's just great to have food, smokes, and a willing woman at my fingertips. I feel like a kid let loose in a candy shop."

She snuggled closer and said, "Me, too, but we've got to study on some plans, Joe. You ain't the sort of boy who kisses and tells, are you?"

"Hell, no! You don't have to worry about me giving your reputation away. I got more sense than that."

"Good. It's getting late and I think you'd better leave well before dark. Folks are funny that way. They never seem to suspect anything when a man comes and goes in broad daylight. We'll finish this smoke and make love again. Then we'd best get dressed and go over to see about the Morgans in the livery. Naturally, you'll have to visit me from time to time to, uh, discuss our business dealings."

"Yeah, I'd like that. I'll get back here as often as I can."

"Not too often, dear. We mustn't be greedy and it wouldn't be discreet. I think we'll be able to get away with one or two visits a week. Any more would have the neighbors talking, and, of course, you dasn't come to me after sundown, ever."

He nodded but frowned. He had in fact planned things the other way, for he had chores out on the homestead and daytime was the best time to work. But he saw the common sense in her words and, what the hell, once or twice a week would hold a sensible man and he could always chore on the sabbath. Folks might talk about that, too, but they couldn't accuse him of anything worse than breaking the sabbath if they noticed him working the fields.

As if she'd read his mind, she said, "I'll make it

up to you every time we can sneak some time together, dear. I'm so glad we have our relationship
worked out pragmatic."

He said "I hope I got it straight. It's my understanding that what we've got here is a sort of, uh,
partnership? We're just pals, right?"

"Exactly. No strings. No jealous notions. I'm too
old for you to get serious about and I don't want
to hear any foolish talk if you see me on the porch
of an evening chatting with other old friends, like
Sheriff MacLeod. He just enjoys talking to a
woman he can talk to sort of man-to-man and I
won't say again there's nothing like this going on
between old Ewen and me. But if there was, you'd
have no right to object. In return I won't act silly
if I hear any more tales about you and that Russian
gal or some other young goose."

"Do Jesus, have folks been saying I'm sparking
old Nadja Ivanov? I've never been alone with the
fool girl!"

She snubbed out the smoke and said, "It
wouldn't vex me if you had, dear. I told you this
was pure friendship between understanding grown-
ups." She reached to fondle him again as she added
with a roguish smile. "I mean to send you home
in no condition to get another gal in trouble. But
it's jake with me if you court others, as long as you
save some for me!"

He laughed and rolled over on her. This time he
was partly showing off, as he'd about exhausted
the possibilities for now. So, for the first time in
his life, Joe found himself just doing it for the hell
of it, without the usual excitement. He liked that,
too. It still felt better than anything else he could
think of and it somehow made him feel closer to

old Gloria to do it so calm and friendly. He now had a model for his uncalled-for cravings and she didn't remind him of any naked bodies he wasn't supposed to dwell on. He knew if he could get some of this at least once a week he'd be able to work his claim and sleep at night with a less worried mind. Hell, it wouldn't fluster him so the next time old Yasha and Nadja came over. He could mayhaps josh a mite with the pretty Rooshin gal and if it gave him a hard-on it wouldn't be as upsetting. Hard-ons were sort of interesting when a man had some notion what to do with them!

His distraction made for a longer than usual and steady canter in the saddle of old Gloria's friendly thighs and she seemed to like it, for she started to move more excited. He wanted to please her. She was just about the nicest old gal he'd ever met up with. She'd saved his day for him between the offer of a team and now this. It was too good to be true. He'd come to town desperate and now he seemed to have it made.

Gloria flushed from throat to nipples as she had her climax and when he kept going she moaned and said, "Oh stop, I can't take any more." But she must not have meant it, because she came again as he finally managed. He lay limply in her arms, getting his breath back, and she stroked his hair and spine as she sighed and asked, "Did I really please you, darling?"

He kissed her and said, "More than I thought possible. Jesus, this must be what it's like to be married up. I know it wouldn't be proper for you and me to even study on it, but if I was a mite older—"

"Don't talk dirty, Joe," she cut in. He chuckled

and said, "You sure have funny notions, Gloria. You don't seem to think there's all that much wrong with sex-talk, but you say marriage talk is dirty."

THE WELL-MATCHED Morgans he'd gotten from Gloria Palmer pulled a John Deere plow like they enjoyed it. Joe enjoyed it, too, for the land was flat and though the virgin prairie sod was thick and tough there were no rocks or roots to contend with and the mouldboard turned an even furrow as straight as a string. He was working the southwest forty in the cool of morning whilst Ma and Jessie prepared the noon meal in the soddy to his north. The Morgans pulled in step and he enjoyed the beauty of their strong brown hindquarters as he guided the plow behind them with the reins tied around his neck. The Morgan was a short all-purpose horse, famous for being smart and willing to try most anything. They were a mite small for plow brutes and built sort of cow pony for a proud rider to show off as a saddle mount but they could handle either job. Both were geldings and seemed twins, like the Mackail brothers. They didn't have the mismatched brains of his neighbors over the horizon to the north-west, though. A man had to just holler gee or haw and the two sweet critters just swung in the traces as if they had one mind betwixt 'em. He sure owed old Gloria. Any one of the favors she'd done him would have put a gent in debt to her. He knew the team was the only favor of her'n he should be thinking about this day, since they'd agreed he wasn't to come calling until Thursday at the soonest. She'd said few settlers from outside of town came in during the week and that he ought to buy some things in town afore he dropped by on his way home. He could hardly wait. For though she'd wrung him out like a dishrag the other day, he'd somehow gotten his second wind soon after getting home. He'd thought having a steady place to get it would calm a man down, but it didn't seem to be working out that way. Like most youths who'd discovered real sex Joe was rather preoccupied with it.

He spied a horse and sulky on the wagon trace as he neared the west end of his field. He stopped his team in the turn-around and rested them as he wiped his face and draped the reins over the plow handles. The sulky driver was the Swede, Gus Olsen. He, too, reined in as he drew abreast of his distant neighbor. Joe said, "Morning," and Olsen nodded, gazed past him at the forty acres he'd laid out and said, "Good morning. I see you don't have your land fenced yet."

Joe said, "They won't sell me no poles either. I figure there's time to catch a crop of barley afore the first frost."

Olsen shook his head and said, "You can't grow

crops without fencing. I understand a cattle drive will be coming through here in a month or so. They'll go after fresh green-up even if their drovers try to control them. I've been told they seldom try to."

Joe said, "First things first. I can get the seeds in whilst I'm waiting for the poles. I'll string some wire betwixt now and the fall roundup. I only need to fence this one forty. They're welcome to any other grazing on my claim, for now. Grass ain't doing anything important out yonder and the cows'll leave us some fuel for the winter."

Olsen grimaced and said, "It's not tidy, no offense." Joe noticed he didn't have a furren accent, even though he looked and acted like a Swede. He said, "We're fixing to eat in a few minutes, neighbor. You're welcome if you care to join us."

Olsen shook his head and said, "No, thank you. I just ate with my family at the hotel in town. I have chores to do out at my place. Unlike yourself I did manage to buy some poles the other day. They were salvaged from a deserted claim and the man who sold them to me ought to be ashamed of himself. But what's done is done and I mean to fence my quarter section properly before I move my kith and kin out there."

Joe shifted his weight and said, "I hear tell there's a water hole on your spread," and Olsen nodded. He said, "Yes, we were lucky. There's a clay measure under our property as keeps the water table high out there. It's my understanding the hole's an old buffalo wallow, widened over the years by other critters coming to drink there. It's not a big pond, but it saved us digging a well."

Joe said, "Seems to me you'd find it easy to dig a

shallow well nearer your house, inside your fence."

Olsen said, "The water hole will *be* inside my fence, once it's up. It's on my claim and my claim is a square quarter section. If you mean to repeat that Deputy Brody's suggestion about a foolish looking dog-leg in my property line, forget it. I told him I have no intention of setting aside a public drinking fountain on that corner of my land."

"Well, the law don't say you have to, but I suspicion that's what I'd do if I was in your shoes, Olsen. Since you talked to Brody, you know those cowboys are likely to find your attitude unfriendly. They've been using that water a spell, now."

Olsen shrugged and said, "They should have filed on it then. It's not my fault they never planned ahead. I filed fair and square on public domain. I'm entitled to all hundred and sixty acres of it and I'd be a fool to leave a couple of acres outside a ragged-ass fence line."

Joe was about to say he was acting foolish the other way, but he saw the man was one of them stubborn kinds of Swede, so he said, "You has the right. It's your land, legal. So we'll say no more about it."

Mollified, the Swede asked him about the likely price of barley in the fall and after a few more words of small talk he drove on. Joe glanced up at the sun ball and saw he had time to run another furrow, so he clucked to the Morgans and they started one. He got to the far end, swung around, and unhitched the team to leave the plow where it was. He mounted the near horse, sitting sideways, and said, "You boys did fine and I'm proud of you. We've all earned a rest and some grub for now."

Gloria Palmer had named the Morgans Damon and Pythias, which seemed fair enough to Joe, but the names had suffered a sea-change when Jessie had mockingly started to call them Demon and Pittypat and Ma had laughingly gone along with Jessie, either to make up with her or to spite the widow Palmer and her "high-falooting ways". Joe had held out for truth and justice until he discovered the horses really didn't care what you called 'em, as long as you didn't call 'em late to breakfast. So he rode Demon back to the barnyard with Pittypat in step as well as in harness. As he drew nigh, he saw Nadja Ivanov turning in sitting alone at the reins. He tethered his plow brutes by the empty watering trough he'd improvised from planks he'd salvaged from the abandoned claim over the horizon to the east. He went to help Nadja down and unhitch her own team for watering as Jessie came out of the soddy to greet her. He decided to let the gals jaw and giggle a spell before he asked why Yasha had let his kid sis drive so far alone. He was afraid he suspected the reason.

The gals went into the soddy while he drew a couple of buckets for the critters. Jessie had already fetched cooking water, of course, and he noticed the water was muddy again. He glanced at the sky. It was a big inverted bowl of cobalt blue without a hint of cloud in it from skyline to skyline. He'd been studying on that booklet from the general store and as a skilled smith and fair mechanic he didn't see as a windmill would be all that hard to throw together out of scrap. But the pipe would be a bitch.

He went to the house and washed up at the
slop sink outside the door before stepping inside.
It was a mite cooler out of the sun. As his eyes got
used to the shade he saw that the Rooshin gal
looked upset. But when he asked her what was
wrong she said she was just tired. She said her
brother was feeling poorly and that she'd been
choring some.

Ma told him to set and say grace, for she was
hungry. So he did. He knew Jessie had done most
of the work and it was a pure mystery how an old
woman who didn't do anything but bitch could
work up such an appetite, but of course he didn't
say so.

Nadja bowed her blonde head and closed her
eyes as he said grace Calvinist-style, keeping it
short. The Rooshins weren't Calvinists. As near as
he could figure they followed some furrin faith
that was a lot like Christianity, and they seemed
good sports about Americans following the True
Faith.

The meal was simple and there wasn't enough
for seconds. Like most farm folk, they ate in silence
and got it over and done with before they jawed a
mite over coffee and apple pie. Ma had made the
pie. It was too sweet and she'd missed a few seeds.
Back home in Penn State she'd made a pretty good
pie, but her cooking was getting careless, too,
since she'd started acting funny. Hoping Nadja
wouldn't notice, he asked her if they'd planted
yet, for he knew they had their quarter section
fenced and watered and it was late in the season.
Nadja said her brother meant to plow and plant
in a month or so.

Joe frowned and said, "I know Yasha's been feeling poorly, Nadja, but plowing next month would be a pure waste of effort. The barley I'm fixing to drill in right about now only has a fifty-fifty chance of ripening afore the first fall frosts."

Nadja nodded and said, "Is true, Josef. Yasha says you Amerikansy are wasting efforts with summer plantings."

"He does, huh? Meaning no disrespect, I reckon us Yanks ought to know a thing or two about farming our own country."

Nadja looked sort of mournful and replied, "Begging pardon, Josef, we came out here with Tovarichki because this part of Amerika was so like own country. What you call prairie is steppe, in old country. Same kinds grass. Same kinds weather. In Russia grows much wheat, *da*?"

"I don't know what in tarnation you used to grow back there, girl, but you sure didn't grow much planting this late or later in the season. They tell me it can snow out here as early as October."

"*Pravda*, we have been out here three years, Josef. You will see. Climate is just like on steppes of Russia. Always, back home, we planted in fall."

Joe stared at her in total confusion and asked, "Now what in thunder can you plant in the infernal *fall*? Are you sure you ain't got your seasons backwards? Nobody since Adam has ever planted in the fall!"

Nadja shrugged and said, "Maybe you English-speaking people farming that way. In Russia *nyet*. Season is too short."

"Well of course the season is short. The crops need every bit of warm weather they can get and there ain't all that much in a short summer. What's this fool crop Yasha figures to plant and harvest in a month or less?"

"Wheat," said Nadja, simply, adding, "We have red wheat from steppes of Turkistan for planting. Boris, our old leader, said English wheat you Amerikanski grow is no good for out here."

"He does, huh? Well, in the first place, I've seen a few fields of wheat as was planted early this spring afore we got started and it's almost starting to head up. I'll allow it's nip and tuck as to whether it'll be ripe enough to harvest before it's nipped off. You're right about the short summers and it grows slow as the devil in this dry heat. You could be right that some furrin grain could do better out here, for I've seen the grass is different from back east. But your red Turkish whatever ain't about to sprout and set seed in any one durned month."

Nadja dimpled and said, "Silly Josef, Russian wheat is harvested in spring time, not fall. You are planting in fall, harvesting in spring, see?"

Even Jessie knew better than that, and she *liked* old Nadja. She smiled across the table at their guest and said, "Honey, you must be mixed up. They say it *snows* a mite out here in the winter. Everybody knows the winter kills all green things that grow, save maybe pine trees."

Nadja shrugged and said, "In Russia, we plant in fall and harvest in late spring. Has always been so."

"Don't it snow in Russia?"

"*Da*, of course. Very much. Like out here in Nebraska."

"Then this tough old Rooshin wheat of your'n is supposed to grow in snow?"

"*Nyet*, of course not. Let Nadja explain. You plant seeds in fall, *da?* Is dry in fall. Seeds lie quiet in earth until fall rains. Put down maybe little roots. Grow maybe tiny first leaves before snows are coming. Then wheat is resting and waiting under snow. Red wheat is tough. Does not grow in cold, but cold does not kill. In early spring, when snow is melting and fields too wet to work, roots go crazy, follow the water down as soil is drying. By time top of soil is hard and dusty again, wheat has grown deep deep roots, much deeper than Amerikan wheats you have to plant in spring. Red wheat stalks grow strong and tall in first warmth of sun. By time fields are dry and Amerikanski are plowing, Russian wheat is setting heads. You harvest by July. Sometimes even in June."

Jessie looked across at Joe. He frowned and said, "A man could catch a crop of summer barley on the same land, if it worked that way. But old Yasha must be funning us."

"Nadja, here, says she's seen it, Joe."

"Well, she's a gal. You gals don't do the plowing and reaping and she was just a kid when they left Rooshia."

Nadja looked hurt and insisted, "I was almost woman and I helped in fields back home. I know we have different calendar, but I know when is spring and when is fall, *nyet?*"

Joe said he'd ask Yasha about it the next time he saw him and went out to resume his own chores as the women folk cleaned up—or rather, as the two younger gals did the housework whilst Ma sat in the doorway dipping snuff and muttering to herself. It seemed to cheer Jessie to have another young gal to talk to and he knew Nadja came over because she was only human, too. But whilst Ma kept bitching about her lack of neighbors, she didn't seem to cotton to the Rooshen gal lately. Joe couldn't see why. Nadja was friendly as a pup as well as being a pretty little thing.

He rode the Morgans out to the plow and hitched 'em up again to finish the forty. He'd told Nadja to stay put with Ma and Jessie and that he'd run her home in time to fix supper for her brother. So the blonde made herself useful and by mid-afternoon she and Jessie had the house neater than it had been in recent memory and were out weeding the yard together, jawing and giggling the way young gals did. Jessie had planted the dooryard with flower seeds to cheer Ma, and though Ma didn't seem too cheered, the sprouting sun flowers still had to be watered and weeded. As he cut a furrow he saw Nadja fetching a bucket from the well. She'd shucked her shoes and kilted her skirts to work serious. She was a strong old gal and moved sort of graceful with that bucket. Her hips were wider and more shapely than Jessie's and they swayed sort of interesting as she leaned agin' the weight of the water. They were well-covered with her pleated cotton skirt, of course, but he couldn't help picturing her bare-assed and down on her hands and knees, like old Gloria. Do Jesus, that was a picture to give an old boy something to think about! He wondered if she'd ever done it that way, or if she'd done it at all. She wasn't married, but neither had that Crawford gal been and she'd started younger than Nadja was right now.

He grimaced and told his team, "We're sure

getting dirty-minded. Leastways, I am. You boys don't know the advantages of having your balls cut off in childhood. Makes it a mite easier to concentrate on a straight furrow."

Jessie had asked him if he liked old Nadja, sort of teasing-like. He'd said she was all right and changed the subject. A man had no call starting up with a gal unless he meant to do right by her. He had too much on his mind right now to study on how he felt about the tall blonde neighbor gal. He had a willing woman to pleasure him on the sly now, and even if he hadn't, old Nadja was likely a durned old virgin.

What was that the dirty old sheriff had told Gloria about kinfolks cooped up lonesome? He shook his head and decided it didn't seem likely. Yasha was crazy, like most furriners. Joe suspected his recent spells of poor health might be coming from a bottle, for he'd noticed Yasha drank pretty good on occasion. He had crazy notions of farming, too. But Joe just couldn't picture him acting indecent with Nadja. He wondered who Yasha did act indecent with. If he didn't have anybody, that likely explained his drinking and other foolish ways. Joe knew his own nerves were steadier now that he'd found a source of supply. He knew he'd feel even better if he could get at old Gloria more often. Damn, that Nadja had a nice round backside.

In another part of the county, the nightriders were on another mission of bedevilment. Since it was still broad daylight and they were far from the homestead they'd picked as a target they rode without their feedsack masks and officially they were searching for stray cows if anyone should see fit to ask.

As a smudge of smoke rose from a soddy on the horizon ahead the leader frowned thoughtfully. They hadn't been this way recently and he hadn't known yet another infernal nester had staked a claim on this stretch of prairie. He pointed at it with his chin and asked the confederate on his left, "How long have those sod busters been here? I thought I had every one of 'em pinpointed."

The other rider shrugged and said, "It's a big county, Cap. The bastards are coming in like locusts into Egypt Land and it's getting hard to keep track."

Another rider asked, "Do we go around 'em or push on through? They're likely to remember us, should the fool sheriff pass this way asking the usual questions afterwards."

The leader looked around at the empty sky line as they neared the isolated homestead. He prided himself on the guerrilla tactics he'd learned fighting for another cause. The Gray Ghost of the Confederacy had taught his followers to make careful plans and stick to them. On the other hand, old Mosby had been flexible on more than one occasion, raiding up and down the Shenandoah. It was true those unexpected nesters would be able to place them in time and space for the law, even if they swung wide. For if he could see the windows of that hated soddy, someone peering out had seen them by this time. One of his men growled, "Looky there, they've got forty acres of half-growed wheat. Them dots beyond are the infernal nester, busting more sod with his woman."

"I likes women," said another nightrider grinning as they rode in. The nester and his wife were working with hoes, for they had no team. The one field they'd sown that spring had been plowed by a roving contractor with a gang plow and it had cost them too much to repeat the notion. They were hoping to catch a few rows of late cabbage with their back-breaking work under the hot summer sun. As they saw the riders approach the man straightened up with a worried frown. He hadn't gotten around to fencing in his wheat yet. They'd told him the roundup was a month off. Cows had no sense about property lines. Men on horseback were supposed to avoid riding over a crop, if they were neighborly. The dozen-odd strange horsemen didn't slow as they rode in. The farmer gasped in dismay as the nightriders came his way, trampling the wheat under hoof. His young wife shouted, "Stop that!" and ran toward them, waving her hoe, as he called out, "No, Martha! Stay put!"

The girl, for she was little more than that, ran to the edge of the wheat before she stopped, hoe upraised, and suddenly had second thoughts as she spied the evil grins and determined movements of the vandals trampling their hard-won crop. The nightriders spread out, like a wolf pack, as the farmer realized sickly that his only gun was in the distant soddy. He yelled, "Martha, run for the house!" as a rider cut him off from the same, shaking out a coil of his saddle rope and yipping a taunting coyote call. The farmer started to make a break for the soddy, keeping an eye on the would-be roper. So he was caught by surprise when a second noose dropped over him, catching him by the throat and jerking him off his feet.

As the laughing nightrider began to drag her

husband the girl called Martha ran madly into the wheat field, screaming in terror as she heard the sound of hoofbeats behind her. The wheat stems lashed her bare shins and impeded her progress, but in truth it would have done her small good had she been able to run faster. A rider passed her to cut her off, laughing wildly. She cut to one side as a second rider leaped from his mount to roll with her flat in the wheat, pinning her on her back among the high stems all around. She sobbed, "Let me go! What do you want?"

He leered down at her as he unfastened his pants, saying, "Hell, you *know* what I wants, gal! What's a pretty little thing doing, wasting her time on a damned sod buster? It's time you was serviced by a *man*, and I aim to do you the honor, hear?"

"No, please, not that!" She gasped as she struggled wildly. She was a strong, determined girl and her attacker only had two hands. But then his companion dropped down to grab her wrists and pin them to the sod above her head, laughing, "Let me help, old son. You reckon there's enough here for both of us?"

"Shoot yes," the first one grinned, grabbing the collar of her thin cotton dress and yanking hard. The worn cotton ripped and as he shucked her body like an ear of corn he whistled and said, "Hot damn, don't she look nice with the sunlight shining on her little white tits like that?"

"Yeah, she oughtta be ashamed of herself. You ashamed of yourself, gal?"

"Oh, God, please, God, *help* me!"

But there was no salvation forthcoming and the young mother bit her lower lip and closed her eyes as he raped her. It couldn't last forever, could it? Just let it be over, please God, and let Sam and the kiddies live through this nightmare, too.

A million years later the second man had finished using her and she opened her eyes as a more distant voice said, "If you boys are through fooling with that slut I'd like you to stand clear."

The girl in the wheat opened her eyes to stare up at a mounted man staring down at her with eyes as cold as the keel of a Viking ship. She rose on one elbow, red-faced, to draw the tattered remains of her dress over her shame as she sobbed, "What have you done to my husband and my—"

"We've kilt 'em, ma'am," he cut in conversationally as he raised the gun in his hand. As she stared in dawning horror into the unwinking eye of the muzzle he added, "Man don't last long, drug along by the neck. As to your boy, I just gunned him as he run to help his father, yelling foolish."

"Oh, my God, he was only six!"

"Do tell? Well, it's been a pleasure talking to you, but you see the way things has to be, so—"

"Please don't kill me! Please, I don't want to die!"

"Nobody wants to die, ma'am. You and your'n should have thought of that afore you come out here to mess up our range."

"No, wait, I'll do anything you say!" she pleaded, exposing herself to him in a last desperate hope. He smiled thinly and said, "You already did that for my sidekicks, ma'am. You ain't bad, but I'm a serious cuss."

He fired. His aim was true and she died fast, for he didn't consider himself a cruel man. It seemed only proper to kill the women and children clean.

* * *

Ma followed Joe out to the corral as he was hitching Nadja's brute to her wagon. She said, "I see no call for you to escort that sassy snip home, Joseph. She got here on her own. Let her get home the same way."

He sighed and said, "Now, Ma, that ain't like you. You know the sun ball's low in the west and if she was to have a breakdown on the road the dark could catch her alone. I mean to ride along on Demon and see her safe to her door. I'll be home in time for supper, most likely."

"You don't fool me, Joseph Barrow. I know what you mean to do as soon as you're alone with that furrin woman."

"Ma, I won't be all that alone with Nadja. Her brother, Yasha, will meet us at the other end and there's nothing improper betwixt here and there."

"You'll be alone on the prairie with her, won't you?"

"Sure I will, on a county road in broad daylight. What in thunder do you figure we can do out there, Ma?"

"You know damned well what you can do, Joseph. I heard about you and that Crawford girl back home."

"Well, that was back home and Nadja's last name is Ivanov, not Crawford."

"Pooh, I seen the way you two have been looking at one another. I heard the way she and Jessie was whispering together as they weeded."

He turned to frown down at her and say, "Young gals always whisper. I doubt like hell that they was whispering about her doing anything sassy with me."

"Are you saying Jessie has reason to be jealous, Joseph?"

"Now how in hell can a sister be jealous of her brother and another gal?"

Ma looked away and muttered, "She ain't exactly a sister. I've seen the looks that pass between you and Jessie, too."

He glanced at the house to make sure they weren't being overheard as he said, soberly, "Ma, you gotta stop tormenting yourself with fool notions about ever'body. You know blamed well nothing funny has been taking place anywhere but in your head. You sleep in the same bed with Jessie, durn it."

"You were alone over at that other soddy the other day."

"Oh, hell, we asked you if you wanted to come along and help salvage."

"Mebbe, but I didn't go. I told you I was feeling poorly, and you said you'd be right back and you was gone for hours."

He snapped, "Oh, sure, have it your own way. I had my own kid sis on the prairie in broad daylight!"

Then he saw how stricken she was staring up at him and soothed, "I'm sorry, Ma, but you're riling me with that fool talk. You see, I know what you've been saying ahint my back and, damn it, it's a dirty bird that soils in its own nest. You gotta stop talking like that, hear? Folks will think you're touched if you go on accusing everybody of all sorts of dirty things."

Ma looked down at the ground and sobbed, "I never said for sure I suspicioned you and Jessie, Joseph."

He patted her shoulder and said, "Let's drop it, then. I'll just run Nadja home and be back directly."

"You swear there's nothing going on between you?"

"Ma, if there was, it would be our own business, but there ain't. I like old Nadja. I think she's a handsome gal. If she offered I'd likely take her up on it, for a man is a man at a time like that. But she ain't been flirting with me. I ain't been flirting with her. So let's say no more about it."

Ma started to say something else. Then she covered her face with her apron and ran back to the house, sobbing.

Joe swore softly and finished getting the brutes ready. Nadja and Jessie must have been watching, for they came out, holding hands. Jessie said, "I've a mind to ride along and keep you company, Joe. I could ride Pittypat, couldn't I?"

Joe said, "You could, but you hadn't better. Ma's having one of her spells and it's best one of us stays with her."

Jessie sighed and said, "Oh, Lord, what's she accusing us of this time?"

Joe didn't think it would set right with two young gals if he told them the truth, so he just shrugged and said, "Didn't say. Likely she swallowed some snuff and it's made her sick."

He helped Nadja aboard her wagon and as she wheeled it he untethered Demon and mounted up while Jessie walked back to the soddy, sort of dragging her feet.

Nadja waited until they were well down the wagon trace, with Joe riding abreast of her, before she said, "Your mother is very strange, Josef."

He said, "We've noticed."

"Yasha says he knew old widow like that back home. I knew her, too, but only boys talked about her, uh, not nice."

"Yeah, well, Yasha can keep his thoughts to hisself, no offense. I know what's wrong with Ma, but she's still my ma, so let's drop her."

Nadja looked hurt and clucked her brutes into a trot. Joe was willing. She made him uneasy, too. He dropped back a few paces to avoid having to jaw with her for a spell. She was sitting stiff-backed and the way her hips jiggled as the wagon jolted was uneasy-making, too. She wore almost as much as an American gal, so there wasn't much of her hide to see. But he'd noticed how pale the line between her tanned upper works and the peek-a-boo along the hemline of her pleated blouse was. So he knew she was milky white where the sun never shone. Her hair was the color of manila rope and when he thought of the way it had to be under the soft-looking lap of her skirts it got him too excited for comfort. He'd thought getting a good look at one naked lady would lay such thought about others to rest, but for some reason it had only given him a clearer notion of what he was about whilst he undressed other gals with his eyes.

He thought of his grotesque conversation back there with Ma and realized Ma had been thinking dirty longer than any of them. She likely undressed menfolk with her own eyes, too. He wondered if all gals did that. It was a sobering thing to consider. He wondered if Nadja had a mental picture of him without no pants on, and what she saw there. He knew there was no way on earth he was about to ask her! She likely had no such notion, being a good girl and all. Old Gloria had told him she'd known right off that he was hung like a hoss, but old Gloria was a salty widow woman who knew what menfolk were built like to begin with.

Joe spotted a rider ahead on the sky line and moved up by Nadja without comment. He hadn't brought his rifle or scatter gun, but of course he wore his sidearm. Nadja pointed out the stranger and he soothed, "Yeah, likely just a cowboy riding home from town. He's alone and it's a public right-of-way."

"You will protect me if he is bad, *nyet?*"

"Sure, but let's not cross bridges afore we come to 'em, Nadja. Like I said, he's likely just coming from town."

"I am not so afraid, Josef. I feel safe, always, with you."

Joe didn't answer. Nadja talked funny, and he recognized the other rider now.

It was Trinity Mackail. The half-owner of the Double M figured out who he was about the same time. He sat his mount warily as they approached one another, for they'd exchanged some ugly words in the past and they were out of sight of anyone else on earth as they rode to meet on the open prairie. Mackail drew off the wagon trace and reined in, either to let them pass polite or to be set for whatever. Joe heeled his own mount ahead of the wagon and reined in near Trinity, saying, "Howdy. We're headed for Miss Nadja's spread, if that's all right with you."

Trinity shrugged and said, "It's a free country. Have you seen a dapple gray stud with a white blaze and stockings?"

"Sure, you was riding him the other day. It struck me at the time your stud was marked unusual as hell."

Trinity said, "Only hoss like that in the county. He's run off. I've been all the way to town and back looking for him. He knows the trail and he's been getting sweets from, uh, a gal I know in town. But that ain't where he went."

"Hmm, you reckon he's been stole, Trinity?"

"It's starting to study that way. None of the boys working for me would be about to ride him without my say so, and I never offer. If he ain't at the spread when I get back, I'd best put out a flier on him."

"That makes sense. Hoss thief dumb enough to steal such an odd-marked mount sure deserves to get caught."

Nadja, seeing they were jawing polite, drove up and stopped. Trinity touched the brim of his Texas hat to her and Joe said, "Mister Mackail thinks his favorite horse has been stolen. You two know each other, don't you?"

Nadja said, "Yes, he is cowboy my brother had fight with, *da*?"

Joe shot her a warning look and said, "We got that straightened out, Nadja. We're all friends now. Ain't that right, Trinity?"

Trinity said, "Friends is a mite strong, but my brother asked me to be peaceable, for now."

Joe smiled and said, "That's good enough for me, Trinity. I don't need much help with my plowing."

Trinity scowled, and Joe added, "I hope you find your stud. It's been nice meeting you, Mackail."

The cowboy rode on, muttering to himself. Joe turned to Nadja and said, "You've got to learn to let bygones lay, Nadja."

"Bah, he is afraid without his friend, Spike. But he still hates you."

"I had that figured out, Nadja. The point is that he didn't have anyone to back his play this time, and the more times you pass a man polite, the harder it gets to start up with him again. Let's get it on home, your brother will be worried about you by now."

But when they arrived at the Ivanov spread they didn't find Yasha worried. They found him dead drunk, sitting at the kitchen table with half a bottle of gin. There was no mystery about where the rest of it was. Another dead soldier lay on the earth floor, near the stove.

Nadja swore under her breath in Russian and shook her brother's shoulder. Yasha opened his eyes and he seemed to have trouble focusing without his wire-rimmed specs. He mumbled something at her in the same lingo and tried to rise. It wasn't a good notion, for Yasha went over backwards instead, chair and all.

Joe stepped around the table, bent to pick the drunken little Russian up, and asked the mortified girl, "Where do we put him, on yonder bed?"

Nadja nodded and said, "He has nothing to do and too much time to do it." Joe picked the smaller man up and carried him over to the bedstead in the corner. He lowered Yasha to the feather mattress and turned around before he said, "Yeah, you told me he plants his crops in the winter. You want to come home and sup with us?"

"*Nyet*, I can't leave him like this. You go, Josef. I will make myself something to eat."

"Where do you figure on sleeping? He's got that bed pretty occupied, for such a little runt."

Nadja pointed to what he'd taken for some curtains hanging flat on the sod wall and said, "Is my room, over there." So he knew the soddy was bigger than his own, and it answered a couple of improper questions, if she had a separate bedroom.

She moved to the big brass samovar near the tile stove and felt it before she sighed and said, "Is cold. I am sorry. I wanted to offer you glass of tea before you rode all way home."

He saw she was putting a pot on the stove to boil. He said, "I'll just put your team away and wait a spell 'til that water boils, Nadja. If you have any other chores . . ."

She started to cry. He said, "I wish you wouldn't do that, Nadja."

But she didn't stop. So he went out to unhitch her team and rub them down before he watered and oated them. He told Demon he'd have to settle for water 'til they got home, adding, "I'm likely missing supper, too, but we can't ride off and leave these folks in this fix, Demon."

He went inside. Nadja had partly recovered and was making coffee. She said tea only tasted good if it was made in her big brass whatever. He didn't think much of her coffee. But being a tea drinker she likely didn't know what that was supposed to taste like. He sat and sipped with her anyway, to be polite, and when Yasha yelled something in his sleep across the room he asked, "How long has he been like this?"

Nadja said, "Since night of fire, when he ran away. Once before, in old country, Yasha stay drunk all winter. That was winter they tell him he got to go for soldier in spring."

"How'd you ever sober him up that other time?"

Nadja shook her head wearily and said, "Is impossible to sober Yasha up before Yasha is ready to sober self. Last time, just before they come for Yasha he waking up one morning. He is saying, *Nyet*, very loud, and we are on way to Amerika."

Joe frowned and said, "I sure keep meeting up with folks whose minds don't work like mine since I come out here. Brought Ma from Penn State and now she's acting touched, too. There ain't nobody coming to dragoon Yasha into no army. But it's starting to appear old Yasha runs, one way or the other, when he feels boxed in by things he can't stand up to."

Nadja bowed her head and stared down at her hands in her lap as she said, "*Pravda*, is weak little man, poor he. Sometimes Nadja think she should have been brother and Yasha sister in this family."

Joe chuckled and said, "Well, you're bigger than Yasha, but that's easy. You're still a might too rounded and she-male to make much of a big brother."

Nadja frowned, not looking half as stern as she doubtless intended, as she said, "I am strong like ox. Strong as any man. Work hard as any man, too!"

"Well, I'll allow you're a sturdy enough gal and I know you ain't lazy. I'll bet on you agin' maybe your average townee. But any man might be putting things a mite immodest, no offense."

Nadja put her elbow on the table between them and said, "I show you. You know arm wrestle, Josef?"

He laughed incredulously and said, "Sure, but you can't be serious. I'm too durned big for you. It wouldn't be fair."

"Hah, all you men say that. What is matter? Is Josef afraid girl might beat him?"

He said, "Not hardly" as he placed his own elbow on the table and they locked hands. Her hand felt sort of nice and he wasn't ready when she gritted her pretty jaws and poured on the coals. She had his wrist halfway to being pinned to the table before he'd gotten set for it. He grimaced in surprise and some discomfort, for in truth the girl was seven times stronger than any she-male had a right to be, and as he braced himself it almost looked like she had him!

Nadja looked surprised and pained some too as his hand slowly rose despite all she could do to stop it. She raised her hips from her chair, which was cheating, and he winced as she threw her back into it, moving him back a few inches before they locked, faces reddening and teeth gritted at each other across the table.

He didn't want to hurt her. He didn't even know what he was trying to prove. He wasn't sure how he'd gotten into such a fool fix or if letting her win wouldn't be the sensible way out. He suspected her confidence had come from other gents in the past letting her do just that. It might be a kindness in the long run to teach the fool gal a lesson. She could get in real trouble if she ever bet money on her queer notion.

Nadja's eyes widened as he slowly forced her arm over despite her blatant cheating. She gasped, put her other hand against her wrist to brace it and then removed it, shamefaced. He said, "Go ahead, I'll take you two to one" and she swore under her breath and threw the strength of both her strong wrists against his. He was sort of sorry he'd bragged, for Nadja was one strong gal. But Joe's lone wrist was whipcord and whalebone from working forge and farm since he'd been old enough to try, and despite her desperate effort the outcome was inevitable. It took some doing, even for Joe, but he forced her arms flat on the table. It threw her off balance and she would have flipped over to land on her back on the floor had not he moved quickly to reach forward with his free hand to steady her. He caught her in time, but he didn't catch her half-proper. For his hand had her under the off armpit with his wrist against her breast and there was no way he could let go without dumping her until he'd rolled her the other way and braced her down side against the table as he rose. He moved part way around to haul her upright and that put her in his arms, panting hard against him as she looked up at him, mad, confused, and pretty as a picture until he just naturally kissed her.

She kissed back, wrapping her arms around him and hugging like she was still trying to prove how strong she was. He knew it was wrong to tongue a nice girl, so he didn't, but it was almost as hot a kiss as he'd ever had from old Gloria and that was going some. She had all her duds on and she was likely mad at him besides, from the way she was moaning in his embrace, but she felt more she-male than anything he'd ever held this way and that was going some, too.

In the corner, Yasha groaned, too, and Nadja stiffened to pull away with a frightened glance toward her brother sleeping it off over yonder.

She said, "Please, Josef, we must stop this silly business, *da*?"

He let her go, reluctantly, as he grinned down sheepish and said, "I'm sorry, honey. I tends to lose my head when I wrestle with gals."

He noticed she blushed some as she replied, "I, too, am losing head. But now we are back from stars, I think!"

"You think? Don't you know?"

"Please, don't mix my head worse with words I don't always understand. You are very strong, Josef. I don't know why that excited me so, but I see it mixed you up, too. Now we must sit down, drink coffee and behave."

He nodded and moved back to his seat, wondering why she was looking at him like that. Didn't gals expect you to sit down when they asked you to?

Nadja took a seat across from him. Neither touched their awful coffee. Her face was scarlet and she couldn't look at him. He said, "Maybe I'd best be going, Miss Nadja. I'm sorry if I upset you. I could say no harm's been done. But I can see you're flustered and I reckon we'd best just move it down the road."

She looked up at him, big blue eyes bewildered pools a man could drown in, though cheerful, and said, "Friend Josef, I don't know what I want, right now. Brain is telling me you should go. Heart is telling me to ask you to stay. You are strong and good. You must think for silly Nadja, *nyet?*"

In the corner, Yasha rolled over and belched sickly. Joe smiled crookedly and said, "I reckon big brother just answered for both of us. I would have put it more delicate but it made a heap of sense."

As he rose, Nadja looked at her drunken brother and said with a weary grimace, "Yasha is brother. I am supposed to love him. Sometimes I love him like I love pig."

Then she laughed and added, "Nice little pig, but still pig, silly Yasha. Jessie is so lucky she has brother like you, Josef."

"Shucks, we've had us a few good scraps in our time."

"*Pravda?* I bet when you and Jessie fight, you always win, *nyet?*"

"Golly, we don't have out-and-out tussles, I mean, like that foolishness just now."

Nadja lowered her lashes and said, "Poor she. Was *fun* making tussle with you, Josef."

He frowned at Yasha over in the corner and asked, "Do tell? How often do you and your brother go at it like that?"

"Oh, Josef, Yasha and I don't fight since children. I have been able to beat him since six." She looked up at him sort of starry-eyed to add, "You are first man ever beat Nadja in arm wrestle."

He laughed and said, "I'll have to give you another chance, sometime. It was sort of fun, now that I've had time to study on it."

She looked away and said, "*Da*, was fun, but I don't think we better do it anymore. Not until we study, like you say, what we are doing."

He nodded and went to the door. She followed him outside. The sun was down and the sky was the color of an open furnace door to the west. The praire all around lay burnished gold in the gloaming and everything that cast a shadow was cool purple on one side and blushed warm shades of red and gold on the other. Nadja walked him to his mount, and as he untethered Demon she said, "Is late. Jessie and your mother will be wondering what is keeping you so long."

He smiled crookedly and said, "Yeah, I figure to catch pure hell and I ain't sure I don't deserve it."

He looked wistfully at the sunset and added, "Ain't it funny? In one way it's late and in another it's sort of early. The day is over and the night's just getting started."

She said, "*Da*, this time of day is always making me sad and happy. All looks so pretty and air always hushed at sunset, like world is holding breath. I wish this time of day lasted longer."

"That's the trouble with pretty times. They don't last long enough."

He reached for her to kiss her again, but Nadja turned her face away and said, "No, Josef. Not now. Is time you went home, I think."

"Don't I get a kiss goodbye?"

"You had kiss already. I liked it, too. Would be easy to kiss you again. Maybe too easy, in pretty sunset when lonely night winds coming soon. You must go, now. Time for silly games is over."

"I ain't so sure we was all that silly, Nadja."

"I know. That is why we must think before we are getting serious."

Joe noticed the commotion about the courthouse when he drove the buckboard in a few days later, but he paid it no mind, for he didn't mean to draw attention to his visit to town. He parked the rig in front of the general store, where he meant to leave it. He went in and bought a few items that weren't worth stealing and left them under a tarp in the back. He went across to the hardware and to his surprise they had his fence posts. Not enough for the whole boundary of his claim but enough to fence off the barley. So he had to go to the bank and draw more money. Then he had to load the bailed posts in the buckboard and worry about someone stealing them while he was with old Gloria. For he couldn't leave the horse and rig in front of her house and fence posts were well worth stealing.

He covered them good, hoping they'd be there

when he got back, for it had been a long time and he sure needed her bad. He'd had a God-awful dream the night before and neither Jessie nor Nadja would ever talk to him again if they heard about the queer things that crept into a man's dreams these days. The hell of it was that while he'd never seen Nadja without her duds on, she'd looked real as hell in that dream as he'd had her stark naked with Jessie laughing at them all the while.

He found it easy to move along the walk to Gloria Palmer's without anyone paying him any notice. She'd told him he dasn't slip in the back way like he'd offered, for that would have raised her neighbor lady's eyebrows for sure. She'd said to just drop by casual, like he was coming to talk to her on business and that was the way it went. Just about everyone in town was gathered out front by the courthouse, sort of growling. He noticed most of the crowd were farm folk, like him.

A smaller knot of townees and some cowboys stood a mite apart, looking uneasy. He mounted the steps of the widow woman and she let him in, saying, "You're late, darling. We've only a little time. It's going to be awfully busy in town by suppertime."

He said, "Yeah, I noticed something's up. What's going on?"

"Hadn't you heard? Trinity Mackail's been arrested. They're holding him for the circuit judge in the courthouse. Ewen MacLeod's afraid of a lynching and the town lockup's not very sturdy."

Joe whistled silently and said, "I noticed a mess of nesters just now. When the cowboys start to gather, as they get the word, I'd say MacLeod could have his hands full. What did old Trinity do this time?"

"They say he was with some riders who murdered and burned out a homesteader and most of his family. It happened Monday afternoon, over near the sand hills. The nightriders didn't know that one of the children was still alive when they rode off. A little girl was hiding in the tall wheat. She was pretty hysterical when neighbors came over to investigate the smoke rise. But she was able to give a good description of Trinity's gray stud. It's the only mount like that in the county, so . . . Where are you going, dear?"

Joe stopped with his hand on the knob and said, "Courthouse. They made a mistake."

"Really? Well, what about us? Can't your story keep for a few minutes, Joe? I need you and it's not like Trinity is going anywhere right now."

He said, "I want you, too, but a man locked up for a thing he never done must be hurting, too. I'll try to get back directly, Honey."

"Joe, you may be tied up for hours and I'm expecting company this evening. Come on, let's have some fun. You told me you didn't like Trinity, anyway."

"I don't like him. That's why I got to go. I couldn't enjoy it, with that poor dumb cowboy on my mind. If we can't make it this afternoon, what about tomorrow, Gloria?"

"I'm going to be busy out at my spread. We're hiring extra help for the roundup next month. It's now or never, damn it."

"Never, Gloria?"

She hesitated, eyes hurt and testing their power as she stared up at him. Then she sighed and said,

"You know better, damn you. But you're sure getting spoiled and it's not fair. How am I to get through the week-end without a few coals lingering in my grate?"

He chuckled and said, "I know the feeling all too well. I'll sure try to get back here directly."

He kissed her and left before she could tempt him further. He knew he'd made her sore. He was sort of sore at himself. He knew Trinity would laugh like hell if the shoe was on the other foot.

He went to the courthouse and another homesteader he knew to talk to said, "Howdy, Barrow. You ain't got a rope with you have you? That nogood skonk in there raped a woman and gunned a little boy!"

Another man growled, "Hanging is too good for him. I say burn him at the stake with coal oil, after we geld the son of a bitch!"

Joe nodded politely and pressed through, surprised at the number of other farm folk. He knew lots of others were filing on the public lands but, spread out as they were, you had to get them all in one place afore you could see how many there really were. He wondered how many cow men there were in the county. He knew most cowboys figured one of them was worth ten of most any thing else, but the anything else was mad as hell and a mess of them was packing guns.

He got to the doorsteps where Deputy Brody and two others barred further progress. Brody had a shotgun cradled across his arm as he nodded, morose, and said, "Afternoon, Barrow. I was hoping you'd have more sense."

Joe said, "I do. I want to talk to the Sheriff. Is he in there?"

"Sure he is, old son. He's hoping the state troopers get here afore the riders from the Double M, Bar Seven and such. This is a pisspoor time for a social call if you ain't with this mob."

"I got to see him, I think they calls it giving evidence."

"You know something about the Treadwell murders? Their spread wasn't anywhere near you'n, son."

"I know. That's the evidence I has to give."

Brody nodded to one of the other deputies and said, "Take him in to see the Sheriff, Hank."

So Hank did. Joe found the Sheriff and some other deputies in a top story room, loading riot guns. Trinity Mackail sat on a cot in the corner with his hands cuffed together. He was scowling fit to bust and didn't notice who Joe was until Joe said, "You can't hold Trinity Mackail, Sheriff."

Ewen MacLeod seemed a mite surprised, too, as he snapped the breech of his scatter gun shut and looked up to ask, "Do tell? I was expecting his kith and kin to tell me some such lie, but I'm surprised to hear it from you, considering."

Joe said, "There ain't nothing to consider, sir. The same afternoon them homesteaders got hit, a good twenty miles or more away, I met Trinity on the trace betwixt the Ivanov spread and my own. Nadja Ivanov saw him, too, if you want to ask her."

Trinity stared at Joe as if the farmer had hit him across the mouth with a wet fish. But he said, "That's the truth, Sheriff! Damn it, I told you I was out searching for my pony!"

Joe said, "I met him riding a bay. He did say he was missing a gray."

The Sheriff held up a hand for silence and said, "I may look sort of dumb, but I can see that if he wasn't riding the gray he had to be riding something, damn it. The little gal said one of the men as kilt her kin was a cowboy, which only stands to reason. She described Trinity's gray right down to its white socks. He has been saying someone stole it on him, but that seemed a likely thing for any man to say. A knowed nesterhater saying he wasn't aboard his favorite hoss in evil company is one thing. A nester hater with two nesters witnessing for him is another!"

Joe said, "That's why you got to let him go. He couldn't have done it. His mount wasn't lathered from running any twenty miles and he was coming from town when we met him shortly after the killings."

MacLeod looked thoughtfully at the prisoner and said, "Well, you ain't seen that boy ride, but it do seem to be cutting it thin."

The Sheriff rose and went to the window. He stared morosely out and said, "I wish the election was this fall instead of next. I've got me a mess of angry voters out there, and by the time I stand for re-election you blamed homesteaders will have the edge. I just can't let Trinity loose. That mob will tear him limb from limb, no matter what you say, Barrow."

Trinity grinned and said, "Just wait 'til my brother and our riders hit town. Nobody's about to stop me from walking out the front door, then."

MacLeod shot him a disgusted look and said, "That's what I mean. He's just too dumb to set himself up a slick alibi even if he could ride that far and fast. I've got a pure bear by the tail and that's a fact. I can't turn him loose afore his friends ride in, and the jail and courthouse together ain't big enough to hold all the folks I'll have to arrest when they get here!"

One of the deputies suggested, "Can't we escort him home, Sheriff?"

MacLeod shook his head and said, "Not without a running fight ever' mile of the way. They know all you boys and they have you down as cow men. No matter what we tell 'em, they're bound to see it as a whitewash and I noticed a couple of 'em have ropes ready."

Joe said, "I can get him out."

The Sheriff raised a quizzical eyebrow and Joe added, "I can move my buckboard around back. Nobody will expect a homesteader to be siding with Trinity. I'll hide him under my tarp betwixt some fence posting. If he can keep his fool mouth shut 'til we're out of town, his spread ain't far from our'n."

MacLeod said, "I admire a man who thinks on his feet, but you do know the chance you'd be taking, don't you? Those other nesters would string you side by side if you got caught. We can't tag along to protect you lest we give the show away."

Joe looked at Trinity and said, "I'm willing to give her a try if you are, Trinity."

The cowboy said, "I ain't skeered."

Sheriff MacLeod said, "No, you're too dumb to be skeered" as he unlocked the handcuffs and removed them. Joe said, "I'll get my buckboard" and the Sheriff said, "You do that. *You're* dumb, too, but I admire your style!"

So Joe went out the back way and slipped

through the alleyways until he was clear of the courthouse. It seemed sort of stupid, when you studied on it, but most of the farmers from out of town had no true feeling for the way the courthouse was set among the other houses in Pittsburgh Landing. He was able to move the buckboard unobserved behind the building and as he reined in two deputies ran Trinity out, tossed him in the back and covered him over. Joe called back, "Lay still and don't make a sound 'til I tell you to, God damn your eyes!"

He clucked Pittypat into a casual trot and while it seemed to take forever they were soon out of town, unnoticed and unmolested. Joe waited until they were a few miles out on the open prairie before he called back, "You can sit by my side, Littl' Darlin'. We seem to have slickered 'em."

Trinity crawled out from under the tarp and climbed over the seat back to join Joe behind the dash. He adjusted his hat and the gunbelt they'd returned to him before he said, "You know what you are, Joe Barrow? You are one pure damn fool, that's what you are!"

"Thanks, I admire you, too."

"I reckon you think now that I'm supposed to get all weepy and tell you I like fences just fine, huh?"

"I don't care what you do, Trinity, as long as you don't do it on my property. I know how you folks feel about us folks. No offense, but I don't give a hoot in hell."

"You don't, huh? Then why in tarnation did you save my ass back yonder?"

"Had to. I was brung up Christian and it says in

the Good Book that it's a sin to bear false witness."

"Yeah? What would have happened if you'd just said nothing at all?"

"Don't know. They might have hung you. Your friends might have saved you. Either way, innocent blood figured to be spilt. Don't try to figure me out, Trinity. We've already agreed that my ways ain't your ways."

Trinity muttered, "That's for damn sure. I never thought I'd save my hide by pretending to be a bale of fence posting!"

Joe chuckled, then his grin faded as he saw a dust cloud with a couple of dozen riders dragging it his way at a full gallop from the north. He reined in as he said, "Looks like we got you out of there just in time."

Brazos Mackail and the rest of the hard-riding band slowed to a walk as they recognized who sat beside the infernal farmer on the buckboard seat.

Brazos looked relieved but puzzled as he said, "What the hell is this all about, Trinity? Spike here just rode home all lathered to say you'd been arrested for a killing!"

Trinity said, "He told you true. Some dirty son of a bitch was aboard my bronc, acting the owlhoot in broad daylight. Let's go back and teach some manners to them sod busters who was just yelling for my blood in town."

Brazos said, "Let's not and say we did. What happened, Joe Barrow? Old Trinity ain't making much sense."

Joe told him and the others in a few words, for he saw Trinity had taken the position now that he'd gotten out of the scrape all by himself.

Brazos whistled softly and said, "That was sure neighborly of you, Joe. You're going to have to let us pay you back someway."

Joe shrugged and said, "I didn't come forward for any reward. I did it 'cause I had no way out. If you really want to do me a favor, one of you let this fool ride double with you so's I can turn around and get back to town. I've, uh, got some errands I'd like to tend to, if there's still time."

Brazos said, "Trinity, you shake that man's hand and climb up here with me, hear?"

Trinity said, "I'll ride double, but I ain't about to shake with no nester. He just told you it was his duty to say what he did, didn't he?"

"God damn it Trinity, you surely had to have been ahint the door when the brains was passed out and your manners are mighty damn poor, too."

Joe said, "Just get him off my hands and we'll say no more about it, Brazos. I've got kin who've been known to talk dumb, too."

Brazos sighed and said, "He knows he ought to thank you, Joe. He just don't know how. Will you accept my thanks, from both of us?"

Joe said he would and as Trinity got down he wheeled around to drive back to town.

Gloria said there wasn't time to do it right and that they'd just have to tear off a quicky with their duds on. But of course once he had her hot and coming on the bed she changed her mind and they wound up the same as before. The front doorbell rang as they were in the midst of things and he paused atop her, aware she'd told the truth about expecting company.

He whispered, "Damnation, your friends has

come." but old Gloria moved her hips teasingly and said, "Screw 'em, I was fixing to come myself when you stopped. Hurry, Joe, I'm almost there."

So he did and it was sort of funny to consider that, despite her words he couldn't screw the folks standing on the front porch, but he sure was doing it to Gloria back here! He knew she liked to talk dirty when they were alone like this. He found it exciting, too. But it sure was funny how a word could sound so ugly when you used it like she had about her guests, yet feel so good when you were doing it. It was funny how that mysterious man on the gray had screwed a woman he hated bad enough to kill whilst others did the same because they kind of liked a gal. Maybe love and hate was all mixed up in some folk's heads. They was both strong feelings, but a man would have to be crazy to want to kill and screw a gal at the same time, wouldn't he?

LIFE SETTLED DOWN for a spell, now that Joe Barrow had his forty acres of barley fenced and an outlet for his pent-up sexual urges. The barley was already sprouting and the geese were starting to fly south when Yasha dropped Nadja off by the house and walked over to where Joe leaned in his shovel in the south-east forty. Yasha asked what he was doing and Joe said, "Digging post holes, of course. It's too late to drill in any more seed this year, but I may as well get this other field fenced while I wait for the barley."

Yasha grimaced at the green dusting of tiny leaves on the even furrows of the south-west forty and said, "*Nyet*, it will never ripen before first frost, Tovarich. I have started to plant my winter wheat. I have extra seed. I know you think Yasha crazy. You try anyway, *da*?"

"Not hardly, thanks. I've asked around about

your notion. There's some other Rooshin folks down Kansas way who talk like you. I hear tell they've yet to harvest a head of wheat."

Yasha said, "They are not Russian. They are Mennonites. I, too, hear about Mennonite colony in Kansas. You are right about Mennonites being crazy. I don't know about their Russian winter wheat."

"You got me mixed up a mite, pard. Folks I talked to said they come from your old country, yet you claim they ain't Rooshin. What in thunder are they, then, Turks?"

"*Nyet*, Germans. Germans with funny religion that makes other Germans throw things at them. Many years ago, Tsarina Katherina invite Mennonites to come grow scientific in her Russia. All Germans crazy. Good farmers."

"What are they doing over here if they farm so good in Rooshia?"

"Bah, nobody can live in Russia anymore. Tsar is crazy, too. Mennonites' religion teaches no war. Tsar says every village must send young men for his army. Everybody is leaving Russia—Mennonites, Jews, even real people like Nadja and me. But enough of old country and crazy Tsar, Tovarich. Let me show you how to grow winter wheat, *da*?"

Joe said, "I'd be willing to give her a try if I had the time, Yasha, but I don't. It's taken us all summer just to get set up and I've still barely started. I've got me an idea for a windmill, if I could only get some pipe. I'd like to drive a pipe well before frost."

"Why, is well dry again?"

"It comes and it goes. That ain't the problem.

Once cold weather sets in, water in an open well figures to freeze solid."

"So you melt snow for water, *nyet*?"

"That can be dicey. Sometimes snow blows off whilst the ground stays froze, to hear the older settlers tell it. I'd feel a lot more permanent if I had me a steady water supply. Might even be able to run a tap line to the kitchen. Ma and Jessie would like that. Water weighs eight pounds a gallon and we sure lug a mess of it on this spread."

Yasha shrugged and said, "I looked into windmill. Too expensive."

"I know. I've been studying pictures in a booklet they gave me about 'em. I found me a busted hand pump on the town dump a few days ago. Some fool threw it away just 'cause he'd let the leather washers dry and crack up. I've hauled some lumber over from that abandoned claim to the east and found some barrel staves and such in town, too."

"You go lots to town, Tovarich."

"Yeah, it's sort of interesting. The point is that I know I can make a fair windmill fan outten wood and scrap iron. Tower and tank ain't all that complicated and I've figured out how to rig extra bobwire and a cast iron weight to work the pump handle. It's the pipe as has me stumped. I need to drive at least thirty feet down to be sure of an all-year water table."

"Will stove pipe work?"

"No, has to be stronger and smaller-bored. I've hunted high and low for it, but it's worse'n looking for fence posts, and that's a pure bitch. They could order new pipe for us at the store, but there's no way in hell I could pay for it. Maybe I'll just start the windmill blades and hope for some pipe to turn up. That's how I drilled this barley in afore I could fence it. How'd you get all your claim fenced so neat, Yasha? I know you and Nadja have been here a spell, but I was admiring the way you had it proved."

Yasha looked sheepish and said, "Nadja strung fence."

"By herself? That's a lot of work for a man, Yasha."

"*Da*, my sister is strong like ox. Is good she is. I sometimes, how you say, put things off?"

Joe glanced up as a vee of snow geese honked overhead and didn't answer. He didn't want to hear any more talk about planting wheat just before the first snows. Poor Nadja would be lucky if he didn't make her pull the plow.

Over the horizon to the north another man was worried about the flying waterfowl, too. His name was Kinlochiel Dundee, but everybody called him Kilty. He was ramrod for the Diamond E in the sandhill country and was elected trailboss of the consolidated herd he was driving in to ship from Pittsburgh Landing. He was riding point with a score of other riders and two thousand head of summer-grazed beef. The roundup had been a bitch even if the signs of fall weren't coming on early this year. The trails were messed with fencing and other stockmen forced off this flat prairie had crowded into the sand hill range set aside by the government. The trouble with public land was that it was public to anybody. The new stock spooked and scattered the original herds up Kilty's way. Harsh words had been exchanged by fellow stockmen during the roundup. Cowboys from different outfits had had to be pried apart when they should have been working together, like in the old days . . . the good old days before the infernal sod busters came. Like most cow men under forty, Kilty tended to think of the mayfly era of the free and carefree cowboy as an established tradition of the west. Yet in truth there'd been only a few short years between the taming of the Sioux and the coming of the taxpayer.

A calico steer with a mind of its own busted loose from the herd near the trail boss and he yelled, "God damn it, Malone, you're supposed to be riding flank, not sleeping in the saddle!"

The flank rider cut the stray off and headed it back, saying, "He don't cotton to being tenderloin, Kilty. Been having trouble with that one since we left the hills. Reckon he wants to go home."

Mollified, Kilty stared back across the sea of tossing horns and low-hanging dust as he said, "They're getting thirsty. There's water ahead, just over the skyline. We'll bed 'em there for the last night afore we run 'em in to weigh and load. It don't look like wind and they'll be easy to hold by water if none of you bean-eating bastards farts again."

A point rider moved in from his other side as the breeze shifted, slapping them across the backs with the smell and heat of the herd. The calories burned by a herd on the move was an awesome thing the first time a green hand felt it. A really big herd moving at a good clip on a hot day could literally blister the face of a flank rider to the lee. Kilty was trying to drift them in gentle, to save the losses to the owners. But they were hot and thirsty and starting to move at a faster walk. He swung in his saddle and called out, "Watch the leaders, damn it! They smell water clean over the horizon and if you let them cows run over me I'll never speak to any of you again!"

The rider who'd joined him said, "I see smoke ahead, Kilty. Looks like a plume from some house."

Kilty said, "I noticed. Likely another nester. It ain't our problem. We're on a public right-of-way and no fool's about to string wire across a county road."

They could see the roof of Olsen's soddy now. The worried point rider said, "Awfully close to the wagon trace. He 'peers to have nested smack on that public water hole, Kilty."

Kilty said, "Naw, nobody would be that dumb. Not even a sod buster."

He turned in his saddle to call out, "All right, boys, listen tight. I see a soddy up ahead. We're on Sheriff MacLeod's range and I don't want you messing up, hear? We're camping damn near that infernal sod buster's yard, but I want you all to stay clear of him and let's not have any mean-mouthing or busted windows this time."

He turned to his companion to add, "Let's ride in ahead and make sure he has his hounds and kids under control. I never brung cows this fur to lose one to a stampede."

Gus Olsen had seen the dust of the approaching herd long before and was standing by his fence, gun cradled across his arms as Kilty and his side-kick rode up.

Kilty Dundee stared slack-jawed at the three strands of bob wire between the wagon trace and the inviting pool of water. He said, "Howdy, neighbor. My handle is Dundee, Kilty Dundee, and you sure picked a pisspoor place to string that wire."

"My name is Olsen and this land is mine," said the farmer, flatly.

Kilty's eyes narrowed and he said, "I don't give two hoots and a holler about your fenced-in *land*, friend. That *water* is *public*! Always has been and always will be."

Olsen said, "You're wrong. I had this quarter section surveyed legal before I filed claim to it. The water is inside my lawful boundary."

"You want us to pay you, right? I'm leading over two thousand head in. So you can't hardly expect us to pay more'n a nickel a head. But I'll shake on that if you will. We'll just cut a gap and—"

"You touch my wire and I'll kill you," Olsen cut in flatly as he shifted the rifle in his hands meaningfully.

The two cow men exchanged glances. The ramrod glanced over at the house and saw a pale-faced woman staring out at them from behind the lace curtains. He said, "Mister, you have been working in this hot sun too long. Don't you know better than to threaten two growed men, with others riding in to back their play?"

"I'm not afraid of you."

"Yeah, like I said, you been out in the sun too long. Your brains has fried. I'd best explain again who I am, since you seem to have missed it the first time. I am Kilty Dundee. I am ramrodding a consolidated herd 'cause the folks who hired me know my rep better than you do. I know it's wrong to brag, but I had a conversation like this in Dodge, one time, and they're still talking about it. You may have noticed I'm the one who come out alive."

"I marched with Billy Sherman and I ain't impressed. You just take your cattle around and leave me and mine alone."

The rider at Kilty's side looked around and saw the herd was coming in, the leaders bawling as they sniffed the dry dusty air for water and homed in on it. He said, "This is getting serious, Kilty. Them cows is headed for that water no matter what the rest of you say."

Kilty nodded and said, "Yeah, get down and cut the damned fence before they hit it and get all tore up."

"Uh, Kilty, there's a gent standing there with a gun."

"Do as I say, damn it. You don't work for him. You work for me."

The hand took a pair of wirecutters from his saddlebag and dismounted. Olsen said, "I'm warning you!" and the hand said, "Man says he's warning me, Kilty."

"Cut the fucking wire. I'm covering you."

So the hand stepped over to the fence, nodded at Olsen, and said, "Sorry, friend, but you can see how it is."

Olsen fired as the hand put the jaws of the wirecutter to the first strand. The hand staggered back and fell, muttering, "Damn, I wish you hadn't done that" as Kilty drew his own revolver and pumped round after round into Olsen, glaring and cursing in mingled rage and disbelief. Olsen would have died from the first bullet in his chest, but Kilty kept firing as his pony danced, rolling the body in the dust with his hot lead. The woman ran from the house, screaming, as Kilty's hammer clicked on an empty chamber. Kilty shouted, "*That'll* larn you to start a war with *me!*" as he dismounted to kneel by his fallen comrade. The man Olsen had shot was dead, too.

The gunplay had the nearby heard milling and only the scent of water, mixed with gunsmoke, kept them from stampeding as the others fought to keep them under control. Another rider reined in near Kilty and whistled, "Kee-rist! You want me to go after that old gal, Boss? She's lighting out in a buckboard full of kids. Looks like she's headed for the Sheriff."

Kilty rose, ashen faced, and said, "Yeah, cut her off and bring her back. I can't leave the herd and MacLeod will insist I come in to make a statement on these killings. Since we're headed that way in any case, it won't hurt to let the herd and ever'- thing cool off hereabouts."

The rider nodded and spurred his mount to go after the frightened woman. Kilty called after him, "Don't hurt 'em. Just make sure they come back and stay put."

But, in truth, he didn't really give a damn, right now. He was more guilt-ridden than angry as he stared down at the dead men on either side. He told his fallen comrade, "I'm sorry as hell about this, Grogan. How the hell was *I* to know he'd really fire? But don't you worry, old son, if these sod busters has declared war, they picked the right man to declare her on! I never cottoned to them to begin with, and this is surely fixing to make things simpler from here on."

JOE BARROW AWOKE and stared up at the darkness for a time as he figured out who and where he was and what had awakened him. He'd been having a funny dream about arm-wrestling with a naked lady, but it hadn't been that awful and his heart had no call to be pounding so spooky.

He glanced down and stiffened as he spotted a pale, ghostly form standing at the foot of his bed. He didn't believe in haunts, so he looked closer and saw it was Ma. She was just standing there in her nightgown with her hair a wild halo around her head. Neither spoke for a time and he could tell from Jessie's breathing that she was asleep in the bed across the way so he whispered, "What is it, Ma?"

Ma said, "I was just looking and remembering. Jessie says you two aimed to go over to that other soddy, come sunrise."

"That's true, Ma. I need more lumber and I noticed some scrap iron over yonder. Why don't you come along? You can just sit in the buckboard and watch. It's sort of nice over there. The lady who used to live there must have liked flowers and there's some asters starting to bloom about the dooryard."

She said, "I know you want to be alone."

He swore under his breath and swung his legs from the bunk to lead her outside. He didn't want to talk to her, especially out-of-doors in his union suit, but he knew she was fixing to get loud and he didn't want Jessie having nightmares.

He waited until they were outside and said, "Full moon looks sort of nice on the prairie tonight, don't it?"

"Your father was a randy man. Before he marched off to fight in the war he'd messed with half the gals in our old county. Did you know that?"

"I'll have to take your word for it, Ma. You know he died at Shiloh afore I was old enough to talk."

She laughed, a mite wild-eyed, and said, "It's a good thing you was too young to hear half the things as was said. My, he looked so handsome in his cavalry blues with the gold stripes down the legs and all. He had half the gals in town crying fit to bust even *afore* the rebels kilt him!"

"Well, he was your husband and not their'n, Ma."

She looked away and said. "He wasn't. We was never married. We'd posted the bands and all but his regiment was called to the field afore he could do right by me. Mayhaps that's why I've always

felt so mixed up about him and you and ever'thin'.
Do you think I'm crazy, Honey Joe? Jessie says
she thinks I'm crazy."

He put a gentle hand on each of her shoulders and said, "No, Ma, you ain't crazy. You was
hurt bad and Pa, the man you really married,
mixed you up some more by dying unexpected."

"You don't seem surprised at all, Honey Joe. I
thought you'd be vexed at hearing you was,
well . . ."

"A bastard, Ma? I wasn't sure, but I suspicioned
you and my real father hadn't got things sorted
out just right afore he died. Folks mean-mouth in
any small town and when I heard some funny tales
from my friends I asked the county clerk about it.
They had my real dad's birth and death on file.
Nothing about him ever marrying up with anybody. But it was a long time ago and who cares?
Jessie's lawfully birthed, for I looked that up,
too."

"She ain't a real sister to you, you know."

"Well, half is better than nothing, Ma. Why
are you tormenting yourself like this? Any scandal
about me being birthed to you a mite before you
married Pa Barrow legal died a long time ago.
Folks don't talk about married neighbor ladies
any more than they does about dead hero gents
who never came back from the war. It's over, Ma.
Over and done with a long time ago. It's time you
studied on here and now. The past ain't just dead.
It's gone. There's no way you can even lay a flower
on the grave of a dead year. The time we live is
always now. In no time at all the future will be
now, so *now* will be dead and done with, too."

She took his hand and said, "Mayhaps you're

right, dear. Let's walk out a ways from the house. We mustn't wake Jessie."

It felt sort of dumb to be walking hand-in-hand in the moonlight with his own mother, even if they hadn't been barefoot. They strolled toward the barley and he filled the awkwardness by telling her he thought the odds were good they'd have a catch crop before winter-kill. He sure wished there was a place to sit down out here.

Ma said, "I know you've been trifling with women. I'd have known even if I hadn't had a little bird tell me. You're so infernally like your father. It's hard to believe you ain't him, somehow back from the grave."

"He's been in his grave quite a spell, Ma. But as long as you aim to jaw about it, how come you two waited so long after posting the bans and all? I mean, with *me* on the way."

She laughed and squeezed his hand as she said, "Oh, Lord, if you only knew the saucy things we did that winter. But you likely can guess, you naughty boy."

He didn't answer. He'd stopped suspecting the stork a while back, but it didn't seem proper to talk about his own folks doing things like that.

She said, "It was another gal as come between us. She was my best friend. At least, she said she was. The three of us had known each other since our school days and I reckon she was jealous. Women get awfully jealous, Honey Joe. He looked so dashing in his new uniform and, well, women are jealous and men are weak. She tried to steal him from me, using the only weapons a woman has. I caught them together, laying in the lovenest he'd said only me and him in all the world knew

about. It was awful. I can still see it. They was
going at it hammer and tongs, naked and laughing. I ran home and cried myself sick for a week,
refusing to see him when he come calling to
explain. Later, when I was ready to listen, it was
too late. He'd left us both for the biggest whore
of all. They calls her War."

Joe nodded soberly and said, "I can see how a
thing like that could put a young gal off her feed."

"He wrote me from the front, Joe. He told me
he loved me best and that he'd make it all up to
me when he got back from the fighting, only he
never. I showed that other gal the letter and I
reckon *she* cried some."

"Yeah, I can see what great chums you must
have been. I reckon you still hate her, huh?"

Ma shook her head and said, "No, not no more.
I'd tell you who she was, but you'd never believe
me. We got over our fuss and we was friends
again after your father died. You see, we had a lot
in common, once you studied on it, and I mind a
couple of times we laughed sort of naughty about
what had happened. She got married years ago
and died not long afore we left Penn State. So
you're right about it being over. But I can still see
them, locked together like that. How can anything
that feels so wondrous when you're a part of it
look so dirty and ugly when it's someone else?"

"Don't know, Ma. Mebbe that's why folks do it
in private."

She shuddered and said, "If I ever come in on
you and Jessie like that I don't know what I'd do."

He grimaced and said, "Ma, that's never happened and it never will."

"You swear that, Joe? You swear you've never

even thought about making love to Jessie ahint my back?"

"Jesus, Ma, you're talking wild as hell. I know some trashy folks have been said to sink that low. But I have too much respect for my kid sis to even consider such a notion."

"What if you was on some desert island, like that Robinson feller?"

"We ain't on no desert island, Ma, we're in the middle of Nebraska." Then he grinned and added, "Come to think on it, though, I always wondered about old Rob and that Friday feller. They was alone out there a fair spell and Friday was always kissing his feet, in that story."

She sighed and said, "Oh, Lord have mercy, you even talk like your father, when you're teasing in the moonlight."

She swung around in front of him and said, "Hold me, Honey Joe. Put your arms about me and hold me like you used to."

He put his hands on her shoulders and said, sternly, "Ma, there's no *used to*, here! I ain't my dead father. I'm his son. Just like you're my Ma."

"You kiss Jessie, don't you? Kiss me, Honey Joe. Is that too much to ask?"

He said, "Yes, it is. I don't kiss Jessie all that much, no more. I don't know why they made the rules the way they did, for it ain't true a man feels nothing when he kisses any handsome woman. But those are the rules, Ma. I reckon we'd best go back to the house now."

"Are you saying, if I wasn't your mother—"

"It don't make no matter what I might say, Ma. We're still going back to yonder house and we'll forget this conversation, total, for a man could take some of it a mite wild if he was less understanding."

"What if neither me nor Jessie was kin to you? Which one of us would you like best?"

"Ma, you're talking crazy. You know I love you both. It ain't a sort of dumb contest."

"If you could have either one of us, as a woman, Joe, who would you choose?"

"Oh, for God's sake, how should I know? Maybe I wouldn't want either one of you. Maybe I'd want you both. As long as we got to dream I may as well have me a harem of wild and wicked gals. But dreams like that ain't fitting, so let's say no more about 'em. I'm headed back to the house, Ma. Are you coming or do you aim to stand out here in the moonlight, talking to ghosts?"

She sobbed and fell against him, crying fit to bust. He snorted in annoyance and picked her up to carry her back to the house in his arms. She felt little and soft and it was hard to believe a big thing like him had ever come outten a little thing like her. But he had, and the reasons for the laws agin' such notions made sense when you studied them.

He knew of course that a gal snapped back together right after she'd birthed a baby. That one older gal back home had born a child out of wedlock one time and she was tight as any other. He wondered how a man would fit in the small woman he was carrying and he was shocked as hell to feel what it did to his groin to even think about it!

He carried her inside and placed her gently on

the bed next to Jessie. His other kinswoman woke up to ask what was going on and he said, "Go back to sleep, Sis. Ma and me was just talking about a dream she had."

THE OLD HOUSE still had two-thirds of its roof because Joe had been too busy to salvage all that much in the first place, and the folks who'd built the soddy had meant it to remain standing in the second. They'd carefully clinched each nail and used a lot of them to hold the boards to the beams. It made their giving up all the sadder and at the same time explained some of the troubles they'd had. Joe could see the other nester had spent a full growing season on the house and garth afore he'd gotten around to planting the crop the grasshoppers had robbed him of. He'd put too much time and money into getting started to survive the loss. Out here a man had to have three hands and a mind that could foresee forks in the road ahead. Joe knew there was a good chance he'd lose his catch crop of barley. So he wasn't counting on it. He needed it bad, but if worst came to worst they'd make it through the winter and spring planting on what was left in the bank. Once he had a standing crop of wheat he figured he could borrow enough on it to feed them all through the harvest. The town merchants seemed afraid to give him part-time work, but the bank didn't give a damn what the cowboys thought. The bank held a knife to *their* throats, too.

He was up on the roof, crowbarring a stubborn plank, so he couldn't see Jessie as she called up from below, "There's a coil of haywire down here, honey. Can you use it for your windmill?"

He yelled, "Throw her in the buckboard" and went on working with a frown. He'd asked her not to call him Honey and he'd told her not to get under him whilst he worked up here. The roof was solid enough, but the walls were sod and the whole shebang swayed some when he put his back into it. He doubted he'd get hurt bad if the soddy collapsed under him, but he didn't want anybody on the bottom of the pile.

Jessie walked over to the buckboard where Pittypat was grazing content betwixt the shafts. She had her fool skirts kilted and her bare legs were showing again. He knew if he mentioned it she'd just ask him who in thunder was going to see her. It was true you could see folks coming over the prairie long before they came near enough to tell if you were naked or not. But the gal should have had more sense, especially since he knew Ma had been talking the same way to her ahint his back. Joe took his eyes away from Jessie's trim figure as his nose wrinkled at the memory of his mother's crazy talk of the night before. Ma couldn't have meant some of that the way it had come across. But he knew she'd accused Jessie of unsisterly notions and there the fool gal was with her legs exposed nigh to the knee and wearing flowers in her hair. She'd plucked and strung a wreath of blue-violet asters to set on her red hair and the gaudy clash of colors made her look sort of dance-hall. Her thin cotton print was a faded blue that didn't go with her green eyes and red hair, either. Joe didn't consider himself an expert on women's duds, but he'd noticed you could tell a towns-woman from a farmer's daughter more by the way they fit things together than by the likely cost of what they wore. Old Gloria's duds all went with her coloring and made her look lady-like even in her underwear. He wondered if the widow woman could give Jessie some pointers on how to dress right. He didn't think he'd better ask. Old Gloria talked dirty about brothers being interested in their sisters' looks, too. Folks sure were dirty-minded. It seemed the less opportunity they had to do something sinful the more they liked to jaw about it. He was all alone out here with Jessie and he didn't feel a bit like leaping on her. He knew Yasha drank and Nadja was one good-looking gal, but he somehow knew they weren't living in incest over to their place. It was the folks who didn't have close kin to get at who speculated on what others might or might not be doing. Sheriff MacLeod didn't have a sister or any other she-males but his old wife living with him, yet he seemed to suspect everyone, like old Gloria did. Sure, that was it. The Sheriff was full of it. More common than murder, indeed. How the hell would anybody know if, like he said, it was the most *unreported* crime? MacLeod was just guessing dirty. Nobody who lived alone with kin ever talked like that.

Except Ma, and she was touched.

He finished freeing the plank and made sure Jessie was clear before he tossed it over the side. She came over from petting the Morgan by the buckboard and asked if he wanted it in the wagonbed. He told her to leave it be, explaining, "I aim to leave most of the light lumber for now. It's the roof beams I'm after. I need at least five for my wind tower, if I ever get around to her."

"Five? Don't you mean four, honey?"

"If I'd meant four I'd have said four. I'll cut the fifth beam for cross bracing, and stop calling me Honey."

Jessie went to the corner where the beams he'd already freed stood against the sod wall. She climbed up to join him, saying, "Let me help, then. Why can't I call you Honey?"

"I don't need no help, but you can stay up here if you stay out of my way. I told you folks think it's funny for a brother and sister to talk mushy. That's why I don't want you calling me pet things, dammit."

Jessie moved over onto the sod still covering the part he hadn't started on and sank to her knees, saying, "We're alone out here. So who's to hear or think anything, honey, I mean Joe?"

He worked the nail notch of his crowbar under a spike head and growled, "It don't matter if you're alone or in a crowd, to the Lord. He knows what you're up to, no matter what."

"Oh, for Heaven's sake, what terrible sort of sin

are we supposed to be up to, Joe? You're as crazy as Ma!"

He started on another spike, not looking at her as he said, "All right, mebbe we'd best turn over the wet rock and have it out in daylight. We both know what Ma's as much as accused us of."

"She thinks we've been wicked together. It makes me feel funny, just thinking about it."

"Yeah, it ain't natural to have such thoughts, but the way you kills dry rot is to let some air and sunlight reach it. I 'spose things like she's talking about have happened."

Jessie grimaced and said, "Yes, we have to face facts, Joe. It happens in the best of families."

He shot her a shocked look as she added, simply, "There's no getting around it, our poor old Ma is out of her head. You don't know the half of what she's said to me about you, me, her and ever'-thing."

He looked relieved and said, "I had a funny talk with her last night, whilst you slept. I mean, she talked *real* funny."

"Oh dear, I was afraid she might. Did she get dirty with you, Joe?"

"Sort of. She mostly talked about my Pa. I mean my real Pa, the one who got kilt at Shiloh. She, uh, seems to have me a mite mixed up with him."

Jessie looked down and began to pluck dry stems from the sod as she sighed and murmured, "Oh, poor you. Poor me, too. She's all mixed up and jealous-hearted, now that you're full-growed, Joe. She told me one time that had she knowed how much you'd favor your real father she'd have never kept you. I asked where in thunder a woman could put a baby she didn't want and she laughed wild as anything and said something about the river and then she slapped me and we didn't talk about it no more."

He gave the crowbar too strong a jerk and broke a nailhead. He swore and forced himself to start over with more care. He said, "The Widow Palmer tells me she heard some wild talk from Ma whilst you two stayed with her. We're going to have to see about a doc for Ma, once we're on our feet."

Jessie nodded and asked, "Are you still seeing Gloria Palmer, Joe?"

"Well, I have to talk to her about business and all, you know. We got a neighborly deal from her on the Morgans and she's interested in my, uh, efforts."

Jessie said, "Ma has you being wicked with her, too." She smiled.

"What do you think, Sis?"

"It ain't my nevermind. Fair is fair and I know Ma's wrong about you and me. The widow woman has a funny reputation in town and that's likely where Ma got her queer notion. She said if you were like your father you'd sniff out any willing she-male in the county and Gloria Palmer's said to be as willing as most."

Joe frowned, wondering why he felt a pang of what felt like jealousy. He and old Gloria were just pals and they'd agreed either was free to come or go as they pleased. He knew he wasn't about to turn down a roll in the feathers with anyone younger and prettier, like maybe Nadja for instance, if she hadn't been so proper. It seemed only fair that old Gloria could have her own turn at bat and he didn't get into town that often. He asked Jessie, "Have they got the poor woman all that willing with anybody in particular, or is she just taking on everyone in town?"

Jessie said, "Lord of mercy, do you think I go about asking questions like that?"

"You say she has a bad reputation. Who's she being so bad with? You can't be bad all by yourself, can you?"

Jessie blushed and giggled before she said, sort of defiantly, "Onan managed, in the Good Book. But nobody ever catches a widow woman at that. Nobody's out-and-out caught Gloria Palmer doing anything wicked with anyone, but they do say she favors young men. She's been known to hire a room to a good-looking cowboy or three, come roundup time. They say it's funny how all the younger hands at her Circle 5 seem to be better-looking than you'd really need to be to rope a steer."

He grimaced and said, "Old biddies likely know more about the sins of Onan than they let on, too. That's silly as well as jealous talk if you ask me. Of course she hires rooms. That's why they call it a boarding house. Extra hands hired for the round-ups would naturally have to stay someplace, and we know for a fact she gives a better deal than the hotel or other boarding houses. As to the boys on her spread, she hardly ever goes out there."

"You don't have to convince me, Joe. I don't care who she's fooling with or if she's fooling at all. I don't mind if you're fooling with her. I told Ma no gal has any call being jealous of a man she can't marry up with. She's the one who's all hot and bothered about the widow woman. I said it was only natural a growed man should have some fun. Then she got mad and throwed a dish at me."

He laughed and said, "You're a good old gal, Sis. I'm glad we can talk like this. For to tell it true, Ma's crazy talk has been setting my teeth on edge and it's good to get things out in the open."

Jessie said, "All right. Fess up. Have you been wicked with that old lady or is it the Mex gal I keep hearing about?"

He whistled and said, "You gals *do* talk as bad as us, don't you?"

"That ain't answering my question, Joe."

"I know. I don't mean to be sneaky, but it's not right for a gent to say if he's trifled with a woman or not. So I won't. If it will set your mind at rest, I do have a, well, she-pal in town and we'll say no more about it."

"Have you been messing with Nadja? Ma says she thinks that Rooshin gal would let you."

"Oh, Kee-rist, forget it! Nadja ain't the sort of gal a man fools with unless he aims to marry up with her."

"Do you like her, Joe?"

"She's all right. I ain't ready to study getting serious with any gal, though, until I have our homestead earning its keep. You sure are a curious critter, for someone so clean-minded."

Jessie plucked another grass stem and said, "A body can't help being curious about something ever'body's so excited about. Would you get sore if I asked you a question, Joe?"

"Don't know. You'd have to ask it first."

"Well, I don't reckon I ever want to do it. Leastways, not until I marry up and that 'peers to be a long ways off, but . . . what's it like, Joe? It sounds just awful, but since ever'body seems to want to do it, I must be missing something! Don't it make you feel sort of disgusted to . . . you know?"

He looked away and said, "I reckon it ought to, but it don't. Not once you've started. I follow your drift, 'cause I know how I felt when the other boys first told me about it. But it ain't as bad as it sounds."

"Tell me what it feels like, then."

"I can't. In the first place this conversation is getting downright indelicate. In the second I couldn't explain it to another man if he'd never *done* it. It'd be like describing chocolate to someone who never tasted it, or like telling a blind man what the sunset looked like. It's a feeling you have to just up and feel afore you'd have any notion what it felt like."

"It sounds sort of scarey. I'd have to like a boy an awful lot afore I'd ever be able to give her a try."

"I know. That's why gals say no so often. Gals like you and Nadja don't find out afore you're married up. You're likely lucky that way."

Then he said, "Let's not talk dirty no more, Sis. I'd explain that to you, too, if I could. But I can't, so let's just change the subject."

She said, "All right, but it sure is nice to have a big brother you can ask questions. Ma gets all silly when I ask her about the facts of life."

"Don't talk to her about 'em, then. I suspicion she's already thinking too much about the subject."

"You reckon Ma wants to *do* it, Joe?"

He started to snap at her, for she was ignoring his order to talk about safer subjects. But then he nodded and said, "I fear that's about the size of it. Some folks needs it more'n others."

"But Joe, Ma ain't got no man."

"That's what I just said. Mebbe after we settle in some she'll meet some nice old cuss. Meanwhile don't pester her about it. She has enough on her plate."

He threw the plank down and saw he almost had the beam clear. He might take a few planks back. Even split they'd make good kindling. But the beams and the nails he was putting in his pocket were the important reason for coming over here.

Jessie pulled her knees up and hugged them before she said, "Honey, I got another question. I know you don't like to talk dirty but it's been bothering me and when I asked Ma she hit me."

"All right, but call me Joe, damn it."

"Joe, I know the Good Book says it's wrong for a man to pleasure his own kin. But why? What's so wrong with doing it to a relation when you're allowed to do it with almost anyone else?"

He frowned and said, "That's incest, damn it. Incest is about the worse sin there is."

"I know that, Joe, I read it in the Good Book. But the Good Book says knowing strange women is wicked, too. That Mex gal is painted wicked and must be awful dirty. Do you like her better than me or Ma?"

"Shoot, I've never been with that Mex gal and you just *hesh!*"

"I'm trying to understand, Joe. Suppose that Mex gal or some other lady in town was to come up to you, sort of bold, and tell you she wanted you to make her feel good. Would you do it?"

"Not with that whore down by the depot, not unless I was mighty desperate. Some nice-looking strange gal . . . well, I reckon I might."

"That's what I hear tell you men are like. Sometimes you go after gals and make 'em act wicked even if they don't want you to. What's got me all mixed up is this incest notion. I can see it's wicked, for you can't marry up with kin, under the law, but it's a sin to do it with anyone you ain't married up with. So what's the infernal difference?"

He gave her a look of extreme disapproval and said, "Jessie, you just hesh. You don't know what you're saying, girl!"

Jessie knew that look—and knew that the subject was closed.

KILTY DUNDEE rode point with a worried mind as the herd approached the Barrow place. A couple of the boys were holding the Olsen family back at their spread until he could get into town and pen the cows before he reported what had happened to the Sheriff. The hysterical woman had yelled all sorts of dumb things about murder back there but it had been a clear case of self-defense and it wasn't like he had no witnesses. They figured to rain fire and salt on him for what he'd done to that fool Swede, but it didn't seem likely he'd serve time for it. First things coming first, the herd had to be delivered afore he settled with the Law. They hadn't elected him trail boss to lose God-only-knowed how many pounds if they weren't drifted in gentle. Some lead critter always spooked when they got near the tracks, as if the fool steers knowed where they was going and didn't like it

much. He'd see 'em penned and watered good
and he'd talk to the buyers afore he mentioned
his shoot-out. He doubted MacLeod would jail
him, but the owners bet on sure things and if the
buyers thought he might be in trouble they'd use
it to beat the price down.

As he eyed the new homestead to the left of
the wagon trace he saw they'd fenced some barley.
A buckboard was coming out of the east, a few
miles away. A blonde woman was coming outten
the soddy with a shotgun. Kilty called out, "Watch
the leaders and left flankers as we pass that sprouting greenery, boys." Then he spurred his mount to
ride toward Ma.

Ma waved the shotgun at him and said, "Don't
you dare drive those critters through here!" and
Kilty called out, soothingly. "We're trying not to,
ma'am."

He saw the jasper at the reins of the distant
buckboard had whipped his horse into a trot. He
had a red-headed gal on the seat beside him. What
in thunder had got into all these sod busters? How
the hell was a man to get his herd to market if
they all acted crazy?

Kilty moved his mount between the woman and
the passing herd, saying, "You'd best move back
some, ma'am. They do move spread and they do
move sudden. They ain't used to seeing folks afoot
and it spooks 'em some."

A spotted black longhorn headed for them, sniffing like a dog, and as a rider cut it off and hazed
it back into the main herd Kilty said, "There you
go. Steers is curious critters. That flapping skirt

and yaller hair of your'n has 'em wondering, no offense."

"Get them away from here!" she demanded, awed by the sheer numbers of the passing brutes. Their hooves were churning the wagon trace into a wider path as she watched and the hot dust was drifting like fog closing in about her. But she could see well enough when a longhorn reached the corner of the barley field and hooked the fence with its horn. She yelled, "Stop that! Joe worked too hard!" and Kilty swung in his saddle yelling, "Collins, Murphy, don't let 'em at that crop! We'll never get 'em out if they fall on that fresh fodder!"

A younger hand on a roan gelding cut between the cattle and the fence line, waving his hat at them. A determined range cow caught the pony a glancing hook and the roan shied, ripping the rider's leg on the wire as they crashed through it together. As the embarrassed rider reined in, his mount's hooves trampling the young barley, Ma raised her shotgun and fired at him, screaming wildly.

The range was too far to worry her target, but the noise sent a shock wave through the herd and Kilty gasped, "Oh, shit!" and rode at her to keep her from firing the second barrel. He didn't make it. Ma fired point blank into the breast of his mount and the mortally wounded horse reared and fell over backwards as its rider slid sideways to land sprawling in the dust. He rolled to his hands and knees as someone shouted, "Stampede!"

Kilty Dundee had been on the wrong side of a stampeded herd before. So he was up and running, not looking back. As he reached Ma, she tried to hit him with the barrels of the gun in her hands. He slapped it aside and grabbed her around the waist to throw her over his shoulder like a sack of feed, yelling, "We might make that corner of your house and we might not, but you just hold still and let me try, God damn it!"

The herd was going every which way now. One bunch spilled into Joe's barley and since the hands saw the far side was fenced they let that bunch go. They'd likely still be there, grazing on the lush sprouts, when and if they ever circled the leaders and milled the main herd to a halt.

Kilty got around the corner and put Ma down. She dashed over to the door way and picked up a broom as Joe, driving within earshot, yelled, "Leave that woman alone, you son-of-a-bitch!"

Kilty saw the gun in Joe's hand, so he drew his own and they both started firing at long range. The added gunfire didn't do a thing to steady the nerves of the cows on the roadway.

The trail boss saw a man wasn't safe in these parts so he backed around the soddy, snapping shots at Joe who in turn handed the reins to Jessie at a safe distance and leaped off to charge the rest of the way on foot. The dust was adding to the confusion as it settled around them both, making it nearly impossible to see. Kilty glanced over his shoulder, saw the nearest cows were headed away from him and spotted one of his riders coming. The man reined in and fired his own gun in the general direction of the soddy's dim outline in the dust cloud. Kilty ran to him and said, "Never mind them. Give me a hand-up and let's get out of here!"

He swung up behind the rider and grabbed his belt, shouting, "Straight south. Got to make sure the boys have them turned."

But the stampede was a mean one and the herd ran nearly three miles before they had them under control, bunched in a bawling tired mass as the dust slowly settled. Kilty got a spare mount from the wrangler and said to his segundo, "Son-of-a-bitch. That was close! You hold 'em here and I'll take some boys back to gather the strays in that damned barley field."

He didn't know, of course, that one of the stray shots three men had exchanged without much thought had found a target in the dust. But back at the Barrow homestead Joe was reloading his .44, ashen-faced, as Jessie knelt by Ma in the dooryard. Jessie said, "Joe, I think she's hurt bad."

He said, "I noticed. I don't reckon we'd best move her. You get a quilt and pillow from inside and see if you can make her comforted until I get back."

"Where are you going, for the doc?"

"Among other places," said Joe, moving over to the buckboard to remove the Winchester from its rack on the back of the seat. He hefted it and headed for the corral to saddle Demon. Jessie looked down at the woman in the dust and said, "Don't do it, Joe. Just get the doc."

He said, "I aim to, after. I can catch those bastards long afore they make it to town with them critters."

"Please, Joe, don't leave us alone like this! I fear she's done for."

"I said I noticed! You do what you can and I'll do what I can, Sis."

He saw he had Jessie crying, so he strode back and into the house to fetch a quilt and pillow. He brought it out, knelt, and gently raised his mother's head to place the pillow under it as Jessie covered her. She opened her eyes and said, "Oh, my darling Joe, you did return to me, but where's your uniform tonight?"

He said, "Take it easy, Ma. I'll be back directly."

"Don't go. You just got here and it's mortal dark outside, darling."

He looked bleakly at Jessie and said, "Do what you can."

But, as he rose, he saw there was no need to saddle up. The God-damned fools were riding back. Four of 'em, leastways. He recognized the initialed chaps and flat hat of the one who mattered. He started walking, growling low in his throat, to meet them.

Kilty and his riders saw him. Kilty said, "You boys round up them cows and get 'em back to the main herd."

"Man's coming with a rifle, boss."

"I noticed. Do as I say."

Joe was in a murderous rage, too angry for his own good. Kilty Dundee had ten years on him and he'd won more than one fight in his time by fighting as cold-nerved as he herded cows. He drew his own Henry .44 from the rifle scabbard on his saddle and dismounted methodically to stand his ground as the men cut cows behind him. As Joe approached Kilty levered a round in the chamber and said, "That's close enough, pilgrim. I'll pay you for the damage we done your crop, but let's keep this friendly."

Joe raised the Winchester and fired.

It was the last thing he remembered doing for a while.

He awoke with a hollow roaring in his head and an awful pain in his side to see Jessie's red head above him, outlined against the blue sky. His voice sounded tinny to him as he said, "Howdy. How's Ma?"

Jessie said, "Dead. I was afeared they'd killed you, too, you poor fool! Does it hurt bad, Joe?"

"Yep. Did I get that son-of-a-bitch in the flat hat?"

"No, he gunned you down like a dog and just rode off with the others."

Joe struggled to rise and Jessie held him down, saying, "They're long gone, Joe, you've been out for almost an hour. You're gunshot in the ribs and you've bled all over creation. If you'll just lay still I'll get the buckboard and we'll get you to the house."

"Don't aim to go to no fool house. Got to ride into town and kill me some cowboys."

Jessie started to cry. He tried to sit up again, gasped in pain and surprise, and said, "Mebbe I'd better restudy on that. That bastard shot me pretty good, didn't he?"

"Joe, you was swatted like a fly, no offense. I don't know why they didn't finish you off, but they didn't, and I want you to promise me you'll stay away from them from now on."

"Are you crazy, girl? You saw them kill our Ma!"

"Joe, I don't know who shot Ma. You was all shooting wild as anything! It might have been an accident. It don't matter if it was or not. I saw you just now from a distance, Joe. That man you picked a fight with wasn't just good. He was impossible perfect! He nailed you with his first shot, swinging his rifle gun up like it was a pistol and firing from the hip."

"He's likely had more practice. I should have gotten closer afore I opened up."

"Honey, it wouldn't have done you a speck of good. I keep telling you I saw it, and he was spooky! He just dropped you, stood there thoughtful for a minute, and just got back on his horse and rode off not looking back. I've heard about professional killers. If he ain't one, I hope I never meet the real thing!"

"I'll be more careful next time."

"Joe, there ain't to be a next time. It won't bring Ma back, even if you win, which ain't possible. You'll just get killed and then who'll I have and what's to become of me?"

Joe said, "Get the buckboard. I said I'd study on it some afore I got around to doing anything."

He heard her walking away through what was left of their barley. He tried to open his eyes to watch her, but it seemed awfully hard to do that, right now. He reached up to touch his eyelids. He winced in discomfort as he realized his eyes were open. They felt better closed and it made no difference. He'd heard losing blood could do that to a man.

He dropped his suddenly heavy arm to his side and saw Jessie had told him true about that, for the earth at his side was wet and sticky. He ran his fingertips over the sprouting barley and wondered how much of his catch crop was left.

He wondered why that was important to a dying man. Nothing seemed really important, when you got right down to her. In a year or so it wouldn't matter if the barley was ruined or if it grew a bumper crop. Sooner or later the sun ball would burn out and this darkness would close in on everything and everybody and what in tarnation were they all working so hard to accomplish in the end?

He smiled blindly and said, "Hell, dying ain't as bad as I suspicioned. I ain't scared after all."

He wondered if his father had felt like this, in those last minutes on the field of Shiloh long ago. He hoped he had. It made a man feel close to his dad, dying the same way.

But Joe Barrow saw he was still alive the next time he came to inside the house. He was naked in the main bed with his chest bound in white linen and Ma's quilt over him. He saw Jessie and Nadja Ivanov brooding over him like a pair of hens and asked, "Who took my duds off? You gals had no call to undress a man without asking."

Jessie said, "Yasha put you to bed, Joe. He'll be back any minute with the doc from town. You've been out a while. It's dark outside."

Nadja said, "I fed you chicken soup but you didn't wake up, poor Josef. Bullet is still in you, but we don't think you lose lung."

"That's all right. I got two. What's been done about . . . Ma?"

Jessie said, "Yasha took her in with him. The coroner will likely want to see her afore he gives us burying papers, Joe."

He nodded and Nadja asked him if he wanted her to fix them some coffee. He said, "Not hardly, thanks just the same. I'm sort of sleepy. Why don't you get Jessie to show you how to make coffee? No offense, but you could use some lessons."

He dozed off for a time and when he awoke again a total stranger was hurting him like hell. The man said, "Hold still, damn it. I'm Doc Smiley and if this ain't bone I have in my forceps it's the ball that hulled you."

Joe gritted his jaw and told the doc to do his damnedest and in a million years Doc Smiley held the mashed .44 slug up to the light and said, "You got good ribs, son. Lead stayed in one lump and if you ain't infected you'll likely live."

"How long am I going to feel so puny, Doc?"

"You'll be able to get out of bed in a few days, if it heals clean. God only knows if it festers. I don't want you lifting anything heavy for at least a month, either way."

He turned and said, "He's all yours, Sheriff," and Joe saw Yasha and Sheriff MacLeod were sitting at the table near the stove. The Sheriff came over and took the doctor's vacated seat by the bed. He said, "I took Kilty Dundee's statement when your friend, yonder, told us what happened out here. Like to hear your side of it, son."

"Who in thunder is Kilty Dundee?"

"Trail boss as shot you and your Ma. This sure has been a rough trip for old Kilty. He had a shoot-out with your neighbor Gus Olsen too. You boys sure have been acting moody out here."

"Jesus, he gunned Olsen, too? They'll hang him sure, right?"

"Doubt it. He's got witnesses as say Olsen fired on them first fatal. They tell me you folks opened up on them first, too. I'd like to hear that from somebody who doesn't work for Kilty, though. So how about it?"

Joe told him what had happened, as well as he could put it together. The Sheriff nodded and said, "Well, it's nice to hear some agreement for a change. I'll tell Kilty he'd best head back to the sand hills and stay there for a spell."

"My God, don't you mean to arrest him?"

"Don't see how that'd do any good, Mister Barrow. The grand jury ain't about to return an indictment on open-and-shut self-defense."

"Self-defense hell! I don't know what happened over to the Olsen place but he gunned my Ma and when I went after him he gunned me, too!"

"I know. He says he disremembers shooting at your Ma. He didn't know she was hit until your friend brung her in. Even if he's lying, your Ma blowed his pony out from under him with a shotgun before she got hurt. As to his shooting you, you fired first with intent to kill. Ain't a jury in this land would find a man guilty for shooting back."

Joe scowled and said, "I see one cow hand washes the other in these parts. Well, I'll be up and about in no time and we'll just see if he can do her a second time."

MacLeod said flatly, "Kilty can. But you're not to go gunning for him in any county I have a say in! I asked him if he aimed to press charges agin' you and he said it was over as far as he was concerned. But you're lucky neither of you was killed, Joe Barrow. What Kilty did was lawful. What you was out to do was pure homicide. If his riders hadn't avenged him on the spot, I'd have had to take you in. I'm putting a peace bond on you, son."

"You put anything you want on me, Sheriff. That son-of-a-bitch gunned my Ma right in front of me!"

MacLeod shrugged and said, "Mebbe he did. But mebbe it was you or that other jasper blazing away like fool kids at targets none of you could see. I know you're too het up to think straight right now. But I want you to study some before you go doing anything dumb again. Kilty Dundee says he's sorry and that he won't go for you if you don't go for him. I'd feel better if I heard the same from you. But that can wait. Meanwhile, I'd best give you some facts and figures to mull over. Kilty's a good old boy, but he killed his first Comanche down in Texas when he was eleven years old. He ain't a big bad bad man as brags and notches his six gun, but the latest reckoning is that he's put eight men in the ground, not counting Mexicans or Injuns."

"I ain't afraid of him."

"Then you're a bigger fool than I took you for. I've done some fighting in my time and I'd sure be afraid to go up agin Kilty Dundee with or without a badge to back my play."

"That's why you was afraid to arrest him, huh?"

The older man's eyes narrowed but his voice stayed calm as he replied, "I'm going to forget you said that, son. It seems sort of surly to hit a wounded man. If I had grounds to arrest Kilty Dundee I'd do my best, scared or no. I'd have a better chance, too. I ain't arresting him 'cause there's no just cause for an arrest, and you can take that or lump it. The point I'm trying to make is that if you go after him again you'll likely die."

"And if I don't die?"

"You'll hang for it if you bushwack him. Getting him any other way is just a daydream. I know how you feel, son. I had a mother once. The Kiowa got her when I was a kid and I was cut up pretty bad. I didn't commit suicide, though. It wouldn't have brung her back worth mention. If you just can't carry on without your Ma, put a gun to your head and pull the trigger. It's a free country."

"I might get kilt trying, but I know what I must do, Sheriff."

MacLeod got to his feet and said, "This is getting tedious, Doc. You aim to stay here a spell or are you riding back to town with me?"

Doc Smiley said, "I've done all I can, here. The rest is in the hands of the Lord." He turned to Jessie and said, "Try to keep him quiet and let me know if he starts to run a fever, ma'am. I've cleaned and dressed his wound as well as I know how. But gunshot wounds are serious. Most folks die more from the after-effects than they do from the first shock. He'll feel better in a day or so as his blood pressure builds back up. He'll want to be up and about. Don't let him. He can go to the outback. He can sit up to sup. You let him chore before we have some laudable pus to cheer us and you might have two funerals to pay for."

Jessie grimaced and asked, "Laudable *what*, sir?"

"Pus. From his wound. There's always some infection in a gunshot wound. If it drains a sort of straw-colored pus there's nothing to worry about. If it looks like greenish mustard and smells sort of sweet, well, we'll cross that bridge when we come to it."

"Oh, dear, is there anything you can do if he blood-poisons bad?"

"Nope. If it festers ugly it's up to how strong he is and how the Good Lord feels about him. Don't worry about it tonight. I'll come out again in a day or so. Hardly anybody dies any sooner than that, if the bullet don't kill 'em right off. I'm leaving you some sleeping powders in case he gets restless. Keep him warm and rested as you can. He'll need all his strength if it goes bad on us."

It did. Joe felt almost strong enough to rise the first morning after he'd been shot, but Jessie wept and pleaded him back in bed after he'd been to the outback. The Rooshins came back that evening and the two gals took turns feeding him. He laughed and told them they were acting foolish.

By midnight he had a raging fever and his side felt like there was a big rotten apple under the bandages, itching like hell. He knew Nadja was spending the night when he tasted the awful coffee laced with sleeping powders. The doc had said the powders would assure him a restful night. The doc was full of it. He'd never had such nightmares in his life before. He seemed to be in hell and naked ladies were dancing about him in the flames of damnation. Some of 'em looked too familiar for comfort and he was ashamed as hell to be doing this with his own Ma whilst the devils laughed and jeered at him, but he couldn't stop and, God damn it, he couldn't come either.

Along about dawn he had convulsions and it was all the two gals could do to hold him in bed.

He was dimly aware both of them were in their nightgowns instead of naked and in hell. He tried to fight them off and one or the other gasped when he grabbed a breast, but they wrestled him back down and Nadja, being the strongest, held him whilst Jessie lashed him to the bed with a rope, ignoring the ugly things he was calling them both.

The next time he came up from Hell it seemed to be daylight out and Yasha was sitting next to him. Yasha said, "Lie still, Tovarich. Chores are done. Nadja and me help Jessie. How you feeling?"

"God awful. But I reckon I'll last 'til the doc comes back."

Yasha said, "Doc was out here yesterday, Tovarich. He drained wound. Was right about it smelling sweet. Nadja go outside and throw up. Nadja strong like ox, but still woman."

Joe tried to sit up, saw he couldn't, and said, "You're talking crazy, Yasha. Doc said he wasn't coming back for a few days, remember?"

"*Da*, Yasha remember. Joe don't, I think. You have been out for nearly week, Tovarich. Doc say you are strong like ox, too. He say if infection don't killing you in next few days, you might live after all. He says you beating odds for such bad wound."

"Jesus. How the hell did I heed the call to nature if I've been dead to the world all this time?"

"You shit bed a lot. Girls clean you. Put fresh sheets under you."

Joe explored his flesh under the covers with a hand and flushed as he realized he was stark naked, save for the fresh dressings. He said, "That's awful. They must have seen my privates."

Yasha said, "*Da.* So did Yasha. You hung like horse, lucky you. One time you got nice hard on when they are washing you. You having wet dreams, *nyet*?"

"Oh my God! I didn't *say* anything dirty, did I?"

Yasha shrugged and said, "Is all right. Everybody is knowing you are out of head with fever."

"Come on, what did I say?"

Yasha grinned and answered, "Ha, what did you not say, you mean! You talk very dirty. Ask Nadja to sucking you. Ask Jessie if she has ever done with dog or something. My English not so good and you talking fast and crazy. Is not to worry. Doc say people say worse things with brain full of poison."

Joe groaned and said, "Oh, God, how in hell am I to ever face either of them again? I want you to know I've never been wicked with Nadja, Yasha."

Yasha nodded and said, "*Da*, I know that already. Forget silly talk from fever. Listen, I just planted red wheat for you out back. Had own finished so thought what the hell, like you Amerikanski say."

"I'd forgot all about my crops. Have you taken a look at my barley?"

"*Da*, is mess. Maybe couple of bushels if frost don't nip on stem. Last few nights cold as Siberia. Saw some frost on grass this morning. Not killing frost, yet. But any night now. People in town say winter coming early this year, they think. But you not listening. I told you I put forty acres wheat in for you."

"That was neighborly as hell, Yasha. Even if it don't work."

"Will work. You will see in spring. Turkish red tough like hell."

"Yasha, the ground freezes solid three feet down out here in the winter."

"*Da*, so in Russia, too. That is why English wheat no good out here. Strong wheat from old country laughs at cold and just goes to sleep like bear. You will see in spring."

The two girls came in before Joe could argue about the stubborn little Rooshin's fool notion. They didn't look sore at him, considering.

He said, "Yasha tells me I sort of acted ornery whilst I was out of my head. I'm sure sorry, but I know there's no way in hell I can take it back and make things right again."

Nadja shot her brother a dirty look and said, "Silly Yasha was not supposed to tell you" and Jessie said, "It wasn't so bad. I didn't understand half of what you said and I talk better English than Nadja. What is going sixty-nine, Joe? You kept asking us who wanted to give it a try, but neither of us knowed what you was talking about."

Joe laughed, despite his horror, and said, "Never you mind. If you didn't get it outten me in my sleep you ain't about to find out now! But, honest, gals, I'm sorry as hell."

Jessie shrugged and replied, "You already said that. I've been showing Nadja how to make coffee American-style and she's been waiting to show you her stuff."

So Nadja poured him some tolerable Arbuckle and when she asked him if it was as good as going sixty-nine he only spilled a little of it.

They laughed, too, albeit looking a mite confused. After he got through laughing 'til he damned near cried, Joe suddenly sobered and said, "You too gals are real gents and that's a fact I'll never forget."

But his friends hadn't even started nursing him. He got his supper down and felt a mite better for a time. But later that night he had a relapse and this time he went too deep to even dream. It was Yasha in the end who saved him. About dawn, when Jessie jerked awake in her chair to find Joe breathing funny she put a damp cloth to his forehead and felt his pulse. She sobbed and that woke up the others. Jessie said, "He's acting just like Ma did, at the last. His pulse is all fluttery and he sounds like he's breathing in a bucket."

Yasha came over, tasting his teeth experimentally with a bottle in his hand. He raised the quilt and felt the dressings. It felt like Joe had a big hot coal smouldering under the bandages. Yasha pulled the cork with his teeth and Jessie said, "He can't drink nothing. He's out of this world."

Yasha said, "Is not for Joe. Is for Yasha. You girls go outside, leave door open. Yasha got to lance big lump and let Death out."

Jessie regarded him dubiously, for she knew he drank too much for his own good and Joe said he had a lot of queer notions about a lot of things. She said, "I reckon we'd best send for the doc, Yasha."

But the Russian insisted, "No time for riding to town and back. Nadja, take her outside." He added something in their own language. Nadja blanched and then she nodded and took Jessie by the arm, saying, "Come, we take walk. See if frost is on grass."

Jessie didn't want to go, but she wasn't certain

she wanted to stay and the blonde girl was stronger than she was. So she let Nadja win and, as Yasha had asked, they left the door open.

It was a crisp morning and Yasha felt gooseflesh under his thin shirt. But the wind through the door smelled good, for while dry cow manure burns well enough, it does little for the atmosphere in a cramped one-room soddy.

Yasha took a stiff jolt of gin, put the bottle down, and told the unconcious man on the sweat soaked mattress, "Last time I do this was horse. Now we find out if it works on peoples."

He gingerly uncovered the crust-and-pus-covered purple mass in Joe's side and after he'd swallowed the green taste in his mouth Yasha swallowed some more gin. As long as he had the bottle open he poured more gin over the blade of his pocket knife. Then he placed a folded sheet of newsprint on the bed below the massive infection, took a deep breath, and stabbed.

He stabbed a full inch deep, using his forefinger as a measuring guard. As his fingertip punched into the soggy purple sack of inflammation a gout of evil-smelling mustard-colored pus shot out and spattered his hand to the wrist. Yasha gagged and placed his other hand against Joe's side with two fingers on either side of the knife blade as he gently pressed. Something gave inside and this time there was blood mixed in with the pus as it ejaculated against the front of Yasha's shirt. He knew he was going to vomit and he had to have a drink. But he couldn't do either. So he didn't. He withdrew his blade, still pressing with his other hand as awesome amounts of the vile fluid pulsed from the wound in a slowly decreasing stream. He saw he was getting nothing but blood, now. He kept squeezing it out, allowing Joe's own blood to bathe the oozy crust from the new opening. Then he reached for the dressings Jessie had washed and dried the day before and poured more gin over them before poulticing the wound with them and wrapping Joe back up. He cleaned up as well as he could and threw the disgusting paper and old dressings in the stove before he rose, went to the door, and stepped outside to vomit, bracing himself against the sod wall.

He looked around sheepishly. He saw Jessie and his sister over by the corral, feeding or petting the horses with their backs to him. He went back inside and helped himself to a deep draft of straight gin.

On the bed, Joe stirred fitfully and muttered, still asleep, "What's going on? It's sure cold down here in hell this morning."

Yasha gently covered him with the quilt. They had enough to worry about without pneumonia.

He patted Joe and said, "Sleep, Tovarich Joe. I got to wash Yasha, now."

There wasn't much he could do about the mess he'd made of his shirt, but he could roll up his sleeves and wash his hands at the basin by the door. The water was cold and the air blowing in smelled like snow.

The two girls came back, their feet crunching the brittle frosted grass stems. Jessie gasped at the blood and worse on Yasha's shirt and asked, "What happened? What did you do? How's my brother?"

Yasha said, "Yasha did what had to be done. Joe's pulse is stronger, now. I think I got it all."

Jessie darted over to the bed and placed a hand

on Joe's brow. She smiled and said, "Oh, he don't feel as hot. I'd kiss you for what you done if you wasn't such a mess."

Yasha shrugged and said, "Maybe some other time."

THE NEXT FEW WEEKS would always remain a confused blur to Joe Barrow. It took him that long to start making sense again. He'd wake up fairly clear-headed, drink some coffee or maybe even eat something and then fall back into fitful sleep as his strong young body repaired itself.

One morning he woke up to hear the soft kitten claws of snow against the windowpanes as Jessie prepared breakfast. He asked her how long it had been snowing and she said off and on for a few days. She asked if he was warm enough and he said, "Too warm by half. Open the door and let some air in, Sis. It smells like a sick room in here."

She said, "That's what it is, you fool. The doc says I'm to keep you warm. I hauled some dry lumber over from that old soddy and we're snug as bugs in here. The snow's starting to stick, but it ain't deep. It's the wind as cuts through you outside. The folks around here calls it the Wolf Wind. I'm starting to see why. Last night it was howling around outside the door like a mean old hungry wolf."

"How's the water in the well?"

"Froze. Don't worry, I gathered clean snow and it makes tolerable coffee water."

He asked her to fetch him his tools and the windmill fan he'd started as he tried to sit up in bed. She told him not to be an idiot and as she pushed him down he was surprised at how strong she seemed to have gotten. He couldn't seem to be able to lick her lately.

He ate and managed to stay awake a while before he dozed off again. The next time he awoke it was because someone had come to the door and Jessie was letting them in.

It was the Mackail twins, Brazos and Trinity. Brazos came over to sit by his side as Trinity sat, awkward, near the stove, holding his big hat in his lap and watching Jessie make coffee. Brazos said, "We brung a side of beef over. It's hanging outside."

Joe told him that was nieghborly, considering, and asked how much they wanted for it. Brazos said, "I know you've been stove up, but that's no reason to talk dirty, Joe. We figured you might be a mite hard up, getting shot and having your barley stomped and frosted."

"Well, I can't say we got no use for your beef and it sure beats beans and flapjacks, no offense, Jessie."

Brazos laughed and said, "There you go."

Trinity had been staring at the improvised windmill vanes in the far corner. He suddenly blurted, "What's that you're making yonder?" and Joe told him. Trinity said, "Not hardly. We got us a wind-mill at the Double M and that ain't what it looks like. Your blades is supposed to be sheet iron, boy."

Joe said, "Didn't have no sheet iron. Used old barrel staves. I doubt the wind will know the dif-ference."

Trinity said, "It's still crazy-looking," and Brazos said, "Leave it be, Trinity. It's a free country and he ain't asking you to like it."

Joe said, "That's all right, Brazos. I can't seem to finish it in the first place and I got no pipe for it in the second."

Brazos nodded and said, "I was talking to Kilty Dundee the other day."

"The jasper as shot Ma and me?"

"Well, he allows he shot *you*. Says he'll do it again if you ever come at him with a gun again. He says he don't know who shot your Ma, but he wants to make it up to you some way."

"I see. You boys are acting as his go-between, right?"

"Sort of. Our own Ma was a Dundee, so old Kilty's sort of kin."

"Does that mean you'd have to back him if . . . you know?"

Trinity looked over at Joe and said, "If you bushwacked him we would."

Brazos shushed him with a look and said, "We'd stay clear of a fair fight, Joe, but there's just no way any man will ever take Kilty in a fair fight, so Trinity has a point, surly as he may sound."

Joe said, "It sure gets tedious hearing how good your cousin is. Sheriff MacLeod told me how awesome he was, too."

Brazos smiled pointedly at Joe's chest and said, "It's sort of surprising anyone has to tell you how good he is, considering. But let's get back to his offer. He says he feels it's only fair to pay you for your barley crop. I said I'd pass along his offer to you. What do you say?"

"No. Three reasons. In the first place it wasn't his fool cows as did most of the damage. It was the early frost. I didn't see it, naturally, but my Sis here tells me she went out one morning to find it froze and only six inches high. In the second place, I don't need charity from any man."

Brazos waited for Joe to name the third place. Then he saw what it had to be and said, "I admire your style, but whether you think it's right to let a man you aim to kill do you a favor or not, I still wish you'd drop it."

"Worried about your kinsman, eh?"

"Not hardly, Joe. But I like you, leaving your way of living aside. Next neighbor might not make such good Arbuckle."

Jessie said that speaking of Arbuckle, it was ready. She poured cups all around and offered them some apple pie she'd made to go with it. Trinity tasted experimentally, then said, "You don't have no apple trees worth mention, ma'am. How'd you get this pie to taste so good? Our cook uses dry apples and his pie tastes like it."

Jessie dimpled and said, "I soaks the dried apples overnight in vinegar water with a speck of sugar in it. It helps bring back the fresh taste afore I bakes it."

"Do tell? Well, it sure works."

Then, as his brother smiled at him knowingly, Trinity lowered his eyes and fell silent, remembering his moody manners.

Joe asked if they wanted their side of beef back, since he'd refused the peace offering from their kinsman. Brazos said, "You're as sulky as my brother and I thought I'd seen sulky. Your feud with Kilty ain't our'n, long as you conducts it fair and square. We brung the beef 'cause we was butchering and had plenty to spare. You ought to try stock-raising some time. Cows hardly ever frost off when the fall comes early."

After the Mackail brothers had left Jessie said she suspected Joe had Trinity all wrong and that his poor manners were shyness. So he told her she was full of it and went back to sleep.

A few days later as Jessie was pinning up laundry out back she saw the surly Trinity turning in out front driving a light dray. She went to greet him as he reined in. She said her brother was asleep but that he was welcome to set a spell and have some cake and coffee. Trinity said, "I ain't got time. Where you want this stuff I got in the back?"

Jessie asked what he was talking about and Trinity said, "Pipe. Lengths of waterpipe for your brother's fool windmill. We had some extra laying about. I figured I may as well drop it off on my way to town."

"Why, ain't you the sweet thing, Trinity Mackail? How much do we owe you for it? Joe's been trying to buy pipe all over the county."

Trinity said, "Aw, mush, I'm a cow man. I sells

cows. I don't sell pipe. You want it or don't you, ma'am?"

She climbed up beside him on the dray and said she'd be pleased to show him where they could unload it. But when they got around by the well he refused to let her help, saying it was man's work. So Jessie waited until he'd dropped the lengths of pipe with a scowl on the brittle grass before she said, "You don't fool me, Mister Cowboy."

"Ain't trying to fool nobody, ma'am.'

"Oh, no? Then why do you go about acting like a growly bear when anybody with sense can see you're really a nice boy?"

"Dammit, woman, I ain't no boy. I'm as old as your brother. I bet I could lick him."

Jessie had no idea how to answer that. So she didn't.

Trinity lined a pipe up neater with his boot tip and stared down at it as he added, "You don't have to worry about it, though. I don't mean to pick another fight with him. He acted decent that time I got in trouble with the law."

Jessie looked relieved and said, "Well, I reckon Joe will figure you're even when I tell him about this pipe. Did you ever find your lost horse?"

"Yep. One of the hands found it out on the range, spur cut and limping. I'd purely like to get my hands on the skonk who'd treat a horse like that. My brother Brazos says he don't think I'd best ride Old Gray for a spell."

"I see what he means, Trinity. Folks might think you was a nightrider if they saw you on a mount seen near a nightriding."

Then she lowered her own lashes and asked,

"I've been meaning to ask about that name. Is Trinity your real name or what?"

Trinity said, "Our Ma named us Peter and Paul when we was birthed at the same time. Our Dad said Peter and Paul sounded sissy. So he always called us after Texas rivers."

"Are you Peter or Paul?"

"It says Paul on my birthing papers. Brazos is Peter. I'm *Trinity*, durn it!"

Jessie laughed and said, "Heavens, nobody hereabouts is aiming to throw you down and brand you Paul, Trinity. Who on Earth put that awful chip on your shoulder?"

Trinity scowled at her and said, "You're talking dumb. I don't go about looking for trouble. Trouble just naturally comes my way. I've just had to larn to deal with it. You'd be a mite testy, too, had you met up with half the trouble *I* have."

"What kinds of trouble, Trinity?"

"You want it numerical or by the alphabet? Folks have been picking on me all my days. I don't know why. They just have."

"What about your brother, Brazos?"

"Aw, Brazos seems to get along better with folks. Hardly anybody starts up with Brazos. Don't ask me why. I don't know. It's just one of them facts of life, I reckon. Brazos has the knack of making friends. All I seem to make is enemies."

Jessie said, "It can't be your looks, for you and your brother are spitting images. Have you ever thought it might be your attitude?"

"What's wrong with my infernal attitude? I pays for the drinks when it's my turn. I don't cuss in Church. I'm willing to leave folks alone if they'd jest leave me alone, but they won't."

"Come on, Trinity, you know you started hazing Yasha Ivanov with no encouragement at all. That Rooshin boy wasn't bothering you."

Trinity shrugged and said, "Sure he was. He come out here uninvited and strung bobwire across a quarter mile of open range, didn't he?"

"He had the legal right, Trinity."

"Mebbe. Nobody asked *me* if he could do it, and it bothered me a heap. I pay taxes and obey such laws as make any sense. Ain't *I* got rights?"

Jessie sighed and said, "I'm not about to argue the Homestead Act with a cowboy, Trinity Mackail. My brother Joe says he don't think you're a nightrider and that's good enough for me."

Trinity started to spit, decided not to, and said, "That's kid stuff. If I aim to fight a man I come right out and say so. I don't have to put a feedsack over my head."

She nodded approvingly, but said, "Pretty mean for kid stuff, when you consider the folks they've killed. You sure you don't want to come in and set for a spell? It's bitter cold out here and you have a long drive ahead of you."

Trinity might have answered one way or the other, but just then they both spied another vehicle coming and as it swung off the wagon trace across the snow-frosted sod they saw it was the Widow Palmer from town. Jessie waved and when Gloria Palmer waved back, Trinity said, "Another time. I got to git."

He drove past Gloria's rig as Jessie moved afoot to greet her. Gloria nodded to him and called out, "Good day, Trinity" as he passed, nodding curtly to her. As he left, Gloria got down and sighed at

Jessie, saying, "He's always been like that. I've known both boys since they were little."

Jessie said, "They sure match odd, inside their heads. Brazos is so easy going. Trinity goes about looking like he just bit into a sour lemon. I suspicion he's sweeter than he acts, though."

Gloria Palmer said, "Don't bank on it, honey. He's been in one scrape after another all his life. A lot of people have made the mistake of hoping to find the good side of him. I don't think there *is* a good side to Trinity Mackail. But I never drove all this way to talk about a boy who must have been dropped on his head as a baby. I brought some vittles and such. How's Joe?"

As she took a basket from her surrey boot Jessie told her Joe was still weak but starting to recover a mite. The last time she'd changed his dressings his wound had looked less ugly.

The widow woman shook her head wearily and said, "You kids sure have had a hard row to hoe out here. How on Earth can one woman hope to manage with both the housekeeping and the nursing?"

Jessie said, "I let the housekeeping go. The place is a mess, but come on in anyway."

She ushered Gloria Palmer inside and took the friendly parcel from her as she called, "Joe, wake up, we got company."

Joe opened his eyes, ran a hand across his face, and then as he saw who it was he perked up and said, "Howdy, uh, Miss Gloria. I'm sure surprised to see you all the way out here."

Jessie said the coffee pot was full and that she had to finish hanging her washing. Gloria sat by

Joe's bed and as Jessie went outside she took his hand in hers and said, "I've missed you, darling."

He said, "I missed you, too. But I don't reckon we'd best hold hands. Jessie will be back any moment."

"Oh, is she likely to be jealous?"

"That's a fool thing to say, woman. You know she's my sister."

"Then why are you so shy? I'd think a loving sister would want her big brother to be happy."

"You're funning me, I see. I ain't ashamed about you and me. But I thought you wanted to keep my visits to you a secret."

"Who's she going to tell, Joe? Who'd know what went on out here, no matter what, if nobody told?"

He didn't like the funny glint in her eye, even though he knew she was teasing him. Old Gloria liked to tease and flirt with being found out. He still remembered the time she'd asked him to stand behind her with the curtains hiding him as she leaned out the upstairs window with her skirts heisted, waving to folks passing by down in the street whilst he gave it to her standing from behind. It'd seemed foolish as hell to him, but she'd said it was something she'd always wanted to try.

But when Jessie came in with her empty laundry basket Gloria had her hands folded prim in her lap and was jawing about the Morgans she'd let them have. Joe said, "I know I said I'd pay you partly from the barley crop" and Gloria quickly cut in, "Don't be silly. It wasn't your fault you got shot."

Jessie said, "We're still discussing that" as she poured coffee, adding, "Mebbe you can talk some sense to him, Miss Gloria. You likely know this Kilty Dundee gent."

Gloria nodded and said, "Quite well. I've spoken to him recently about the misunderstanding out here. He's assured me he means you no further harm. I think he'd feel better if I could tell him you felt the same way, Joe."

Joe said, "I've been studying on what happened. Lord knows I ain't had much else to do. I'd still be bound to go agin him if I was sure in my own heart he kilt Ma deliberate, or even I could swear for sure he kilt her at all. But for all I know it was my own bullet as done the deed and, let me tell you, that sort of notion puts a man off his feed!"

"Then Kilty is forgiven, Joe?"

"I can't say if he is or not. That's up to Our Lord in the end. For all I know I'll have to answer to the murder myself some day in the Great By and By. All I know for certain is that it ain't up to me to punish anybody for what happened to Ma, for in truth I just don't *know* what happened in all that confusion."

"What about his shooting you, Joe?"

"Been studying on that, too. I can't say as I've enjoyed the experience all that much, but fair is fair. If a total stranger came at me with a gun and missed me with his first fool shot, I doubt like hell I'd give him a chance to fire twice. I didn't pay much mind the first time Jessie pointed out he had the chance to finish me off and passed on the notion. I reckon we was both doing what we thought was right at the time."

"I'll tell him you want to be friends, then, Joe."

"Hey, let's not get mushy about it! I said I wasn't studying on going after him again. I never said I wanted to drink with him."

Gloria laughed and said, "I think that will be

good enough for Kilty. He doesn't like homesteaders, either."

"I noticed. What ever happened to the survi-
vors at the Olsen spread?"

"The widow and orphans went back east, Joe. I
bought their claim at a fair price."

Joe frowned up at her and said, "You bought it?
I thought you was a cow gal, Miss Gloria."

She said, "I am. No offense. I wanted that waterhole, not the silly little homesteading notion. You'll
be pleased to hear the garden they'd started was
killed off by the first frost, too."

"I ain't pleased, but I ain't surprised, neither.
Gus Olsen started later than us. That was already
too late. What do you figure to do with that waterhole, sell it? It's way out of the way for your own
cows on the Circle Six, Miss Gloria."

She nodded and said, "I'm deeding it to the
county as a public pond. Lord knows we've few of
the same and there's been enough trouble over
one muddy puddle, if you ask me."

Jessie said, "That sure was generous of you,
ma'am" and Gloria smiled sort of Mona-Lisa-like
at Joe as she shrugged and said, "I can afford to
be generous. I've enough for my own creature
comforts. In the end that's all anyone needs."

Jessie didn't notice how Joe was blushing as she
handed out the cups and said, "Well, it was a
handsome gesture in any case. If half the other
cow folks were as nice as you and the Mackail
twins, things would be a heap nicer out here."

Gloria raised an eyebrow and said, "One Mackail twin, dear. I keep trying to tell you Trinity is
... funny."

Joe frowned and asked how they'd gotten on the subject. Jessie said, "Oh, I forgot to tell you. Trinity Mackail just dropped off a load of pipe. He said is was a gift free and simple. Said you might use it for your windmill if you ever get it built."

"Old Trinity did that? Well, it just goes to show, you can't tell a book by its cover."

Gloria Palmer said, "Listen to me, both of you. I'm old enough to be the Mackail twins' mother and I watched those boys grow up. Grow up from their teens, leastways. Brazos is all right. Trinity is twisted up inside. Sure, he did you a favor just now. That don't mean much, with Trinity. I made the same mistake you're both making when the boys came up here with their late father to start the Double M. I sensed that Trinity was a loner and a mischief-maker but I was nice to him. I mean, I thought it my duty as a Christian-hearted woman to make a strange young boy far from home feel welcome. So, one day I spied him riding by on his pony and I invited him in for sweets. I thought little of it until he insisted on doing some chores for me to pay me back. You both know my house and there's always something for a strong back and willing hands around a well-kept house. I let him move some furniture for me and allowed we were even. I mean, I didn't work him hard or abuse him in any way and he only did a little work about the house."

Joe said, "I understand. What happened?"

"What happened was my front window. He came back and heaved a brick through my front parlor window, just like that!"

Jessie gasped and said, "That's awful! Are you sure it was Trinity?"

"Of course I am. I saw him out front when I ran to the sound of the crash. He was sitting his pony with a silly grin, as if he'd done something proud. I asked him had he been moonstruck and he made an ugly gesture at me with his finger and rode off, laughing fit to bust."

She sipped her coffee and added, "His father was still alive, then. Later, he and the other boy came by to apologize and pay for the damage. Brazos offered to sweep up the glass for me, but of course I'd already done that. The father said he'd tan the boy good when he caught up with him. I begged him to give Trinity another chance, but Mister Mackail said he'd used up his other chances in Texas. Later I learned that Trinity had set a schoolhouse on fire when he was a tad down Texas-way. The tales of his cruelty to animals are sickening as well as endless. What kind of a boy would soak a cat with coal oil and set a lit match to its tail just for fun?"

Joe said, "He sounds sort of crazy" and Gloria nodded and said, "That is the point I've been making. Keep Trinity Mackail at arm's-length and don't turn your back on him. That's the secret of getting along with him in this county!"

Jessie frowned thoughtfully and said, "Just now when I was talking to him Trinity said he was sore about somebody mistreating his horse. That don't sound like a man who's mean to critters."

Gloria shrugged and answered, "Mayhaps he resents *others* being cruel to critters. Or maybe he just gets spells. I said he acted decent *some* times. I was completely fooled by his act when he helped me move furnishings a short time before he decided to ventilate my front parlour with a brick."

Joe said, "I just read a magazine story about a gent like that. It was calt Doctor Jekyll and Mister Hyde. Some Englishman writ it. It was spooky as anything. There was this old doc across the water who drunk some sort of stuff and turnt into an awful brute. I mean, he was a decent cuss when he was hisself, but then he'd start acting like a lunatic. You reckon that's what Trinity is like?"

Gloria grimaced and said, "The boy who helped me move furniture was Trinity Mackail and the boy who busted my window was Trinity Mackail, but you could say they acted like two different persons."

Jessie asked, "How do you know they weren't? Peter and Paul Mackail are identical *twins*."

Gloria laughed incredulously and said, "That's even crazier, honey. I follow your drift. You're not the first person who's thought of that. But they can be told apart, if you know them well enough. In the first place, Brazos has always acted right. In the second he was with his father right after his brother rode off jeering me. They each had their own pony and they've never dressed exactly alike. Trinity has tried that, too. He's as much as said some of the things he's done were done by someone trying to make him look bad."

Jessie said, "Someone surely tried to frame him with that stolen horse. It would have worked, had not Joe and Nadja met Trinity that time by pure chance. What happened the time he broke your window, ma'am?"

"Call me Gloria. He got a tanning, of course. His father dragged him to my door by the ear and made him say he was sorry and that he'd never do it again. It must have worked, for he never did."

"I see. Then you was never friendly to the boy again, eh?"

"Friendly? Not hardly. Oh, I still say howdy to him on the street, but, as you likely noticed, he's never been able to look me in the eye again."

Jessie murmured, "Poor boy. He said nobody liked him. I didn't know 'til just now what he meant."

Gloria shot Joe a helpless look. He nodded and said slowly, "I stumbled on a weasel in a trap one time, back home in Penn State, Jessie. Some poacher had set the trap on Uncle Seth's wood lot, which made me sore, and the critter was alive and only hurt a mite, which made me feel sorry for it. Young weasels are cuter than they sound. I thought mebbe I'd make a pet outten it or something."

"I don't remember you having a pet weasel when we was little, Joe."

"I know you don't. Nobody's ever made a pet outten a weasel. I reached down and smoothed the critter's hair and it just looked at me, little beady eyes not telling me nothing. I figured I'd gentled it. So I opened the jaws of the trap to free its paw. That's when the little so-and-so bit my finger to bone and scampered off, likely laughing to itself."

Jessie wrinkled her nose and said, "That must have smarted, but what's the point, Joe?"

Joe looked at Gloria Palmer and Gloria said, "You're right. Some folks are just too kind-hearted to be set loose without a leash. You're just going to have to tell Trinity right out to stay clear of your sister, for your sister ain't got a lick of sense about weasels."

IT WAS SNOWING in the moonlight as the night-riders passed the deserted Olsen homestead by the waterhole. One of them pointed at the frozen pond and called out, "Old Kilty beat us to yonder chore. But if you ask me he done a half-ass job. Fence is down about the water but a lot of wire still stands strung and nobody's burned the soddy yet."

The leader said, "Mebbe later, on our way back. How many times have I told you boys how me and the Gray Ghost done it in the Shenandoah? You don't burn going in. You burns coming out. Wouldn't we look just fine riding down this wagon trace towards town outlined by fire on the skyline?"

Another rider asked, "Ain't your Colonel Mosby the gent as started that Ku Klux back east after

259

the war? I'll bet that's where you got this notion about our masks, huh?"

The leader said, "Nope. Folks was wearing masks long afore the Gray Ghost started scaring Niggers and Yankees with those get-ups the Kluxers are said to wear Old Mosby was a damn good Confederate raider, but to tell the truth, a mite dramatic, like that Yankee, Custer. I ain't out to scare no infernal nesters. I mean to wipe the bastards out until it comes to the minds of those left that Nebraska-by-God is cow country!"

The one who'd suggested torching the Olsen spread said, "It's hard as hell to see in this snowstorm, but the Barrow place is next down the road. Kilty started another job he didn't finish there. Doc says he don't know how, but the Barrow kid looks like he's going to make it. Got a nice-looking redhead living with him. Alone. Just the two of 'em, alone out here in the night. Him flat on his back and the gal good-looking."

Another rider hooted and said, "Hot damn. I like redheads no matter what color hair they has. I'll bet she's a virgin, too."

"Shoot, old son, the only virgin you'll find on any infernal farm is a gal who can run faster than her father and brothers. Them trashy sod busters is lower than Red River Breeds."

"I know, but let's screw the redhead anyway. She's sort of pretty."

There was a chorus of agreement and the leader snapped, "Keep it down to a roar, God damn it! We're on a public highway and you can't see a hundred infernal yards betwixt this snow and the light."

"Hell, if we come on another rider we can just shoot the son of a bitch."

"We can, but we won't, 'lessen we have to. We got to do this thing more scientific, boys. We got the weather on our side tonight and Lord knows when we'll get another crack at folks so close to town."

"Yeah, you can see the Barrow spread's chimney smoke from the Sheriff's window. But Old Benedict Arnold MacLeod won't see the smoke tonight, so we can make it a good smoke, after we take care of the two of 'em."

The leader said, "First things first. The Barrow boy is stove in and ain't got his claim half proved. Them pesky Rooshin's just beyond 'em is our main target, for they've fenced and planted."

"Hot damn, the Rooshin gal is pretty, too! After we get's done at the Rooshin place, we can get the Barrows coming back, right?"

The leader considered before he said, "May as well. Ain't likely to get a better night afore the snow's too deep for nightriding. By spring thaw, that pesky Joe Barrow's likely to have his strength back. He's got more sand in his craw than most nesters and I wouldn't want none of you boys getting bruised."

The others laughed and one said, "Only thing as figures to get bruised is that redhead's ass, time we get through gang-screwing her! Lord of Mercy, getting both the Rooshin blonde and that sassy redhead in one night is a thought to give a man a real hard-on, ain't it?"

The leader swore softly to himself as he rode, eyes squinted against the snow. He knew some of his followers were serious about this business, but you always had a few assholes in any outfit and it wouldn't hurt to let 'em rape the nester gals. It was a reward for his men and punishment for the sod busters that everyone in the county could grasp with little effort. He knew the nester men might get their backs up and talk tough about the killings and burnings, but their women folk would nag at them about the rapes. It'd prey on the minds of every nester with a pretty young daughter to think about. The whole point of terrorism was to get folks terrified.

The full moon was high and it was getting easier to see as the snow seemed to be letting up. The leader reined in and raised his free hand to halt the column, squinting ahead through the slits in his feedsack mask. One of his followers asked what was up and he said, "I can see the light of the Barrow place, ahead."

"So what? We knowed it was there."

"We're half a mile from it and that's mighty good seeing in a snowstorm. Snow's letting up."

The other rider looked up at the moon and opined, "You're right. Clouds over the moon ball have started to clear and I can even see me some stars. We'll have us a regular hunter's moon tonight."

"Don't want a hunter's moon. That fucking MacLeod hunts too good without help. We're going to have to call her off, boys. We'll ride together back to the crossroads north of the waterhole afore we splits up and heads for home."

There was a collective mutter of protest. A self-appointed spokesman said, "God damn it, we've come from far and near to ride with you this night and now you're telling us you want to call her off?"

The leader said, "Don't want to. Have to. Look at the prairie all about us, you idjets. There's a fresh inch of snow over ever'thing, just right for tracking. I figured the falling snow would cover for us on our retreat. But as you see, the snow is stopping. So that means no snow over our hoof-marks. Just neat dotted lines leading to each and ever'body's home spread, should anyone care to follow them."

The protester shot a worried glance at the snow-covered wagon trace they were on and said, "He's right, God damn it. We dasn't do a thing that'd make Ewen MacLeod and his deputies question hoofprint one, for we're leaving 'em clear as hell." Then he asked their chosen leader, "When do you figure it'll be safe to try again, Pard?"

The leader shrugged and said, "When the ground is clear and firm, of course. It pains like hell to say it, but I reckon nightriding season is over for this year."

NAPOLEON NEVER TRIED to march an army across the Nebraska prairie in the winter time, but if he had the results would have been much the same, for as Yasha said, the climate of the Great Plains and the Russian Steppes are much the same. Having Russian neighbors that first awful winter was a Godsend to Joe and Jessie Barrow. Even if Joe had been up to snuff they'd have had a hard time of it. The derisive western term of "greenhorn" didn't just apply to city slickers from back east, for many a farm-bred newcomer had to learn, the hard way, that the old rules didn't apply out here.

The Ivanovs were life-savers as well as friendly neighbors. Nadja showed Jessie some tricks to keep the soddy warm and suggested others Jessie said she'd have to study on. Yasha took the two Morgans over to his spread to share the warmth of his sod stable with his own team. Fortunately

Jessie kept no chickens yet, so she didn't have to let them run about inside the house like Nadja did, pecking at food scraps and stinking up the place. Nadja showed her that many layers of thin cloth kept a body warmer than one layer of heavier wool, so she put extra sheets between the quilts on the beds. When she told Joe what Nadja said about the notion of the two of 'em sharing the same bed he said it sounded trashy.

Jessie said, "Nadja and Yasha wear all their clothes in bed together, Joe. I didn't think it was fitting to ask, but I don't think they do wicked things in bed together. It's jest to keep warm when the wolf wind blows."

He said he wasn't no durned Rooshin and suggested she take back the big bed, now, as he'd be warm enough in the smaller bunk she'd been using. But Jessie said, "No, you'd best stay put. You're staying awake more, lately, but you purely thrash about some nights and you need the room. You sure cuss dirty when you're nightmaring, Joe."

"I'm sorry. What did I say that bothered you?"

"Shucks, I ain't bothered. I just wish there was something I could do to help you sleep better. You sure has silly nightmares, from the way you talk in your sleep."

He frowned and said, "I disremember most of my dreams. What did I say so silly?"

"Oh, all sorts of fool things. You keep yelling at that Kilty Dundee how you aim to fix his wagon and the other night you told poor old Gloria Palmer what a great lay she was. What's a lay, Joe?"

"Never you mind."

"That's what I figured it meant," she grinned, adding, "It's a good thing she couldn't hear you. Poor old widow woman would likely fall down in a dead faint. How come you had wicked dreams about her, Joe?"

"Hell, how can I explain a dream I disremember?"

"You wouldn't trifle with that poor old woman, would you, honey?"

"What do you think, Sis?"

She laughed and said, "It's too foolish to think about, now that I've studied that the widow woman's old enough to be our Ma. Old folks don't act wicked, do they, Joe?"

"How in thunder should I know? I ain't old yet!"

"I did hear old Gloria has a beau on the sly, last time I was in town. He's been seed slipping in and out her back door by a nosey neighbor lady. But he'd have to be old, too. It sure sounds dirty. Two old folks acting wicked together."

Joe felt an odd wave of coldness sweep through his groin as he kept his face desperately calm and asked, "Anybody mention who this other jasper is, Sis?"

She said, "No. Neighbor lady's never got a good look at him. She says it ain't the first or only time the widow's been bad. I don't understand. I like old Gloria and she don't look bad. I thought wicked women traipsed about with painted faces and big plumed hats and such. You reckon that neighbor lady's just being spiteful, Joe?"

"Mebbe. Mebbe she's jealous."

"Don't see why. She's married, hon."

"That'd do it. One thing nobody can abide is someone else having some variety to their life when they can't."

"Do Lord, you reckon old Gloria is still young enough to do . . . you know?"

He looked away and said, "Ain't my business one way or the other. If a gal's not married up with a man he has no call to say who she sees or what she does when he ain't about."

"Is that why folks get married up? So's they can have each other all to their ownselves?"

"Reckon so. It sure has other disadvantages."

Before Jessie could probe deeper into the mysteries of life she heard the distant clop of hoofbeats on the frozen ground outside and went out to see who was passing. Joe lay alone in the gloom. For while it was broad day out and the sun was dazzling on the snow, they'd followed Nadja's suggestion about newspapers tacked over the window glass. Joe's mind was gloomy, too, now that he knew Gloria had another lover. He told himself he was being foolish. He knew no gal as horny as Gloria Palmer was about to wait him out all winter unless he asked, and he hadn't. But it was funny how, as his wound slowly healed, his old pecker was starting to bother him. He didn't know that the breeding instinct is a natural response by the body of any male mammal, for Mother Nature assures the survival of the species by driving the injured male to a last chance to leave its seed in the nearest female. He only knew he was horny as hell.

The inaction enforced by winter as well as his incapabilities was what he blamed his trouble on.

It was too cramped indoors to assemble his home-made windmill head, even to see if the blades would spin on the wagon wheel hub he'd salvaged. It was too cold to work on it outdoors. There wasn't anything else to do. He couldn't even go back to sleep, God damn it, and if he jerked off, Jessie would catch him, for she'd be back any minute.

He was wrong. Wintertime on the Great Plains is a series of freezes interspersed with fine crisp days when the sun shines down from a cloudless sky through the thin dry air. This day was one of those almost balmy ones and Jessie was quite comfortable in her ankle-length skirt and the sheepskin jacket she'd thrown on before stepping outdoors to satisfy her curious young mind.

The rider approaching was Trinity Mackail. He had on a sheepskin coat and a brand new pair of mohair chaps, as white as the snow all around.

He reined in near Jessie and started to unfasten a feed sack tied to his saddle horn as he said, not looking at her, "I shot me a mess of snow geese I caught tarrying late. Early snows likely surprised them, too. Anyway, I brung you a couple."

Jessie took the sack with a delighted smile and said, "How thoughtful of you, Trinity. It's a smart ride here from your place, too."

"Aw, it ain't all that fur. I'm dressed warm."

"I can see that. I sure admire them woolly chaps, Trinity."

He smiled for the first time since she'd known him and didn't look really crazy at all as he said, "Got 'em from Chicago by mail order. You don't think they look sort of sissy?"

"No, *sissies* don't wear chaps, Trinity. Now, if you'd rode up wearing a lace dicky or a lavender frock coat, *that* would look sort of sissy."

He laughed, quite boyishly, considering, and said, "That sure would look funny, wouldn't it? You're a funning gal, Jessie Barrow, but you ain't mean with your funning, like some I could mention."

"Well, you can have fun without being mean, I reckon. You want to come in for some coffee?"

"Not hardly. Your brother don't like me."

"He never said that, Trinity."

"You mean he does like me?"

"Well, to tell the truth he never said that, neither."

"That's what I mean. I can tell when folks don't like me. I'll chore outside for you, if you like. You must have some work about, with your brother laid up and all."

Jessie started to say she couldn't think of a chore that needed doing. Then she saw the hopeful look in his oddly haunted eyes and said, "Well, I was about to fetch me some well water, if it ain't still froze."

Trinity dismounted eagerly and followed her as she walked over to the well head. Their heads were close together as they looked down into the well together. It made Jessie feel funny. She said, "Solid ice, durn it. But that's all right. I got some snow melt inside."

Trinity stared down the shaft and recited, "Little Willy, raising hell, threw baby sister down the well. Pa said, later, drawing water, gee it's hard to raise a daughter."

Jessie laughed uncertainly and said, "That's an

awful poem. Where on earth did you ever larn it?"

He shrugged and said, "There's a whole mess of poems 'bout awful Little Willy. I reckon him and me has a lot in common."

Jessie placed the game sack on the planks between them and said, "Tell me about it, Trinity."

He frowned and asked, "Tell you about what, Little Willy?"

"No, tell me about Trinity Mackail and what makes him so awful."

He looked away and said, "Aw, I'm just a dumb old cowboy. I can barely read and write, to tell the truth. Funny thing, though, I'm good with figures. I tally the cows right, and when we go to sell 'em, Brazos lets me do the talking. Believe it or not, I'm better at bargaining beef than my smarter brother."

"How do you know he's smarter, then? Some folks are better at one sort of figuring and some are best at others. Maybe your brother's just better at words and you're better at numbers. Did you ever think of that?"

He looked at her, meeting her eyes, and said, "No, as a matter of fact I never. It ain't hard to see why he's better at reading and such, though. He never got in trouble at school like me. It's hard to learn your letters when the teacher keeps stropping you. I spent more time playing hooky than I did with book larning."

"Why didn't you try to get along with the teacher, like your brother and the other kids, Trinity?"

"Hell, I mean, shucks, I *did*! Mean old teacher just kept picking on me and picking on me. They even tried to have me put away for setting the infernal schoolhouse afire one time."

"Why'd you do that, Trinity?"

He looked confused and said, "Why? 'Cause I hated that durned school, I reckon. That's the only thing as makes any sense, don't it?"

"I don't know. I wasn't there. You're the only one as can say why you done it, Trinity. Was it 'cause the teacher vexed you or some other reason?"

He looked around, as if afraid of being overheard before he leaned toward her and almost whispered, "Can I tell you a secret?"

"Of course. What is it, Trinity?"

"Aw, you'll laugh and say I'm a lunatic, most likely."

"Cross my heart I won't. Wouldn't be Christian for a gal to laugh at a boy who'd just brung her a present."

His face softened as he glanced down at her hand on the rough gunny sacking. Then the haunted look returned to his otherwise clean-cut features as he said, "I get spells."

"What sort of spells, Trinity?"

"Don't know what you call 'em. Been to a couple of doctors. They don't know, neither. One doc asked me all sorts of fool questions and banged on my head and hide with a little rubber hammer. He said I was uneducated but intelligent, whatever that meant, and that he couldn't find nothing wrong with me. So docs don't know ever'thing."

"I know. They thought Joe was fixing to die, too, but he never. What do you do when you have them spells, Trinity? Do you fall down, have a fit, or what?"

His face was a study in misery as he replied, "I don't know what I do. I can't ever remember, afterwards. It's like I been asleep. Only I don't lay down and close my eyes. I reckon I just go . . . crazy."

She moved her hand to place it on the back of his as she said, "Oh, you poor cuss. It must scare you half to death."

He stared down in wonder and his eyes filled with tears. He wiped his face with an angry gesture and said, "Aw, much you know. I'm too ornery to know fear!"

She pretended not to notice as she soothed, "Maybe a *man* could stand up to spooky spells like you has, but I know *I'd* be scared. How come you think you go crazy when you're having them? Maybe you just wander around sort of drunk-like. When Joe had the fever he acted like he was drunk and he sure talked crazy, but he didn't do anything crazy."

"I do," said Trinity bleakly, adding, "Folks tell me, afterwards. You know why the widow Palmer hates me?"

"No," Jessie lied, "I didn't know she did."

"Well, she does. I throwed a brick through her window after she'd been nice to me. I reckon that was sort of crazy, wasn't it?"

"I can't say it was nice, Trinity. But why did you do it?"

"Damn it, I just don't know! I don't even remember doing it! I did some chores for her and headed home. It was a hot day and the sun was in my eyes. I don't remember blacking out, but I must have, for the next thing I knowed my Dad was just about killing me and the widow woman said I done it, too. I was sorry as anything, but what could I do or say to make up for it? I've just sort of avoided her, ever since, like she avoids me."

"What about the time they say you set a cat on fire?"

He looked miserable and said, "I done it. It was a nice cat, too. It used to rub agin my leg and purr, for I gets along with brutes, when I'm my own self."

"Do you remember setting the cat on fire?"

"Of course not. Who'd do a thing like that if he knew what he was doing?"

"Well, what about the fights you got into with my brother, Joe?"

He looked sheepish and said, "Guilty, your Honor. I remember me and old Spike hazing that Rooshin feller. We didn't mean to really hurt him. Just trying to run him out of Nebraska gentle. As to wanting to fight your brother for butting in, I know how I felt about that. I felt mad as a hornet. Maybe I got a temper. You'd have one, too, if folks picked on you all the time."

She patted his hand and said, "Joe can be sort of bossy. How 'bout the time you tried to draw on him?"

"Yeah, I was thinking clear, that night at the fire. Thinking, leastways, I was too het up to say for true I was thinking clear!"

"Would you have really slapped leather, Trinity?"

"I hope so. I surely tried to get him to! I meant it, too, even if he is your brother and I'm sort of sorry, now. He was making fun of me and you said he acts sort of bossy and sure of hisself."

"Tell me one thing true, Trinity Mackail. Did you mean to kill him?"

He met her eyes and nodded, saying, "I did. My mind was filt with pure hate. I didn't draw on him 'cause I was waiting for him to draw on me. But if he'd fit me, I'd have tried to kill him."

"Why couldn't you draw first? Is there some rule you menfolk have that I just can't grasp with my she-male mind?"

Trinity looked away and said, "I ain't sure I could gun a man cold. I've never done it, yet. I've challenged more'n one for rawhiding me, but if they won't draw, I can't seem to do it, neither. I just can't get up the sand in my craw to kill cold. I could likely kill in a serious fight I knew was live or die. But I'm missing what it takes to be a real gun slick. I reckon that's another weakness I has to larn to live with."

Jessie said, "That ain't no weakness, you big fool, that's a kind heart. What's wrong with you men? Why jaw on about how tough and ornery you all are? Don't you know there ain't a gal on Earth who wouldn't pass up every badman in the territory for one shy boy who'd likely make a kindly father to her childer?"

"A man's supposed to act like a man. He ain't supposed to let folks bully him. He ain't supposed to let folks call him a lunatic, even if he is one."

"I don't think you're a lunatic, Trinity Mackail. I think you're a nice boy, or, have it your own way, a nice man."

"Even when I set cats on fire?"

"Well, just don't never do that around me and we'll get along better. You ain't been doing that lately, has you?"

He shook his head and she said, "There you go. Maybe you've outgrowed your spells. When's the last time you had one?"

He thought and said, "Not for years, come to think on it. I mean, I'm still sort of ornery, but, praise the Lord, I generally know what I'm doing when I knock somebody down for looking at me mean."

"I sure wish you'd stop doing that, Trinity. How are you to ever make any friends if you go about acting so surly all the time?"

He shrugged and said, "I don't know how to make friends. I've never had much practice."

She dimpled and said, "It ain't hard. You just come by all sulky-faced with presents and after a time folks notice you ain't biting them on the leg, despite your growling. Why don't you come in the house and try making friends with Joe?"

"Another time, mebbe. I got to study some on this. Are you saying, uh, that we could be friends, Jessie Barrow?"

She said, "We are, ain't we?"

Trinity looked down at her for a long sober moment. Then he swallowed hard and said, "I reckon it beats fighting with you."

"Wouldn't be fair to fight with me, Trinity. I'm only a girl."

He laughed, looking surprisingly handsome all of a sudden. Then he said, "All right, from now on you and me are friends, even if you are a sod buster and I'm sort of insane. You tell me if anybody pesters you and I'll just lay them low for you, hear?"

"Don't you have any other ways to show a gal you like her, Trinity?"

He said, "Nope. Didn't know there was any."

JOE'S PROTRACTED RECOVERY was a lot like the Nebraska winter. They'd get a spell of dry chinook winds that evaporated the snow in patches to leave the prairie looking like the hide of a pinto pony all the way to the horizon and it'd be warm enough outside to chore dressed light. Then they'd get a howling blizzard lasting three days or more and Jessie praised him more than once for locating the door south at right angles to the wind. The snow didn't pile up much on the wind-swept flatness all about, but it duned from roof to the ground in the lee of their soddy and they'd have been in a fix if it had duned over the doorway. Joe allowed Jessie's advice on small north windows had been a good one when the wind would shift another way and send the wolf wind south across the snow. The wolf wind was the worst. It carried no snow in its teeth, but the teeth bit deep and drained the

279

warmth out of everything it touched. The sky would be a brilliant blue so deep you could see the brighter planets like Venus in broad daylight. When you breathed outside your breath formed snow flakes on its way to the ground. You could see your breath indoors no matter how hot they kept the stove, and that wasn't always easy. But just as you figured the wolf wind had you, the weather would change and it would either snow or warm up some.

Joe's infection acted the same way. He'd wake up all bright-eyed and horny, hardly noticing the bandages itching under his night shirt and wondering if Gloria would let him in if he managed somehow to get to town through the drifts without a horse. The first couple of times he said he was going to town Jessie argued with him. He soon learned not to really plan any desperate moves, for a few hours later he'd be weak as a kitten or out of his head again with a raging fever.

Nadja Ivanov came over as often as the weather would let her. Her coffee was getting better and a hundred years or so back they'd have likely burned her as a witch in the old country, for she was a tolerable folk doctor. She said few of the herbs and simples growing in these parts reminded her of the medicine plants back home, except for the tumbleweeds she said were like the ones on the Russian steppes. But she doctored him with licorice root when his kidneys backed up on him and refused to flush more poison out of him. He had no idea how she knew he hadn't peed for a few days, for he'd surely never told either gal a thing like that. But the licorice root worked just after she left, praise the Lord. She brewed willow bark tea that tasted worse than bile, even with lots of sugar in it. She said it was good for fevers. When he felt better he allowed he'd rather have a fever, but when his face got flushed and his brain started boiling inside his skull the willow bark did seem to help.

One morning after a long bad night he awoke to find himself alone with Nadja. She said it was ten in the morn and that Jessie had taken her own wagon over to the deserted soddy to gather firewood. He nodded and propped himself up on one elbow, running the other hand over his stubble as he said, "I don't know how we'd have ever made it without the kindness of good neighbors, Nadja. This winter has been a pure bitch and that's a fact."

Nadja went on carefully measuring the coffee she intended to get right, this time, and said, "Winter is not over, and wait until you see spring. Spring is killing time on steppes, Joe. Most people start winter with food and fuel enough. By spring all food and firewood used up. Weather still cold and wet. Nothing to eat until harvest. Harvest far away, even with winter wheat in ground."

"You paint a cheering picture. Is that why you folks plant your grain so crazy? You figure you can't wait until fall for a harvest after a long hard winter?"

She shrugged and said, "Is impossible to live on steppes without early food in late spring. Harvest wheat, plant cabbage for fall harvest. Maybe cabbage lives through dry summer if you water lots. If cabbage fails and tax men take too much spring grain, is bad for village. Somewhere, every year, somebody starves on hungry steppes of Russia. Is hard land with hard government."

"Well, I can't say I've found Nebraska all that soft."

"*Da*, Nebraska tough place, but you got no cossacks or tsar, so maybe we all make it, working together. Yasha come over later to help chop wood Jessie bringing from other place."

He nodded, gratefully, and said, "You and Yasha have been good friends, Nadja. Best friends I can remember. Although, fair is fair and the Mackail brothers have been pretty decent, considering."

"*Da*, Trinity Mackail with Jessie right now, helping her tear boards off other roof."

Joe blanched and gasped, "Jessie rode off across the prairie with that crazy cowboy, alone?"

Nadja nodded and said, "*Da*, she says he not crazy, just lonely. What you doing, Joe? You go crazy, too?"

Joe had his legs off the bed and was trying to rise as the strong blonde came over and forced him back down, saying, "Stop it, Joe. You too weak to go anyplace. You got call to nature, I get pot, *da*?"

"Don't talk dirty, damn it! I got to get out there and make sure my kid sis is all right. I told her I didn't want that fool Trinity hanging about. But she won't listen and—"

"Listen, Joe, be still. I think I hear wagon coming back. You lie there while I look, *da*?"

He subsided slightly, and Nadja went to the door to peek out. She turned with a smile and said, "See, silly Joe? Jessie is back with load of wood and cowboy is helping her unload. What are you expecting him to do, scalp like Indian?"

"Not exactly. You sure she looks . . . alright?"

Nadja closed the door and came back to him, saying, "They are both smiling, like happy" as she sat on the edge of the bed and covered him, firmly, with the quilts. She patted his cheek and added, "You rest. I make coffee for all of us. Why you so worried about Trinity? I think he likes your sister and she likes him."

"There's likings and there's likings. They say Trinity is touched in the head."

Nadja moved over to the table and said, "I hear this, too. I don't think he is bad as they say. One day, in town, he is helping me put chicken feed on wagon. He is saying he is sorry he picked on my brother. He is saying if I am friend of Jessie is enough for him. He talks strange, even for cowboy. But we have madman in our village back home. He did not have same kind of eyes as Trinity Mackail. Maybe he was just bad boy, and now he's grown up and don't want to be bad any more, *da*?"

Jessie came in, red-cheeked and sort of dimply-looking. She said, "Oh, Lord, it's cold out there even when you're choring. But we got us enough wood to last a spell. Trinity says the cow turds under the snow don't burn good unless you leave 'em by the stove to dry, and then they smell just awful."

Joe growled, "He had no call to talk about things like that to no woman, Jessie. Where is he, now?"

Jessie removed her sheepskin and hung it up to join Nadja as she replied, "He said he was riding into town. I invited him in for coffee but he said he was trying to turn over a new leaf for me and stay outten fights."

Joe snorted in disgust and said, "I told you I wouldn't hit him if he come inside like a man instead of skulking about outside like a damn coyote."

Jessie said, "I reckon he's shy, but that ain't why he won't come in. He says he ain't scared of you, Joe. He said he'd fight you over me fair and square when you felt better. But he's afeared of causing more trouble for his brother and the other riders on the Double M."

Joe frowned and asked, "What are you talking about, girl? I ain't seen any riders from the Double M for weeks, and even if I did, they have no quarrel with me."

Jessie said, "I know. Trinity says Brazos and his other friends are in trouble with the nightriders already for not being willing to join 'em. He says he likes me and wants to be my pal, but he's afeard the nightriders will start up with him and hissen if he get's too thick with you or any other infernal sod buster. I'm sorry, Joe, that's what he called you, an infernal sod buster. I asked him what about me, and he said gals didn't count in a stand-up fight betwixt men."

Joe said, "Them nightriders failed to leave more'n one gal out of their fighting in recent memory. Mebbe they figured since a massacre wasn't a fight so they didn't have to be gallant."

Jessie looked uneasy and said, "Well, even Trinity says the nightriders are mean, and you know how surly he can get when he's not among friends."

"I noticed. He must know who the nightriders are, if they've tried to recruit him and his outfit.

Seems to me he'd be in a fair way to collecting the reward that's been put out on them by the Grange."

Nadja asked, "What is this Grange, Joe?" and he said, "Farmer's association. Ain't you and Yasha been asked to join?"

"I don't know. Yasha does all business talk for us. But I interrupt. You two talk, *nyet*?"

Joe shrugged and said, "It ain't all that important. I doubt Jessie got many straight answers from that cow boyfriend of her'n."

Jessie flushed and said, "You take that back, Joe Barrow. Trinity and me are pals, is all. He ain't my boyfriend."

"Whatever. Folks so chummy with those nightriders make me broody, even when they ain't pouting outside in woolly chaps like a love-sick schoolboy."

"Trinity ain't lovesick. He's misunderstood, and he don't know who the leader of the nightriders is. He said one of their hands rode with 'em a couple of times and then Brazos found out about it and called him to the main house for some explainings. The hand allowed he had pals in the nightriders and asked the two brothers if they wanted to join up. Brazos said no but that he'd fire him if he wasn't in the bunkhouse the next time he heard about a raid. He said the Double M raised cows, not hell, and Trinity said he agreed with his brother for once. Nightriding may be all well and good for trashy rascals with nothing to lose, but quality folks is above such ridiculous behavings in the first place and have too much to lose in the second. He said the one rider they had in the outfit dropped out after Brazos rawhided him good."

"Yeah? That sure sounds law-abiding, but I notice they never turned him over to the Sheriff!"

"Oh, Joe, you know they couldn't do that! I'll bet if you had something on Yasha or the widow Palmer you'd keep it to your ownself, wouldn't you?"

Joe lowered his eyes and said, grudgingly, "Well, I don't know anything I could turn either over to the Sheriff about. We're talking about killing folks, Jessie."

"I'll bet if Yasha kilt somebody and you knowed, and Yasha said he wouldn't do it no more, you couldn't go to the law about it."

"Mebbe you're right. It do sound sort of sneaky. But just the same it's Jake with me if Trinity steers clear of me. I wish you'd do the same."

Before the argument could get heated, Yasha himself came in, stamping his feet and rubbing his hands together. He said, "Is like old country outside. Cold like devil. I just passed Trinity Mackail on road. We all alone on prairie and he doesn't shoot me, so Nadja must be right about what he told her in town."

Jessie handed him a steaming cup as soon as he removed his outer clothing. Yasha came over and sat on the edge of Joe's bed. He said he'd seen the weathered planks Jessie and Trinity had salvaged but that he'd make firewood out of them later, when he could feel his fingers moving again.

The two girls fell to talking between themselves at the table by the stove, now that Joe had male company, for in truth they were both more interested in she subjects than he subjects and neither could follow all the details of the menfolk's politics and market prices back east.

Yasha glanced over at them and told Joe, casually, "Was in town this morning. At land office."

"Do tell? You've fenced all the land they'll allow one man to file on, ain't you?"

"*Da*, Yasha maybe get mixed up on something. Thought there was enough in bank to feed us until harvest sold."

"You mean you're running short, Yasha?"

"Got enough to feed Nadja and me. Got enough to pay land tax they say I forgot to pay last year. Don't got enough to do both."

Joe whistled silently and said, "I was wondering how you'd set up so elaborate, considering. Folks got to eat. But it smarts to lose your land."

"Land is all we got, Joe. Yasha got no trade but farmer. Yasha good farmer. But how Yasha farm when Yasha got no farm? Land office peoples say they will take claim back if we don't pay taxes."

"Won't they give you an extension? You must have paid the first year's tax, right?"

Yasha looked sheepish and said, "*Nyet*. I think money they ask for when Yasha file claim is all they want."

"Hell, Yasha, that was only the filing fee, and you got to admit it was modest, considering. The way the Homestead Act works is that you take out a sort of low-cost mortgage with Uncle Sam. You don't get a quarter section of virgin land for nothing, old son! The money up front pays for the legal papers and such. To prove your claim you're supposed to live on the land and make improvements, like houses, fences and such for a few years. The land tax is figured a mite steeper than if you already owned the land fee-simple, but you're still getting a whale of a bargain. Cost you ten times as much if you wanted to just up and buy the land right out from the Department of the Interior."

"They tell me all this at land office. I think they think Yasha stupid immigrant. They say if we don't like the way they do things in this country why don't we go back where we are coming from. They say I got ninety days for pay taxes in full or they give my land to someone more deserving. Can they do this thing, Tovarich?"

Joe grimaced and said, "I fear they can, Yasha. I'd sure like to help you out. But the last time I looked at my own bank balance it made me feel a mite green around the gills."

"Hey, Joe, you think Yasha putting bites on you? You are knowing me and Nadja better than that."

Joe looked over at the two gals jawing happy at the table. He said, "I know you both right well, Yasha. Let's find us a pencil stub and get some facts and figures down. We'll add up what you got, and subtract what you owe the land office."

"You would do this, Joe?"

"Don't see what else I can do, you crazy Rooshin. My own taxes are paid. I'll be wiped out in any case if we don't raise some damned thing or the other this coming summer. One hand washes the other, like they say, and even if I didn't like you, I'd still owe you and Nadja."

A look of sheer relief swept over the Russian's face and he happily called out to his sister in their native tongue. Nadja gasped and rose to join them, her face pale as she shouted down at Yasha in Russian and then told Joe in English, "You must not do this, Joe! Is not your fault Yasha is fool!"

From the table, Jessie called out, "What's all the fuss about?" and Joe said, "Ain't no fuss, Sis. The Ivanovs owe some back tax money and I just said we'd see if we could help 'em out. Is that Jake with you?"

Jessie said, "Of course. How come you never told me, Nadja?"

Nadja started to cry and Joe said, "Aw, mush" as Jessie rose to come over by the bed and comfort her. Joe said, "It sure is getting crowded around here. Help me over to yon table and fetch me some scrap paper, damn it. Since we're all agreed, it's time to stop talking about it and see if we can do it!"

Nadja protested, "*Nyet*, is asking too much, Joe. You two must also eat."

Joe sat up and said, "That's all right. Your chickens will just have to buckle down and lay more eggs than usual."

THE SECRETLY LUSTY Widow Palmer let her other secret lover in well after dark and when he kissed her he noticed the coolness of her embrace. He said, "Well, are we to stand here in this dark hallway all night or could we get outten this ridiculous vertical position? Let's go in your room and light the lamp. I likes to watch us in the mirror, old gal."

Gloria grimaced and said, "Just like that? What do you think I am, one of those whores you've been trifling with down by the depot?"

"Damn, who told you about that?"

"A little birdy. That's not all I've been hearing about you lately."

He tried to kiss her again and when she turned her head he said, "Don't be shy with me, honey lamb. You know I got what it takes to pleasure you betwixt my chaps. I was only funning with that Mex gal. She don't mean nothing to me."

"Does anyone? You use us all the same way, don't you?"

"Aw, hell, what's got into you tonight? What am I supposed to do, come calling with flowers, books, and candy?"

"It might help, but I doubt it. I don't want to make love to you this night, cowboy. Why don't you go down by the depot and have another helping of hot tamales? Don't you have the three dollars to spare? I'll stake you to it, if you'll just leave me be."

He cuffed her back against the wall and growled, "Watch that mouth, you old bawd! Nobody talks to *me* that way!"

Gloria put a hand to her cheek as she stared up at him with disgust and said, "Oh, my, ain't we ever brave, and we're not even wearing our mask this night."

His voice grew wary as he pasted a smile across his face and asked her, "What's that supposed to mean, old gal?"

"Thanks for the compliment. You know damned well what it means. I've got lots of little birds as tell me things. I know you've been riding with them other silly kids, all dressed up like Halloween and proving your manhood the easy way. Are you one of them as raped that homesteader's wife that time?"

"Hell, no, I'm too pretty to have to rape gals. Is that what's got you off your feed tonight, Glory? Let's just go in there and let me show you how I've saved all my jizz for the gal who's always craved it most."

"Oh, Jesus, you're so romantic I think I'm going to vomit."

"Come on, Glory. Stop funning about with me. I don't understand you at all tonight. You and me has never exchanged no vows. You agreed we was just pals, remember?"

"I remember," she sighed, with a pang of self-loathing as she added, "I was intrigued by you once. It's no secret I like good-looking young studs."

"Yeah, that's me, all right, and I'm better than any man you ever bedded with afore, too. Ain't that right?"

She smiled thinly and said, "Not hardly. But that's not the point. You're a brutal lover, but that can be fun. Your manners are God-awful, but that's to be expected. I could maybe forgive you an occasional dish of hot tamales on the side and take my chances with catching something off you. But you're a nightrider. That's where I draw the line."

"Damn, are you siding with them infernal sod busters, Glory?"

"No, I'm siding with the human race. The homesteaders have cost me money. I liked it better when the range was all open and the grass was free. If there was some way to get rid of them I'd subscribe to it, but—"

"Hell, Glory, we're *getting* rid of them. Soon as the snow melts we'll start getting rid of 'em some more."

"I ain't finished, damn it. Your way's not only nasty, it's pure foolish. There's an election coming up next year. Ewen MacLeod is running again. We all know he's a fair and decent man. But right now there are more farm folks than there is cow folks in this county. The Grange is going to run a Populist candidate agin Ewen for sheriff. You nightriding idjets are playing right into their hands. You've got the new nesters so riled that if Ewen MacLeod don't catch you afore the election he'll be outten a job."

"Hell, MacLeod ain't about to catch anybody. Besides, he's cow, like ussen!"

"He's cow, but he's honest and decent and he's going to get you. I don't want a nightrider within a county mile of me when he does. So you just put on your gunny sack and ride, cowboy. I left no light in my window for you this night and—"

He hit her again. This time hard, with his fist. Gloria's head cracked against the wall and she started to slide down it, dazed. He grabbed her by the hair and dragged her into the bedroom by it, spurs ringing as he swaggered. She moaned, "Oh, God, what's happening?" as he rolled her on the bed and started to tear her clothes off, growling low in his throat. As she groggily recovered he was saying, "What is happening is that you talks too much for your own good, old lady."

She said, "Please, don't hurt me again. If you want it that bad, for lands sake, I'll give it to you! But let me take my clothes off right. You're just ruining my dress."

He tore the last of it off and smiled down to say, "That's all right, you ain't never gonna wear it again."

Gloria's eyes widened as she stared up in the semi-darkness at her brutal visitor. The light from outside shone through the lace curtains on his face, painting it with leopard spots of light and darkness. He tore her drawers off as he unbuttoned his fly and as he forced her legs apart she gasped, "Good heavens, in chaps? If we have to do it, let's do it right, honey."

"Don't sweet talk me, old woman. I heard what you said the first time and you're right. This'll be the last time we screw."

Suiting brutal action to brutal words, he thrust his erection into her and winced with the effort, saying, "You're a mite dry tonight, Glory. Don't you like me no more?"

"Please, I'm trying to respond to you, but I'm scared. Don't be so rough and maybe—"

"The change is sort of interesting and we both likes variety. You likes this variety, you old bawd? Feels bigger when you ain't gushing for a nice innocent boy's hot dick, don't it?"

She laughed, uncertainly, as one part of her mind told her she was being raped and another wondered if one could call it rape when the man in question had come in your mouth on less frightening occasions. He started pumping as he warned, "Don't you go laughing at me. You had no call to twit me like that about some other man having a bigger dick. I reckon an old slut like you is an expert on the subject, but I've swum nekked with most of the hands in this county and if there's a jasper hung better than me I'd like you to name him for me."

In a last friendly gesture to Joe Barrow, Gloria groaned, "I was teasing you. You're the best."

"Then why'd you turn agin' me, dammit?"

"I'm scared. Scared you might get me in trouble." Then, using the last woman weapon a desperate woman has, she started moving her hips as she added, "Let's forget it, darling. Do it faster, for I think I'm coming."

He laughed and used her body selfishly to relieve his own tension and as he ejaculated in her she thought it might be all right. Then she felt his hands around her throat and as she grabbed his wrists and started fighting for her life, eyes wide with horror, he grinned evilly down at her and said, "*Now* you're moving good, old woman. You think I can't tell when a gal likes it or not? You was dry as a sock until I come in you just now. But that's all right, for you'll lie to me no more and I got you slick and wet inside. Do Jesus, that feels good. Your old twat is clamping and fluttering on me like a virgin's on her wedding night."

Gloria couldn't answer. The world was spinning around and her eyes were filled with pinwheeling stars as she fought for just one breath, Please God, and realized through her utter horror that she was having a climax of sorts as she blacked out. Her unconscious body, still fighting to survive, convulsed and voided itself as the strangler finished his brutal assault.

Joe Barrow didn't hear about Gloria's murder for two days, for the wagon trace was lightly traveled now. A wandering peddler man stopped by to warm up and give them the news as he tried to sell Jessie a new ribbon bow for her hair. Being in mixed company, the peddler didn't fill them in on the nasty details. He just said the widow woman had been found in her bed, strangled. The Sheriff's posse had been flummoxed by a fresh snow later that night that had covered the tracks of anyone riding out of town and, of course, for all anyone knew, the killer was still in town. Lots of no-account niggers and such down across the tracks, you know.

The peddler man said he was famous and that everyone in Nebraska knew him. Joe said they'd just come out and that was likely why the name meant nothing to him at first. The peddler said, "Well, you know me now. You ask about if any man in Nebraska has an unkind word to say about Moses Stocking. For I have been all over and done most everything there is to do out here. I've run cows and I've run sheep. I've planted more turnips and swapped more hosses than any white man living."

Joe said, "I believe you. You say the Sheriff has no notion at all about who murdered Miss Gloria?"

Stocking said, "He says he don't, and he's nigh as smart as me. I tried to sell him a doctored pony one time and he just laughed. Said he'd arrest me did I sell it to anybody else in the county, so I had to unload it on the Injun Agency up north. Them ribbons the young lady is admiring is the real thing, though. Pure silk, all the way from Paterson, New Jersey. Let you have 'em cheap."

"Cheap ain't low enough. We're about busted. You ever try homesteading, Mister Stocking?"

The self-styled famous Moses Stocking said, "Yep. Didn't like it much. Only thing as saved me was turnips. Got the seed off a medicine man I cured of the ague with this here patent tonic I sells on the side only to good friends. He said he was grateful but the seeds must have been bad, for only five turnips come up afore frost. One in each corner of my quarter section and the other in the middle."

Jessie looked up from the box of ribbons on the table and said, "My, how on earth did you ever manage with only five turnips, Mister Stocking?"

Moses Stocking grinned and said, "Oh I had to eat two of the smaller ones. For it was a long winter and I've a big appetite. I sold one to the Union Pacific to use as their depot in Omaha. Most folks think that big dome is made of gold, but it's really one of my turnips, painted gilt. I donated another to a boy's school on the Platte. Took the kids two years to eat out the inside and they're still living in the shell."

"Heavens, those must have been big turnips."

"I told you I got the seeds offen a medicine man. It was the big turnip as made my fortune. I blasted a hole in the side with dynamite and let my sheep eat their way in. Only way I got 'em through the winter. By the time a blue norther came down from the pole my sheep and other stock was all inside that big turnip, sheltered from the wind and eating what was left of the pulp."

Jessie said, "Aw, I bet you're just funning me" and he nodded and said, "Yeah, it's sort of a hobby of mine."

Joe asked, "What really happened to your homestead claim, Moses?" and he shrugged and said, "Texas and grasshoppers took turns eating it out from under me. I makes out better peddling notions than any gol-durned fool ever made farming out here."

Joe grimaced. Helping the Ivanovs had taken more than he'd figured and he hadn't even told Jessie what a bind they were in. He knew he wouldn't have to pay poor Gloria for the team now, but he'd sort of hoped she'd be an ace in the hole, once he was able to get about again. She'd offered more than once to stake them to credit at the general store until they were out of the red. He'd been too proud, then, to take her up on it. It was too late now to reconsider her offer. It was starting to hit him that he no longer had a safe outlet for his other needs. He wondered why that made him feel ashamed. He said, "I wish I knew who kilt old Gloria. She was a nice woman."

Moses Stocking nodded, but said, "You're the gent as had the fight with Kilty Dundee, ain't you? How's that hole he put in you coming along?"

Joe shrugged and said, "It comes and it goes. I'm getting stronger ever' day and I ought to be up to spring plowing."

Stocking said, "Don't plant corn, this fur west. Corn grows good in east Nebraska. I could tell you a tale about some corn I got stuck with one time, over in Cass County. But I don't think this young lady believes my tales. Anyway, even I couldn't get corn to grow out here on the prairie and if I can't, nobody can."

"You ever hear of winter wheat, Moses?"

"Heard some Mennonites has tried it, down Kansas way. Them furriners is mighty weird."

"Nobody's grown it around here, huh?"

"Nope. Make you a fortune if it'd work like they say. Oats and barley is about the only things I've seen ripen in one summer out here. But you know they sells for half what wheat costs on the market."

Joe said, "I sure has to grow something. I'd best drill in more barley as soon as it starts to thaw."

The peddler nodded sagely but warned, "Don't plant too soon. Make sure the winter's gone for keeps. An early chinook can fool you out here. I've seen me more than one late blizzard flatten a sprouting barley field in these parts."

He took out an Ingersoll on a gold-washed watch chain and looked hopefully at Jessie as he said, "I got to be on my way and I thanks you for the coffee and sweet smile, little lady. See anything you like?"

Jessie said, "They're all pretty, but my brother is right. We can't throw money away on play pretties."

"Ribbon bows ain't play pretties, missy. They can be pure necessities to a gal stuck in a sod house. I'll tell you what I'm going to do. I'm going to pay you for your hospitality with the ribbon bow of your choice, free gratis and don't you ever tell on me, hear?"

Jessie looked hopefully across the room and said, "Joe?"

Joe said, "We ain't asking for charity, Moses Stocking."

"Shoot, I ain't offering any, son. I reckon a man has a right to bestow a ribbon on a pretty lady in a free country. You got nothing to say about it. They's my ribbon bows and I'll do as I durned please with 'em."

Joe laughed and Jessie said, "Oh, they're all so pretty and I don't know which one I like best."

Moses Stocking said, "Let me pick, then. This pale green one goes good, but, no, this one here's the very color of your eyes. If you won't take that one, the deal is off."

Jessie rewarded him with a radiant smile as she took the gift and got up to tie it in her red hair in front of the mirror. Joe nodded at the peddler and said, "I can see why you're famous, Moses Stocking. I thank you. It ain't been easy for Jessie out here."

The older man said, "It's a hard land. I may be dropping by Kilty Dundee's spread in the next few days. He's got a wife who likes my ribbon bows, too. Is there anything I can tell him as will make it a mite easier on all the women folks, hereabouts?"

Joe said, "I've already said I'd stay clear of him if he stays clear of me. That's the best I can do. I don't aim to ride up to the sand hills after him. If he ever tries to drive through me again I aim to kill him."

"That sounds fair. I'll advise him to use another trail, next time he comes to Pittsburgh Landing. What happens if you meets him in town, Joe?"

"Don't know. Sheriff frowns on gunplay along Main Street, but I sure don't aim to belly up to the bar with him."

The peddler rose and put his wares away in his pack. Jessie led him out, the ribbon ends fluttering from her tied-up hair. As she walked him to his wagon she asked, "Is that patent tonic of your'n really any good, Mister Stocking?"

He smiled down at her and said, "Child, I saved the Union Pacific with it one time. Injuns put a bullet hole in a locomotive boiler. Things looked bad for the iron horse, 'til I poured my patent tonic in the boiler water. Naturally, it healed the punctured boiler good as new and—"

"I'd like to buy a bottle for my brother" she cut in, adding, "He's taking so long to get well and I've been so worried about him. I got some pin money saved and—"

"Hush, now," he cut in, smiling wistfully at her as he asked, "How old are you, honey?"

"Seventeen going on eighteen, why?"

"Never mind. I ain't gonna sell you any medicine, Miss Jessie. Your brother don't need anything I could give him from a bottle, even if it was real. His wound will heal if it ain't kilt him by now. His wound is the least of his worries. I tells tall stories, but I really had dreams like his, one time when the world seemed more innocent to me. I know all too well what money worries and this country's other cheerful pranks can do to a proud man's insides. You wouldn't know it to look at me, but I used to be a proud young man, Jessie Barrow."

She looked confused and said, "You ain't that old and you don't look licked, Moses Stocking."

He swallowed and said, "Thank you, child. I'd best be on my way, but afore I go, has anybody ever told you you got angels dancing in your sweet green eyes?"

"I ain't sure I know what you're talking about, sir."

"I know. None of you ever does, 'til some ornery cuss wises you up and them angels all fly away."

BOTH THE IVANOVS and Moses Stocking had warned Joe and Jessie about the treachery of winter on the Great Plains. But by the time Joe was able to stay on his feet most of the day and do some simple chores it looked like they'd seen the last of it. The first warm winds of April melted the snow into the thawing ground and the tough prairie grass had already begun to green under the last snow. Everything was soggy. The sod squished underfoot like wet sponge. All bare earth was ankle-deep mud the consistency of glue. But Joe walked over to the forty acres Yasha had planted, anyway, and, as he'd expected, the plowed field was a quagmire of bare wet mud. The water in the well was high. He knew it wouldn't stay that way, so he took his improvised windmill makings outside and began to assemble them seated on a box as Jessie took

303

advantage of the warm spell to air the house and do some dusting.

Trinity Mackail rode in, eyeing Joe warily as he reined in and sat his mud-spattered mount. Joe noticed he had mud on his fancy chaps, too. He said, "Howdy, Trinity. Ain't it a mite warm for them woolly chaps?"

Trinity said, "It was cold when I rode in. Might get cold later tonight."

"You want to light and coffee up, Trinity?"

"Mebbe, if it's all right with you. I just got deputized in town. The Sheriff said he'd get me a badge later."

"Do tell? Where does that put you with your nightriding friends?"

Trinity dismounted and said, "They ain't my friends. Especially not since they kilt Gloria Palmer. I went after one man I knowed was a nightrider, but he lit out after my brother fired him. Brazos is sore about what happened, too."

He moved closer and made sure Jessie was still inside as he whispered, "They said the skonk as kilt her did worse than kill her. You know what I mean?"

Joe grimaced and said, "I do now. It's good to see we agree on some things after all, cowboy."

Before Trinity could fill him in on more distasteful details Jessie came out. She smiled at Trinity and said to come in and set a spell. But he said, "I can't stay, Miss Jessie. Got to get back to my outfit. This sudden thaw will have the cows messed up in the head. They ain't got much sense. If they wander all about getting mired fur from home . . . well, never mind. What I really dropped by for was to jaw with Joe, here."

They both looked surprised. Trinity just looked awkward as he said, "I heard a gent in town saying he figured to salvage the fencing from the Olsen spread, as soon as the roads firmed some. They never took nothing with them when they left the county and there's lots of stuff out there in their soddy. I figured it was only fair you'd get first crack at it, Joe, you being nearest and all."

Joe smiled up at him and said, "Thanks, Trinity. You changing your mind about fences?"

Trinity said, "Not hardly. But as long as you're here, you may as well fence off your crops. Be spring roundup, soon. Young cows running all over the prairie trying to keep from being branded. Anything you plant is sure to get stomped."

Joe saw the Told-You-So look in Jessie's eyes and grudgingly said, "I take your warning neighborly, neighbor. Mebbe I'll take the buckboard up there in a day or so. The Ivanovs just brung back my Morgans and the chore will do 'em good after laying about lazy all winter."

Trinity looked at the sky and said, "I ain't sure it's over, but we've likely seen the worse of her for this year."

There was an awkward silence. Then Trinity said, "Well, I'd best get it on down the road" and Jessie said, "I'll walk with you to the wagon trace."

"Mighty muddy, ma'am."

"I'll walk you anyway."

Joe watched bemused as his kid sister strolled the few yards with the spooky cuss. She laughed at something Trinity was saying. Joe's eyes narrowed. Then he caught himself and said, "Don't be jealous, you fool. She's your sister, not your woman."

But he didn't like the way she was smiling when

she came back to join him in the dooryard. It was funny, but he'd never thought on Jessie getting married up to some infernal cuss some day. Now that he did think on it, he couldn't come up with a less likely rascal he'd choose for a brother-in-law!

She asked, "How's the windmill coming, honey?"

He said, "See for yourself. It ain't hard to see how the blades fit on the hub. What's vexing me is how I'm to keep 'em there in a smart wind. If I can pull a blade free with my bare hand, the wind'll do it easier."

"There might be some hardware you could use up north at the Olsen place. Why don't we go right now, Joe? There's nothing much to be done here and—"

"And your cowboy friend's still in sight, so he'd naturally rein in and ride along with us, huh?"

"Well . . ."

"The road's too muddy and the Ivanovs are coming over this afternoon. You know Yasha's been drinking again? Nadja told me, the other evening, she seemed a mite cut up about it."

Jessie nodded and said, "She's still ashamed they had to pester us for money. She told me she fears *we'll* be ruined. I told her we had plenty in the bank, Joe."

He snorted, and she said, "I know. I told her anyway. But she's worried."

"What about? I know he paid the land tax. I was with him when I drawed the money from the bank to give it to him that time we all rode in to town together, remember?"

Jessie said, "I pointed that out to her. She's still

scared. She says she just knows you'll never talk to her if Yasha acts up again."

He shrugged and tried to see if the haywire holding a blade to the hub of his contraption would hold. It wouldn't. Jessie said, "I think Nadja likes you, Joe."

"Well, we've been good neighbors. Why shouldn't she like me?"

"Silly, I mean she *really* likes you. I asked her if she was studying on being your woman and she got all flustered and yelled at me."

"Hell, of course she would have. What made you ask a fool question like that, Sis?"

"I just wanted to know. Be sort of nice if we was always, you know, close. If you married up with Nadja it'd work out neat, don't you reckon?"

"Shoot, next thing, you'll say you aim to marry up with Yasha!"

"No, not Yasha. I like Yasha, but not that way."

"Who, then? There ain't another farmer in these parts I can say is single."

Jessie said, "I know" and sort of flounced into the house.

Joe went on working at his windmill head. It was big and awkward standing on edge like a wagon wheel on the ground, though he knew it would look smaller than most if he ever put it up in the sky to catch the wind.

The Ivanovs came over to share dinner with them at noon. It wasn't much of a dinner. They were all running low. Even Jessie made her coffee weak, these days. So they'd et and coffeed it down before anyone was satisfied.

Yasha went out to see how his so-called wheat

was doing. Joe was too polite to say he was crazy when he came back and said it looked good. Yasha pulled out a pint bottle and offered Joe a swig. Joe said he didn't cotton to gin and the afternoon began to drag.

The two gals worked in the house together. Joe went back to his homemade windmill. Yasha proceeded to get drunk.

A million years later the two gals came out and Nadja spoke sharply to her brother in Russian. Yasha growled back at her sort of dirty in the same lingo. Joe sure wished they'd go home.

Jessie must have sensed it. She told their guests about what Trinity had told them about the Olsen spread and suggested a treasure hunt. Yasha seemed to think it was a grand notion. He volunteered to drive her up there in his wagon. She said, "Joe?" and he shrugged and said, "You all go on if you've a mind to. I got work to do and to tell the truth I ain't feeling so good."

So Yasha escorted Jessie to his wagon with mock courtesy and they drove off, laughing. Nadja found a nail keg and dragged it over to sit near Joe. He asked, "How come you didn't go with them, Nadja? Ride might cheer you some."

She said, "You said you didn't feel good. What is wrong, Joe?"

"Oh, I'm not going to roll over and die on you, girl. Matter of fact, I'm almost better. I just ain't up to poking about in old houses and they face a long, jarring wagon ride."

Nadja looked relieved and said, "*Da*, how long you think they'll be gone?"

"Gee, I don't know. Even if they poke around a

couple of hours they'll be back in time for supper.
You sure worry a lot, Nadja."

"*Pravda*, I got lots to worry for. Yasha getting
funny looks in eye again."

"I noticed the bottle. That's why I let 'em go.
There's nothing like a long cold wagon ride to
sober a gent up, and there's no way they can get
in trouble, drunk or sober. There ain't a tree to hit
or a ditch to fall in betwixt here and the Olsen
claim."

She leaned forward and said, "Joe, what if
Yasha run away again?"

"You reckon he aims to?"

"I hope not, but he is acting so worried. He is
not strong like you, Joe. When peoples are hound-
ing him for money and things don't look good
Yasha is not fighter. Yasha runs."

"You told me all that before. But who's hound-
ing him for money? We paid the taxes on your
spread, Nadja."

She looked down and said, "Is for liquor. Nadja
is so ashamed. Silly brother owes money to saloon-
keepers in town. Is so easy to get credit in this
country. In Russia, nobody will give drink to town
drunk unless he pays."

Joe whistled softly and said, "I'll have a talk with
'em. Don't you worry about 'em bothering you out
to your homestead. I'll take care of it."

She looked hopeful, but asked, "How, Good Joe?
Even if you could pay money to saloon-keeps for
what Yasha has already drunk, Yasha will just run
up more bills, *nyet*?"

"No. I'll explain that to 'em. I'll guarantee they
get paid, one day or another after I catch a crop

out here, if they'll agree not to serve him no more without our permission."

"Our permission, Joe?"

"Well, you're his sis and I'm his friend. If he needs a drink to celebrate a good reason or to doctor a cold or something we might let him have a snort. But if we gang up on him, he can't get drunk enough to matter, right?"

For some reason that made Nadja lean forward more and kiss him. But he didn't mind. Nadja kissed sort of nice.

THE DESERTED OLSEN homestead was a treasure indeed, next to the closer soddy Jessie knew. The widow Olsen had of course taken everything folks back east found valuable when she vacated the premises, but in a dead flat land where the only natural resources were earth, water, air and grass, a door hinge or an empty mason jar seemed worth their weight in gold and few people had explored the place over the winter. They were far from other homesteads and passing cow hands took little interest in such things as mason jars, save perhaps for target practice.

But if the Olsen homestead seemed worth the trip, there were other disadvantages. Yasha hadn't been sobered by the trip. In fact he'd produced another bottle from the wagon box and was about to pass out by the time they got there. Jessie left him semi-comatose in the wagon as she let herself in the house. She found a whole box of empty jars in a corner by the remains of a cheap metal bedstead and carried them out to the wagon. Yasha was sprawled asleep across the seat as the team nibbled moist sod. She shrugged and as she turned back a snowflake fell against her cheek.

Jessie shot a quizzical glance at the darkening sky as she re-entered the soddy. It was darker in here, now, and it looked like they were in for more snow. She knew it was time to be getting home, but there were so many things here they could use. Surely there was time for a few more loads?

She found some unopened boxes of matches and a writing tablet. Joe would like that. He liked to figure things on paper. He was smart.

She opened the drawer of an abandoned dry sink. It was filled with almost new cakes of soap, some candles, and a ball of twine. She wondered if she could get the whole dry sink out to the wagon without Yasha's help. She moved it with her full weight and, yes, it seemed like she could walk it out the door a few inches at a time. It just took patience. She gasped when she bumped the door open with her hip, for it was snowing hard now, and the wagon was a blur a million miles away. She moved around to the far side, took a deep breath, and put her back into dragging it across the snow-dusted grass. She got it to the tailgate and went to ask Yasha to help. He cursed her in Russian and refused to move.

Jessie cursed back, for they were alone, and went back, grim of jaw, to manhandle, or womanhandle, the dry sink up into the wagon bed. She closed and latched the tailgate, saying, "That's enough.

I'd best get that fool Rooshin home afore we both freeze solid out here."

She brushed off her hands and smoothed her hair before climbing up to drive. That's when she noticed her new ribbon bow was missing. She said, "Oh, no! It must have fallen off inside."

She headed back to the house. She hadn't heard anyone ride up, but there was a barely visible cow pony near the soddy, standing head down in the falling snow with its rump to the wind. She frowned and took a wary step closer to peek in through the window. She saw a familiar figure in white woolly chaps and Texas hat. He was holding a lit candle aloft like a torch, as if looking for something.

Jessie smiled and stepped inside, saying, "Trinity, I never heard you coming."

The cowboy turned, staring blankly at her and there was something about the way the candlelight played on his features that made Jessie uneasy. She licked her lips and said, "You likely guessed I'd come out here, huh?"

He moved between her and the door as he smiled, with no mirth, and said, "Yeah. This'll be the icing on the cake, for I owe your brother."

He put the candle on the windowsill and moved toward her, spurs ringing. Jessie took an involuntary step backward and stammered, "What's got into you, Trinity? Why are you looking at me like that?"

"Just wondering. Wondering why your brother had to mess with my woman when he had something as good as you at home. You didn't know he was loving Gloria Palmer, huh? Well, neither did I. 'Til recent."

"Trinity, you're talking awful! I thought you never went near the widow Palmer."

He laughed, evilly, and said, "I didn't in public. We made up a long time ago for the brick I throwed through her window as a boy. I got to know her real good, as a man. You want to get to know me, Jessie?"

Jessie felt the sod wall against her shoulder blades as she stammered, "Trinity, you're having a spell! Wake up, you hear?"

He reached for her, saying, "Baby, I knows exactly what I'm doing, and you're gonna like it!"

She didn't. But there was no stopping him. As he took her in his arms she tried to struggle free, but he shook her as a terrier shakes a rat and when she still kept resisting he punched her in the jaw, knocking her semiconscious. When she came to her senses she was on her back on the dirty straw and as she realized what the rough wool chaps between her bare thighs meant she gasped, "My God, you're . . . touching me!"

"Honey, I ain't touching you, I'm making love to you."

Jessie sobbed in mingled pain and horror as she felt him brutally enter her. She tried to struggle free but he had her wrists pinned over her head with the whip end in his left hand. As she arched her back he hissed, "Yeah, darlin', move that sweet body and give it to me right!"

"Trinity, I swear I'll tell my brother on you if you don't stop right this instant!"

He laughed and proceeded to pound her until he'd ejaculated in her. Then, as he laughed down at her tear-streaked face he said, "You just saved yourself what Gloria got for talking less sensible,

Jessie Barrow. I was gonna do you the same. I come here to burn this snake's nest down and figured as long as you was here you could pleasure me and burn along with it."

"Trinity, you ain't yourself tonight! I can't believe this is happening."

He thrust deeper and chortled, "Oh, it's happening, and I want you to go home and tell your brother all about it, hear? Yeah, you tell him Trinity Mackail just loved you good, and let's see what he aims to do about it!"

She started to say something and he cuffed her brutally and said, "Shut up, you trashy sod busting scum. I aims to have you again and if you don't do it right this time I'll kick the daylights outten you!"

"Please, Trinity, I don't know how you does this. You're hurting me!"

He laughed and started to pound her, grunting like an animal until he stiffened, closed his eyes, and growled, "Hot damn! How do you like both barrels, baby?"

Jessie didn't answer. She couldn't answer. She just wanted to die.

But then he stiffened, darted over to the candle and snuffed it before opening the door a crack. Jessie heard the hoofbeats, too.

He went outside and Jessie heard him ride off. The others must have, too. A voice called out, "Who's there?" and Jessie called for help before she'd had time to consider.

She tried to rise, but her legs refused to obey her. The door opened again and a man peered in, "Who's there? What's going on?"

Jessie didn't answer. But he heard her breathing. He struck a match. She saw it was Kilty Dundee and fainted.

The husky Dundee gasped as he took in the scene. He put the match to the same candle stub and knelt beside her as another hand came to the door and asked what was going on. Kilty said, "It's that little redhead from the Barrow place where we had the trouble. She's been beaten up and mebbe worse. Look at her dress."

"Yeah, right nice body, too."

"That's no way to talk, God damn it. Go to my saddle and fetch me a blanket. We got to get her warm wrapped and carry her home."

The first rider left. A second who'd stopped outside in the snowstorm had heard enough to put some of it together. He said, "Her brother's the gent you had words with, ain't he, Kilty?"

"Yep. I wonder how in thunder she got out here. Heard a pony ride off, There's nothing else out there. We're a smart ride from her homestead, too."

The other man came in with the blanket. As he was wrapping her in it, Jessie moaned and opened her eyes. She focused on the rough-hewn features of the man who'd gunned Joe and gasped. He said, "It's all right, gal. We're on your side. What happened, or, should I ask, who done it?"

She stammered, "I don't know. I was looking for things to take home. Something come at me in the dark. Mebbe it was a wolf or a bear or something."

The hand who'd brought the blanket said, "*Bear*, on the Nebraska prairie? That's a hot one!" But Dundee said, "Hush your fool face. If the little lady wants to say it was a bear, a bear is good enough for me."

Then he picked Jessie up and said, "I'll get you home. But if you don't mind some advice, I'd stick with mebbe a wolf or a stray hound tearing you up like this. I never calls a lady a liar, but as you just saw, some folks are likely to find a bear hard to swallow."

"Listen, is Yasha coming with your sister at last," said Nadja, getting up from the table and going to the door. She didn't open it just yet. It was snowing blue blazes outside now. Joe, sitting at the table, cocked his head and said, "Sounds like your wagon, Nadja, but it don't seem to be stopping."

Nadja frowned and said, "*Is* wagon. I know sound of wheel silly Yasha put on wrong." She opened the door and snow flew in around her as she called out into the blackness in her own language. Then, as the oil lamp near the table flickered she shut the door and turned to say, dubiously, "Somebody else? They drove by, very fast."

Joe shrugged and said, "Likely trying to beat the snow drifts home," in a casual tone he didn't feel. He didn't want to worry the girl. He could worry well enough himself. It was after dark and even a drunken Rooshin knew better than to stay out in a blizzard all night.

Nadja sat across from him and said, "Joe, I am frightened."

He reached across to pat her wrist as he said, "We'll give 'em another half hour. Then I'll saddle old Demon and mosey up to see what's keeping 'em."

"Joe, you can't ride yet. Better *I* go, *da*?"

"Nope. Then I'd have two gals as well as Yasha

to fret about. They could be waiting out the blizzard inside, up to Olsens. In which case they don't need neither of us. If they've broke down on the road they'll need me to help."

"You are still weak from long healings. I am strong like ox."

"I don't want to arm wrestle you just yet. But I reckon I'm better at fixing a busted wagon whatever."

Nadja lowered her lashes and blushed as he reminded her of another time they'd been alone together. Not quite as alone, as a matter of fact, for tonight they had no sleeping chaperone in the corner. Nadja was suddenly very aware of the empty bed nearby. She knew that in the old country the village gossips would already be talking about her and this handsome unmarried man she'd been visiting so often. If anyone looked in the window and saw them alone in the same room as the bed . . .

Joe noticed the blush despite the soft lamplight. He knew why, for he'd often relived that wrestling match they'd had, alone in his bed with the sound of Jessie's she-male breathing coming from the other. He knew he was likely just using Nadja to keep his mind on the right tracks when he thought dirty. But thanks to the way her pretty blonde head fit old Gloria's body in his fantasies they were a heap more natural lately. Rough as hell on his glands, but at least a man could daydream with less shame about a composite love partner he wasn't related to. He lowered his own eyes to their hands across the table, for he was suddenly sort of flushed about the neck his ownself. He could smell the natural odors of a healthy she-male in the stuffy confines of the soddy and whilst snootier folk might have wrinkled their noses, he had a countryman's nose for honest nature.

Nadja said, "Was our wagon I heard, Joe. Please don't be cross with silly Yasha, but I think he's done it again."

"Done what, run away? How could he, Nadja? He's got Jessie with him. No matter how drunk and mixed up he was, Jessie'd never let him just drive on by."

"Maybe he run away and leave Jessie? You have never seen Yasha when Yasha like that. That time the Indians come he almost leave me behind."

Joe got up and reached for his sheepskin and hat, but he said, "I'm sure you're mistaken, but I'd best ride up there and make sure."

"I come too. You got two horses, *nyet*?"

"I have, but I only got one saddle and you'll be warmer here."

Nadja rose with a determined look and insisted, "I ride bareback then. You can't go out in snow alone. You not well yet. What if you fall off?"

He laughed and said, "Right, you're strong like ox. Come along then, if you're bound and determined to freeze your nevermind."

But as Nadja was wrapping up they both heard hoofbeats and he said, "There you go. We got all het up over nothing." Then he cocked his head and said, very quietly, "Nadja, go over there by Jessie's bunk and hunker down."

She stared at him, ashen-faced, and he nodded and said, "Yeah, I make it about a dozen riders too. Do as I say."

He crossed the room and took his gunbelt down

to strap it on. He saw Nadja take the shotgun off the wall pegs and asked, "What do you think you are about to do, girl?"

"Two guns better than one, if nightriders coming."

He started to object. Then he remembered what had happened to other gals in other soddies. His mouth felt dry as flannel as he nodded and said, "All right. We'll douse that lamp. You crack yon window and I'll man the doorway. Don't go off half cocked. The Sheriff has deputies patroling, too."

He blew out the lamp, plunging them into darkness, for the wan light through the windows wouldn't have mattered much even if they hadn't been covered with paper. As he opened the door, Nadja carefully unpinned the paper and opened the sash. One part of his frightened mind noted wryly that even when she was scared she was neat.

He stared out into the swirling snow, gun drawn. They were turning in, all right. A voice called out, "Barrow, you in there?" and he answered, "I am. Who are you and what do you want?"

There was a moment's hesitation and then the mysterious rider called back, "Hold your fire, Joe Barrow. We got your sister with us. She's been hurt. I'll bring her in to you if you'll be neighborly about it."

Joe called, suspiciously, "Jessie?" and the man he couldn't see replied, "She can't answer. She's fainted again. We found her up to the Olsen place. We didn't do it, boy. You fixing to let us approach or do you want her to freeze stiff in this fool blanket of mine?"

"Bring her in. No more'n two of you until I get a handle on what's going on."

There was the sound of mutterings and dismountings and now he could see a bulky figure carrying something toward him with another man trailing him.

Kilty Dundee clomped inside, holding Jessie in his arms and said, "She ain't hurt bad. Just roughed up and fainted. Where in tarnation do I put her down? It's black as a bitch in here."

Joe struck a match, gasped as he recognized Dundee and saw at the same time how swollen Jessie's face was. The gun in his hand moved and Dundee said, "Don't be an idjet. If I'd done it would I bring her home to you?"

Joe said, "Put her on the bed there" as Nadja moved to help, leaving the shotgun propped out the window. As Kilty Dundee lowered Jessie gently to the mattress he said, "You can keep my blanket for now. She's sort of nekked under it. You folks expecting visitors?"

"Thought you was nightriders, no offense. You say you found her up to the Olsens?"

"Yep, me and the boys was riding to town when we heard a commotion. Knowing the place was supposed to be empty, we rode closer for a look-see. Found this little lady inside on the floor. Now you knows as much as we do. She sure faints a lot, but from the little she told us, somebody, or, rather, some *critter* jumped her as she was poking about out there. She allowed she didn't get a good look at . . . it."

Joe looked bleakly at Nadja and the blonde gasped, "Oh, no!" as she made the sign of the cross. Joe turned soberly to Dundee and said, "You likely heard it repeated that I said I'd never drink with you."

"That sounds reasonable."

"I ain't finished. I was wrong. You and your friends is welcome to come in and warm up whilst I scout up a bottle."

Kilty Dundee glanced at the blanket-covered figure on the bed and shook his head. He said,

"We're in a hurry to beat the drifts betwixt here and town, thanks. What I done was only natural. Mebbe some day you can buy me a drink in town. Right now don't hardly seem the time, but . . . are we even, Joe Barrow?"

Joe held out his hand and as the burly Kilty shook it he nodded and said, "We are. Fair is fair and I'll never know for sure if you killed Ma or not. But I know you just saved my sister's life and I'm obliged to you, Kilty Dundee."

"I only did what I had to, but my wife is surely going to be cheered when I tell her I shook with you. We'll be going now. I can see you all got family matters to talk over."

He started out. Then he turned and said, "Uh, Joe?"

"Yeah, Kilty?"

"The little lady said it was a *critter* who tore her dress like that. Uh, nobody will ever hear different from me and my riders, hear?"

"I thank you, Kilty. Others has told me you're a gent, but I'm a slow learner. I'll take care of the critter my ownself and we'll say no more about it."

Dundee and his sidekick left and as they rode off Joe shut the door grimly and turned to see Nadja bathing Jessie's bruised face with a wet rag.

His voice was glacial as he said, "How bad is it?"

Nadja couldn't look at him as she replied, "She has, what is word, concussion? Heart is strong. She just needs to stay warm and sleep for now."

Joe moved closer and reached for the blanket to lift it. Nadja grabbed his wrist and said, "Don't. Jessie would not wish you to see."

But he raised the blanket despite her effort to stop him. His breath froze in his chest as he saw her half-naked body inside the torn-away dress. He said, "He pulled her drawers off. I figured as much."

Nadja covered Jessie again and the unconscious girl winced at the touch and pleaded, "Please don't. I ain't that kind of gal."

Joe holstered his gun and went over to sit on the smaller bed Jessie had been using while he was recovering. He sat down and ran his fingers through his hair, trying to think. Catching up with the little bastard was no big deal, blizzard or no, but how was he to leave Jessie here like this?

Nadja came over and sat down beside him. She said, "Joe, I am so ashamed."

He shrugged and replied, "Why? You didn't do it. It's as much my fault as anyone's. What sort of a fool lets his sister ride off with a drunken furriner?"

"What will you do with Yasha when you find him, Joe?"

"Only thing a man can do, no offense. I know he was likkered up and I know all too well how tempted a man can feel sober. You remember that time we was sort of funning over at your place, Nadja?"

She lowered her lashes and said, "*Da*, I remember, Joe."

"I'm going to tell you something then. I wanted you that night. Wanted you so bad I could taste it. I'd just whipped you fair and square at arm wrestling. So you know I could have done anything else I wanted to, don't you?"

She couldn't answer. He nodded anyway and said, "What a man wants and what he does is the difference betwixt a man and a brute. If Yasha had tried fair and square, and Jessie had let him, I wouldn't have call to kill him. But you saw the way he beat her black and blue, God damn it! No man has any right to do that to no woman, even if he's married up with her."

Nadja sobbed, "Please, Joe, silly brother was too drunk to know what he was doing."

"He knew enough to drive off after, and leave her there half kilt and nekked to freeze. She'd have died for sure if them cowboys hadn't come along. Rape is bad enough. Murder calls for a hanging. I can't take him to the law without shaming my sister, so I'll have to kill him personal."

Nadja slid off the mattress to kneel before him, taking his hand in hers as she pleaded, "Listen to me, Joe. Please listen, even if you hate me."

"I don't hate you, girl. Don't really hate old Yasha all that much. We've been good friends and I'll keep that in mind when I catch up with him. I ain't out to kill him cruel. But there's some things a man just can't get out of doing."

"Listen, Joe, is maybe way out. You are angry because Yasha is shaming your sister, *nyet*?"

"Jessie's got nothing to be ashamed about. I doubt like hell it was *her* ideal!"

"*Pravda,* but that is still what makes you mad the most. I got good way for you to get even with Yasha without you having to shoot him. You listening to me, Joe? Please listen!"

He frowned and said, "I'm listening" and she blushed beet-red as she hung her head above his knees and said, softly, "If Yasha do bad things to your sister, you could get even by doing same bad things to his, *nyet*?"

"That's foolish talk, even for a furriner. I just told you I don't go along with raping women, girl."

Nadja shuddered, took a deep breath, and said, "I know. I will let you. You take me now and do bad things like Yasha do to Jessie. Just don't hurt my silly brother."

Joe touched her blonde hair lightly with his free hand and said, gently, "You sure do love your brother, don't you?"

"Is only brother I have. Can we put out light before I am taking clothes off for you?"

"You leave both the light and your clothes on, girl. You don't know what you're saying."

A tear rolled down her cheek and splashed on his other wrist as she sobbed, "I know. I am frightened. I have never been bad with man before."

"We'd best keep it that way, for now. I sure thank you for the offer, but—"

"You don't want me? Oh, how you must hate poor me for what has happened."

He said, "I don't hate you, honey. That's the whole point. I think too much of you to even think about revenging myself like you say. Even if old Jessie didn't wake up in the middle of it all and cuss me out for being a brute, I'd know I was a brute my ownself. A man don't abuse a woman to get back at anyone. It ain't natural."

"You wanted to make love to me that night at my house, *nyet*?"

"I did. That was a friendly wanting, Nadja. If I wasn't feeling all fire and ice inside right now I'd still want you friendly, for you're a right handsome woman and I admire you for other reasons."

"We turn out lamp and be friendly, *da*? Maybe, after you have way with silly Yasha's sister—"

"You ain't listening, sweetheart. What Yasha done wasn't silly. It was pure evil. I can't go after him tonight, for I mean to see that Jessie's all right afore I leave her. You'd best stay here, too. There's room for the both of you in yon big bed and she'll likely need some womanly comforting when she comes around. You don't have to worry about me trifling with you. I'll tell you straight out that I'd like to. A meaner-hearted man than me would take you up on your offer and then go ahead and do what he had to after he'd enjoyed your favors. But I ain't that sort of cuss. That's why I can't ever consider having you, now."

He rose and went over to the window to remove the shotgun from the sill and lower the sash all the way. He put the gun back on its pegs and said, "It'll be colder once the snow stops. I'd best poke up the fire."

He knelt to open the stove and shove in a chunk of scrap Trinity and Jessie had gathered at the distant spread. He grimaced as he remembered how worried he'd been about her going off alone with the cowboy everyone said was touched. It just went to show you couldn't judge a book by its cover. The last man on Earth he'd have expected to attack his sister had been the one to do it. He closed the stove with a sigh and turned to rise. Nadja was standing there with the double-barreled twelve gauge trained on him.

He shot her a defeated bitter smile and said, "I should have knowed. You was both reared by the same family."

Nadja licked her lips and said, "I will kill you if you don't promise me you won't hurt my brother."

He shrugged and said, "I've always been a man of my word, Nadja."

"Please, Joe, I don't want to kill you. I think I love you. But Yasha is my brother."

Joe looked past her at the girl in the big bed and said, "Jessie's my sister. Half sister, leastways. Wouldn't really matter if she wasn't. No man has the right to do what Yasha done to any woman."

"I am meaning it, Joe."

"I mean it, too. You still don't understand me girl. A weaker man would have lied to you when you tried to stop me the other way. It's sort of tempting to lie to you right now. I could say what you wanted to hear easy enough. I'll be damned if I know why I ain't saying it, but I ain't. There's a chance I won't catch him. If I do, I aim to pay him back. So we knows where we stand and the next move is up to you."

Nadja raised the gun and he tensed expectantly. Then she lowered the muzzle, tears streaming down her face, and said, "I can't. You know I can't."

He moved over and gently took the shotgun

from her. As he put it on its pegs he turned with a crooked smile and said, "You almost disappointed me, but you're all right, Nadja."

She came to him and wrapped her arms around him to bury her face against his chest as she sobbed, "You crazy big fool. How you know I couldn't shoot you?"

He patted her back and said, "Easy. I took the shells out afore I put it up. But it sure was an interesting experience."

She stiffened in his arms and gasped, "Oh, you trick Nadja, wicked Joe! I thought gun was loaded."

He said, "Yeah, I reckon I could have kept quiet and let you think I was braver than I am, but—"

"Don't you ever lie, Joe?"

"Not to my friends."

She looked up at him, big blue eyes filled with adoration and fear and he kissed her, gently, and said, "Lord knows I'd like to be able to lie to you, right now, for you're pretty as the first rose of summer and you fit agin me just right. We'll probably never be able to get married up now, but if it's any comfort, I have strong feelings for you, too. I sure wish this hadn't happened, Nadja. But it did, and there's nothing we can do to heal the gap your fool brother put betwixt us."

On the bed across the room, Jessie suddenly gasped in fear and then she said, "Oh, I'm home! How'd I get here?"

Joe let go of Nadja, awkwardly, and as the blonde sat down beside her he said, "Kilty Dundee and his riders brung you."

Jessie looked owlishly up at Nadja and said,

"Oh, I remember. Did Yasha get back all right?"

Joe said, "Not hardly. We heard him drive by, going sudden. If I don't find him at his place he'll be in town, for there's no train out 'til morning."

Jessie said, "He must have woke up, looked in through the window, and lit out scared, poor little cuss."

Joe frowned and said, "I'm missing something. I know you kept it in the family by telling them cowboys you was mauled by a critter, but wasn't it Yasha?"

Jessie gasped, "Of course not! Why on earth would Yasha want to hurt me?"

Nadja looked up at him with a hopeful smile and he said, tight-lipped, "Who was it, then, if it wasn't Yasha?"

Jessie lowered her eyes and said, "It was dark. Them cowboys allowed it might have been a wolf."

"I know what they allowed, damn it! Wolves don't hit folks with their fists, girl. I saw what he did to your duds. How, ah, much else did he do?"

Jessie blushed and said, "The cowboys came just in time. Please, Joe, you're getting me all mixed up. I ain't hurt. I was just sort of roughed up a mite."

"I noticed. I'm still waiting for a name, Sis."

Jessie said, "It was nobody I knowed. He acted like a total stranger."

"Could you point him out if you saw him again?"

"I don't reckon," she lied, "It was dark and it all happened so sudden."

"And then Yasha woke up and came to the window and he didn't see nothing either, eh? All right, we'll say no more about it until I catch up with him. He knows more menfolk hereabouts than either of you gals. You try to get some rest, Sis. Nadja's going to stay here tonight."

"Where are you going, Joe?"

"No place, in a damned blizzard. I can see what got into Yasha, now. He'd have never run off had not he recognized the skonk he saw with you and been afeared of him. When he gets over his gin and fright he'll either be at home, or he'll come back here and we can sort it out. I'll just bed down in my old bunk and you two gals can share that'n."

Jessie said, "Oh, I wanted to take me a bath."

"A bath, at this hour?"

"I feel sort of . . . soiled, Joe."

He looked at Nadja and the blonde said, "Is water heated in kettle on stove. I can help her."

He said, "This sure is a funny time to go for a walk, but I'll see how the horses are taking the snowfall."

He threw on his sheepskin and wool scarf, put on his hat, and went out, muttering to himself about fool she-male notions. Nadja smiled and said, "I fill wash tub and we make quick bath, *nyet*?"

Jessie said, "I can sponge off quick enough, I reckon. But . . . do you know what a gal does when she don't want to have a baby, Nadja?"

"Oh, *Bokh protif plakhoy*! He *did* go all way?"

"I was too ashamed to tell Joe. It was just awful, Nadja. I don't know how a gal could ever want a thing like that, even if she liked a boy. He shot all that terrible stuff in me and I'm all messy down there and still throbbing. I got to get clean again and you got to show me how to keep from being in trouble, for I fear I may be."

Nadja looked helpless and said, "I don't know how to do that. Was old woman in village who could stop babies. But she was wicked and I never spoke to her. You did not know man, Jessie?"

Jessie frowned and said, "Not as well as I thought I did. I dasn't tell anyone, for Joe would surely go after him."

"*Pravda.* Joe told me this already. But maybe Joe and Yasha together can, how you say, take him?"

"No, they mustn't. In the first place he has too many friends who'd avenge him."

"And in second place, Jessie?"

"I ain't sure it'd be right. He's . . . sort of sick. I ain't sure he'll have any notion what he done come morning. Wouldn't it be awful if he was just standing there, grinning friendly, when Joe slapped leather on him? They'd hang Joe for murder if that other never made a move to defend his own-self, wouldn't they?"

Nadja nodded. She was smarter than Jessie and had a pretty good idea what they were talking about now.

She didn't want Joe killed, either. So she fixed a quick bath and helped the ravaged girl clean up as well as they could manage. By the time Joe knocked discreetly on the door Jessie was bathed and back in bed in a clean nightgown.

He came in, growling, "Snow's dying and the wind's turning bitter. I got the Morgans bedded as well as possible. I don't know about you gals, but I'm sort of tired and I got an interesting day ahead of me. So I'm turning in."

He hung his things up and went over to sit on the smaller bunk to haul off his boots. Nadja blew out the light and he could hear her removing her heavy skirting. She likely aimed to sleep in her underclothes and he didn't see what business that was of his'n.

He stripped to his union suit and got under the quilts, punching the pillow up to fit better against his weary head. He felt a lot better about Yasha now, but the little Rooshin still had a lot to answer for. He knew Yasha wouldn't back his play. But if he could just point out the son of a bitch and stand clear, Joe aimed to forgive him.

The fool gals in the other bed was whispering. He couldn't hear what they were saying and he couldn't tell them to shut up. He turned his face to the wall and tried to ignore them. But it sure was crowded in here tonight. The one-room soddy was filled with the odor of soap and fresh scrubbed she-male. He knew most of what he smelled was forbidden kin. But it was hard to ignore. He hadn't had a woman since he'd been gunshot and now that old Gloria had been murdered he didn't know when he'd ever find another so willing and randy. His eyes narrowed in the dark as it suddenly came to him that men who attacked women were a rare breed anywhere. There weren't all that many men in the whole county. The son-of-a-bitch who'd tried to rape Jessie was more than likely the one who'd done old Gloria in!

Sure, it had to be! Jessie had been even luckier than he'd first thought, for if those riders hadn't come along, just in time, her attacker would have left her dead. Like Gloria! It had to be a man fairly well known in these parts. That's why he'd killed his other victim. Gloria knowed everybody. Jessie was more a stranger in the county, but sooner or later she'd spy the rascal, and he had to know that, too!

Joe got out of bed and went to the door. Nadja whispered, "What are you doing?" and he said, "Just making sure the door's barred. I think I locked up, but . . . there you go, we're snug as bugs in the rug. Go back to sleep."

He returned to his own bed. He heard the rustle of cloth and knew by the smell of her hair it was Nadja sitting down beside him on the mattress. She whispered, "Jessie is asleep again. Bath tired her and she has bruised head to rest. She will sleep a lot in next few days, I think."

"Yeah, I know. What can I do for you, Nadja?"

She was silent for a moment before she said, "Before, when you were mad at me, you said you liked me a lot."

"I told you I don't lie worth mention."

"Is true you think I'm pretty as rose?"

"Mebbe prettier. I know you smells more exciting."

"Then kiss me, Joe. I like it when you are kissing me, but every time we are kissing we seem to be having fight. I don't want to have fights with you any more, Joe."

He sat up, drew her to him, and kissed her eagerly, lowering both of them to the mattress as she responded warmly, albeit a mite shy. He moved to make room for both of them on the little bunk and as he ran his free hand over her he discovered that she wore only a thin cotton shift. He slid his hand up to cup her breast and she started breathing faster. She put a hand on his wrist and gasped, "Not wicked kissing, Joe. Not yet."

He let her slide his hand down to a proper but

still encouraging position on her ribs. He could feel her heart pounding. His was sort of loping, too. He said, "You was only funning when you said you'd go all the way, huh?"

She didn't answer for a time. Then, as he kissed her throat, she said, "I am frightened and happy at same time. I think I am in love for first time, too. I am, how you say, mixed up, dear Joe. You must think for us both. I do what you want because I love you."

He said, "Words like that sort of stick in a man's craw, honey. But I reckon we'd best go along with what *you* want."

"*Pravda*? You won't get angry again if I speak true? I always hear all men want same thing and is duty for woman to please man she loves."

"Well, this is America. It says in the constitution that you got some rights, too, even if you can't vote. A man's got a duty, too. He's supposed to please the gal he's fond of. If I follow your drift, I'm moving too swift for you, right?"

"I don't know, Joe. Part of me is saying this is wicked and that Jessie might wake up again. Other part is wanting you so close is frightening to think about. Can't you just . . . hold me for little while?"

He snuggled down and nestled her head on his shoulder, saying, "How's this?"

She sighed and said, "Heaven won't be better if I ever go there. You sure you not angry I'm afraid to go farther, tonight?"

"Now who'd get sore in heaven, honey? Just lay sort of still, though. I'd explain why, but I'm trying to be delicate."

She giggled and said, "I, too, feel wiggly. But this does not scare me so. You think, after married peoples do wicked things, they snuggle nice like this?"

"If they like each other they do. The other parts ain't as awful as you might imagine, but it's sure nice to just lay quiet like this with someone you, well, sort of admire."

He chuckled and said, "It's funny, considering, but all of a sudden I feel close to you, like we've already done the other stuff."

"I feel close and so happy, too. Maybe, when I get used to being in bed with you, I can get up nerve to be bad, but—"

"Hush," he cut in, "We've said all that, honey. You said you wanted me to think for both of us. Are you feeling trusting, Nadja?"

"Of course, Joe. I know you would not hurt me. You are so strong, but so gentle."

He said, "Well, here's what we'd best do then. I'm going to kiss you good. And then I'm sending you back over to that other bed."

"But you said I could trust you, Joe."

"I know. You can. But if we was to fall asleep like this and Jessie awoke to find us so in the morning, she'd never in this world believe this."

He kissed her, long and lingeringly and this time when he ran his hands over her she didn't resist. He started to run his hand down her flank, checked himself, and said, "I don't know as I'd believe it, neither. We'd best stop right here and now."

She sighed and said, "I know what you mean. But, are we lovers, now, or what?"

He said, "I reckon we're as loving as two folks can get, decent. We'll talk about it some more later."

She sat up, changed her mind and bent down to

kiss him again before she got up and moved away. He didn't know how she felt, but he knew he was going to have one hell of a time getting to sleep, now.

He was throbbing with excitement and as he lay there listening to the two gals in the dark he wondered why in thunder he'd acted so damned decent.

But somehow he was glad he had.

THE DRIFTED STREETS of Pittsburgh Landing were deserted at dawn as Yasha huddled on the platform of the railroad depot. The ticket office was closed and the cold had sobered him. Yasha was still frightened but the morning train would be here soon and his first blind panic was fading. He knew he ought to go home. What must his sister and the Barrows think of him? He had run away like a coward. How could he go back and face them? How could he explain? Seeing Trinity Mackail attacking Jessie had been bad enough, but the hellish scene had been seen through the flame of the candle on the window sill and in his drunken stupor it had seemed as if the big cowboy was raping her amid the flames of hell.

Now, in the cold gray light of dawn, even Yasha thought it was crazy. He'd long since realized that what he'd seen had only been a close-up candle, distorted by the dirty glass and flickering on the walls beyond. But it was too late. It was always too late when he came to his senses again after one of his blind panics.

He heard a distant train whistle. The station master hadn't come yet and he remembered Pittsburgh Landing was only a flag stop for the cross country trains. He could buy a ticket once he got aboard to anywhere, but how was he to stop the train? When people had no tickets the station master flagged the train. But Yasha had no ticket and no flag. Maybe if he waved his hat?

Across the street a door opened and Yasha shot a casual glance. He knew it was the crib of that bad Mexican woman. Maybe the station master had paid her an early visit? But it wasn't the station master coming out of the whore's crib. It was Trinity Mackail!

The man in the white mohair chaps saw him at the same time and looked around. Yasha wondered where he could run, but there was no place to run and suddenly, as the man started walking toward him, Yasha didn't feel like running any more.

The cowboy clumped up on the station platform, spurs ringing, and said, "You're out early. Ride far?"

Yasha met his eyes and said, "*Da*, all the way from Olson place, last night."

There was an odd flicker in the other man's eyes. Then he smiled and said, "I heard you drive off. See anything interesting out there, friend?"

"I am not your friend, Trinity. Maybe I am coward, but I am still man."

"My, my, ain't we feeling peppery this morning?

What do you think you saw out there, little feller?"

"You know what I am seeing. I am little fellow like you say. I am ashamed. I was going to take train out and never come back."

"Now, that's the first sensible notion I've ever heard outten you. You might have just saved your own life, Rooshin. We wouldn't want to wake the town with gunplay now would we?"

Yasha nodded and said, "*Pravda*, you can't shoot anybody with Sheriff's office just up street. I think I am going there, now, to tell Sheriff what you did to Jessie Barrow last night?"

"Do tell? I got a gal across the street as can swear I spent the night with *her*. That makes it my word agin your'n, don't it?"

"Not if Jessie says same thing, Trinity."

The other scratched the stubble on his jaw with a thumbnail and said, "Yeah, that would make it two solid citizens agin a whore and a boy some says is loco. But, like they always say, there's more'n one way to skin a cat."

The innocently raised fist shot out and caught Yasha flush on the jaw. The smaller man went down and rolled as a boot collided with his head. Yasha shook his head to clear it, but then the boot hit again with a dull thud and jingle. Yasha fell unconscious against the snow-dusted planking. His attacker looked around, saw nobody had observed the short, silent struggle, and grinned. He rolled the unconscious man off the platform, onto the tracks below. The snow between the steel rails muffled the crash of Yasha's body on the ballast. He lay with his legs and hips between the tracks with a rail under his arched spine and his head and shoulders almost under the platform. If the rail hadn't busted his back the train coming over the horizon would cut him in two. The man who'd rolled him off the platform crossed it, not looking back. He was up the street mounting his tethered pony as the train whistle wailed and he heard the desperate scream of locked steel wheels, slding on the snow-dusted rails. As he looked back, he saw the locomotive stopped, a couple of car lengths *beyond* the depot. He chuckled and rode off as doors and windows began to open all around. Nobody seemed to notice him as he rode out of town. He felt pretty pleased with himself, for he'd thought fast. Now the only witness was a gal who'd be ashamed to tell anyone but her brother, and her brother would be too proud to go to the law about it. It sure figured to be an interesting gunfight when it came, as come it must.

Sheriff MacLeod brought the news from town in person, riding with Brody and another deputy. When Joe let the sober-faced lawmen in, MacLeod spied Nadja at the table with Jessie and said, "I figured Miss Ivanov might be here when we failed to find her at her own spread."

Nadja looked up and asked, "You are looking for me? What is wrong? Is it about my brother, Yasha?"

MacLeod said, "I'm afeared it is, ma'am. I wish there was a better way to put it, but he's had an accident. A bad one."

Jessie moved over to Nadja and Joe asked, "How bad an accident, Sheriff?"

"As bad as they can get. Train run over him. He, uh, smelt like he'd been drinking, no offense, ma'am. Nobody saw it, but as near as we can fit it together, he was on the platform for some reason and lost his balance as the westbound flier came in. Engineer tried to stop when he spied him on the tracks, but . . ."

Joe took his sleeve as Nadja covered her face with her hands. He led the Sheriff outside, saying, "We'll take care of her. You're sure it was an accident, Sheriff?"

"Hell, he was just laying there, sleeping off more gin then you could shake a stick at. Give us credit for doing our homework, son. The coroner says he was alive when the train cut him smack in twain. There was nobody else anywhere near him. What makes you suspicion foul play?"

Joe looked down and said, "Don't know. He was a homesteader and they've kilt more'n one of us in this county, lately."

The Sheriff glanced at Brody and asked, "You hear tell of any nightriding lately, Deputy?"

Brody shook his head and said, "Not with snow on the ground. They ain't been all that subtle about their killings, up to now."

MacLeod said, "There you go, Mister Barrow. That Rooshin was a known drunk and the flier was moving good. I'm glad that young blonde gal was with friends when I caught up with her. I sure hate to bear news like that, but it goes with my job. You'll tell her that for me, won't you?"

"Yes, me and Jessie will take care of everything. I'll come in later to see about the burying, after I find out how she wants it. They're not regular Christians."

"So I hear tell. There's no hurry. It's cold in the undertaker's shed and you understand it'll have to be a closed casket service?"

Joe grimaced and the Sheriff said, "Long as I'm out here, mebbe you can clear something else up for me. I was talking to Kilty Dundee's foreman in town this morning."

"Me and Kilty has buried the hatchet, Sheriff."

"So I hear, and I'm mighty pleased to hear it from you personal. But they said they found your sister, Miss Jessie, out to the old Olsen place, sort of tore up. Kilty's foreman says she told them some sort of *critter* knocked her down and tore her dress."

Joe nodded and said, "Yeah, must have been a wolf, to hear her tell it."

The Sheriff turned to Brody and asked, "You notice any wolf sign lately, Deputy?" Brody shook his head and said, "Not recent. Ain't seen a wolf in these parts for some time. They sort of went with the Sioux."

Joe said, "Might have been a dog. She says it was dark."

The Sheriff raised an eyebrow and said, "I see. You, uh, aim to hunt it down, Barrow?"

"If I can cut its trail. Lots of snow last night."

"That's what I figured you say. You don't need my help in tracking it, eh?"

"No thanks, Sheriff. It's likely long gone by now. If Jessie can point it out to me, I'll get it when it comes sniffing around again."

"I follow your drift, son. But be careful lest you, uh, shoot somebody's pet, hear?"

WHOEVER SAID that April was the cruelest month had Nebraska in mind. The snow melted away and turned the prairie to a bog as the melt water looked for places to run and couldn't find any. Joe used a spell of fine weather to erect his windmill as Jessie and Nadja watched. They'd invited Nadja to move in with them, but after she'd gotten over the first shock and stood frozen-faced to watch them lower Yasha's pine box in the churchyard, Methodist or not, she'd said her brother would want her to carry on at their spread. So while she visited a lot, she spent most nights alone at home. Joe had to admit she had a point as well as gumption, for some of Yasha's creditors came out like vultures and likely would have stolen her chickens if she hadn't been there to chase 'em with a broom.

Joe climbed down from his pole tower and released the brake wire. The primitive-looking contraption spun smoother than it looked like it should, for he'd spent a long winter balancing each and every blade. As the pump started splashing water into the galvanized tank he'd set up both of them clapped their hands and Jessie, "Oh, that's wonderful. I was getting so durned tired of cranking that old bucket windlass, Joe."

He stared up thoughtfully and said, "Well, it seems to be holding up for now. Naturally, it's easy to get water when you got too much of the fool stuff. The real test will be the dry season."

As three of them stood admiring his handiwork, they heard a hail and turned to see Trinity Mackail ride in, wearing plain jeans for a change. Joe didn't notice the look on Jessie's face as he waved and said, "Howdy, Trinity. That pipe you gave us was just what we needed. Even if the fool mill breaks we can still pump by hand."

Trinity reined in and said, "I never thought I'd live to see it work. Howdy Miss Nadja, Jessie?"

Jessie licked her lips as she stared at him and said, "I see you're your old self today, Mister Mackail."

He looked puzzled and said, "Sure I'm my old self. Who else would I want to be? We've finished marking and branding, out to the Double M, and I've been meaning to drop by. Uh, there's to be a church social at the First Methodist, next week. I'm a Baptist, my ownself, but if you'd allow me to take you, Joe permitting, of course . . ."

Joe started to say it was Jake with him, but Jessie was running for the house, not looking back. Trinity stared after her in hurt wonder and muttered, "Shucks, she could have just said no."

Joe said, "She's feeling poorly, Trinity."

"Do tell? She sure looked pale, like she'd seen a ghost recent. What's ailing her, anyways?"

"Don't know. Asked her to see the doc, but she won't go. I'll find out and let you know if she wants to go to the church social, Trinity. You want to hang about a spell?' '

Trinity shook his head and said, "No thanks, I got to get into town. Sheriff says he's got my deputy badge and this is a good time to patrol the county roads. Hoofmarks stand out sharp."

"Has there been more nightriding, Trinity?"

"Not so fur, this spring. Sheriff aims to nip it in the bud by asking large bodies of riders who they is and where they's headed."

The cowboy tipped his hat to Nadja and wheeled to ride off. Joe stared after him and said, "Jessie sure acted funny, just now. You don't reckon . . . ?"

"Trinity?" Nadja cut in incredulously, adding, "Silly Joe, can't you see poor Trinity is in love with Jessie?"

"Well, he does act sort of fond of her. But he's sort of rough-cut, too."

"*Da*, like you, darling Joe. Big tough man who would not hurt fly if fly was female. Man in love does not tear girl's dress, Joe. Man in love makes nice cuddles and treats her with respect, like some peoples I know."

He smiled and said, "Yeah, let's go inside and coffee down afore I rides you home to respect hell outten you."

But Nadja said, "No, dear Joe. I drive home

alone to do afternoon chores. You come over later, maybe, if Jessie doesn't need big brother's shoulder."

"What are you aiming at, girl? What have you and Jessie been whispering about all this time?"

Nadja looked away and said, "You go, comfort her. Is family matter."

"You know what it is?"

"*Da*, but I not family, yet."

He shrugged and helped her to her own wagon, which of course had been recovered in town long ago. As she drove off he went in the house to find Jessie face down on the bed, crying.

He sat down and put a gentle hand on her shoulder, saying, "Hey, Sis?"

Not looking up, Jessie said, "I ain't your sister. Didn't Ma never tell you that?"

"Well, half sister if you want to get snooty on me. What in thunder's got into you, girl?"

She shuddered and said, "Joe, I'm going to have me a baby."

He clenched his jaw and then, knowing how upset she was, he chose his words carefully as he said, "I figured you might. It don't make no difference in the way I respects you, honey."

She rolled on her side and peered up at him through her disheveled red tresses as she said, "Joe, I got to get married up durned soon. For I'd die before I bore a bastard child!"

He said, "I know how you feel but dying seems a mite drastic. You don't know who the father is, huh?"

"No," she lied, adding, "If I did I'd hardly marry up with him! I may as well tell, it wasn't exactly a critter as tore my dress off over to the Olsen place. Not a four-legged critter, leastways."

"I sort of had that part figured out. Why didn't you tell us you'd been raped? We might have been able to do something about it. But it's been over two months, now."

"How did you think I knowed I was in a family way, you durned old boy? There's nothing to be done. Nadja don't know how and we don't know the doc that well."

She sat up and asked, soberly, "I don't reckon you'd marry up with me, would you, Joe? We've always got along just fine."

He blinked and said, "Don't talk foolish, we're blood relations."

"Would you be willing if we wasn't, Joe?"

"Mebbe, I don't know. It don't matter. You're my kid sister. Half sister, anyway. Our Pas was different but we shared the same Ma."

Jessie shook her head and said, "No we never. I used to think Ma was talking crazy, but now that I've had time to study on her words it all makes sense. For history is pure repeating, and I know just how your real ma must have felt. I know I'd do anything to git out of having *this* durned baby! She must have felt the same way."

"Jessie, you're mixed up in your thinking. I know my real father sort of jumped the gun with Ma afore he marched off to get kilt in the war. But Ma still had me. Then she married your Pa and had you."

"That ain't what happened, Joe. Ma Barrow wasn't your real Ma. Your father was tempted by her best friend and that's who he got in trouble.

So my ma wasn't your ma and my pa wasn't your pa and we ain't related in no way."

Joe blanched as some of the crazy things his ma, or Ma Barrow, had said to him sank in. He said, "Hold on, what sort of a fool woman would bear the shame of another for her? She did tell me, one time, about catching my real father with another woman. But that surely couldn't have made her *fond* of the gal!"

"She never done it for her friend, Joe. She done it for your real father, out of love for him and to keep him out of trouble. Your real ma was a sort of high-toned gal whose father could have made trouble for everyone if he didn't marry up with her damn sudden. Ma, I mean *my* ma, didn't want him to marry that other gal. She knew what had happened was a fling they both regretted. So, after the two young gals made up, they went off together and when your real ma had you, *our* ma brung you back as her own. She never figured your father would die in the war. After he did, she was stuck with you. But fair is fair and you got to admit she raised you like your own ma would have."

Joe sat thunderstruck as pieces of puzzle cascaded down around him to fall into place of a sudden. He asked, "Did she say who my real ma was?" and Jessie said, "No. She said she'd swore she never would and that the lady died a spell back. She said something else that was just pure awful, but you my as well hear it. She said as you got bigger it got harder and harder to treat you like a son, for you looked just like your real father and she still loved him. She said that was what made her so jealous. You know how she used to get after us about being alone? Well, that was 'cause she feared we knew we wasn't really brother and sister, and that you'd be like your real father. He seems to have been a sort of salty rascal around pretty gals."

Joe groaned aloud and said, "Jesus, I wish I'd known, afore she died I mean. I was starting to think the poor old woman was touched."

"What would you have done, Joe, make love to her like she wanted?"

"Jesus H. Christ, no! She was my mother, Jessie. Leastways, she was the only mother I'd ever known. Even if she didn't birth me, I never could have trifled with her."

Jessie said, "I know, she was sort of old, even if she was pretty. Do you think I'm pretty, Joe?"

"Huh? Well sure I think you're pretty, damn it."

"I ain't old, like Ma. I'm just the right age for you and if we was to get married up, I wouldn't have to bear a bastard."

He started to say they'd still be kin in the eyes of the law, but he knew a couple of papers from Penn State could clear that up. He said, "It still sounds mighty wild, Sis, I mean, Jessie, whatever."

She said, "I reckon I'd feel sort of awkward, at first, too. But I've always loved you and you've always loved me, sort of family. Don't you reckon we could larn to love the other way?" Her eyes filled with tears as she added, "Joe, I'm so skeered and you're the only man I has now."

He took her in his arms to comfort her and it was funny but despite the fantastic revelations of the past few minutes it didn't feel any different to hold Jessie than it ever had. She felt sweet and desirable and . . . forbidden in his arms.

She took one of his hands and moved it to her breast. He snatched it away and asked, "What in thunder are you doing, girl?"

She said, "Trying to get used to the idea of being more than a sister to you. You don't make me feel wicked when you hold me, Joe. Even after Ma told me we wasn't really kin I never felt no different. But maybe if we practiced some we'd get the hang of it."

He said, "Now just slow down and let's study on this, Jessie."

"I've been studying on it. That other man scared me. I thought I'd just die when he had his way with me. But I don't reckon it was what he did that upset me so. It was the unfriendly way he done it! Since it happened I've been wondering what it'd be like, with somebody you liked. Have you ever gone all the way with a gal, Joe?"

"Yeah, a few. I had their permission, of course."

"Mebbe if we tried it we wouldn't feel so kinful. It's still light out, but we could lock the door and if you started gentle . . ."

His body was betraying him even as he said, "Jessie, you got to give a man time to think. You can't just tell him the kid sis he's always had ain't really his sis and expect him to leap on her like a maniac."

"You wasn't shy with them other gals, was you?"

"That ain't the same. I didn't know 'em all that well and we was just doing it for fun."

"I don't remember it being fun, but I'd be willing, if you figured it would get us over being shy about marrying up."

"Jessie, I ain't sure I want to marry you, no offense. You have to let all this sink in a mite afore I say yes or no. This is all confusing as hell."

"Not to me. I got to marry up with somebody! I like you better than anyone I know. Is there anybody you like better than me?"

He scowled and said, "I ain't sure. I've been thinking more about plowing and drilling in some barley afore I make goo-goo eyes at anybody."

"Are you in love with Nadja? I think she's in love with you, but when I asked her if you was fixing to marry up with her she jest cried. You ain't studying on marrying up with Nadja, are you, Joe?"

"I told you, I'm studying on catching a crop of barley. That wheat old Yasha planted on both spreads is winter-kilt, just like I said it would be. If we don't get some cash crops growing, getting married will be the least of all our worries."

Jessie said, "I'm glad you ain't fixing to marry Nadja. She's about the only gal I'd stand aside for. You study on what I asked of you, Joe. I can see you have to get used to the idea. Took *me* a spell to sort it out, too, and I've knowed longer. Nadja says I got mebbe three months afore I starts to show I'm carrying. So you got plenty of time to make an honest woman outta me."

Nadja was unreasonable, too, when he went over to her place after supper. Jessie's surprises still had him in a state of shock, but he'd gotten used to spooning with old Nadja and while she said she just loved to cuddle with him innocent, it was having a bad effect on his nerves of late.

He told her about his notion to drill in some

barley for her as well as soon as the ground dried a mite. He said, "That field Yasha plowed last fall ought to dry out sudden, with no sod cover. I'll just run the harrow over her and drill in some seed. Don't even need to turn it over with my John Deere."

But Nadja said, "No, darling Joe. Is wheat planted in that forty. Also in forty Yasha plowed for you."

"Honey, I just come from looking at my so-called wheat and it's pure mud. You want me to bust my back along with a mess of virgin sod?"

"I wish you would, Joe. Sometimes winter wheat comes late. Seeds know better than us when winter is over. Give poor Yasha's wheat a chance, *nyet*?"

He said, "All right. I'll do her just to prove you're wrong. Did you know old Jessie's in a family way?"

"*Da*, she tell me everything."

"Do tell? She didn't say who the father is, did she?"

"No, Joe. Even if she knew, she would not tell. She doesn't want to marry such a bad man and she doesn't want you to kill him."

Nadja hesitated and as they sat together on the made-up bed Yasha used to sleep in she added, quietly, "She told me other things, about parents. Did she tell you?"

"About us really not being brother and sister? Yeah, ain't that a bitch?"

"How is this making you feel, Joe?"

"Confused as hell. It come to me, riding over here, that in the eyes of the law I might be cohabiting with an unwed she-male. A notion like that takes getting used to."

"She is very pretty girl, Joe."

He said, "I noticed. There seems to be a lot of that going around." Then he kissed her and fell back across the bed with her.

He'd gotten used to her in his arms and she'd gotten used to him fondling her breasts and allowing a little tongue between her lips, for she was mighty fond of kissing and had the hang of it, now. He waited 'til she was breathing hard before he slid his hand down, exploring her firm but voluptuous torso. This time she didn't try to stop him when he slid his hand below her navel and her belly was sort of hard and soft at the same time. He kissed her hard as his fingers felt pubic hair under the thin cotton and she stiffened in his arms. He held her firmly albeit gently and when she grasped his wrist he just kept going until he had her mons cupped in his palm and could feel the moistness of her privates through the cotton. He started stroking, gently, and she quivered like a nervous colt that had never been saddled, but he could tell she liked it.

But then she suddenly wrenched away and leaped off the bed to stand in the corner, her back to him as she started bawling, quietly.

He got up and went to her, placing a hand on each shoulder to turn her around. But she wouldn't budge and she sobbed, "Please, Joe, I am afraid."

He said, "You wasn't afraid that first night we started this stuff."

"Da, I was too crazy for you to think straight, and you were good. I didn't know, then, Jessie was having baby. I didn't know having baby was so easy."

"Come on, there's certain, ah, precautions we could take, Nadja."

"Easy for man to say. Is woman who must pay consequences like poor she."

"Come on, I won't go that fur again. We'll just kiss and cuddle like usual and I'll stop whenever you want me to."

She shook her head, not looking at him, and said, "*Nyet*, is not so easy to say no for me, either. We got to stop this, Joe. Is wrong for peoples to tease each other if they are not getting married."

He frowned and said, "Lord, when it rains it purely does pour, don't it? All of a sudden I got more damned women wanting to marry up with me than I can shake a stick at. Is that how you figured to rope me, Nadja? Let me get all het up and then hold out for a wedding ring?"

She whirled, eyes blazing, and slapped him hard as she spat, "That is filthy thing to say! You go home now, Joe. I don't want to kiss you no more. I don't ever want to kiss you no more."

He said, "You sure pack a mean punch, honey. I likely had it coming, so we'll say no more about it."

He tried to take her in his arms. She shook her blonde braids and said, "No, not after what you are saying. I just want to be alone. Is silly to cry in front of peoples and you make Nadja very cross."

He let her go and went to pick up his hat. He stopped and asked, "You coming over to dinner tomorrow? Jessie's making a pie."

She said, "Maybe. I don't know. Oh, damning

you, Joe Barrow, you got me all mixed up in heart!"

He shrugged and went to let himself out. Nadja came to the door and said, "Wait. Kiss me good night."

So he did, and she responded warmly. But when he tried to lead her back inside she shoved him away and said, "*Nyet*, go home. You are making us both crazy."

So he left. He mounted Demon and rode through the gathering gloom, muttering to himself, for the man who said he understood womenfolk had to be one boob and idjet. There was just no way to figure the critters and no matter what you expected one to do they always did something else.

He was still arroused and the motion of the saddle against his crotch was no help cooling off. He had to admit he'd acted the fool back there.

But how in thunder was a man supposed to start up with a blamed old virgin gal? You couldn't tell a gal you had a French letter in your wallet ahead of time, could you? Sassy gals asked right out if they could "trust you" at the last minute and you knowed they expected the feller to take precautions. Gals who knowed how to take care of themselves, like old Gloria, never asked. It wasn't delicate.

He sure missed old Gloria. They'd gone at it every way but flying and she'd never asked silly what-ifs about getting in trouble. 'Course, as old as she'd been, she likely hadn't had to worry. Gals who'd reached a certain age were like pregnant women. They didn't have to worry and could just do it like a man, any time they wanted. He'd talked to an old boy one time who'd said he always enjoyed his old woman best when she was in a family way. Other times, she'd fret and say she had a headache, worried about what might happen. But once the damage was done, she was just as rough and ready to go as he was. He said nothing beat a gal in her first few months expecting.

He suddenly realized where his thoughts were steering him and muttered, "Get thee behind me, Satan. What you're studying is just plain disgusting."

But it was a long ride home and a man couldn't help thinking about sex when he'd been shoved out the door with a hard-on by one old gal and was heading home to another who'd as much as said she was begging for it. He knew it was wrong. It had to be wrong. He'd had many a sleepless night to study on how wrong it would be, but that had been before. Jessie wasn't his kid sister no more. Jessie was a willing redhead who'd been broken in and couldn't get in trouble. Couldn't get in any more trouble than she was already in, leastways.

He got home, unsaddled, rubbed down the Morgan, and went inside the soddy. Jessie was in bed in her nightgown, reading. She looked up and asked, "What are you scowling about? You look mad as a wet hen."

He said, "That fool Rooshin gal keeps saying the wheat Yasha planted is still alive. Won't let me harrow them fields. Just thinking about plowing up new sod makes me cross as anything."

"Well don't do it, then. Plant your barley where you figured on planting it, Joe."

"I dunno. May as well do it her way. Only way

to prove a fool is to give 'em some rope. If I planted atop that dead seed she'd just say I kilt it. I reckon I'll just turn over two more forties and show her I know what I'm doing. Grounds nigh firm enough, now. I'll start come morning. Then, after I drill the seeds in I'll wire the extra acreage and we'll see what we shall see."

"Old Nadja's likely set in her ways. You been thinking about our talk this afternoon, Joe?"

He sat down and began to haul off his boots, saying, "Some. Like I said, I got to study on getting you married up. What's the matter with old Trinity Mackail? He ain't much, but Nadja says he's in love with you and he's better than nothing."

Jessie rolled out of bed and dashed over to him, hopping on his bed beside him and wrapping her arms around him to bury her head in his chest.

She sobbed, "No, Joe, not Trinity! I don't like him no more. Why can't it be you and me, like I said?"

He was uncomfortably aware of her firm breasts against him as he tried to comfort her. She said, "Let's do it, Joe. Let's do it right now. I been thinking about it all night, and I suspicion it would help us both."

He said, "You may be right" for a man only had so much strength, she was pretty willing and, what the hell, enough temptation in one night was enough.

He rolled her on her back and bent down to kiss her, putting a hand on her smaller breast. She didn't feel at all like Nadja and she kissed like a little girl. He thought about the light, decided the hell with it, and ran his hand down her flank. As he started to move it between her thighs she crossed her legs and giggled. He said, "I thought you wanted to. Make up your mind."

She relaxed and he moved his hand in position, edging the flannel up as he pet her. She giggled again and said, "You're making me feel so silly."

He stopped what he was doing and said, "That makes two of us. I know what you said, afore, and I believe you. But, no offense, you don't feel like a woman to me. You feel . . . like we're being a couple of naughty kids."

She said, "I know. I ain't at all scared, like the last time a man touched me there. But I sure expected it to be more, well, exciting."

He said, "I know what you mean. And it's ridiculous as hell. I don't know how to put it delicate, but I ain't sure I could, ah, function just now."

Jessie smiled up at him, innocently, and said, "Well, durn it, ain't at least one of us supposed to enjoy it, Joe? I'm willing enough, but for some fool reason, you still feel like my infernal brother."

He sat up and said, "I know. You're likely stuck with being my kid sister."

She sat up to join him, hugging her knees as she said, in a clinical way, "This sure beats all. Ma always worried about us being wicked together and now that we're ready to be, we don't feel right about it. How come, Joe? I've heard stories about real brothers and sisters being wicked and we ain't even cousins."

He said, "This sure is interesting and I think I got it figured out. The folks who wrote the Good Book knew brothers and sisters fooling with each other could lead to all sorts of complications, and they knew most decent brothers and sisters would feel like this in any case. So they wrote a rule agin it."

"But, Joe, if we ain't kin, it ain't incest, is it?"

"No, it's jest sinful. There ain't even the notion of forbidden fruit to tease us into acting dumb. So all we're left with is our natural feelings, and it don't feel natural to feel up a gal you growed up with. It don't matter that we shares no blood, Jessie. You've been my sister all my life. A boy larns to protect his baby sister. I feels downright, well, silly to go poking at her."

She studied him judiciously then asked, "You sure are nice looking, honey. But I'm sort of glad you don't aim to screw me after all."

"I figured you might be. All that talk was to trick me into marrying up with you, right?"

"Sort of. I figured, what the hell, I've already been ruint, and there's nobody else. But where does that leave us, Joe?"

"Well, you can see that us getting hitched would just complicate hell out of things. We'll just have to let you have that fool kid and work something else out."

She said, "I've been thinking about what folks are going to say. I reckon I can take it if you can. They don't like us much anyways, and friends like Nadja will understand. But that's not what I meant, Joe. I meant how can I go on being your baby sister, now that you know I ain't?"

He reached out to brush hair from her worried brow as he smiled fondly and said, "We'll always be kin, Jessie. Nothing anyone can do or say can change that. We growed up together as kin and we've always stood up for one another as kin. So don't you worry about it, little sister."

She swallowed and said, "I sure love you, Joe. But we got to be sort of practical about just how fur this whatever goes. Since you knows you ain't really my big brother, don't that sort of let you out of going after the man who wronged me?"

He shook his head and said, "Don't see how. Didn't I just tell you that you'll always be my kid sister through thick and thin?"

She put her head down and sobbed, "Oh, Honey Joe, I don't know whether I should feel happy about that or cry fit to bust. You're about the nicest brother a gal could ever have. Can't we just forget what happened out to the Olsen place?"

"There's some ways a man can turn the clock back, Jessie, and there's some ways he can't. Since we agreed you're to go on being my flesh and blood or whatever, it's up to me to avenge what happened to you."

"Joe, I'm willing to forget it. Why can't you?"

"I'm likely not as good a Christian. We ain't out of the woods yet by a long shot. I've got an idea about saving your reputation, but the son-of-a-bitch who wronged you will always know, if he goes on living, which don't seem likely when I figure out who he is."

Jessie started to try and think up a way to warn him without giving away Trinity. Then his last words sank in and she asked, "What do you mean you have a way out? I don't think I want to kill the baby, Joe. Not now."

He said, "You'll have it. Over in Omaha or some other big town where nobody knows you. You might say we'll just be repeating Barrow history. I'm sure I can get old Nadja to come back and say the baby is her'n."

Jessie laughed incredulously, and asked, "How on earth could you get her to do that, Joe? She ain't married up, neither!"

He said, "She sure wants to be, with me. So here's what we'll do. We'll all go off this summer on a honeymoon, with kid sis tagging along. I'll leave you both there until the baby is birthed and then I'll give it my name and we'll say no more about it."

Jessie gasped, "Oh, Joe, would you make such a sacrifice for me?"

He shrugged and said, "Have to, I reckon. Sometimes a man just has to grin and bear it."

TIME WAS MONEY. Joe Barrow didn't believe in wasting either of them and he was sort of pleased with his solution to Jessie's problem. So he didn't wait for morning. He saddled Pittypat to go wake Nadja up and ask her what she thought of his notion.

Nadja was undressed and in bed albeit not asleep when she heard the familiar clop of the Morgan's hooves outside. She got up to let Joe in, but said, "What has happened? Is something wrong? Is almost midnight, Joe!"

He said, "I've been mulling it over on the way from our spread. Omaha's too fur. The three of us can't light out until our crops are planted and fenced. I'm going to have to borrow some more from the bank to get us three counties away, but that oughtta do her and Jessie won't be showing for a few months and . . ."

"Joe dear, what are you talking about?" Nadja cut in.

Joe said, "Oh, that's right, I forgot I left you sore at me. But I got to come in anyhow. I just had a long talk with Jessie. Now I got to have another one with you."

Nadja led him over to the table by the stove, the candlestick in her hand, and he admired the view as he followed. The nightgown she had on was thin and the candlelight outlined her pretty as hell. She'd unbraided her long blonde hair and the way the light caught it she looked sort of like he'd always figured an angel must look like, although, come to study on it, he'd never thought an angel could look so desirable. Nadja placed the candle on the table between them as they sat down. Her big blue eyes were red-rimmed and he asked, "Have you been crying, honey?"

Nadja said, "Yes. I am fool, too."

He grinned sheepishly and said, "Well, I reckon we've both been acting sort of dumb." Then he proceeded to fill her in about Jessie and tell her his plan. For some reason it seemed to get her all flustered and he asked, "What's wrong now? I thought you wanted to get hitched, Nadja."

That made her cry some more. So he got up and moved around to comfort her, saying, "Hell, if you want to say no, just say it. You don't have to blubber up about it."

Nadja rose to wrap her arms around him, sobbing, "Oh, darling Joe, Nadja is crying for happy! I thought you were angry and we'd never make cuddles no more. Was crying self to sleep, saying was big silly fool for sending you away angry."

He smoothed her hair as she cried against his

chest and said, "Aw, I was jest horny. I wasn't really mad. You want to lie down and spoon some more afore we start making plans? You do want to make plans, don't you?"

Nadja started to hesitate, for she was all too aware where Joe's huggings and kissings had started leading to of late and she was only wearing a thin cotton gown. Then she led him through the curtains into a room he'd never been in before. Her bedroom. She left the candle on the table outside and the only light was through the slit in the curtains as they sank down on her sheets together and he took her in his arms.

He didn't want to rile her again so he kept his hands polite as they cuddled and kissed. It hardly seemed possible, but Nadja was suddenly kissing better than ever. Just the same, he was surprised when she took one of his hands and placed it on her breast. Her nipple was turgid between his fingers and she sure felt different than old Jessie. He said, "No offense, honey, but I've felt up all the gals tonight a man can without going plumb crazy. I'd best stop. For we've got some jawing to do and a man only has so much self control."

Nadja said, softly, "Is all right, if we are getting married, *nyet*?"

He kissed her again and chuckled, "You sure got a lot to larn about men, girl. Didn't your mamma ever tell you about boys who make false promises to get engaged?"

She said, "*Da*, I mean yes. But I am trusting you. Do you know why I love you, Joe? I am loving you because you are most honest man I have ever met. You are pretty, too, but there are lots of pretty men. Woman needs man she can honor and respect. Man she feels safe with. That is why I was crying and calling poor me fool just now. I was so silly to think man like you would do anything to hurt any woman."

He kissed her but left his hand where it was, which was exciting enough as he said, "I ain't no better than most, if the truth be knowed. I acted like a skonk before. I knowed you was a nice gal and that nice gals never go all the way afore their wedding nights. But it takes time to study on taking such important steps. I reckon I abused you."

"Abused, *nyet*. Scared, *da*! I think maybe I abuse you too. But is all right, now. One thing only is still bothering me. What if *we* have baby, too?"

"We likely will. I don't mean to sleep separate after we're hitched. I got that all figured out. We'll tell Jessie's kid and our'n that they're brothers and sisters or whatever. Jessie won't exactly lose her'n, as she'll be their aunt."

"But, darling, Jessie is not really your sister."

"Sure she is. Don't go getting technical. She'll really be related by blood to the little bastard we're raising for her in any case, won't she?"

"Of course, but child is only half Jessie's. How will you feel about other half, Joe? Part that is the bad man who raped her?"

He frowned and said, "Hell, that ain't the kid's fault. It didn't have anything to say about it. I aim to kill the son of a bitch that fathered it on Jessie so mean. But I see no call to take it out on an innocent child."

She held him closer and sighed, "Oh, you are such nice man, Joe."

"Hell, I only aim to do what's right, as the Lord gives me the power to see what's right."

His hand started to wander again on its own and he added, "Speaking of what's right and fitting, I'd best sit up and have me a smoke. I know I said I'd behave, but my fool body has a mind of its own."

She laughed and said, "Mine, too. Is funny. I am still frightened, a little, but I don't think I want you to stop this time."

He moved his hand down her flank to cup her mons. She stiffened and then relaxed. He began to pet her. Then he shook his head and said, "This don't seem right, if we're getting married up. It's gonna be pure torture, but I can hold out if you can."

She murmured, "I don't know if I want to. How soon are we to be married, darling?"

"Ain't worked it all out yet. Still got the barley to plant on both spreads. Got to fix our place up for you afore you move in with us."

"Can't you and Jessie move over here? This house already bigger and got separate bedrooms."

He started to object. Then he said, "That makes sense. We can claim a quarter section sort of in the middle for Jessie, too, as soon as she's of age. Ain't too fur to work this spread and 'tother. It figures to be one hell of a lot of work, but work never hurt anybody and you keeps saying you're strong like ox. By the time we got it all plowed and planted with mebbe some apple trees out back we ought to have us some fair-sized rascals to help us with the chores and—"

"Joe, dear, before we homestead rest of Nebraska don't you think we should get married first?"

"Oh, you want to set a date? Well, Jessie can't last to the Fourth of July afore folks start talking. By then there won't be much to do but wait for the harvest. I'll have to come back from wherever to watch the property, but I'll have the two of you boarded decent and it won't be too fur for me to visit some."

She put her own hand on the back of his and began to move it between her thighs instinctively as she sighed and said, "So long we must wait? I don't think I can, darling."

She suddenly realized what she was doing and said, "Oh, Joe, you got to show me how."

"You mean . . . now?"

"I think so. I not sure. Is making me frightened and something else at same time, but, *da*, I am wanting to give myself to my man like woman should."

Joe started to roll over on her. Then he said, "We got to do this right. I don't want to scare you and I don't want to hurt you. So, if you promise not to yell at me I aim to get undressed and we'll just take it slow and easy, like we was already married."

So that's what they did. Joe took his clothes off and as she ran her hands over his bare back and crooned endearments he gently removed her gown and soothed her quivering flesh with hand and lips before he eased himself above her and she, without being asked, opened her body to his in warm welcome. She gasped and bit her lip as he deflowered her. Then as the moment of oddly sweet pain passed, she went wild in his arms. For Nadja was a simple girl of sturdy peasant stock and hadn't been burdened by the grotesque myths of Anglo-Saxon Victorian morality.

As Joe thanked the Lord for what he'd just discovered about life, Nadja laughed naturally in his arms and wrapped her strong thighs around his waist to say, "Oh, Joe, is lovely! I never dreamed it would be like this!"

He said, "Me neither" as he skillfully brought her to orgasm and then joined her there as she moaned with uninhibited earthy ecstasy. As he paused to recover his breath and wits Nadja sighed, "Was lovely. Can we do it some more, darling?"

He said, "We ain't started yet. You liked it, huh?"

"Was most wonderful thing that ever happened to me. Was virgin, so was surprised."

"Me too. There must be more'n one kind of virgin. We're going to have to drive into town and see the Justice of the Peace, come morning. If that's all right with you. We might be able to figure a church service, after the spring planting. But we'd best make an honest woman out of you in the meantime."

She moved her hips experimentally and said, "I thought you wanted to wait little while, darling. I don't mind."

"I know you don't. That's why we'd best get to it right away. It's come to me that I loves you, Nadja."

"*Now* you say that?"

"Don't get sore. I told you some words sticks in a man's craw. The point is that I got to protect you now. You'd be in a hell of a fix if you was to find yourself in Jessie's position without a husband neither. I got to marry up with you and put things in your name right off. That way, if something were to happen to me, you'd be an honest widow woman with property."

She held him closer and gasped, "Joe, don't talk so. I would die if I am losing you now."

"I would be dead, too. What we're doing here is just great, but it can't be all fun when folks really mean something to one another. I got to make sure you'll be all right if anything happens to me."

"Oh, darling, you make me frightened talking like that. What is going to happen to you, Joe?"

"Don't know. No man ever does, 'til it happens."

"Oh, no, you are not still going after man who abused Jessie?"

"Might not have to. He might come after me."

So Joe Barrow and Nadja *née* Ivanov were wed in a simple civil ceremony with his "sister" and a strange but accommodating traveling salesman as witnesses. The bride wore gingham and a new straw hat with artificial cherries on it. Jessie noticed the price tag and cut it off in time to save her new sister-in-law embarrassment. After the ceremony he bought them both ice cream sodas and as they were getting back on the buckboard Sheriff MacLeod came over and shook with all three of them. He put his hat back on and told Joe he was lucky. Then he added, soberly, "You'd best get a watch dog, son. One that barks good."

"Nightriders out again this spring, Sheriff?"

" 'Fraid so. Hit a homestead over near the county line the other night."

"Hit 'em bad?"

Lee Davis Willoughby

" 'Bout as bad as folks can get hit. They had two childer, too."

Joe thanked him for the warning and was about to drive off. The Sheriff stopped him and took something from his pocket, saying, "Here, Barrow, this may be a funny wedding present, but my wife'll bake you a proper cake when I tell her the good news. You take this for now. Might come in handy if you has to face a grand jury some day."

Joe stared down at the tiny star in his hand and asked, "Special deputy?"

MacLeod nodded and said, "I've been handing them out to men I figure I can trust not to abuse 'em. Makes it lawful if you has to use a gun sudden. It's my notion some of the settlers as has been hit might have had a better chance had not they been raised to hesitate when strangers crossed their property line, if you follow my drift."

"I do, and I thank you. It's right generous, considering you're cow."

"Joe, this has got past cow and plow. It's decent agin evil. I've deputized both the Mackail boys and, no offense, Kilty Dundee says he's willing to pack one for our side."

"Well, I'd rather have old Kilty on my side than agin me. What sort of duties goes with this badge, sir?"

"You just pack it and use it as you see fit, for now. If I needs you for a posse I'll let you know."

"I'm willing if my plow horses is. You don't have any notion who's behind this nightriding, huh?"

"No, and it's mighty confusing. You see, I know the leader at least is a right smart skonk who's had military training. You knows I rode in the war, so I knows guerrilla tactics when they're used on me. On the other hand, the raiders make no sense."

"I thought the cowboys jest wanted us offen their range, Sheriff."

"They sure do, son. But them nightriders is going about it all wrong if that's their motive. The governor and the Grange is up in arms and talking about moving in troops. You nesters is starting to outnumber us cow folks and this figures to be my last term. So the nightriders ain't helping the stock-raisers either. They've just getting both sides in trouble with all this raiding and burning."

Joe thanked him for the badge again and drove for home with Nadja looking happy and Jessie looking glum for some reason.

It took them a few days to move the Barrow stuff over to the Ivanov claim, but that part was enjoyable and the change seemed to cheer Jessie for she enjoyed jawing with Nadja while Joe worked the fields. He drilled in the barley on both homesteads and used the dead Olsens' fence posts to secure the new forties with three strands of wire. It wasn't as easy as it sounds. So by the time he was done it was the middle of May and Jessie was having morning sickness. Fortunately, Nadja knew a furrin brew that helped Jessie. She said *she* wasn't expecting yet. Joe didn't know why. It wasn't for lack of trying. They were still going at it hot and heavy every night like kids who'd just discovered it, keeping it sort of quiet with Jessie sleeping in the next room, but still enjoying it more than he'd thought old married couples was supposed to. It was funny how, with Nadja, it kept getting better and better instead of tapering off. She said it was because they were in love, and he expected that must be it, but that was funny, too.

He'd always thought folks were supposed to go crazy and act sick in the head when they was in love, but with old Nadja he just felt good. She somehow seemed to get prettier every morning when they woke up smiling at each other. At the same time she got sort of old-shoe comfortable to be with. Each time he entered her after dark it felt like his old horny devil was coming home after being away a spell.

One day a robin sassed them from the windowsill. The prairie was greening up and it looked like summer was coming in at last. But a couple of days later he woke up to see his own breath in the bedroom. When he went outside his boots stomped ground as hard as a tombstone. He went to see how the tender new spears of barley were doing and his face went wooden-indian as he saw what the late frost had done. For the blackened barley was the cash crop he was counting on, but he didn't have it, now.

He stared morosely at the nearby field of winter wheat old Yasha had drilled in a million years ago. It was as bare as ever, with the frost glistening on the sterile furrows of hard, frozen dirt. He shook his head and walked wearily back to the house as Jessie and Nadja were fixing breakfast. Jessie saw his face and asked. "What's wrong, Joe?"

He sat down with a wry smile and said, "I reckon I planted a mite early. Nothing to do but try again when it warms up again. I never heard of frost in May before, but we live and larn."

"Oh, dear, all that work for nothing?"

"It was an interesting lesson. I reckon you just can't figure on plowing before June in this infernal country."

Jessie stared down and said, "We won't be able to, uh, go away until July or so, then."

He said not to worry. He figured he'd keep his worries to himself. They'd have to sell something else if they couldn't sell barley. He couldn't think of anything they could sell but the horses. But if they could just hold out until he plowed a second time . . .

All three of them looked wordlessly at one another as they heard the sound of hoofbeats, lots of hoofbeats, on the cold hard ground outside. Joe rose with a frown and strapped his gun on before going to the door.

He relaxed when he saw Sheriff MacLeod was leading the two dozen riders. MacLeod had Kilty Dundee and Trinity Mackail with him, but that only seemed reasonable. As MacLeod dismounted, Joe invited them all in to coffee and warm. He didn't have to say it twice, for they were all half froze and the front room could just hold them, standing.

As the two gals started handing out coffee, some of it in mason jars, MacLeod said, "The night-riders took advantage of the frost last night. Hit another homestead to the west. Saw the flames from my window, for they're getting mighty bold."

"You want me to go along, huh?"

"If you would, Barrow. Couple of these other men are homesteaders, too. I don't know if we'll be able to cut their trail or not, with the ground like cement. But I've been going about it another way. I mean to ride by every spread and ask questions."

"I said I'd ride with you, Sheriff, but it do

seem anyone who saw anything would have come
forward by now."

"Depends on what they seen. What I'm doing
here is what they calls a process of eliminating. I
know where each and ever' one of these men with
me were last night. Kilty and his men were drinking with Trinity and some Double M boys in
town when I left 'em and went upstairs to see the
fire glow on the horizon. The others all have alibis
or they're married up, like you."

"Nightriders are all single men?"

"Most of 'em has to be. We know there's at
least a dozen in the band and meaning no disrespect to these ladies, I sure doubt a dozen gals
could keep it a secret if their menfolks spent that
much time away from home at night. I got her
down as one or two mean old coyotes and a mess
of ornery wild boys. I know ever' one in the county. So I already have some smart questions to ask
as we ride around it. If we can just nail one who
was in the wrong place at the wrong time, we
oughta be able to get the other names outten him."

Joe nodded and allowed the Sheriff's plan made
sense. As the others stood about warming themselves he noticed Trinity in a corner looking sort
of left out. He called to Jessie and told her,
"Trinity don't have no Arbuckle, Sis."

Jessie hesitated. Then she picked up a jar and
went to hand it to Trinity, not looking at him. He
said, "Thank you, Miss Jessie" and she just turned
her back on him to rejoin Nadja. Trinity looked
hurt but tried to shrug it off. Joe said, "She's
feeling poorly, Trinity."

Then he got his sheepskins and bundled as he
saw the others were ready to saddle up and ride

some more. He got his Winchester down and the Sheriff doffed his hat to Nadja and thanked her as she held the door open for him. Joe followed him and the others out. He didn't notice that Trinity had tarried behind.

Jessie did. As all but Trinity left the room she stared at him like something she'd found under a wet rock and said, "You'd best go after them if you don't mean to be left behind."

Trinity took his hat off and stood there twisting the brim as he said, "I got to get something straight, Jessie. I thought you and me was friends."

"We used to be mebbe. You'd best hurry. They're starting to ride off."

"I can catch up. MacLeod's a slow, methodical cuss. Won't you tell me what I done to rile you, Jessie?"

"Don't you know? No, I reckon you don't, at that. I s'pose you never went near the Olsen place that night. I likely dreamt it or something."

Trinity's expression was impossibly innocent as he replied, "Olsen place? Sure, I remember telling you we could mebbe salvage some stuff there like we done at the other. But the next time I come by you wouldn't talk to me."

"I don't want to talk to you now, and Nadja's getting froze in the doorway, so please be good enough to leave, Mister Mackail."

Trinity started to say something, then he put his hat back on and turned to head out the door, stomping his boot heels a mite like an angry, hurt kid. Jessie watched, lip curled, and Nadja was about to close the door after him when Jessie suddenly gasped and shouted, "Oh my God!"

Trinity stopped and turned with a puzzled

frown. Nadja looked confused, too, for she suspected the reason for Jessie's open dislike.

Jessie pointed at Trinity's boots and said, "Your
spurs! That's the only thing he didn't get right!
Anyone can send away for the same hat and fuzzy
white chaps. But he wore his own boots and spurs,
and *his* spurs *jingled* but *your* spurs *don't!*"

Trinity stepped back inside, puzzled, and Jessie
ran over to him and wrapped her arms around him
to sob, "Oh, my poor dear Trinity! I sees it all now,
and to think I was fooled like everyone else!"

Nadja shut the door dubiously, but stood by in
case her obviously insane sister-in-law needed
help. Trinity held her, puzzled, and said, "I'm
sure glad we're pals agin, but I wish somebody
would tell me what in thunder is going on!"

Jessie smiled up at him radiantly, and said,
"You ain't crazy, Trinity. You ain't never been
crazy and you ain't never had them spells they
even had you convinced of. It was *Brazos!* It was
always Brazos, and, oh Dear God, how he must
hate you!"

"Brazos? My twin brother? What are you talking about, Jessie? Brazos and me ain't never had
no trouble. We gets along just fine. He's a good
old boy. I'm the one who's always got in trouble."

"No, you're wrong. Listen to me. It was never
you. It was always him, double-dealing you whilst
looking like butter wouldn't melt in his mouth!
You mind that story about the time you chored for
the Widow Palmer and how you and her seemed
to be getting along just fine?"

"You mean that time I come back and throwed
a brick through her window?"

"It wasn't you, it was Brazos. He was jealous,

or maybe just crazy like ever'body thought you
was. It was him as throwed the brick and sassed
the poor woman. That's why you never remembered doing it! It wasn't you as set the schoolhouse
or that cat on fire. You *likes* critters. That's why
you wear them smaller gentle spurs. Can't you see
how he worked it on you, honey?"

Trinity started to object. Then, because he
wasn't a stupid man despite his lack of education,
his face went ashen as he said, quietly, "He never
got licked, like I did. He was always such a good
little boy. Mebbe too good to be true. What you
say sure explains a lot I've never been able to
fathom, Jessie, but why on earth would he do a
thing like that to his own brother?"

"I don't know. Mebbe to cover up a mean streak
he hides from the rest of the world. Mebbe to have
the Double M all to hisself. Mebbe 'cause he's
just plain crazy."

"Well, I surely mean to have it out with him
about that cat. But that ain't important right
now. What's important is me and you, Jessie. If
you ain't mad at me, can I come back again,
courting?"

She sobbed and lowered her eyes, saying, "It's
too late. I'm a ruint woman and no decent man
would want me, now."

"I'll be the judge of that. Who could have
ruint you? You ain't been sparking no other gents.
I've asked."

Jessie pulled away and ran in the other room.
Trinity looked at Nadja. Nadja came over to him
and said, "I understand too now."

"Well, for God's sake let *me* in on it, ma'am."

Nadja hesitated. Then she nodded and said,

"Was your bad twin. Out at Olsen place. He is raping Jessie and making her think it was you! Jessie is ashamed. She is going to have baby. Now you know all. You go now, *da*?"

Trinity steadied himself as a big gray cat got up inside his stomach, turned around a couple of times and simmered down, clawing his guts. He took a deep breath and said, "Not hardly." Then he strode into Joe and Nadja's room where Jessie lay face down on the bed, crying.

Trinity sat down beside her and put a hand on her shoulder, saying, "Hey, Jess?"

"I'm all right, damn it."

"No you ain't. Miss Nadja told me. This is taking me a little getting used to, but I see there's only one thing we can do about this mess."

"There's nothing we can do. It's too late."

"No it ain't. You're right about us being a mite short of time. So I'll ask you to forgive a hasty courting. We'll ride right into town and marry up."

"But Trinity, I'm carrying another man's child!"

"I know. Little rascal ought to look like me, since it's my nephew in the first place and its father is my identical twin in the second. We'll say it's mine and nobody will ever know the difference."

She rolled over to stare up at him in wonder as she asked, "You'd really do a thing like that for me, Trinity?"

"Hell, I'll be doing it for me, too. You know how I feels about you, Jess. To tell it true, I'd marry you if the kid was an Injun."

She sobbed and said, "I wish it was. I could mebbe live with that shame."

"You got nothing to be shamed about, Jess. What happened wasn't your fault. It was that in-

fernal brother of mine trying to spoil things for
me again. He knowed I liked you. So he went
out of his way to ruin me in your eyes. But this
time I don't aim to let him get away with it. I
loves you, Jessie Barrow, and this time his dirty
tricks ain't working."

She shuddered and said, "Oh, Trinity, he said
such awful things. He dared me to tell Joe, but I
never."

"I see. He was trying to get me kilt, or hung
for killing your brother after raping you. I'm sure
mighty disappointed about old Brazos. But we're
on to him now. So git dressed and we'll run in
and scare up the Justice of the Peace."

"What about the posse, darling? Ain't you supposed to be riding with them right now?"

"I can catch up, later. I know where they're
going. MacLeod will jaw a spell at each spread.
We'll be all right as long as I makes it back to
them by the time they get to the Double M.
They're riding in a circle."

Jessie sat up and said, "Well, if we're getting
hitched, you'd better kiss me at least once first."

Trinity took her in his arms and kissed her ten-
derly and it didn't feel at all brotherly to Jessie.
He let her go and said, "We'll practice more later.
We got to get cracking if I'm to rejoin the boys
and your brother in time."

"For heaven's sake, I can wait a day or so, darling. I ain't that fur gone."

His face was grim as he said, unconsciously repeating another concerned and thoughtful man,
"Got to marry you today. That way, if there's no
tomorrow, the baby will still have a name."

She grimaced and asked, "What do you think

your brother Brazos will say when you bring me home? I just thought of that and it sure make me feel queer."

Trinity said flatly, "He won't be there when you become the mistress of the Double M. I may be a slow thinker, but I just figured out how come that little gal saw me on my gray when the night-riders hit at her spread that time."

It was late in the afternoon when the posse rode into the dooryard of the Double M. Sheriff Mac-Leod and his men were stiff from the long, cold, and so far fruitless ride all over Robin Hood's Barn. As Brazos Mackail came out to greet them, MacLeod turned to Joe at his side and said, "At least I know where one of them is. Sure is odd how old Trinity dropped out along the trail. I thought he took his deputy badge more serious."

Joe said, "I missed him shortly after we left my place. It's a pure mystery to me, too."

Spike Long and some other hands came out to join Brazos as he called out, "What's going on, Sheriff?"

"Nightriders hit agin last night. We're making sure where ever'one else might have been. Your brother Trinity and some of these boys with me

as works for you were in town last night. Anybody
else leave your spread?"

Brazos shook his head and said, "Nope. Too
cold." He turned to Spike and asked, "Can you say
all these boys was in the bunkhouse, Spike?"

Spike nodded and said, "Sure. None of ussen
could leave without the others noticing." Then he
looked beyond the posse riders and added, "Hey,
here comes old Trinity, now, and ain't he ever
riding!"

Brazos said, "There you go, Sheriff, all us Mackail boys has alibis. But I'll saddle up and ride
along with you a spell to see what others has to
say in these parts."

Trinity loped up, reined in, and dismounted,
jaw set funny. He nodded at Joe and said, "I just
married your sister, Barrow. Any objections?"

Joe's own jaw dropped. But he said, "Not if she
was willing, Trinity. Is that where you was all
this time?"

Trinity nodded and said, "Yep. We'll have a
drink on it later." Then he turned to face his
brother.

Brazos smiled and said, "Congratulations, brother, for she's a nice looking lady. But ain't this sort
of sudden?"

"Had to be sudden. You likely knows why."

Brazos looked sincerely puzzled and went on
smiling, but this time it didn't work. Trinity said,
"Sheriff MacLeod, I know you figure it's your
duty to do most of the arresting in these parts, but
I'm your deputy and this is personal."

MacLeod frowned and said, "I'm missing something, Trinity. Just who are you talking about
arresting? These boys all has alibis."

Trinity kept his eyes on Brazos as he said, "I figured they'd all lie for one another. I was in town with the hands who ain't in on the deal."

Brazo's eyes narrowed but he kept smiling as he said, "Calling folks liars seems sort of unfriendly, Trinity. But you're my brother and I know you're subject to spells, so—"

"It's no good, Brazos. I got you figured now. You're my so-calt spells, you two-faced skonk! I don't know why you done it, but all our lives you been framing me for things I never done, and I was too dumb to see it!"

"Trinity, has you been drinking? You ain't yourself today."

"Oh, I'm myself. My real self at last, now that I know I ain't touched, and why ever'body's always been so mean to me. Are you listening to any of this, Sheriff MacLeod?"

"We're all listening, son, but I ain't sure I follow half of it. I ain't interested in family quarrels."

"You'd better be, in this one. Brazos and these others here are the nightriders you've been looking for. He's done other things of no interest to anyone but me and my new wife's brother, Joe Barrow, but the nightriding ought to be enough to hang these sons-of-bitches."

Brazos started to say something, then he slapped leather as Trinity's eyes left his for a moment. But Joe, behind Trinity, fired his Winchester as Brazos's gun cleared leather. The Morgan wasn't trained for that sort of action, so it reared and spilled Joe, rifle and all, as things got mighty confusing all around.

As he rolled to his knee and pumped another round in the chamber he saw Brazos was down with Trinity standing over him, and Spike Long throwing down on his back. Joe yelled, "Trinity, behind you!" as he saw he couldn't nail Spike without hitting anybody else. Trinity spun and crabbed sideways as Spike fired, missing. Trinity's answering bullet took Spike just under the nose and blew teeth and brains out the far side of his shattered skull.

As Joe rose, Kilty Dundee yelled, "Barrow, duck!" and shot the Double M hand behind him. As Joe hunkered warily on one knee he saw that was about the end of it. Everyone who wasn't reaching for the sky was down, for others in the posse had been active as well. Joe rose and nodded to Kilty Dundee, saying, "Thanks. That makes us more than even."

He walked over to Trinity, who was standing over his dead twin. Trinity swallowed and said, "I always liked and admired him. I always wished I could be good like him. I sure wish I'd killed him."

Joe said, "I know. But someday you'll be glad it wasn't you. Did you and Jessie really get married, Trinity?"

"Yeah, I know what you're thinking. She told me about the kid. That was Brazos's doing, too."

Joe whistled silently and suddenly felt better about gunning a man he'd hardly had time to study killing. He said, "Jesus, that sure explains a lot. But if she recognized him, why didn't she ever tell me?"

"We talked about that, going in to see the Justice of the Peace. She thought it was me. She knowed you'd come after me if she said I'd trifled with her and, I dunno, I reckon she didn't want you to."

"That figures. Let's help the others sort this out and then we'll all go home together and have us a shivareee with the two gals. You and Jessie can use my old spread 'til you're up to staying here again."

"Yeah, it do need some housecleaning, don't it?"

They went over to join Sheriff MacLeod, Deputy Brody, and some of the others, who'd lined up some of the bodies in an oddly neat row. The Sheriff said, "I'll send for a photographer and we'll take us some pictures folks might be able to identify. They didn't wear masks all the time." He nodded at Brody to add, "I forgot to thank you for nailing that one there, Deputy. I only got two eyes and it's hard to look both ways at once."

Brody shrugged and said, "Just doing my job, sir."

Joe stared soberly down at the dead men and said, "So that's them. Funny, I expected horns and a tail."

MacLeod nodded and said, "They say Billy the Kid looked like a little sissy, too. Meanest killer I ever arrested looked like he sat down to piss and sang in a church choir. That's where we found the little girl he raped and murdered, up in the choir loft."

"You reckon this'll make trouble for my new brother-in-law, his brother being the leader of the nightriders and all?"

The Sheriff shook his head and said, "Not hardly. They say Ben Franklin's son was a renegade who sided with the English at that time. Folks understand these things happen in the best of families. Like Cain and Abel, only this time it looks like Abel won."

"Yeah, and the town bad boy turned out to be misunderstood, just like my kid sister said. Funny how she was the only one who had any faith in old Trinity. You need us for anything right now, Sheriff?"

"No, why?"

"Thought me and Mister Hyde might ride back to my place and get to know each other better."

"Mister Hyde? Who the blazes is he?"

"Just funning, Sheriff. It's a new book I just read. Funny, but in the book the two personalities was in one body. Took my dumb innocent sister to see it had to be two men in real life."

JESSIE AND TRINITY didn't honeymoon at the old soddy. He carried her off to North Platte and they checked into a fine hotel that charged a dollar a day. Jessie had never seen such a big city. They even had their pictures taken, Jessie in a fine new dress. She told Trinity he was spoiling her and that it wasn't practical, as she'd soon be too thick-waisted to wear it, but he wanted to buy it any-way, and threw in a hat with real ostrich plumes.

Meanwhile, as the weather warmed up back home, Joe took Nadja in to have a talk with the local Calvinist preacher. He said he didn't know how to conduct a Rooshin church wedding, but that he'd be proud to marry 'em up in the Old Time Religion. Nadja was practical, too. She still had an icon from the old country and if Joe didn't mind it in the bedroom she was well content to see any kids they might have grow up American.

Joe said it was Jake with him and that it might be interesting to have a mother with sort of queer notions on what day Easter came, and what the hell, she only burned a candle to that furrin icon on her sabbath or when she was feeling more thankful than usual.

One day Joe rose early to hitch the Morgans to the John Deere, for the weather had settled down and the ground felt right at last for plowing. Nadja knew her man would be hungry after all that work, so she was baking a jack rabbit pie when he came in from the fields early, looking sort of confused but grinning.

She said, "What is wrong, dear? I thought you were plowing."

He said, "It can wait. Come with me. I want to show you something."

He took her by the hand and led her out across the sunny land to the forty acres her late brother had planted the fall before. They stopped at the edge and Nadja sighed, "Oh, Joe."

The hitherto stubbornly barren field was green with tiny emerald spears of life. Joe said, "It's wheat. I pulled up a clump to look at the roots and the damned roots go half way down to China. Yasha was right. That red wheat from the old country has this new country figured. The seeds must have a clock or brains or something. They send down roots all winter, too smart to stick their heads up to be nipped by the wolf wind. They can take freezing, once their roots is below the frost line, which is where they go by the late fall. *Now* look at the way the stuff is coming up. It's growed an inch during the night and it's still early to plant anything else. I'll still put in the barley and some oats to feed the Morgans and your fool chickens, but if the other wheat on the old claim is up, we've got her whipped, Nadja."

"Oh, Joe, Yasha would be so pleased. You see, darling, silly Yasha was not all useless."

Joe sobered and said, "I know. Is it still too hurtful, or can I talk about your brother, now?"

Nadja looked down and said, "Poor Yasha, poor he, I know what he was, Joe. Drunken man who falls down in front of railroad trains."

"That ain't what happened, honey. You see, that ugly Brazos bragged some to his followers and we took some of them alive. We still don't have some parts worked out, but I know what happened to Yasha. I've been trying to come up with a gentle way of telling you, but there ain't none."

She turned wordlessly and by now he knew her well enough to read her eyes. So he nodded and said, "Brazos killed him. Yasha did panic and run off to leave Jessie to whatever. But later he must have come to his senses, for Brazos boasted that he'd kilt the little furriner and blamed it on the Union Pacific. He was visiting a whorehouse, pretending to be Trinity, of course, 'cause he was Goody Two Shoes to the town. Yasha thought he was Trinity and that Trinity had raped Jessie. So Yasha fit him, Nadja! He never had a chance, of course. He barely come up to Brazo's belt buckle, but he tried, and he died like a man."

Nadja made the sign of the cross and murmured, "Thank you, Joe. Was ugly story, but you have given brother back to me."

"I figured you ought to know. Let's take the buckboard over to the old place and see if we got wheat there, too."

They did have, forty acres, making it eighty altogether, or, at the current price, enough to see them through if even her sunflowers failed.

Later that night Nadja lit a candle before the old age-blackened icon of the Little Mother and Child. They got in bed and as Joe began to take her gown off she said, "Wait, I feel funny, doing that in front of Little Mother, dear."

Joe chuckled and said, "Yeah, she does have sort of knowing eyes. Why don't we blow out the durned old candle?"

"Would be just as wrong, like taking back gift."

"Well, what do you reckon we ought to do, then? I'll go along with a certain amount of sacrifice, but this is ridiculous."

Nadja giggled and said, "I know. In old country is other beliefs left over from earlier times, before my peoples becoming Christians. Church says is wrong, but farmers still do it in Russia to make crops grow good."

"Do tell? What is this pagan notion of your'n?"

"You will laugh at silly Nadja and say she is superstitious."

"Maybe not. Rooshin methods sure work good with wheat. I'll go along with anything that don't hurt."

Nadja laughed and got out of bed, saying, "Come, then. Is wicked something I have always thought might be fun."

He thought they were going to the other bed to leave her Little Mother in peace with the candle. But in the front room Nadja stripped off her gown and opened the door, naked in the night wind. He'd already shucked off his duds, so he was naked too as he joined her dubiously, and said, "We can't go outside like this, can we?"

"Why not? Who is telling, chickens?"

She took his hand and led him out in the moonlight. It was cool but not too unpleasant. Nadja said, "Come, we go to where you intend to plow in the morning, *da*?"

He went, but it sure felt silly, like they were going skinny-dipping, only they had no water hole. Nadja stopped when they came to the virgin sod and turned to face him like some pagan Earth Mother in the moonlight. She said, "Here is where I want you to make love to me, Joe."

"Jesus, on the infernal prairie?"

"On our land, Joe. Land that will always be ours and our children's after us. In old country, before plowing, villagers make love in fields as sacrifice to Mother Earth. I know is pagan. But can it hurt?"

He grinned and said, "No, but you sure are an easy gal to please."

They sank down to the sod and he mounted her, smelling the old raw prairie life that they were destroying to make room for richer promises from the land. As he entered her, she looked up at the star-spangled sky and sighed, "Oh, my Joe, I cry for happy and little stars laugh down at silly me."

They made love in the barley field to be and, what the hell, as long as they were out there acting foolish he took her over and laid her where he aimed to plant the oats.

They walked back, arms around one another with her unbound head on his naked shoulder. They got back in bed and he said, "Oh, that do feel good after thudding around on that sod, don't it?"

She snuggled close to him in the warm feather bed and he ran his hand over her, saying, "Civilization has its good points, too. I don't know about you, but I still want you, honey."

She said, "Me, too. But what about Little Mother? Candle is still lit."

He said, "Well, fair is fair and I think it's only right we do the same for her as we did for the older gods, don't you?"

Nadja laughed and said he was awful, but she didn't stop him when he rolled atop her, and over in the corner the lady in the icon just went on looking sort of knowing and friendly.

JOE WAS PLOWING when the delegation from the Grange dropped by. He asked them their pleasure and the spokesman said, "We're getting together about that cowboy sheriff, Barrow. It's an election year and we got the votes this time to put one of our own in."

Joe skuffed the ground with his boot and said, "I hate to tell you boys this, but I aim to vote for old MacLeod. It seems to me he's doing a good job. I rode with him when he put the nightriders down."

"We know that. That's why we thought you might like the job."

"Me? Hell, I'm just an old farm boy. I wasn't in charge when they arrested or shot those rascals out there. It was Sheriff MacLeod who put it all together, boys."

"No offense, but you're wrong. You wasn't the

only homesteader with that posse, so we all know what happened. It was your brother-in-law, Trinity, who pointed the finger at them. MacLeod didn't know it was them. They had him slickered."

"Well one way or the other he got 'em all, didn't he?"

"We don't think so. Even Macleod says the leader had to be an old soldier and there wasn't a man caught over thirty, so how many wars could any of 'em know about? We think there was others from other outfits."

"If so, they're laying low, too scared to pester folks again."

"For now, mebbe. Young Brazos was what you might call a squad leader, working outten the Double M. The old guerrilla was their captain, and he was never caught. He's out there somewheres waiting for the trials and such to blow over afore he recruits more young fools to come at ussen again!"

Joe allowed they was likely right, but that he had no more notion than the Sheriff on who they might go looking for. He added he wasn't at all interested in standing for office, so they rode off.

Joe went back to plowing for a time as he mulled over what they'd said. He was sure the Sheriff was honest. The Sheriff had been in town talking to Trinity and the other honest riders from the Double M, so he couldn't have been in on it if he'd wanted to be.

Kilty Dundee didn't like homesteaders much, even now. But he had an alibi even if he hadn't been mighty active in that shootout.

Course, a gent riding with the posse playing

innocent would have had to go along when the others started firing. But even so, it couldn't have been old Kilty. He'd been drinking with Trinity when that last soddy was torched.

Joe reached the end of the furrow, still chawing on it, and then he suddenly stopped and said, "Son-of-a-bitch, of course!"

He unhitched both Morgans and led them back to the corral. He ran Pittypat inside and saddled the more reliable Demon. He went to the house and got his Winchester, telling Nadja he'd be back in time for supper. She asked if she could go to town with him and he said, "No." Flat. Nadja was getting good at reading his eyes, too, so she didn't argue, but when he left she went in and lit a candle for him.

He got to the Sheriff's and went in to find Deputy Brody alone in the office, seated at the desk. He said, "I'm looking for Sheriff MacLeod," and Brody said, "He ain't here, as you can see. Anything I can do for you?"

"Yeah, I come in to tell the Sheriff I just figured out who was leading them younger fellers as nightriders."

Brody looked interested and rose from behind the desk, saying, "That's a mighty serious charge, son. You want to tell me who you think it is?"

Joe said, "Yeah. You." So Brody went for his gun.

He didn't make it. Joe had the Winchester loose in his right hand, muzzle down, as he stood there. So when Brody slapped leather he simply whipped it up and pulled the trigger. Deputy Brody slammed against the wall and slid down it, a look of wonder in his dying eyes as he left a red streak on the wall. Joe said, "Larnt that trick from Kilty Dundee. The hard way. I may be a mite slow, but I got a good memory."

Brody didn't answer. Dead men never did.

Joe heard the sound of running boot heels and turned as the Sheriff came in. MacLeod gasped as he saw Brody on the floor near his desk and said, "I sure hope you have a good story, Mister Barrow."

Joe said, "Your deputy was the leader of the nightriders. He was two-faced, like Brazos Mackail. I don't know if he was after your job or just crazy mean with hate."

"You got anything better than a guess to go on, son?"

"Sure. He told me he rode for the South, like you. I knew you were one old rebel raider it couldn't be, so I started thinking how many others there could be. Most of the Texicans in these parts is too young, like me. I remembered something he said to you as he joined the posse after it left my place. I thought nothing of it at the time, but he asked you what was up and you told him. So he couldn't have been in town when you was forming up your posse. A deputy sheriff can ride all over the county and when somebody's asked if they've noticed any strangers riding past they'd all say no. Any homesteader or stock man far enough from his own spread to matter would draw more attention. Besides all that, when I said I knew who it was, he got up and opened his coat to clear his gun. When I said it was him, he went for it. Now you know as much as I do."

MacLeod stared soberly down at the body on his floor and said, "Well, I could say we rode a ways together, but if Brazos Mackail could frame his own brother I reckon we'll skip that part. We'd best get a secretary in here and take down your statement, son."

"Don't you believe me?"

"I ain't got much choice, but we'll have to do this legal."

"You mind if I make a suggestion, sir?"

"Go ahead, you've made a heap of sense so far."

"I ain't trying to shirk going afore the coroner's jury, but you're up for re-election and there's some who say you ain't as skilful at catching folks as you might be."

"You mean, you'd let me take the credit?"

"Credit or blame. Neither one is going to hurt you with the voters this November when they remember how you caught the ringleader in your office, sort of slick."

The Sheriff nodded and said, "This is mighty neighborly of you, son. Didn't you have some shopping chores to do?"

"Now that you mention it, I thought I'd pick up some ribbon bows for my woman. It's been nice jawing with you, Sheriff."

Joe went outside and when a townee asked if he'd heard the shooting and if so what it was all about, Joe said, "Ain't sure. Sheriff got the leader of them nightriders, the way I hear it."

He went to the notions store and figured as long as he was buying Nadja the ribbon bows he might as well take home a box of sweets for her.

He stepped out and heard his name called. It

was Jessie and old Trinity, back from Platte City.
Trinity said, "We just heard a gunshot, Joe. Know
what happened?"

He said, "Yep. Let's talk about it on our way
home. Nadja will be pleased to see you both, and
it sure looks like a fine summer ahead."